MONSTER HUNTER
MEMOIRS
SINNERS

Larry Correia & John Ringo

MONSTER HUNTER MEMOIRS: SINNERS

Copyright © 2016 by Larry Correia and John Ringo

A Baen Books Original

Baen Publishing Enterprises
P.O. Box 1403
Riverdale, NY 10471
www.baen.com

ISBN: 978-1-4814-8287-5

Cover art by Alan Pollack

First Baen paperback printing, February 2018

Library of Congress Control Number: 2016042000

Distributed by Simon & Schuster
1230 Avenue of the Americas
New York, NY 10020

Pages by Joy Freeman (www.pagesbyjoy.com)
Printed in the United States of America

As always
For Captain Tamara Long, USAF
Born: May 12, 1979
Died: March 23, 2003, Afghanistan
You fly with the angels now.

❖

And
Keith Berdine
Born: June 18, 1964
Died: September 21, 2013
Miss you, buddy.

ACKNOWLEDGEMENTS

On the "how you shoot from a helicopter" thing, I had to go back to my buddy Emil Praslick, recently retired long-term NCO in the US Army Marksmanship Unit (USAMU). You might recognize the name as one of the sniper instructors from the Paladin of Shadow series. I figured if any of my various contacts had experience shooting a Barrett out of a helo, it would be Emil. Yeah, yeah, he did.

And I'd like to belatedly congratulate USAMU for beating the pants off of the Marine Corps at Camp Perry lately! Fun part? The Army's primary shooter is SSG Sherri Gallagher (female badass, one each) who Emil specifically recruited from civilian shooting then "dialed in."

Now, if they'd just put Emil in charge of Army's football team . . .

Most characters are based upon someone. They may be "super-characters" but they generally have some basis. As Hemingway said, "Good writers create, great writers steal." Sometimes it's intentional, sometimes you don't even realize it.

It took me until this book to realize that Chad is based in part on a friend of mine from "Back in the Day" named Keith "Duck" Berdine. I first met Duck picking up some jeeps that were being redeployed back from Grenada. Pick up in Wilmington, drive to Fort Bragg. Total *shit* detail and a very long story why. I truly got the big green weenie on that one. God, I was pissed! But on the other hand, got to meet Duck and make friends, so not all bad.

(Being left behind when even the NCOIC went home, guarding a stupid piece of electronics when I had a twelve-hour drive ahead of me was part of the shit detail aspect. Stupid piece of "secure" commo! I could have cut the lock right off, but NO, it was a "secure lock" and had to be...Aaaagh! I had to wait two hours for the stupid duty officer, idiot lieutenants, to find the fricking KEY...Which turned out was in the box RIGHT BY HIS STUPID LIEUTENANT HEAD! Then there was the fact that it was Thanksgiving weekend and a freaking day off for the *entire rest of the battalion* since we'd been in *Grenada* for Columbus Day...Gah! Never mind. Army shit. Most of you get it. Yes, people, been there, done that, *still* pissy about it.)

I ended up riding with Keith in an M151 doing road guard. It was a particularly dark night, black as pitch, back roads of North Carolina. We'd drive up to an intersection and block it to let the convoy pass through. Then Duck would put the hammer down and pass the *entire* convoy, in the left lane, on curvy two-lane back roads, at night, with the speedometer more than pegged, carrying on a conversation the whole way while waving his hands and paying NO and I mean NO attention to the road!

The looks, the crazy, the perpetual joie d'vivre. That was Duck. Wasn't the cock hound that Chad is admittedly.

After years as an Air Marshal he died, really suddenly, of leukemia of all things. He left behind a wife and two children and many, many friends who remember him for his universal bonhomie and kindness.

Miss you, man. But in a way, through Iron Hand, you get to live again.

—John Ringo

We told the story of how the MHI Memoirs books came about in the acknowledgements of the first book. These are John's stories unfolding in a world I created. My main role was to edit them to make sure everything fit what had already been established in the series.

I want to thank Mike Kupari, Whit Williams, and Peter Grant for some fact-checking help. And special thanks to Toni Weisskopf for being an awesome editor.

Most of all I want to thank John for writing these. Personally, my favorite thing about a Ringo novel is the contagious enthusiasm. You can tell that he had a lot of fun writing these, and that comes through on the page. The man is one hell of a storyteller.

—Larry Correia

PROLOGUE
Hell's Bells

A church bell was sounding midnight, wet as a marsh and still hot as the hinges of hell, as I prowled the deserted cemetery. I could hear my harsh breathing, the distant rumble of thunder and the incessant buzz of the fucking mosquitoes in this hell-spawned city. The cicadas were silent, a bad sign for sure. There was hardly any light with the moon stuck behind billowing banks of cloud.

Sweat was pouring down my face from the heat and situation. My body armor was stifling and I didn't dare take my hand off my weapon long enough to take a drink from my canteen.

I was all alone and being hunted by a werewolf that had already killed a half-dozen people.

The elevated tombs of the cemetery crowded around me, blocking my vision and line of sight. All I had was my ears and nose, and I was up against a hyper-advanced predator with ten times my ability with both senses.

Then the howl of the loup-garou broke the stillness, an inarticulate cry, half-human, half-wolf, all bad news.

I was tired of this. I was tired of the heat. I was tired of the mosquitoes. I was tired of being the hunted instead of the hunter. I was one of the best MHI had to offer. That was why I was here. I once took a werewolf this bad in a pair of running shorts with a 1911. I was fucking *Iron Hand* and no fucking devil wolf was going to get *my* heart pounding fucking with me in the dark of this fucking cemetery.

I jumped onto one of the lower tombs then up again onto a higher one.

Standing up there I had a view around. But this loup-garou was cagey. It wasn't going to just to walk into my sights. I caught a flash of moonlight off dark fur and fired a burst in that direction. The silencer on the Uzi muffled the rounds to a dull *thup, thup, thup*. The ricochets and sound of the action working were louder than the rounds.

I reloaded without thinking about it and did a three-sixty. The thing was circling around me and could come from any direction. It wouldn't be bothered by the few feet of height. A jump like this was nothing to a loup-garou. But I might be able to spot it from up here.

No, it was slinking from tomb to tomb. It sensed I was a predator as well. Maybe because all the innocent people it had murdered had a racing heartbeat and mine was slow and regular. Innocent is not a description anyone would use for me.

I was tired of this. I decided to press the issue.

I raised my head to the full moon and howled. I couldn't get the full timbre of a werewolf howl, but it got the picture. I was challenging it. Come out and fight.

I barely caught the skritch of claws on stone, and spun as the loup-garou flew through the air and impacted on my left arm. Somehow, it had gotten behind me. Its teeth sunk into my armor, just under the opening to my vest, but the teeth didn't penetrate. The claws, though, those damned claws. Like nothing on anything natural, they were as long as daggers and tore my armor and legs to hell as I fell off the tomb.

It was too close for the Uzi. I reached down, pulled my 1911, stuck the barrel into its ribs and fired seven plus one into its body in one continuous *thud, thud, thud*.

It let go and rolled away, whining and licking at the wounds on its side. That put it right in the direction of the barrel of my Uzi. I dropped the 1911, clamped the trigger and walked the rounds into its head, riddling it from stem to stern.

I automatically dropped the Uzi magazine and inserted another, then picked up the 1911, reloaded and holstered.

"Good doggie." It returned to human form as it died. The guy was skinny as a rail, probably a crack addict. Well, his problems were over. Absent having really fucked up, he was going to the Summer Lands where it was always green and the temperature was perfect and, I dunno, maybe for him the crack was free and didn't have side effects.

"Go to God, kid," I said. "Surely your sins are forgiven. God understands curses. He sure *allows* enough of them."

I hadn't been bitten, but I might have been scratched. Scratches weren't often infectious, but bites always were. I pulled out my canteen and took a swig of sacramental wine. That might help stave off lycanthropy, or it might just be a wives' tale, but it couldn't hurt. I needed to bandage my leg, then call the coroner.

There was a rush of grinding claws and the *second* loup-garou charged out of the darkness.

I had neither firearm in my hand. As the werewolf flew through the air, the canteen hit the ground, spilling my wine. I stepped backwards between two of the tombs, and Mo No Ken, Sword of Mourning, flashed up from the scabbard and down. I didn't even think about it. Just acted.

Which is why I'm one of the best of the best and had lived through the worst this damned town could throw at me while my buddies were going down the shitter every hellish day.

The werewolf's body continued for another ten feet and its head kept rolling, stopping when it hit a tomb.

I flicked Mo No Ken to clear the blade of blood, took out a formerly white silk cloth, which had already been used that night, and wiped the blade clean carefully. Then I pulled out another cloth from behind my left arm and wiped the blade down, carefully, with holy oil blessed by the Rabbis of Jerusalem.

Ritual complete, I waited to see if another loup-garou was going to appear out of the darkness. Probably not. The cicadas were starting their incessant whining again. Fucking bugs, fucking heat, fucking humidity. Fucking City of the Fucking Undead. I loved and hated New Orleans. Loved the food. Loved a lot of the culture.

They called it the Big Easy. The only thing easy in this town was death. And half the time you ended up working overtime as a zombie or ghoul.

I got up on the tombs again, a bit harder this

time with my left thigh cut to ribbons, and looked around. I howled a couple of times. I could swear I saw movement but no more loup-garou appeared. I sat down and bandaged my wounds as best I could with the small first aid pack I carried. I'd need to do more when I got to Honeybear.

I climbed down and started working my way out of the maze. Somewhere, there was a road through the cemetery and a gate.

I finally found both, unlocked the gate with the big skeleton key I'd been handed, and walked over to one of the NOPD cars parked outside the gates.

"Done!" I shouted through the rolled up window. The cop didn't have the window rolled up just for the undoubtedly pleasant AC. He had it rolled up 'cause the NOPD had a deathly fear of loup-garou. They'd lost too many officers on details just like this one. They weren't getting out of their cars until they were sure Hoodoo Squad had cleared the area. "Call the coroner! Got it?"

The guy made an "Okay" sign and picked up his radio. With any luck Tim would be on his way in a few minutes. Until I'd finished providing security for the Orleans Parish Special Incident Coroner's Squad (SICS), we weren't done—part of our contract with the parish and in this town, it made sense. Coroner's teams had lost people just doing pickup.

I limped over to Honeybear, my personally rebuilt 1976 Cutlass Supreme, opened the trunk, rummaged, got out the big first aid kit and finished bandaging my thigh. Fucking loup-garou. I made a mental note to call Memorial and tell them to have my coffee mug ready. I made actual notes on the action, limped back to the squad car and got the incident number.

I took another drink, refilled my canteens and magazines, closed Honeybear's trunk and limped back into the cemetery.

I started the process of finding the bodies, again. Another maze.

I rounded a tomb and knew right away I'd found the kill site 'cause it was covered in ghouls, ripping the first loup-garou's body apart. The headless one was entirely missing.

A blast of wind hit as the storm reached the cemetery, the heavens opened up and water poured from the sky.

The ghouls turned, hissing at my lights, and got up from their meal.

More were closing in among the tombs. Their outline was revealed as lightning pounded the Big Easy like Thor's hammer.

I was wounded, alone, stuck in a thunderstorm and surrounded by hungry ghouls. Then *another* freaking loup-garou, barely audible over the howling wind, bayed its challenge to the moon...

You might be wondering how I got myself into this predicament. I blame trailer park elf girls and the inventor of the tube top.

My name is Oliver Chadwick Gardenier. Call me Iron Hand.

This is my life. I'm a Monster Hunter.

Note:

This is the second volume of Chad's old memoirs we discovered in the archives. There is a lot of useful information in these pages, so I'm passing it on to you.

Being honest, this one was tough for me. We lost a lot of good people there. I knew many of them personally, and they were some of the bravest men and women I've ever known. Evil loomed, and they held the line.

The Eighties were wild in New Orleans. Something horrible rolled into that town, and the only thing that stopped it from establishing hell on earth was Hoodoo Squad.

Chad loved to tell sea stories, and some of what you are about to read may sound crazy, but I was there. New Orleans really was lousy with monsters. Some of the PUFF collection records set by Hoodoo Squad still stand to this day.

That said, I think Chad totally exaggerated the parts about me. I was never that much of a dork. I've always been as cool and suave as I am now.

> Milo Ivan Anderson
> Monster Hunter International
> Cazador, Alabama

CHAPTER 1
Rebel Yell

How was I to know she was forty? She said she was ninety!

I should probably start with the fact that I make most lounge lizards look unambitious. If it's female and reasonably attractive, I'm going to hit on it. I could blame my father, who never met a coed he wouldn't give a better grade to for a nice roll in the hay. Dr. Nelson—my friend Joan—says it's a way to get back at my much-hated mother.

My excuse is I don't think Hunters should have serious relationships. We die way too often and easy. So surgical strike mixed with the occasional full-on arc light is the only way to go. Using one of the new slang terms in vogue: It's how I roll.

So when I had gone to bribe some trailer park elves for intel, I ended up chatting up this elf girl named Cheyenne.

Man, she was sweet. Five feet if she was an inch. Buck soaking wet. Curly red hair and I do like redheads. Those deep, blue, slightly tilted elf eyes just smoking with banked fires. Shorts, Candies and a seriously overstrained tube top.

Like the song said, she had Betty Davis eyes.

She looked like a fragile little angel and she nearly broke me in half in the backseat of my Cutlass. If I hadn't been so in shape, she'd have killed me.

And I'd *asked* her beforehand how old she was. She *said* she was ninety which is, in human terms all grown up, okay, even by elf standards. I mean, either way it's legal, don't get me wrong.

Thing was, she was forty. Okay, thirty-eight, according to one of her cousins I ended up beating up.

That sort of crosses a line with elves. I tried to make the argument that it wasn't like I was the first one across the goal line. Did not make inroads on their mad. Her brothers and cousins and some of the other elves from the trailer park, who were very distant relations, were out for my sweet little ass.

Don't get me wrong, I'd dealt with some serious nasties before. Her toothless brothers were no problem.

A gang of them? Some of those guys were big for elves and they were all carrying sticks with nails in them. And her mom was casting curses right and left.

It was time to get out of Seattle until the heat died down. Like, say, a hundred years. Elves have very long memories and hold onto grudges harder than the last PBR in the cooler.

So I called the home office. And fortunately I got Ray IV instead of Earl. Ray was in town keeping an eye on Susan in her last trimester. So Earl was running the team and, fortunately, out. Earl was sort of a stick-in-the-mud on this stuff.

"Monster Hunter International, Raymond Shackleford the Fourth."

Ray had to add "the Fourth" part. His dad, Ray III, was still president of the company even after having lost his hand and nearly being burned to death the previous year fighting a lich.

Raymond "Bubba" Shackleford had founded MHI back in 1895 and the business was still family owned and still the premier Monster Hunting outfit on the planet. As next in line, Ray IV was the designated heir apparent if Ray III ever stepped down. Which wasn't going to happen soon. In the meantime he managed day to day business along with Earl Harbinger, the Operations Manager.

I'd never asked Ray how it felt to have so many bodies between himself and the top spots but it never seemed to bug him.

"Hey, Ray," I said, relieved. "Chad."

"Chad, man." You could hear the grin on the phone. Even though he was part of the family of owners, we'd sort of bonded way back when I was a trainee over pumping iron. "Good to hear from you, buddy. I'm sorry about Jesse. I know that hurt."

"Absent companions," I said, shrugging even though he couldn't see it. "He's in a better place. Been there."

A few months before we'd nearly lost most of Team Flaming Warthog taking on a shelob, giant spider mother, and her colony of couch-sized children. The shelob's body was bigger than an elephant and if she'd been able to spread her legs out, they'd have stretched from one side to the other of Broadway. We'd faced her in a maintenance corridor for an old cistern and she nearly filled it. We did for her and her horde of babies with a mechanical ambush. But it had been a close thing. We damned near got overrun.

My best friend, Jesse Mason, had been bitten in the belly, right up under his armor. He was "just" injected with the paralytic toxin, not a full dose of the flesh-dissolving enzymes. But enough enzyme was always mixed in that it meant he was just going to take longer to dissolve. Nothing in human or mystical medicine was going to save him. He'd face weeks of agony while his abdomen slowly melted into goo.

So I gave him grace with a .45 round up under his chin and blew my best friend's brains all over my lap and chest.

His official death certificate said "death due to kinetic trauma (automobile accident)." We never seemed to officially die the way we really did.

Both Jesse's death and the last moments of that battle still had our team, and me in particular, a little shaken. Not that I was going to use that as an excuse.

"Yeah," I said. "It's got me a little off my game. How's Susan?"

"Round and keeps saying she looks like shit."

"Be a cold day in hell." I'm not going to compare myself to Lancelot or anything, but I had a serious crush on my friend and sort-of-boss's wife. Susan was a real foxy lady. Even if she gained a hundred pounds without being pregnant, I still wouldn't kick her out of bed for eating crackers. Not that she would. She was one of those women with the amazing ability to lose every ounce of baby weight within weeks. Probably 'cause, like her husband, she was a workout-aholic.

Of course, later we lost Susan and, in a way, Ray as well. But that's a different story.

"So, you never call, you never write," Ray said. "This must be business."

"Sort of. Look, before we get into it, I *asked* her how old she was. She *said* she was ninety."

"Oh, no," Ray sighed in exasperation. "Fey or elf?"

"Elf," I muttered. "And, seriously, Fey? There's ugly, then there's Fey-ugly! They've got...tentacles and stuff."

"Well, if it had been that Fey princess there'd be nowhere on earth you could hide from *her* mom. And what did I tell you about getting involved with *trailer park elves*, Chad?"

"Don't," I said.

"How old was she?" Ray asked.

"Forty."

"Forty?" Ray said. "Forty? That's what, like seventeen in elf years?"

"She didn't *look* forty! She sure as hell didn't *act* forty! The local elves are pissed."

Ray sighed in exasperation. "Okay, okay. Team Warthog doesn't need to lose another heavy hitter. Especially now. But it just so happens I was going to call you."

"Oh?" Shit. If I'd waited a few days I'd have probably been offered something and never have had to fess up.

"Remember how I asked you if you'd like to be on my team?"

"I'll take Happy Face," I said, immediately. The Happy Face demon was the logo of the company and MHI's premier team. It was run by Earl Harbinger and with Susan out of the loop, Ray III pretty much sidelined and Ray IV watching the store, I could see where they could use help.

The reason I'd turned it down the first time was that I hate heat. Happy Face bounced all over the place; they'd come in as reinforcements for our lich, but they concentrated in the Southeast and South America. I went through Parris Island in summer and learned to hate the bugs and heat and humidity of tropical and subtropical latitudes. I was from Kentucky, which occasionally had pretty hard summers, but the truth was there were few things more beautiful than a Kentucky summer.

Alabama and Mississippi, not so much.

But that was better than sticks with nails in them and elf curses. They can suck a guy's soul into an alternate dimension and shit. I was wearing a neck full of antiscrying charms and they didn't seem to be working. Cheyenne's overprotective mother kept finding me. Then pickup trucks full of redneck elves in tank tops and mullets carrying big freaking sticks would pull into the parking lot and I'd have to jump out a back window. Again.

"Wasn't the offer," Ray said. "We've got bigger concerns. I was thinking about your reason for turning it down. I'm talking about New Orleans."

I'd heard the rumors in the company. New Orleans was heating up in more than purely thermal terms. The word was that their last couple months had been unusually busy. They were making beaucoup PUFF bounties but had the casualties to match.

I wouldn't mind the PUFF. Not that I ever had time to spend the money I made as it was. I was sort of a workaholic when it came to monster hunting. The only time I ever took off was when I was in recovery.

But the heat. The humidity. The bugs.

Dimensions with teeth. Big sticks.

I'd heard the girls were hot. And they called it the Big Easy for a reason.

"I'll take it. I'd take sweeping Hades with a broom at the moment. I'm having to move from hotel to hotel to avoid her mom's curses. And some of those elves are monsters."

"Pack your stuff," Ray said. "You're headed to New Orleans."

I had all my really necessary stuff in the trunk of Honeybear. Clothes, my armor, lots of various guns, ammo, bladed weapons and miscellanea you need in monster hunting. I'd gotten Dr. Lucius to oversee Allied Van Lines packing up my apartment when it became obvious that Seattle was a done deal. I was going to miss the University District. I liked the food, I liked the atmosphere, I liked the coeds, I had lots of contacts.

Big sticks with nails in them. Alternate dimensions with things with teeth.

I hit the road and didn't look back.

It is a long . . . damned . . . drive from Seattle to New Orleans. And most of it seems to be through the driest country in the world. And the freaking mountains. I thought the freaking mountains would never end. Then the plains started and I found myself missing mountains.

That trip took me right past Jesse's home town of Yuma, Colorado. His mom still lived there. She'd lost her husband to a "hunting accident" (werewolf), then her oldest son to a "car wreck."

It was part of the job that families rarely knew what their sons, daughters, fathers, mothers did for a living. I knew Jesse had sent money home. Like me, he made more than he could spend in his limited free time. I knew she had to wonder what he really did for a living. He told me one time he'd told her he'd gotten a job with Microtel. As often as we were over there, it was close to truth. But it would have been hard to explain getting the money with just a high school diploma.

Stop by and reopen that wound? I didn't think she knew me from Adam. I didn't even know if Jesse ever mentioned me. Women, booze and monster killing had been most of our conversations.

And did I violate federal law and tell her the truth? Would she even believe me?

I had the address. I think, in the end, it was a selfish decision. I was looking for some closure. Stupid, but there you go.

Yuma is a small town in the Colorado high plains, not far from the Kansas border. Flat as hell. After two years in Seattle and working in the Cascades and Grand Tetons, the complete lack of relief was disorienting. It was flatter than the areas around Lejeune and that's saying something. Or maybe it was just the complete lack of trees that made it seem that way.

It also was arid as hell. Some of the areas on the dry side of Washington had been like that. Just not as flat. The many empty lots were barren. Most of them didn't even have grass growing in them.

The houses were mostly pretty run-down. The sun and incessant wind just sort of baked them, I guess. Off the two US highways that crossed through town, most of the side roads were unpaved dirt.

I could never figure out what people in a town like this did for a living.

The house was a two-story Cape Cod. The yard was watered and green, well maintained, the house had a fresh coat of paint on it. Windows were clean.

There was a pink flamingo in the yard and for a second I hunched up in the seat and reached for my weapon when I saw a red hat in the bushes. But it was just a plaster statue. Probably.

Might have been a gnome. I'd be able to tell when I got closer.

Probably a statue. If it had been real, Jesse would have plugged the son of a bitch for being on his property the couple of times he went home.

I parked on the street and sat there with the car running and the AC playing on me, working up the courage. There was a battered pickup in the driveway. Jesse had mentioned having a couple of brothers and sisters who were still living at home.

There was someone peeking out the front window. I'd been spotted. I could run like a coward, easy enough, or I could get out and face the music.

I got out and walked to the front door. I went around the neatly manicured lawn.

The doorbell played "There's No Place Like Home."

I tried not to burst into tears.

A pretty teenage girl opened the door. Blonde hair, maybe sixteen, you could see Jesse in her eyes and cheekbones.

"Can I help you?" she inquired in an uncertain tone.

I guess my face was a picture.

"I'm looking for Mrs. Janet Mason, miss," I said formally. "Is she in?"

"I'll get her," the girl said, shutting the door.

A couple of minutes later the door opened again

and a middle-aged woman looked out. She was wiping her hands on a dish rag.

"Whatever you're selling—" the woman said in a stern tone.

"I was a co-worker of Jesse's." I cut her off. "I was just passing through and stopped to offer my condolences."

"Oh," she said, just a bit stunned. "I..."

"Chad." I held out my hand. "Oliver Chadwick Gardenier, ma'am."

"Chad!" she said delightedly. "Jesse talked so much about you! Come in, come in..."

Jesse had talked about me. His mother, and family, knew what he did. They knew how their husband and father had died, but not Jesse.

"Was it quick?" was the main question from Mrs. Mason. She was sitting on the couch in the formal living room and twisted her hands together as she asked it. She'd served tea and cookies after asking if I wanted something stronger. The answer was yes but I said no.

"Pretty quick. He...didn't die in a lot of pain."

"What got him?" the sister, Dauphine, asked, her face pinched.

"Giant spider. It was a nest. Big one. We'd set up a mechanical ambush in a corridor. Lots of directional mines, machine gun, we brought out the works. All the fire beforehand cut the detonation circuits. We managed to get it to blow but not before our position got overrun. Jesse got bit. It was quick. It's a paralytic, mostly. He barely felt it."

I wasn't about to say that I'd blown his head off.

"Portland was about to get overrun. Thousands would have died. He died how he lived. A hero."

"He's in a better place," Mrs. Mason said. You could see it wasn't *pro forma*. She was a believer. But there was a nagging doubt in the tone.

"He is, ma'am," I said definitely. "Been there. It's nice. It's practically the last thing I told him."

"You've been to heaven?" Bobby, his younger brother, said skeptically.

"I died," I said matter-of-factly, looking him in the eye. "In the bombing of the Marine barracks in Beirut, Bobby. Had a chat with Saint Peter while fishing. Got the choice of continue to in-processing or come back. God said he had something for me to do, something important, something about 'being the best candidate.' So here I am. I'd doubt that except there was stuff about a sign, which I later found, and it led me to Monster Hunting. So . . . mission from God, I guess.

"And ma'am," I said, taking her hand, "I know from Jesse that you're . . . pretty fundamental on some stuff. Trust me when I say Jesus is a lot more forgiving than your average small-town preacher. Jesse *is* in a better place. So's your husband. We're the ones stuck here in this . . ." I couldn't say *crap hole* to this woman. ". . . vale of tears. We'll all see him, again, soon enough. Based on odds, I'd say I'll be first," I added with a grin.

"You seem so . . ." Dauphine said, frowning. "Okay with it."

"Did you love Jesse?" I asked.

"Yes," Dauphine said, tearing up.

"Then you have to want what's best for him. And heaven is, trust me, better than this place. Although the fishing is really boring. The fish just swim right up, spit the hook out and go back out to be caught again."

"Now I know you're joking," Dauphine said.

"God's truth," I said. "But it's *so* green. God, it's so green. I miss him, too. I'll miss him as long as I live. But he's the lucky one. And I loved him like the brother I wished I'd had. So I'm happy for him and he'd want me to keep going. So I keep going. Grief is a selfish emotion."

"Where *are* you going?" Mrs. Mason asked.

"New Orleans. They're getting hammered. Based on their activity rate, I'm going to be seeing Jesse *real* soon now."

I wouldn't stay for dinner or stay over. I'd made that commitment before I even stopped. Especially once I saw Dauphine I made up my mind to hit the road as fast as possible.

I made sure Mrs. Mason was okay for money. Jesse hadn't just sent money home, he'd invested it at my insistence. He'd had a nice chunk of change when he died. I could see she was careful with it but I planned on sending some to her as well. I wasn't going to need it.

Then I hit the road and headed for Kansas.

Kansas was Yuma multiplied by a thousand and on steroids. Kansas gives you too much time to think.

CHAPTER 2
Changes in Latitudes

I rolled into the NO area at oh-dark-thirty and got a room in a town called Gonzalez. It wasn't near New Orleans, exactly, but on the map there was nada for miles, then suddenly New Orleans. So after gassing up, I hit a Holiday Inn for one last night of sleep. I had the address for Team Hoodoo. I'd check in with them in the morning.

Just lugging my gear into the room told me I was sooo going to enjoy working in Louisiana. I worked up more of a sweat in those few minutes than I'd worked up fighting trolls in Spokane. I already missed the cool mists of the Northwest. Maybe I should have hid out with the Sasquatch. Surely they could keep me out of range of the elves?

I woke up at 0430 minus a few seconds, courtesy of the US Marine Corps and tutelage before that under Mr. Brentwood. For once I hadn't had a nightmare about spiders. The nightmare was that I had overslept and was late for formation and the senior DI was pissed.

You can take the boy out of Parris Island but you can never get Parris Island out of his head. Zombies, vampires, werewolves, spiders the size of Godzilla, and I was still having drill instructor nightmares.

I did some stretching exercises, pushups and sit-ups, then went out, found a Waffle House and got an egg sandwich, then headed into New Orleans proper. I also got a big Styrofoam cup of sweet tea. That *was* something I had been missing.

I'd grown up, middle school and high school at least, in Louisville, where I'd gotten addicted to sweet tea. You could not get sweet tea in Seattle or anywhere else in the Pacific Northwest. So that was a benefit. I was back in sweet tea zone. And I'd heard the food was good. I doubted I could find a good bento place but there was probably something to replace it.

There was still fairly light traffic that time of the morning and New Orleans looked almost peaceful.

MHI's headquarters in Seattle was in a fairly new office park in a decent part of town. The office in New Orleans was in a ghetto. 3398 Washington Street, corner of Washington and Johnson Streets. The building was a fairly standard New Orleans construction: a brick, nearly windowless structure; lower floor with heavy steel doors on the front and side, and a wooden upper with a balcony overlooking Washington Street. There were bars on the upper windows and a heavy barred door leading to the balcony.

It was covered in graffiti. It looked abandoned. I had to think at this time of day it probably was. I wasn't sure if I had the right address. I looked carefully in the early morning light but there was no sign saying

MHI, not even a discreet one. I wasn't supposed to meet the team lead, Trevor Arnold, until 0830. It was just past seven when I found the place.

I could sit here in the ghetto or cruise around. I decided to sit.

About fifteen minutes later a guy looked in my passenger side window. I had the windows up, the AC on and the stereo playing and appeared to be half asleep. I was a Monster Hunter. Paranoia had better be in your bones or you don't survive. I'd been discreetly keeping an eye on all the mirrors. I'd seen him walk up. He looked nervous, glancing around as he approached the car.

I leaned over and rolled down the window to see what he wanted. I also took an unnoticeable glance around to see if anybody was with him.

The guy was black, no surprise in the South, in his twenties, wearing a ratty T-shirt and jeans.

"Hey, man," the guy said, nervously, flashing a mouthful of broken and snaggly teeth. "You, you know, lookin' for somethin'?"

"Waiting for someone. You know Trevor?"

"Shit," the man said, clearly trying not to piss himself. "You *Hoodoo Squad*?"

He was actively trembling and sweating like somebody with malaria.

"New replacement," I said in a bored tone. "Just waiting for Trevor."

"Sorry, man," the guy said, backing away with his hands out. "Sorry, sorry..."

He turned and ran.

"Well, that was odd," I said, rolling the window back up. I turned on the windshield wipers to get rid of some of the condensation. The last time Honeybear had gotten this steamed up . . .

Damn elves.

Keeping an eye on the mirror, I saw a few other early risers, or late late nighters, giving my car the eyeball. Bit before eight a couple of younger guys with knee-length shirts and ball caps on sideways took up residence catty-corner to the, hopefully, MHI building. Cars started stopping by.

In Seattle the drug dealers didn't usually show up till after noon. Props for the work ethic.

One of them eventually swaggered across the street, coming up at an angle that kept him mostly away from my mirrors, and rapped on the back window. He was looking back and forth, ducking up and down, as if checking to see if he was going to take fire. Body down, body side to side, lean forward. It would have been hard to get a head shot if you were a sniper. Otherwise any decent shot could have pegged his center of mass from fifty yards.

"Yo," he said when I rolled down my driver's side window. "You best find 'nother place park, homie." It was an aggressive tone. He had his hand up under his shirt and was staying back over my shoulder where it was harder to get shot. And easy to shoot someone.

"Hoodoo Squad," I said. "New transfer. Just waitin' on Trevor."

"Shit, homie," the kid said, taking his hand out from under his shirt and holding up his hands. "Sorry, man! Fo'get I say nothin'!" With that he trotted back across the street and engaged in excited conversation with his homies.

So I guess this *was* the office of the Hoodoo Squad.

"Apparently we have a rep," I muttered, chuckling. I could imagine what an MHI monster squad, scarily armed and highly trained, could do to your average shoot-sideways-spray-and-pray drug gang.

Bit after eight a battered, gray, late model Toyota Corolla pulled up behind my car and a black guy got out. Five eight, muscular but not ripped, he had his left arm in a sling. In my mirror I could see him give the group on the far corner a chin up as if to say "Hey." They waved back nervously, ducking again. He was wearing a ball cap for a fishing company and appeared to have a shaved head.

I got out and walked back to his car.

"Trevor?" I asked, holding out my hand. I'd met other team leads but not Arnold. "Chad Gardenier."

"Ben Carter," the man said, shaking hands. "Team Second. Trev's in the hospital, still. He'll be out by noon."

He was tired as hell, I could tell.

"What?" I asked.

"Vampire on Seventh Street," Carter said. "Same stuff, different day. We need to run you down to the parish offices, touch base with SIU, get your permits stamped, maybe have lunch with MCB. You got a place to stay yet?"

"I was going to find a residence hotel till I get somewhere," I said. Lunch with MCB? The FBI's Monster Control Bureau officers were usually our biggest pains in the ass.

"You can stay in the team house." He gestured with his chin. "We'll take my car. Leave yours."

"Uh . . ." I looked around. "I've got about a hundred

thousand dollars in guns in the trunk and a sword that cost more than a new sports car."

"Oh, yeah." Ben reached into his pocket, pulled out a small sticker, peeled off the backing and slapped it on Honeybear's trunk. "That'll take care of it."

The sticker had a shrunken head on it and the caption: MHI Team Hoodoo.

"That's it?" I asked skeptically.

"Nobody in the whole parish is going to mess with any car with that on its trunk." Ben pulled out his keys. "You're driving."

"Okay," I said doubtfully. "But I got to get my sword."

"Feel free," Ben said in an amused voice. "They're technically legal to carry in public in New Orleans."

"You guys have to get into it with drug gangs often?" I asked.

Mo No Ken was in the front seat taking up room. I never left Mo No Ken somewhere unsecure.

"What do you mean?" Ben said.

"I had a couple of . . . approaches. One a street dealer and one of the guys across the street. Both of them freaked when they realized I was, as they put it, Hoodoo Squad. I had to guess you guys have busted heads with them before?"

"Nothing of the sort," Ben said. "Twelfth Street Dons provide mundane security for us. Keep an eye on the building when people aren't around, make sure nobody messes with our cars, not that anybody in this town would, that sort of thing. The gang owns the building we use, so I guess you'd say they're our landlords. Not that they ever ask for rent."

"Okay."

"This is the New Orleans, son," Ben said. "Things are *different* here."

"Got it," I said. I didn't. Not then.

I started to get *different* when I met the captain in charge of the Special Investigations Unit. I'd dated, briefly, the new "special actions" captain for Multnomah County, Oregon (Portland area). Kay Shaw was a hot redhead who was as disinterested in a long-term relationship as I was and especially with a Monster Hunter. She had no employees and an office in the basement.

Captain Otis Rivette was in charge of the New Orleans P. D. Special Investigations Unit and had one corner of the top floor of the parish offices and a full staff. He looked as worn out as Ben. He was heavy-set, had thinning yellow hair, a florid complexion, the nose of a heavy drinker and sharp but tired blue eyes.

"Hope you last longer than the last guy," was Rivette's greeting while shaking my hand.

"I'll try, sir."

Ben had told me if I was that attached to the sword to bring it. Nobody in the offices batted an eye at a guy walking in with a katana. I actually heard cops arguing about whether wights technically counted as zombies or not. Yes. Right out in front of God and everybody.

"Give Candice all your particulars," Rivette said, leading us back out of the office. "We'll have all your permits done by this afternoon. How soon can you be rolling?"

"If you don't care about permits, as soon as I've got my armor on, sir." I was standing there with a sword slung and my 1911 bulging on my hip. I don't think he cared about my permits. "I've got a battalion's worth of guns and ammo in my trunk." *Assuming it's still there when I get back.*

"Good." Rivette patted me on the shoulder. It was the sort of pat an oncologist gives you as you're going out the door after being told you have terminal cancer. "You religious, son?"

"Catholic," I said.

"Might want to stop by church," he said. "Get a confession in before you roll. Maybe communion. State of grace, you know."

"Yes, sir." I was pretty sure this wasn't "fucking with the new guy" stuff. He was serious.

Later I took his advice.

"Let's go meet MCB," Ben said.

Generally the only time Monster Hunter International interacted with Monster Control Bureau—the secret government agency dedicated to witness intimidation, disinformation, and every other dirty trick to keep secret the existence of the supernatural—was on missions when MCB would complain about MHI being too *indiscreet.*

The meeting was in an open-air bar and grill called Maurice's. Three MCB agents, in polo shirts and dark slacks, weapons in holsters and badges on their belts, were sitting at the bar drinking shots of bourbon. All three had shaved heads. It seemed to be the local style. Maybe it was the heat.

Again, Ben said to bring the sword. So I did. Again, nobody batted an eye. And we were still both packing. I'd taken off my jacket because it was just that freaking hot. Okay, almost nobody batted an eye. A few people you could tell were tourists eyeballed us on the way in. "Two guys with pistols on their belt, one carrying a Jap sword! New Orleans is so weird!"

"Bill, Jody, Bob, this is Chad, the new guy," Ben said, sitting down at the bar. The bartender, a shapely brunette, didn't even ask, just laid down the shot glass and poured.

Ben held it up. "Absent companions."

"Absent companions," the three agents said and downed their drinks.

I found myself sitting in front of a shot of bourbon. Oh, well, I'm all about fitting in.

"Where did you come from?" one of the agents asked. It sounded *pro forma.*

"Seattle," I said.

"Tough town?" another one asked.

"I used to think so," I said, considering the newly filled shot. I was driving after all.

"Pretty good with that sword?" an agent asked.

"Fair," I said.

"You look silly carrying it around. Shotgun?"

"I prefer an Uzi .45. I've tricked it up various ways. Works for me."

"Long gun?"

"M14. Barrett for really long."

"Explosives?"

"Military training only," I said. "Marine."

"Pendleton or Parris?" one of them asked, sounding vaguely interested.

"Parris."

"Pussy. Try mountains."

"Try sand flies."

"You flatlanders and your sand flies. Which unit?"

"One-Eight."

That occasioned a moment of silence.

"Beirut?"

"Yup," I said. "Minor miracle. Only miracle in my platoon."

"Okay."

About then a plate was set down in front of me. It contained some chopped up chicken, greens and grits. More were laid in front of the rest of the group. Nobody had asked me if I wanted any.

My mouth immediately began watering. I'd forgotten how much I missed greens and grits.

The chicken, though, was simply amazing.

"What *is* this?" I asked, taking another sip of bourbon. If I was going to be rolling tonight, I needed to be vaguely sober.

"Bourbon chicken," Ben said through his own mouthful.

I held up my cleaned plate to the barmaid and gave her my best puppy-dog eyes.

"More, please?" I asked. "And can I get some sweet tea?"

A guy came in and dumped a bunch of broadsheet papers on the bar and walked out without a word. The barmaid, after placing my order for "more, please," picked a few up and delivered them.

It was an alternative weekly. The *New Orleans Truth Teller*. The printing looked as if it had been done by a kindergartner. So did the spelling. The stories though ...

MAJIC FIRE HURIRCANE RECKS
HAVOC IN NNTIH WARD!

The picture, out of focus, showed what looked like a tornado on fire. It looked badly retouched.

"See you made the front page again, Ben," one of the agents said, perusing the paper.

"That fucking demon," Ben said. "I knew I should have brought nitrogen."

"Loup-garou rampage?" I asked.

"That's what everybody calls werewolves down here," one of the agents said. I had no idea which one was Bob or Bill or...

"Was there, in fact, a loup-garou terrorizing... Meteor?"

"Met-ah-ree," one of the agents corrected. "And yes."

"And you *allow* this to be printed?" I said cautiously. MCB would generally find whoever was printing something like this and slip a wire garrote around their neck, First Amendment be damned.

"You kidding?" one of the agents said, taking a sip of bourbon. "We publish it."

"You *what*?"

Keeping the supernatural secret was the primary mission of the MCB. Not "protect the constitution," not "protect and serve." Keep the reality of the supernatural secret. I'd been told there was a good reason for that from people I trusted. I didn't like it and generally didn't like the MCB. But there was a reason and that was good enough for me. I'm a Marine. If senior people said "There's a reason, Marine," I accepted that even if I hated the order and its effects. Publishing something like this was the equivalent of a Marine squad defecating on the flag. Unthinkable.

"Best way to tell a lie," the agent who'd apparently been a Pendleton Marine said. "Tell the truth. Just tell it badly. Nobody from out of town *believes* any of that stuff. Look at how it's printed, the spelling, the stories. The person who prints it is obviously delusional. Just another piece of New Orleans color. People bring them home to their friends to show them how crazy New Orleans is."

"Traditional MCB containment methods have never worked real well in New Orleans." The agent who said that was a little older and had the aura of being senior. "So we're trying some atypical methods now."

"And the MCB in Washington is okay with that?"

The three agents exchanged amused glances.

"They care about results. You know about the First Reason?" the senior agent asked.

"Yes, sir," I said. "Basically you keep the supernatural secret, because the more people who know about it, the stronger the supernatural gets."

"New Orleans is *why* it's important," he said. "The First Reason exists so that people don't know and won't believe in the supernatural. Because if they know they can curse an enemy with a voodoo doll and some virgin's blood, they'll go find a virgin and get the blood. If they know they can call up an Old One and get a promotion, they'll call up an Old One. The more people get into it, the crazier they get, and Katy bar the door."

"Only in some parts of this city, the locals all *know* the supernatural exists and you aren't going to convince them otherwise," explained Agent Marine. "Half of them are terrified of houdoun, the rest are practitioners."

"I was promoted to SAC of this office recently. The way I see it, this is already the most superstitious city in America. My men aren't going to convince the locals everything they've believed for generations is a delusion. So containment in New Orleans isn't about success or failure, it's more about holding the line and trying to keep the lid from coming completely off."

"The important thing is that we get things shut down before too many tourists get involved," Ben explained. "So Bill here grants certain allowances for us to do our job that would probably be frowned on in other jurisdictions."

"That's a polite way of saying that I'm a lot more lenient to you Hunters than you're used to. You want to keep it that way, don't fuck this up," Agent Boss, whose name was apparently Bill, explained. "Most agents see you guys as a pain in our ass, but I see you as an allied resource. Incidents have been on the rise for a while, which is why my predecessor got transferred. DC wants results; an unorthodox city requires unorthodox methods. That means if Hunters need to make some noise in public, as long as you get it locked down fast, I'm willing to look the other way."

"What do you mean incidents have been on the rise?"

"The graph for New Orleans' quarterly monster attack numbers looks like a motherfucking rocket ship taking off." He downed his drink. "And no. We've got no idea what's behind the recent spike. When we find out, you guys will be the first to know."

That was oddly forthcoming from the MCB. I would find out later that Bill, or Special Agent in Charge William Castro, was considered a cowboy by MCB standards. I would also eventually learn that he was former DEA, had a cocaine habit and a few mistresses, took bribes, made a lot of bad decisions—and he was *still* probably one of the most dedicated MCB agents I ever met.

"Welcome to hell, Marine. Drink up," Agent Three said. "Now, ask us why we all have shaved heads."

"I don't have to. You don't want anybody getting a lock of your hair to curse you. Been there."

"Cursed?" Agent Marine asked.

"Moved here to avoid it," I said.

"Cut your own hair," Agent Boss said. "Cueball."

"Boot style," Agent Marine said, rubbing his head.

"Keep your toenail and fingernail clippings, too," Agent Boss said. "Burn them with your hair. Can't keep from leaving some blood behind but it usually gets contaminated."

The phone rang and the barmaid answered, then held her hand over the receiver.

"Ben, you here?" she asked.

"Shit," Ben said, then waved for the phone. Agent Boss's beeper went off about the same time.

"Shit," Agent Boss said, looking at it. "Tell them we're rolling, will you?"

"MCB says they're rolling," Ben said into the phone. "Yeah. Maurice's. What? Okay. I'll roll . . ." He thought about it and rotated his arm in a sling. "Somebody. The new guy. Yeah. Bye."

"I've got it," I said. "What do I got?"

"Zombies at a school," Ben said.

"Again?" Agent Three said.

"Bullies around here are at least learning to leave nerds alone," Agent Marine said.

"I'll take it but I have no clue where anything is," I said. "And my gear is back at the team house."

"I'll give the new guy a ride over and show him where it's at," Agent Marine told Ben. "I'm out front."

"Roger," I said, standing up and pulling out a hundred. Say what you will about us mercenary Hunters, most of us tip really well.

"I've got it," Ben said.

"Money's already down," I said as Agent Marine started out the door. "Hey, honey, when do you get off?"

"I don't date Hunters," she said, smiling. "I like to have some idea if a guy's going to be around next week."

"Your loss," I said, grinning. I liked a challenge.

CHAPTER 3
Lunatic Fringe

"I sort of missed the introductions," I said. "Chad Gardenier."

"Special Agent Robert Higgins," Bob said, holding out his hand. He had lights and sirens on and was blazing through traffic, weaving in and out and into oncoming lanes. Naturally, nobody was getting out of the way.

"What's the deal with the drug gangs?" I asked.

"Not my area," Bob said. "But what deal?"

"The ones across the corner from the house apparently handle security? I was sort of afraid to just leave my car there but Ben slapped a team sticker on it and said it would be all good."

"Oh," he said, "that. Everybody in this town thinks the supernatural exists. Some are into it, the rest are scared of all the weird shit that's in this town. Even the practitioners are afraid. Just because you're a necromancer doesn't mean you can stop a demon. Having Hoodoo Squad right there is sort of like their own personal luck charm. And generally people think the Hoodoo Squad cars are hexed."

"Hexed?" I said. Keep in mind, I was talking to an MCB agent about people using black magic, and he wasn't shooting anyone for it.

"Minor stuff," Higgins said. "Temporary impotence, that sort of thing. But I don't think they'd mess with your cars anyway. Every criminal in town is terrified of anything supernatural. They're the prime targets of all the stuff we deal with. Loup-garou running wild? Good people are in their homes at night, drug dealers and burglars are out on the streets. Vampires? Same deal. So they're terrified of what goes bump in the night because they have to be out in the night. That includes Hunters, SIU and us. Just the fact that we deal with it puts us in the practitioners field. They think we're the lunatic fringe. When you get a place, put up some shrunken heads and chicken feet in the windows. You want people to know you're Hoodoo Squad. If they break in and find out later, they're liable to freak out. And if you do get a break-in, put the word out and your shit will probably be returned pretty quick. And a body will end up in the river face down."

We pulled up next to my car in a cloud of blue tire smoke. "That is you, right?" Higgins said.

"Yes," I said, climbing out.

"Think you can keep up?" It wasn't a challenge, it was a question.

"Probably," I said. "Some of the turns might get me."

"Just try to keep up," he said.

"I have to check one thing," I said.

I checked the trunk. Everything was there.

"We keepin' a good eye on it, Mr. Hoodoo!" one of the thugs yelled.

New Orleans.

❖   ❖   ❖

Keeping up had been difficult. Other people thought following a car running lights and sirens was a good way to slip through traffic. I had to practically sideswipe one guy. He flipped me the bird. I pointed at my trunk. In the rearview I saw him go white and pull over.

We needed our own color lights. Like purple or something. I was starting to get the feeling that the locals might not get out of the way for the FBI, but they would for us. Agent Boss said he was unorthodox, so it wouldn't hurt to ask.

We pulled up in front of a brick school. Two NOPD cars were parked outside, lights on. The officers were in them, buttoned up. Ben Carter's car was already there. The other members of MHI were either occupied or too far away to wait for.

"You get anything on the radio about numbers?" I asked as I got out.

"Report is initially three," Higgins said. "They announced it and had the classrooms lock down. Active zombies on premises. They don't know if all the classrooms locked down in time or how many victims there might be."

"Shamblers?" I asked, opening my trunk.

"Yeah, a couple. Sounds like they're contained though. Carter already went in the back."

"I've got this side," I said, pulling out the Uzi and the designated vest. I had a load-bearing vest for whatever weapon was my primary. The Uzi was my preferred weapon for shamblers, slow zombies in other words. They shambled. Could get into a nice fast run on a flat, which school hallways would be, but they weren't really dangerous if you could dodge at all and had enough firepower.

"No armor?"

"If it's a horde, then, yeah, armor. But a few shamblers?" I hefted the Uzi. "Ask me sometime how I got into this." I slammed the trunk lid. "And time is the enemy with shamblers. More people that get bit or killed, more that rise."

"Right answer," Higgins said. "Go. MCB has the perimeter."

There were big glass double doors on the front of the three-story school. I entered and assessed. The AC felt good was my first assessment. There was a wide entryway, tiled. On the right was an office marked "Nurse." On the right was another marked "Office."

I went to that one.

"Hoodoo Squad," I said, banging on the door. "MHI, Team Hoodoo," I added. I added *shave and a haircut* to the hammering so they'd know I was human. Sentient. Whatever.

There were three locks on the door. They slowly clicked one by one. The door cracked a bit to reveal an elderly black woman.

"MHI, ma'am," I said politely. "Any more word on numbers or location?"

"They was up on the second floor," she said, glancing nervously through the door to make sure there weren't any zombies around. "Couple of 'em."

"Wouldn't happen to have a map, would you?"

She shoved a mimeographed map that read *New Students Orientation* into my hands.

"Thank you, ma'am," I said, tipping my nonexistent hat. "Go ahead and lock back up."

They hadn't just been on the second floor. There was a body sprawled in the corridor that, according to the map, led to the stairs. Older black gentleman. He'd been pretty badly torn apart but in short order he'd be up and tearing others.

As I passed I put a .45 round in his medulla. I kept walking.

"Hoodoo Squad in the building," a voice announced over the loudspeaker. "Stay in you classrooms till we tells you."

There was a faint cheer from pretty much every direction. That sort of made me straighten up. It's always nice to be liked.

The difference was bizarre. MCB had not only given me a ride, they'd shown me the way to the site. Lights and sirens, no less. Nobody asked what the hell I was doing creeping through the halls of a school with a gun. I was Hoodoo Squad, there to get rid of the hoodoo. Like you'd call a pest control company to come take care of a raccoon in your basement.

Difference being raccoons don't, by and large, eat people then cause them to rise from the dead. Except, you know, zombie raccoons. And let me tell you, brother, those things are a bitch and a half.

At the top of the stairs there was a corridor running directly away from the stairs, then a corridor heading left. The one to the left had windows on the stair sides, the other had no doors, and a plain wall littered with posters and photographs. There appeared to be a small shrine with pictures and cards around it. Someone had died who recently attended or worked at the school.

At the end of that corridor there was another, turning right. The shamblers had to be down that hall. I could hear them battering at something, probably a door. They sure as hell weren't down the one I was looking at.

I kept to the left, by the windows, and heel-toed forward until I was looking down the corridor. There were two shamblers, battering at a door to one of the classrooms. The doors were sturdy. They weren't making much headway at the moment but they'd eventually batter through.

There was another body on the floor between myself and them. Female student. Very torn up.

I silently heel-toed up till the not-yet-risen corpse was on my right, lowered the Uzi and put a bullet in her head.

A suppressed .45 isn't that loud. Unless it's fired in a tile-lined corridor where most of the building was being as quiet as church mice to avoid attracting the hoodoo.

The shot attracted their attention away from the door. Which was the point.

I took an offhand stance, left foot slightly forward, leaned in and began targeting. I fired. One round hit a zombie in the eye and it dropped like a rock. Another shot. Another penetration. It went right through the forehead. You can't just do minor damage to a zombie brain and kill it. Isn't how it works. You've got to pulp a lot of brain. So after everybody got one, I went back and served up seconds. Just to be sure.

I automatically did a 360 as soon as the threat was eliminated and double-checked the girl at my feet. Still dead dead. Nothing on my six.

Ben was clearing the other side of the school. I wasn't used to working solo. I was used to a brother at my back. "Cold is back without brother to warm it." I tried to remember which culture had that as a quote. Spartans? Solo hunting was a good way to get killed. No matter how tough you are, you can only look in one direction at a time.

I continued heel-toe down the corridor, around to the cross corridor and back. Another body. Adult female. Bullet in the head. *Pop.* Heel-toe.

I cleared the second-floor corridors then up to third, quick walk around second in case of infiltration, down to first. All clear.

I walked back to the office and did shave and a haircut again.

"Are there any other areas than on this map?" I asked the black lady. "A basement, maybe?"

"There ain't no basements in New Orleans, son," she said. "It all done?"

"Yes, but the police would probably prefer you stay locked down till they clear the corridors," I said. "There's bodies. Especially on the second floor."

"You get 'em all?" the lady asked, querulously. "You gotta put bullets in the haid all them as is bit."

"Yes, ma'am," I said. "I put bullets in all their heads."

"That bitty gun gonna do it?" she asked. Now that the threat was gone she was back to school-office-manager mode and I had always been a bit baby-faced. She probably thought I was right out of Monster Training School or something.

"Yes, ma'am," I said. "Not my first rodeo. I've got to go get the police, now. If you'll excuse me."

"Thank you, young man," she said as I walked away.

I'd marked the map and pointed out the location of bodies.

"Two shamblers, one victim. I cleared the victim. One victim here. And here. Both cleared."

"Cleared?" The guy asking the question was slightly chubby with a flabby face and hands, wire-rimmed spectacles held on with a piece of string to keep them from slipping and wearing a blue coverall marked "Coroner."

"I shot them in the head to keep them from rising," I said. "They were all bitten."

"Chad Gardenier," Agent Higgins said. "Dave Boswick, Coroner's Special Incident shift lead. Dave, Chad. Chad is MHI's new guy."

"Pleased," Dave said. He didn't seem to be. "You're sure you shot them all?"

"Sure," I said. "I don't make mistakes about putting down undead, sir."

"Your contract specifies staying on scene until we're clear," Boswick said.

"Okay," I said. Ben was talking to some of the cops, but that sounded legit. "Quick question. We usually take samples on site. What's the procedure here? For the PUFF."

"Dave gives you a receipt for each of them," Bob said. "That's mostly how it goes. Keep the receipts, turn them in to MHI. You'll need an incident number, you can get that from the on-scene cop or Dave or other shift leads. MHI submits the receipt number and incident. We verify. You get paid."

"That's . . . almost efficient," I said.

"We've suggested it nationwide," Bob said. "Hunters don't trust it because it depends on us and coroners verifying. And most places the coroners aren't as experienced so that causes problems. Here, it works."

"You ready?" Dave asked.

"Sure," I said.

In Seattle I'd dealt with coroner teams a few times. They generally turned up with a stretcher. The New Orleans coroners had a lift on the back of their truck and a large, wheeled cargo flat piled with body bags.

I followed them in. Dave stood by making notes and filling out paperwork as his two assistants, both burly black men probably in their forties, loaded the bodies into body bags and stacked them on the flat.

They had to just carry the body bags upstairs and get the corpses that way. Finally, all the bodies were cleared and Dave handed me a slip of paper stamped with the parish stamp and his squiggle.

"That's it?" I asked. The paper was full of codes. I recognized the one for Undead, Zombie, Human, Slow.

"That's it," Dave said. "Five shamblers."

"There were only two vertical."

"Five shamblers," Dave said. "Just take the receipt."

I took the receipt and carefully put it in my wallet so I wouldn't lose it.

"I guess we're done," I said, walking out to the MCB car.

"You got another call," Bob said, grinning maliciously. He'd reparked his car under a live oak and was looking cool as a cucumber. "Some sort of little fire imp or something over in Lafayette Cemetery."

"You're joking," I said. I'd been checked in for about four hours, gotten a bit buzzed for early lunch, was still burping bourbon chicken, cleared a high school of zombies, and I had *another* call?

"Nope," Bob said. "Call came in on the radio."

"Somebody has to stay with the coroner." Carter said. "I'm not even supposed to be out of the hospital yet. You want this one? I can catch up."

"So, is MHI gonna take the call or not?" the MCB agent asked.

"We don't do imps," Dave the coroner said as his helpers maneuvered the loaded flat down the steps of the school. "All they leave is ectoplasm."

"Those you take samples," Bob said. "Want me to lead you over, new guy?"

"Sure. Lemme put this stuff away. Then we'll play car tag."

There was exactly zero shade in Lafayette Cemetery Number Two. The aboveground burial plots and tombs caught what breeze there was and trapped the heat. It was a furnace.

A furnace in a maze. Most of the burial plots were single and just raised. The water table was so high that you couldn't bury someone six feet under. The raised single plots were about knee height and looked somewhat like Egyptian sarcophagi.

But there were dozens of mausoleums as well. The mausoleums were mostly about a story in height and elaborately made. They were all in bad repair but they'd been pretty when new, you could tell. In addition, many of the plots had statues on them, the Virgin Mary and weeping angels featured prominently.

Between the plots and mausoleums were broad walkways and narrow gaps. Both were choked with weeds ranging up to waist height. Each walkway, in turn, was filled with more kinds of bugs than you could find in the entire Pacific Northwest.

Somewhere in this maze there was, supposedly, a small fire demon. Things which were on fire were often best dealt with by cold. I'd stopped at an industrial supply store and picked up an industrial carbon dioxide fire extinguisher. About then I wanted to just play it over myself.

There was a squealing and chattering from around a small mausoleum with . . . six people in it according to the inscription. I had the fire extinguisher in one hand and my other on the pistol grip of the Uzi.

A few small demons were ripping at another corpse. This was an old woman, dressed for church, in a nice dress—well, formerly nice—good flat shoes and a hat. By her right hand was a vase with flowers and water spilling out of it. She was pretty well torn to bits at this point and thoroughly cooked. There was a smell of burnt pork in the air.

One of the demons squealed as I appeared and sent a blast of fire my way. The fire breath barely warmed my already warm shins.

"HOODOO SQUAD!" it squealed. "HOOF IT!"

"Oh, no, you don't," I said, hitting the lever on the extinguisher.

One of the demons managed to get out of the area of effect. The others wailed and screamed as the cold hit them, then one by one turned to statues.

I hit them with a burst from the Uzi, hip fire, and they shattered like glass, and immediately began to deliquesce.

That left the one that got away. It had darted across the walkway and between two mausoleums, headed for the street.

My only choice was to follow it directly. After

reloading, I squeezed between the mausoleums. Beyond them to one side was a mausoleum, on the other side one of the regular burial plots. I ran across that, apologizing under my breath, until I got to the next walkway and looked both ways.

About that time there was the honk of a horn. I went that way.

There was an NOPD car parked on the next street over. The officer pointed across the road to *another* cemetery on the *other* side of the road.

"You've got to be freaking kidding me," I muttered, crossing the road. I was still carrying a thirty-pound fire extinguisher in my left hand.

I heard screams in the cemetery and headed that way as best I could. Another freaking maze.

It was a group cleaning up one of the plots, four young women and a boy, probably ten, pulling weeds off one of the sarcophagi.

"Did you see..." I said, panting. Fucking heat. "Demon..."

"It went that way, Mr. Hoodoo," the boy said, pointing between another couple of mausoleums.

By this time I was starting to notice the occasional scorch mark. Jesse had taught me the rudiments of outdoor tracking and I realized the little demon was leaving sign. The scorching was from whenever it touched some of the burial plots and mausoleums.

It turned eventually—it had been going straight as an arrow as far as I could tell—and then turned back. At that point I lost it for a bit but picked up the trail again near the road.

I found a scorch mark that still had a faint trace of sulfur to it. I was getting close.

The trail all of a sudden went crazy, going in and out between mausoleums. Like it was chasing something. Finally I found it.

The demon was huddled between a mausoleum and a sarcophagus, worrying on the body of a rat.

"OH, NO!" it squealed, dropping the half-eaten rodent. "I DON'T WANNA GO BACK!"

I sprayed the remains of the fire extinguisher over the imp. One kick and it shattered.

"Six flame imps," I said, holding up the plastic sandwich bags containing traces of the ectoplasm of each. "Four people who saw one of them. One victim. Need coroner. I give these to Ben?"

"I'll take them," Bob said, pulling out a ticket book. "I'll take your word for it. They might get tested, they might not. We're sort of backed up."

He gave me a receipt with the incident number and receipt numbers for each baggie.

"'Nother call came in while you were chasing that last imp," Bob said. He had, again, somehow managed to find shade. "Might want to rig up for this one. Remodeling crew in Metairie found what sounds like a nest of vampires in a building."

I looked up at the sun. It was still well high.

"And they didn't just stake them?" I asked hopefully.

"Not after one of the workers got his throat ripped out. Like I said, might want to rig up."

CHAPTER 4
Hit Me with Your Best Shot

It was another mad dash through the streets of New Orleans with MCB in the loud car. We got up on I-10, the way I'd come into town, and made good time. The site was an old strip mall on Metairie Road. It looked not unlike the one where I'd enlisted in the Marines.

The original anchor store had apparently been out of business for some time. The area looked as if it was improving and apparently it was time to clean it up and do things like take the plywood off the... HOLY SHIT! VAMPIRES!

What appeared to be a survivor was babbling. It was a patois that was entirely impenetrable. And I'm a noted linguist in some circles.

"Epi li Coolie chire gòj li soti!"

"And then it just ripped the boss's throat out," the Metairie PD officer said, in a bored tone.

"San! San!" the man cried.

"Blood, blood."

"Vampire," Bob said, nodding his head in a knowing

48

fashion and wagging one finger. "Bet you dollars to donuts." He turned to me. "Sounds like you're up."

"Again," I said, walking back to the trunk of my car and starting to rummage.

"I'm just messing with you, man. Carter's stuck in traffic but will be here soon. My guys should be too. Just relax. They aren't going anywhere before sundown."

I reappeared with my .45 in a tac holster, a double-barrel sawed-off in a chest holster and bandolier with stakes and a dozen shotgun shells in loops. I had on a dog collar with spikes I'd picked up to get into punk clubs. Mo No Ken was slung at my side. I started walking toward the building.

"Seriously," Bob said. "No joking around. You don't want to rig up for this one?"

"Too damned hot," I said. "Where's the open door, Agent Higgins? And somebody do me the favor to pull down a couple more of these plywood sheets, please."

The door was in the shade. I thought about it and decided I didn't like the door option. The sun was shining from the other side of the building. There were windows on the sunny side. Take a couple of pieces of plywood off and I'd be golden. But if I entered by the door, everything would be in shadow and my vision would be horrible. Better in from this side through the windows.

Since none of the workers were willing to go near the building and MCB Bob wanted to wait for backup, I rummaged in the car again and came up with a Halligan tool, crowbar and ax.

"What all do you *have* in there?" Bob asked, amused.

"Well, to find out we'll need something that requires C4, claymores, and a LAW," I said, grinning.

Bob found a seat in the shade and was writing up an incident report. It probably read: foolish new MHI guy went in solo and got eaten by vampires, the end. "One vampire will fuck you up. There could be more in there, you know."

A few minutes' work with the Halligan tool and I had the first sheet off the windows. I took down two more and decided that was enough. It was too hot to do this shit. And I had to remember to fill my canteens.

I broke out one of the grimy windows, threw a blanket on the chest-high sill and stuck my face up to it.

"Hello! This is your friendly welcome wagon! I don't suppose you'd like to just come over and get staked?"

"Go away, blood bag," a female voice hissed from the darkness. "Or I will drink your very soul!"

"Come out here in the sunlight and say that, fang."

"You come in here."

"Okee-dokee, artichokee," I said. "Take your best shot!"

I smashed the window all the way out and looked around.

"Hey, Bob, I need you to bring your car up here on the sidewalk," I yelled.

"Why?" he said.

"So I can stand on the hood."

"Stand on your own hood," he said, indignant.

"I gotta pay for damages to my car," I pointed out. "Besides, I did most of the bodywork myself. I don't want to damage it. Yours is issue. Be a pal. Once a Marine, always a Marine!"

"Touché," Bob said, getting up.

Only I had said all that for the vampire's benefit. I backed up, put in a couple of earplugs, pulled a flash-bang out of my pocket, pulled the pin, flipped the spoon, waited two seconds, and threw it through the window as hard as I could. Then I ran up, put my gloved hands on the sill and vaulted through the window just as the flash-bang went off.

The secret to a flash-bang is to know it's going to happen and have been around it before. They are loud, they are scary, they are very bright. But if you know it's coming, they aren't so bad. If you don't have super-sensitive eyesight and hearing like a vampire, that is.

The vamp was expecting me to climb up on the hood of a car and climb through the window. She was up against that wall, crouched down to avoid reflected sunlight. Her plan was to grab me as I came through and rip my throat out. She probably heard the pin coming out of the bang, but odds were good that she wouldn't know what it was until it was too late.

I could see her clearly as I came through the window. She was crouched down, pressed against the wall, screaming, her hands over her ears and eyes tightly shut. The image was briefly superimposed on my eyelids as I landed.

I took one step forward and Mo No Ken flashed.

No more vampire.

A few minutes later I climbed back through the window carrying a skull in a mesh bag.

Vampires deliquesce quick.

"This do for proof of kill, Agent Higgins?" I asked, holding up the bag.

I was more or less covered in blood from cutting her head off. It's the only way you can kill a vampire. Staking them only paralyzes them.

"Ought to," Bob said. I swear some of his "you ain't from around here" attitude was starting to wear off.

I was also standing on a fairly major road and traffic had picked up as schools let out. People were slowing down to figure out why the police cars were parked here. Some people were staring, dumbfounded, at the blood-covered guy. Some were surprised but mostly I was getting horns honking, people holding up thumbs, things like that. A pickup with a bunch of rednecks in the back, including a couple of teenage cuties holding beer cans, went by and I heard an excited "Hey, look y'all! Hoodoo Squad!" and a female voice yelled "Wooooo!"

"What was that you were saying about Parris Island Marines?" I yelled, holding one hand up to my ear. "I'm a little deaf from all the monster killing and big 'splosions. I know I heard *something* about Parris Island Marines."

"I'll get a trash bag," Bob muttered. "Get out of sight before you make my job any harder than it needs to be."

"I hate fucking heat," I shouted. "I want to go back to Seattle!"

And that was the daylight part of my first day working the Big Easy.

Trevor Arnold was a big guy, from his head to his feet. Big bald head, big shoulders, big chest, big gut, arms like tree limbs and legs like trunks. He could barely fit into the office chair in the MHI team leader's office. One of those tree-trunk legs was currently in a size ogre soft-cast that was propped on his desk. A cane with a silver-demon-head top was leaning on the desk as well.

The desk was covered in paper. I could tell it was in "this has got to be done, this should be done if I ever get a chance, this is never going to get done" piles. There were more piles around the office. You could tell MHI New Orleans was having a hard time keeping up with the minor shit.

"I hear you did pretty good today," he said.

He had green eyes that reminded me of a Jamaican guy we had in my platoon before Beirut and what might be called café au lait skin. Other than that, his features were more or less Northern European with maybe a dash of Mediterranean. He had a big nose to go with the big everywhere else and high, Scandinavian cheekbones.

"Fairly well, sir," I said. I pulled out the sheaf of receipts.

He ruffled through them, nodding, then shook his head.

"Even for around here that's a rough first day," he said.

The air conditioning was a window unit that could barely keep up. It was probably eighty degrees in the office. If Trevor noticed, it wasn't apparent. The interiors of the offices were more pleasant than the exterior. There was a nice team room in the front by the balcony that was finely carpeted with wood paneling, comfortable furniture, projection TV and a full wet bar.

Trevor's office was even well set up. More like a lawyer's office than a Monster Hunter's. There were custom bookshelves on the walls and the desk he had his foot propped on looked to be an antique. On the wall behind him was a shadow box with a Special Forces beret, jump wings, various other Army doodads

I mostly didn't recognize. One was a diver's helmet I was pretty sure was SCUBA school, and an awards set surmounted by the Silver Star. There were a bunch of Vietnam decorations I recognized but didn't know what they meant.

"If it wasn't for the heat, I'd say I enjoyed myself, sir." Which was true. Say one thing for New Orleans, I wasn't going to be sitting on my hands. And that one day of Perpetual Unearthly Forces Fund bounties was what I'd usually make in Seattle in a month.

"Plus most of those will count as solo, so you'll get one hell of a check. But about that..."

I got ready to be chewed out for going in alone on the vampire. "The situation was—"

"Shut up, Chad. I don't care. Every good Hunter has a different style. You want to lone wolf it, and you get killed because of that, that's on you. You're a professional. Use your brain. It's better to wait for help, but if you can't, you can't. This is a job, not a suicide pact, but the man on the scene has to make the call. That said, you get somebody else hurt because you aren't where you should be, that is all on your head, son. And I will remove it from your shoulders."

"Understood, sir."

"Good. Joan Nelson called me to talk about you. By the way, she loves you and thinks you're a brilliant Hunter, but she also said you've got a lot of self-destructive tendencies, delusions of invincibility, and possibly a death wish."

"Well she is a psychiatrist."

"I told her with a resume like that you'll fit in fine in New Orleans. I asked Ray to shake the trees and find us some more help—you're hopefully the first of many—but until then we're short-handed, and everybody but you has something injured. I'm hopping on one leg, Ben shouldn't be moving that arm at all yet, but Shelbye should be up for light hunting tonight. You two will be on call," Trevor said, pulling out a beeper. "You got a cell phone?"

"I've got a radiophone, sir."

"Probably won't work around here. Soon as you can, get a cell. See if your radiophone works. Maybe keep both. You'll need them. If it is something the two of you can't handle, you call me. Gimped up or not, I can still shoot. Keep Shelbye from getting in close if you possibly can. That's not her thing."

"Close is sort of my specialty, sir," I said. "Be nice to have someone at my back."

"Here's the deal," Trevor said, as if he'd repeated the briefing too many times. "New Orleans has always been one of MHI's busier postings, and it has a history of going nuts on the full moon. You've got to have your shit together here, or you will not last. I've been here for the better part of a decade, but lately everything has been getting worse."

"The MCB agents said the same thing. Any idea why?"

"Nope. We've got bodies popping out of graveyards, loup-garou moving in, and fucking vampires think this city is Mecca, but we've always got that. Lately? It's like the black magic spells suckers are always trying have actually been working, which gets more suckers trying them. The darker it gets, the more it riles up the monsters. The more folks talk, the more some asshole is going to be tempted to play with magic. MCB isn't doing their regular scare-or-shoot-the-witnesses thing lately, so we'll see where that gets us."

"Agent Castro says he's a lot more lenient than regular MCB. I was covered in blood and getting honked at today, and there was an agent just sitting there."

"Enjoy it while it lasts. I've seen SACs come and go. He could get replaced tomorrow by an agent with a stick up his ass. Until then, this is probably the one place in the country where we can get away with being identified as Monster Hunters by the locals and it isn't the end of the world. But we still try to keep our business away from the public as much as possible, because when we make the MCB's job easy, they'll make our lives easy."

"Yes, sir."

"Carry a notebook. Log every incident with notes on what you killed and where. Always get the incident number from NOPD or the Sheriff's office. There's times when you're going to have to roll before the paperwork is complete. Always stay on site while the bodies are cleared to cover coroners unless you're sure it's completely clear and coroners agree. They'll lose people if you don't and they get nasty when they lose people. Don't expect any help from anyone. Sheriff's will but it's rare. NOPD will watch you get ripped to pieces before they'll get out of their cars. We're contracted to protect coroners. Everyone else is just regular folks. But protect coroners. Any questions like *what the hell is going on around here?*" he finished with a grin. He had big, white teeth.

"No, got that," I said, still looking slightly puzzled. "I need to find someplace to live."

"We've got a bunk room here," Trevor said. "We generally hold here most nights and when we're up to full roster we'll keep an alert team on standby twenty-four until things get back to normal. So bunk here for now. I've already got a real estate agent ready to meet at your convenience. She's, pardon, a wizard at finding the right place. Next."

"When I cleared the zombies, the coroners gave me a receipt for every corpse, including the ones that hadn't gotten up yet."

"Ah," Trevor said, nodding. "We usually try to ease people into that. This is New Orleans."

"I saw the sign on the way in, sir."

"Everybody is on the take," Trevor said. "And I do mean *everyone*. Well, except MCB. I think. We have to pay the coroner's office for prompt response or we'll be sitting there for hours especially on the full moon. Then there's the Sheriff's office, local politicians to keep our contracts. It's a long list. So the coroner's will add a couple of PUFF here and there."

"Ah," I said. Given the rest, what was another major violation of federal law? "Thank you. Clarified, sir."

"Just roll with it," Trevor said, shrugging. "And welcome to the Big Easy."

Shelbye turned out to be a brunette white lady in her thirties. Curly brown hair pulled back in a ponytail, scarred, rode hard but nice body from what I could see under the body armor. She had an American flag bandana tied on her head as a do-rag and was walking with a slight limp and favoring her right ribs. Flesh golem.

We'd rigged up and were in the team room hanging out. Our cars were out front in case we got a call-out. I'd borrowed Trevor's Wahl clippers and now had a boot buzz for the first time in years. I'd put on a do-rag as well. Helmet in direct contact with buzz was uncomfortable and it would help keep the sweat out of my eyes.

The sun had set and business was booming for the drug dealers across the street. There were even a few Beemers passing by with decent suburban folk picking up their evening blow or weed before they headed home to their nice, safe, suburban homes and got the hell out of New Orleans.

Shelbye wasn't talkative and I let her have the silence. We mostly watched the evening news. Several people had died in a gas leak at a high school. There was nothing about a demon in a cemetery or...

"And in news of the weird," the anchor said, grinning with that look of someone playing a joke. "There were reports a vampire went shopping in Metairie!" There was what looked like a stock photo of a strip mall. It wasn't even the same strip mall. "Police were called to reports of a vampire in a small store in Metairie! When they checked it out, it was an old clothes dummy *dressed* as a vampire."

"Gotta love the Big Easy, Paul," the anchorwoman said, shaking her head and laughing.

"And that's the news this night," the anchor said, smiling. "Good night."

"And they're clear," Shelbye said. "And they'll shake their heads and shudder. The producers probably know the actual story, but run the cover faxed to them by MCB."

"People were waving when I came out," I said, shaking my head. "It's different. I know, welcome to the Big Easy."

"Only thing easy here is dying," Shelbye said fatalistically. The phone rang. "And it starts."

CHAPTER 5
All Along the Watchtower

Notes from my first night working the Big Easy.

0017 Rpt "sumpin big wif scales an teef" Bayou St. John. Naga. Term. Y-313-248-R. Receipt.

0234 Oh, you've got to be freaking...Ghouls in Merritt Cemetery, Violet. Term. Inc# 254-96, Parish. Receipt.

Okay, some fill-in.

The naga was freaking big. Think snake man. Ten feet long and it weighed a ton. It had broken into a home and tried to kill the family. When cops responded to a report of domestic dispute, it ripped one of them wide open while the other ran. Then it proceeded to begin its reign of terror.

It probably *could* be called a "domestic dispute." The man in the house was shacked up with the lady who lived there and whose family—four kids, one his—lived in the house. His wife had taken exception to her man sleeping around and, according to later reports, dropped a very nice insurance settlement she'd recently gotten from slipping on a grape while "going grocery" on a houdoun woman for a big curse. Said houdoun woman summoned the naga—or local houdoun equivalent, a giant water moccasin instead of a cobra—to show that man not to sleep around. Unfortunately, three of the four children were killed, one eaten. The fourth made it out the window and hoofed it.

After the fleeing officer radioed it in, Captain Otis called us.

When we got there, the naga was slithering through the neighborhood, terrorizing everyone. It kept trying to get into houses but there were more reasons than burglary for bars on the windows of houses in New Orleans.

We split up in our cars, looking for it. As I was crossing Lopez, I saw something down the street to my right. A quick turn, up on the sidewalk for a bit but Honeybear don't do sharp, and the massive reptile man was in my headlights.

I gunned it.

There was a *THUH-BUMP*! and it felt like going over a speed bump.

"Hey," I radioed, backing up. *THUH-BUMP*! "It's over on Lopez by..." I looked up at the street sign... "Dumaine."

I backed up and took a look. It was still writhing. I'd broken its back but apparently nagas regenerate. And now it was headed my way and it was pissed.

I backed to the end of the street, gunned it and hit the reptiloid with my front bumper doing about forty. It was maybe doing ten so say, combined, about fifty. Say what you will about American cars, I have my pet peeves, but there's nothing like a couple tons of Detroit steel to put the fear of God into a monster.

I was a bit afraid it was going to come through the window but it got flipped under the car instead and dragged along the street. I could hear it hammering at Honeybear's undercarriage as I drove. Finally I dislodged it by driving into a driveway then up on the curb.

I backed up and assessed. Still moving.

"*I got this,*" Shelbye radioed. The naga's cottonmouth head exploded as a rifle round went through it. "*Thet'll make a nice little trophy.*"

I wasn't sure if she was serious. She was. When I got invited to her place, she had taxidermied monster heads or other bits on every wall.

Then it started to get back up again. They regenerate. You have to take the head off.

"I think this is going to be my trophy." I got out, pulled Sword of Mourning off the floor where I'd jammed it. I had been riding around with my Uzi on its sling.

The naga was fast. It charged right at me, hissing, its muscular human arms held wide. Its humanoid, scaled torso was broad as a musclehead's and the arms reminded me of Trevor's. There was another shot but this time Shelbye missed the moving target. Head was bobbing and weaving, not her fault.

On the other hand, it was headed right at me, and a really big target. I aimed the Uzi low and let the slight recoil carry it up, stitching the naga from the base of its humanoid torso to its head.

I trotted forward, drawing Mo No Ken as it was getting up again.

Before it could orient itself, or I could take the head, another .308 round went through its skull.

"Hold off," I radioed, standing at high port. I waited for it to start rising before I took its head off. "You can still have the trophy."

"*Why'd you wait?*" Shelbye replied. She was lying

across the hood of her Dodge Charger, rifle set up on a bipod.

"This sword costs about as much as a Ferrari." I wiped down Mo No Ken. "I wasn't going to slash it into the ground now, was I?"

"Gotcha. I'll remember for next time."

"Fuck, it's hot," I muttered, taking a swig of water out of my canteen.

The door to the nearest house opened up and a woman peered out. Black, round and in her forties, she was wearing a flowered dress and curlers in her hair.

"It daid?" she shouted.

"It daid," I yelled.

"Hoodoo Squad done kilt it!" the woman shouted in the house.

In a second it seemed like the deliquescing naga was surrounded by people oohing and ahhing.

MCB was going to flip.

About that time, MCB showed up, lights flashing, along with NOPD. NOPD set up a perimeter but it was to keep out cars. Locals were flooding out to see what Hoodoo Squad had caught.

Agent Three walked over and waved his hands as if driving chickens. "Go on now, folks," he said in a New York accent. "Nothing to see here."

"What was it, Mr. Hoodoo?" one of the boys asked. The naga was almost entirely deliquesced at this point.

"You'd have to ask the FBI," I answered. "Sorry, kid."

"What I wants to know is who gonna clean up this *mess*!" the woman from the house asked angrily. "I ain't havin' no snake goo all over my driveway!"

"We'll take care of that, lady," Agent Three said tiredly. "You and your family just go on back in your house."

"Somebody ought to do somethin' 'bout all this hoodoo!" the woman said. "Streets ain't safe! We pay our taxes!"

Based on the houses in this neighborhood, I doubted most of them paid much in taxes.

"Yeah!" someone in the crowd shouted. "Too much hoodoo! We got rights!"

It took the MCB agent a few minutes to get the people calmed down and back inside. He came back, looking tired. "Can you see now why in some neighborhoods around here Castro skips the whole coerce and intimidate thing?"

"Works for me. I sort of missed the names at the bar. Or forgot it with all the shots. Chad Gardenier, MHI." I held out my hand.

"Special Agent Jody Buchanan. Naga?"

"Cottonmouth, but yeah," Shelbye said. She bent down to get a sample and winced.

"Let me get it," I said. I pulled out a baggy and scooped up some of the goo.

"You kinda fucked up your car, man," Jody said.

Honeybear's grill was seriously trashed, but that was about all.

"I can bend it out," I said. "Assuming I get any time off to do so."

"I know a good body shop," Shelbye said. "Cousin runs it. Fix it up in no time."

"I guess I'll have to go that route. I usually do all my own work."

"Won't get no time," Shelbye said.

I handed the sample to Jody and got a receipt. In the middle of the mess was what looked like the spine and head of a snake. I added that to the sample bag.

"Hey, y'all," one of the NOPD officers said. "Gots 'nother call. Over Vilet."

Make that Violet, Louisiana. Which was on the other side of the freaking city.

We were in Arabi on Louisiana 46 going like a bat out of hell, with me following Shelbye, who drove about like Bob but without a red light stuck on top of her car, when a state trooper pulled in behind us with his lights on. We were weaving in and out of traffic, blowing through red lights and going about twice the posted 45-mile-per-hour speed limit so it made sense.

I slowed down, getting ready for the ticket. I figured part of our payoff money was to cover tickets and such. Back in Seattle, generally the Sheriff's office we were responding to would handle it for us.

The trooper pulled in close behind me, practically tailgating, then pulled over and up to my window and made a motion for me to roll my window down. Shelbye was, at this point, long gone.

"You heading Vi'let?" the trooper yelled.

"Yeah!" I yelled back.

He sped up and got in front of me to clear traffic. We eventually caught up to Shelbye whose Charger, sorry, wasn't nearly as good as my Cutlass or his Impala. I'd done some work on Honeybear.

The trooper pulled off when we saw the blue lights ahead and joined the blockade around the cemetery.

We pulled further forward on State Road 46 and Shelbye stopped her car right in the road. Traffic had been stopped in both directions, not that there was much this time of night. I pulled in behind her.

The small cemetery consisted entirely of sarcophagi.

Big concrete and marble things. It didn't have the scenic aspect of the older one in town but it was in much better condition. There was a chain-link fence which had also been missing in the in-town cemeteries.

Oddly, from my perspective, it was planted right next to a small ball field. It just seemed like an odd place to put a cemetery. I suspected it was the disliked chubby kid who had to go retrieve the errant pop flies. "I'm not going into the cemetery to get the ball!" "You hit it, you have to get it!" "Let's make *Larry* get it!"

Shelbye got out, holding a hand-held spotlight that had seen some use over the years, and shined it into the cemetery. There were no lights in the area. Even the field lights were shut down. The closest light was some sort of port facility about a quarter of a mile away on the other side of the road.

I got out and walked over.

"There they at," she said, spotting the ghouls. They were feeding, of course. Their heads were bobbing up and down as they ate, occasionally glancing at the spotlight and hissing. They looked for all the world like some weird deer herd being spotted at night. Or a lion pride. "Shit."

I counted four. In Seattle we'd have a five-man team. I was starting to realize in New Orleans this was not a big issue.

"They down," she said. "Cain't get no shot."

She looked back down the road to the roadblock.

"Be right back."

She got in her car and drove down to the road-block, then a few minutes later came back driving a Fish and Game pickup truck.

"Told the poacher man I needed his truck," she said, grinning. She had a very obvious plate replacing her front teeth. Good work. The reason it was obvious was the condition of the rest of her teeth. "You come on in from over left," she said. "I'll cover."

"Works," I said. It was at least getting cooler. Not cool, mind you, just not blazing hot.

I filled my canteens from the five-gallon can of holy water in my trunk. It was rubber-tasting but it was water. I drained one, filled it, took a piss, something I'd been dearly needing since the naga incident, then headed out into the darkness.

Shelbye had used the spots on the Poacher Man truck to illuminate the ghouls. I was coming in from out of the darkness.

But they were about done with whoever or whatever they were eating and I was fresh meat. As soon as I got close they started to get up.

There was a series of cracks from the direction of the road. Say what you will about Shelbye, the girl could shoot. She dropped one, but immediately the rest were ducking and weaving like one of the gang-bangers across the street from headquarters. They were headed right for me. Ghouls are tough. A head shot, even from a silver .308, did not necessarily kill them. Just ruined their night.

I started putting bursts into the oncoming ghouls. Short bursts to the heads. I'd long ago learned one .45 round just sort of pissed them off.

I kept that up, had to reload, and moved forward. They were badly chewed up by the time I got to the group, so I pulled out Mo No Ken and more or less worked my way through the four that way.

"That's a pretty nice sword you got there," Shelbye radioed. *"Right nice."*

"Wouldn't believe how much it cost," I said. "And I got a deal."

Ghouls don't deliquesce. We were left with four dismembered bodies. In a cemetery, which was convenient.

They'd been eating a deer.

When the coroner team arrived it was led by a guy named Tim Best. Best way to describe Tim is John Cleese as an undertaker but without the humor. Tall, he had a faint Commonwealth accent and a distinguished manner. I never saw him except at scenes.

"You're *sure* it's clear?" he asked as he approached the bodies.

"If it's not, Shelbye's on overwatch and I'm here," I said.

The assistants were a set of burly black men in their forties. Same size, same build, same looks, they never really talked. Just did the job.

The scene was cleared and I walked back to my car. It was pushing four A.M., about the same time I'd gotten up the previous day, and I was bushed.

"We have another call?" I asked when I got back to the cars.

"Nope," Shelbye said. She'd switched her Charger out again when the scene was being cleared. So much for being on overwatch. "We're green. Back to the Hoodoo Shack."

The wet bar had a keg on tap. Now I knew why. I pulled a sixteen-ounce cup of Budweiser and just about drained it. Shelbye was right behind me.

"I got to reload magazines," I said. I was still in my ghoul-ichor-covered armor.

"Got a room downstairs," Shelbye said.

The ammo room had something I'd never seen before: mag reloaders. There were three that could be switched out for various calibers and with attachments for various magazines.

Shelbye put one of her M14 mags in the reloader, the reloader had a well just like an M14, dropped a bunch of .308 rounds into the hopper and pulled a lever. Mag reloaded.

"We don't got one for your Uzi," she said. "We'll get that fixed. Like it, by the way. Where'd you get it?"

"I built it," I said. "Want one?"

"I'll stick with long guns," she said. "Stayin' back's the only way I've survived this long. Gettin' up close and personal generally don't end well."

"What got you started?" I asked as I started reloading mags. I needed to clean my weapons as well, soon. But ammo first.

"Humboldts," she said darkly. She'd broken her 14 down and was cleaning it. "Hit our camp out the swamp. Killed some family. Took off with a cousin of mine. Didn't know nothin' 'bout Humboldts back then. I took off after her. Stupidest damned thing I ever done in my life and that's saying something. They nearly got me but I found her. Turned out she was already one of them. She'd gone just plumb crazy.

"I was in it bad when MHI showed up. MHI fella put her down. He was right nice about it. Explained and everything. The green glow should have been a clue. Got a call from MHI a couple weeks later. They'd done the paperwork for the Humboldts they could find I'd done for. Asked me if I wanted a job. Been doin' this for four years."

I'd never dealt with Humboldt Folk but I heard they were pretty horrific. "That's a tough introduction."

"You?" she asked.

"Shamblers," I said, frowning. "At a tent revival of all things. Long story why I was there. I had a .22 converter for my Colt. I just ran around popping them. I was really busted up at the time. That was about the only problem I had with it. Not as hard as your story."

"Was pretty bad," she said, shrugging. "Nobody else was willing to go. 'Fraid of the hoodoo. It was stupid but I ain't never been known for my smarts."

"You're damned good with that," I said, pointing at her rifle with my chin.

"Been huntin' and shootin' since I was a kid," she said, shrugging. "But I'll leave the stubby guns and swords and axes for y'all men."

I was done reloading and pulled out a pack of gear to sharpen Mo No Ken. I always started with that when cleaning weapons if Mourning had been used.

The kit consisted of a tiger shark skin sharpening strap and another of cloth. I considered the edge and skipped the shark skin. I hooked the cloth, which was attached at both ends to hardwood dowels, to one of the tables and started swathing the blade on the cloth strap.

"You sharpen it on cotton?" Shelbye asked.

"Silk," I said, continuing the sharpening process. "That's why it goes through limbs like butter. I've put this through the arms and necks of trolls, wights, and both legs of a vampire. And the neck, obviously. You name it, Mo No Ken has killed it."

"Mo No Ken?" she asked.

"Sword of Mourning," I said. "Yes, it has a name. It's a two-hundred-year-old, three-soul blade."

"Okay then. Gotcha," she said, reassembling her M14. "You all into that Oriental stuff?"

"You could say that," I said, smiling slightly. "The way of the warrior is the way of duty," I added in Japanese.

"Huh? I ain't into all that mystical bullshit. I just shoot the monsters and get paid."

"I got into it in high school," I said, completing the sharpening. I anointed Mo No Ken again and put it away. "My unofficial foster father was into it. He'd had a buddy killed by a sword in World War II and got into it after that. He taught me kendo, the Japanese sword art. And about guns. Even gunsmithing; he was the school shop teacher which was where we met. My family was and is very fucked up. He and his wife were and are my real parents.

"Later I kept studying. When I decided to get into this, he helped me do the Uzi redesign and to find Mo No Ken. I've studied all sorts of martial arts, Oriental as you put it, and European. It's all useful tricks."

I broke down the Uzi next and did a rough clean. I wasn't going to bother breaking down the silencer or the trigger group. It didn't need it.

"Is there some point at which we can put down our heads?" I asked, reassembling the Uzi.

"Might as well," Shelbye said. "Seems to have calmed down."

I took a shower in my gear, hung it up to dry, took another out of gear, hit the rack and passed out like a light.

Thus ended my first day with New Orleans Hoodoo Squad.

CHAPTER 6
Hungry Like the Wolf

"Eat..." Trevor said, holding up a thumb. "No, no, *drink*. Water. Maybe beer, but something that keeps you hydrated..."

I had been in New Orleans for a few weeks. We were having our pre-full-moon team meeting at the Hoodoo Shack. It was ten A.M. on the day before the full moon and we were eating barbeque courtesy of Monster Hunter International.

"So...drink," Trevor said. "Not liquor. Keep hydrated. Eat," he said, gesturing at the barbeque. "Kill monsters."

"Sleep?" I said. "Shower? Clean weapons?"

"That's for when the moon's past," Jonathan Baldwin said. "You got a replacement for your Uzi?"

Jonathan was from NYC like Agent Buchanan. Jonathan was a bit chubby-looking but he'd already smoked me at running, chasing down an imp on Front Street. Brown hair and eyes, he was a fair shooter but not much at close range fighting. He'd been with MHI for less than two years after killing a nest of kobolds in a building where he'd been the super.

"Two," I said. They were still in my trunk and, no, nobody had messed with them. I was still bunking at the office.

I hadn't found a place to live. Someone, possibly something, was looking for me.

My second day, Trevor had given me a card and directions to Madam Courtney's Real Estate.

Madam Courtney's office was in Bayou St. John. She had various voodoo items hanging in the window but the sign plainly said REAL ESTATE.

There was more hoodoo in the front room which had a reception desk. A pretty young black woman led me into the back through, yes, a bead curtain to meet with Madam Courtney.

Madam Courtney was in her fifties wearing a flowing native African dress, bright crimson shawl and a colorful rag wrapped on her head. She was about covered in various houdoun charms and amulets. The dimly lit office featured only a table covered in black cloth.

"Sit, Hunter," the real estate agent said. "Sit, sit." She pronounced it *seat*.

I sat at the table wondering where the crystal ball was.

"You need a home," she said, her arms wide, as if calling the loas for guidance.

I forbore to say that's generally why people come to a real estate office.

"You," she said, drawing it out. "You who have never known a true home. You, speaker to the saints! You, with the *mission*!" Meeeeeshuuuun! She was leaning back with her arms wide and her head thrown back, her voice rising. "You, player of women! Wordsmith! Bard! Gifted in tongues!" She was shouting and shaking.

"A home for the warrior not a saint! I call upon the loas! Find this warrior a hooooome!"

She calmed down, panting, and wearily pulled out a deck of tarot cards.

"We shall read your path," she murmured. She shuffled the tarot then drew the first card.

"The Fool," she said, setting it down. "This is your past. A new beginning."

"I got a transfer."

"More than that," Madam Courtney said. "Did you have a near death experience?"

"More like a dead death experience," I said.

"This refers to that," Madam Courtney intoned. "The Fool is a powerful card for you, Oliver Chadwick Gardenier. You are a man renewed and returned. The loas do not do such without a reason."

She drew the next card.

"The Hanged Man," she said. "This is not a sign of death but a sign of a change in focus, a change in perspective. This represents your new home here in New Orleans. There is much change in perspective in New Orleans. Some things will be revealed to you here that make you understand your purpose in life."

She drew the third card.

"The Four of Cups," she said. "This represents your needs in the present. A place to rest, recuperate, heal. This represents what I must find for you with the help of the loas.

"The Eight of Cups," she said. "This represents present obstacles. You must find a new path and give up the known. You must seek a higher perspective. This does not mean you must change your ways in terms of becoming more moral. It seems to indicate you must become *more* of what you are. You must strive to become *greater* in your skills, in your doing. You must become the most *fierce* warrior possible. To focus on becoming a living weapon."

"A sword saint?" I asked. "Ever seen *The Seven Samurai?*"

"Yes," Madam Courtney said, nodding. "Thus you must have the home, a life, that will *support* that. You must *focus*, Oliver Chadwick Gardenier. You must focus on becoming *more*."

I hoped that included being more of a lady's man.

She drew the fifth card.

"The Hermit. A need to take stock of your current condition. To put it in modern terms, you need to find yourself. Understand yourself."

"Uh, sure?"

"The Three of Pentacles," Madam Courtney said. "You will have opportunities to grow and improve. To become greater in your skills."

She drew the last card.

"The Seven of Wands. So, the others become clear."

"Why?"

"The loas are preparing you. There shall come a great battle. Not any of the normal ones you will engage upon. No matter how great, these are but the training, the tests. A great battle, one that will turn on the edge of a knife and if your side fails, it will mean the end of all things. It is *that* battle for which the loas prepare you, forge you like a sword to their destiny. A living weapon. In that battle, you will have one task for which you must be prepared. In that battle, you must become greater. You must be the *perfect* weapon. Or the world will fall into darkness."

"Okay," I said when she was done. She hadn't asked me about location, style, square footage, anything. I had no idea what any of it meant in terms of finding me a place to live. I knew some houdoun worked. I was a Monster Hunter, after all. But I wasn't sure it was up to finding me an apartment. "I was just sort of looking for a good apartment. Fairly central. Decent neighborhood would be nice."

"No," she said, in a deep, strained voice. "No apartment for you! Your destiny is here for many years. You need a fine home to return to after your battles. You are a seer. You need peace to contemplate the mysteries of the universe."

She shook herself again and took a deep breath.

"There's no fee," she said in a perfectly normal tone. "My cut is half the broker's fee which is paid by the seller, not the buyer. How's your credit?"

"I don't really have much. I generally pay cash."

"To get a mortgage you'll need your last two years' 1040s," she said. "Are you a get-it and spend-it type?"

"I've got some investments if that's what you mean. I could probably cash those in for a decent house much less a down payment. Even if I wanted to buy a house, which I'm not sure I do, you haven't asked me how much I want to *spend*?"

"This is up to the loas," she said, spreading her hands again. "I do not find the home. The loas find the home."

"Okay," I said dubiously.

"You, a seer, returned to us from the lands of the dead, you doubt the loas?" she said with a merry laugh. "*Trust* the loas."

She led me out and said she'd give me a call in a

few days, couple of weeks max. That had been two weeks ago. A paralegal had turned up from a law firm looking for documents on my financials. I'd given them to her. That was all the contact we'd had since her tarot reading.

"If this full moon is like the last one, pretty much you nap in your car," Shelbye said. She was over the limp and her ribs had healed.

"Keep a cooler in your car," Alvin Nunez said. "That's what I do. Drinks, some food."

Alvin was a "native born Texican." He was definitely Hispanic but his family went back in Texas to before they'd broken away from Mexico. He didn't have an ancestor at the Alamo but he did have some in the army that avenged it.

He and Jonathan had both been out, injured, when I first arrived. They'd since been cleared back to duty.

Trevor's injured leg was still slowing him down so he would be handling the phones at the office.

"How many magazines you got?" Trevor asked me.

"Ten," I said.

"Not enough," he said. "You need more than ten. I'll make some calls. Get some more for you."

"You probably need about thirty," Greg Wise said. He'd only been with the New Orleans team for three months. Difference being he'd come straight from MHI training. "If this is like our last full moon … you won't believe how much ammo you go through."

He was right.

We were all still hoping that the last full moon had been a fluke, and that things would return to normal, or at least *normal* by New Orleans standards.

"The moment the moon rises over Lake Pontchartrain, God kicks the dust of New Orleans off his sandals and Satan comes to town," Trevor said. "Be ready. This ain't Satan's town. It's ours."

I wasn't on shift for the day if there was a call. I'd been handling calls day and night for the last week and a half. I had the afternoon off. So I started what was to become a tradition for me whenever I had the chance. I called it Last Rites.

First, I would take a very long shower. I would scrub myself practically raw and shave, eventually, pretty much my whole body. Ended up using Nair on most of it. Some people react poorly to Nair. I never did.

Then I would check all my equipment meticulously. I would make sure everything was in as perfect working order as was possible given the circumstances. Sometimes it had been a bad month and I had to roll with stuff that wasn't fully repaired. Shit happens. But I'd fix it as well as possible.

Then I would go to church. I'd go meet my father confessor, make my confession, and take communion.

Then I'd go have a really good meal.

I'd thought the food in Seattle was good until I got to New Orleans. Hated the heat, the job was, obviously, a little too profitable; hated the bugs—damn, some of the *regular* cockroaches and spiders in New Orleans should count for PUFF—but the food. My God, the food!

But at this point I was still new. Working one day with Shelbye, she'd taken me to a Creole place over in Faubourg Marigny called Sasson's. It was sort of a hole-in-the-wall, just a concrete building with a kitchen in it and an order window off Spain Street with some tables outside. Couple were shaded by live oaks. It was busy so we ended up sweating out in the sun.

I looked at the menu and had not a clue. I spoke French but this wasn't French. Shelbye ordered for me.

Andouille gumbo. It was like being back in heaven again.

The traffic and the heat were not my idea of a perfect setting, but the food!

So a few days before the full moon, I called and asked to speak to the owner or head chef or somebody. It wasn't a "chef" sort of place, but the food was chef-worthy.

Note, this was about the time that Paul Prudhomme was making big waves in cooking circles and putting New Orleans on the map for gourmets.

I've eaten at K-Paul's, met Prudhomme and even been invited to eat at his chef's table in the kitchen. Prudhomme is good, don't get me wrong.

Sasson's made Prudhomme look like a ham-handed *côme*. (That's French for junior cook.)

Anyway, I called Sasson's and ended up talking to the owner and chief cook and bottle washer Jean Sasson. I told him I was Hoodoo Squad and was planning on having a late lunch, early dinner at his place.

"I would like to ask a favor," I said in meticulous Parisian French. "I do not know your strengths. If you were condemned to death and told to cook your last meal, what would *you* cook?"

"It will be the day of the full moon, yes?" he asked seriously. "I shall serve you only my best."

"Merci, monsieur. Vous comprenez."

So at three P.M., under the shade of a live oak

tree, I found myself sitting at a concrete table, eating a seven-course meal that would have made Escoffier weep to be able to replicate. I didn't have to go to the order window; Monsieur Sasson's pretty daughter (and protégé) served. So I also got a pretty face to look at.

It was hot, it was noisy, I was sweating my ass off, it was delicious.

Then I would go home—at that point the barracks—and carefully kit up. When I was done, up to and including having my Uzi rigged and Mo No Ken slung, I would stand in front of a full-length mirror.

"I am the warrior elite," I would say to myself. "Satan had better watch his ass."

Last but not least, I would get in Honeybear and drive over to Breakwater Park on Lake Pontchartrain. I would crank up the AC, put on some tunes, slide my seat all the way back and watch the moon come up. People would be out fishing. Young couples would be walking hand in hand along the lakeshore.

I would be waiting for the first call. And about the time the moon was fully exposed over the lake, it would come in.

"Momma, I was gonna go over to Randal's," James Robinson, sixteen, said trying not to fume. "I can eat there."

"You're going to sit down and eat the supper I made or you're not going out at all tonight," Ginger Robinson replied sharply. "I don't think that boy's a good influence, anyway. You're always getting into fights when you go out with him. Now go set the table before your father gets home."

The Robinsons lived in Metairie. Metairie was a fairly

standard middle-class suburb. It had its problems, what town didn't, but by and large it was in the safer part of the New Orleans area. Houses were painted, lawns were mowed, cars were in good condition. People kept up appearances and worked hard to make a better life for their children. American Middle Class.

And the Robinsons were a perfect example of that. Mr. Robinson worked at the Port of New Orleans as a stevedore. That might sound like a minor job but he ran one of the massive on-, off-load AT-AT cranes and made good money. Mrs. Robinson was a homemaker and worked at the church doing all the little things like getting the altar clothes cleaned and pressed, and polishing the offertory vessels that needed to be done and someone had to do them. Their daughter, Kristina, fourteen, had just missed getting on the JV cheerleading team and was hoping to make it next year. She just had to train harder and suck up enough to Coach Jermaine.

"It's Kristi's turn to set the table," James said angrily.

"If it is or it isn't, it's your turn now!" Mrs. Robinson said.

While James was angrily throwing silverware on the table, Mr. Robinson came home from his day shift and set down his lunch box. Every morning Mrs. Robinson packed his lunch box for work.

Mrs. Robinson would not be packing that lunch box on the morrow.

You see, Mrs. Robinson had a point in her disdain for James' new set of high school friends. James hadn't mentioned that they'd been going out to roadhouses that were a bit lenient in regards to drinking laws. Nor that he'd gotten into a fight, just last week, with some crazy biker dude who had bitten him. He'd covered up the bite with a bandage and told his parents he'd gotten scratched at shop class.

It had healed remarkably fast, anyway. It was barely a scratch. Hardly broke the skin.

Mrs. Robinson didn't like to dump on her husband when he just came in the door, but she was on her last nerve with James, and a man's problems—and James was fast becoming a man—were best solved by a man.

"You have got to talk to that son of yours," she said, turning the fried chicken in the pan. "He is out of control."

"I'll talk to him, *cher*," Mr. Frank Robinson said, trying not to sigh.

Ginger stopped turning chicken and got him a beer from the fridge.

"You go sit down for now. Dinner's in about ten minutes."

"Thanks," Frank said, popping the can and taking a sip. "He's just feeling his oats, *cherie*."

"There," James said, stomping into the kitchen angrily. "The table is set!"

"You do not use that tone with your mother, James," Mr. Robinson said. Clearly, Ginger wasn't exaggerating. Teenage mood swings. He'd had them. Who didn't? But a man learned to control them. "Apologize to your mother!"

"The hell I will!" James shouted. "Is it that big of a deal I want to go out with my friends tonight?"

"You want to go out ever again, you're going to apologize to your mother," Frank Robinson said, putting down the beer can.

"Or *what*? What are you going to do? Get out your belt to teach me a lesson, old man?"

"Oh, it's going to be like that, is it?" Frank Robinson said, rolling up his sleeves. "I think we need to take this out back."

"Now, boys," Mrs. Robinson said.

"I don't think we need to take this *anywhere!*" James roared and, with both hands, hit his father on his chest with all his might.

Frank was picked up off his feet and thrown across the kitchen to impact painfully on the bar. He was briefly knocked out.

"I'M NOT LISTENING TO YOU ANYMOAARRR!"

James Robinson looked at his lengthening fingers as his bones started to crack and realign. He screamed in agony. "Oh, nooo!" It turned into a howl as his mouth started to lengthen. The pain was excruciating. "Mommaaaa! Mommaaaa!"

"No, no, no, no," Mrs. Robinson said, squatting down to look into her son's eyes. They turned gold as she watched. "Not my baby. Please, God, not my little baby."

"Momma, what's happening?" Kristina asked, running into the room. She'd been in her bedroom with her Walkman on but still heard the crash as her daddy hit the bar.

"Ginger," Mr. Robinson said, standing up and shaking his head. He saw what was happening to his son and was the only one there who realized just how bad things were about to get. "You and Kristi, you go and get in the closet in the bedroom. Right now. You lock the door to the bedroom and you *stay* in the closet."

"Jimmy, no," Mrs. Robinson begged.

"You go right now, *cher*," Mr. Robinson said. "You and Kristina. You go. *Go now!*"

He knew what was happening, had even seen it

before for himself in his distant youth. There was no time for sadness or panic or denial. Mr. Robinson was a bedrock Louisiana American and that meant guns. And he knew it was probably going to be no use. But the monster that had, until a moment before, been his son was not going to get to his wife and child without some 12-gauge double-ought in its belly. And it was not going to get to them until Frank Robinson was stone dead.

It takes a new werewolf a fair amount of time to change. Enough time for Mr. Robinson to go to the spare room, take down his already loaded pump shotgun, grab a bag with some shells in it from his last hunting trip, and walk back out into the hallway.

The hallway led from the kitchen and living room to the bedrooms. Ginger by now would be in the closet of the bedroom they'd shared for fifteen years. The bedroom where they'd made little Kristina, his pride and joy. Her 20-gauge was in there. He'd heard that even if you didn't have silver, sometimes you could put enough hurtin' on a loup-garou to put it down. If not, maybe Ginger could finish the job. If she could kill her own son.

He knew it wasn't his baby anymore. It wasn't the boy he'd taught to fish, to catch a football, it wasn't the boy he'd taught how to be a man.

It was a monster and if he didn't stop it, it was going to kill his wife and daughter.

He took his stand as the loup-garou slunk around the corner, yellow eyes glowing...

My cellular car phone rang as the final sliver of the moon cleared the waters of the lake.

I had two, now. Turned out there was a radiophone company in New Orleans that even used the same system as the one I'd gotten installed in Seattle. It had more range than the newer cell phone I'd also had installed but was less clear in the city. So I had two.

"Where you at?" Trevor asked.

"Breakwater Park," I said.

"Possible loup-garou in Metairie," Trevor said. "1512 Houma Boulevard."

"On it."

While Honeybear was in the shop, I'd had a couple of installs done. I now had a siren and a dash light. The dash light was a powerful strobe with, yes, a purple, more violet, cover. I thought it being violet was both useful and appropriate. So I now had a purple emergency light to signify that, no, I wasn't a cop or a volunteer firefighter.

I was Hoodoo Squad. And you'd best get out my way.

Special Agent in Charge Castro hadn't cared, because getting to the incidents faster meant there was a lower body count for him to cover up. I cranked up Honeybear and peeled out. I damned near hit one of those couples holding hands as I did.

"Sorry," I yelled.

I don't think they heard me.

I got lost twice.

CHAPTER 7
Holding Out for a Hero

I knew I was there when I saw the blue lights.

"Finally," I muttered. It had only taken about ten minutes but that was five minutes longer than it should have taken. This fricking town was a fricking maze of canals and if you didn't know where the bridges were...

"Took you long enough," the Metairie PD officer said as I pulled up next to his car. He'd cracked the window but only when I was right alongside. "Just you?"

"So far. I caught on the scanner we got another one down in Ninth Ward and I doubt that's the last. Where is it?"

"Right up the road was where it was last seen," the officer said. "I see so much as a dog I'm taking off."

"Got it."

I drove down the street, slowly, until I got to 1512 Houma Boulevard. It was a pleasant ranch-style house, single story. Bars on the windows which wasn't universal in Metairie but was common. Well-kept yard. Bit of a pull-around in the front. I pulled into the driveway and got out.

"Any werewolves around?" I asked.

There was a crashing from inside the house. That answered that question. One of the front windows smashed and a furry paw extended out. There was a deep, bass snarl.

"Hey, doggy," I said calmly. I turned on the mini-mag on my Uzi, walked over to the window and looked in. The werewolf took a running start and slammed into the bars, shaking bits of mortar out of the connecting rods. It had blood all over its muzzle.

I set the selector switch on semi, laid the sight on the beast's forehead and put one silver bullet into its brain.

The loup-garou flopped over on its side and stopped. Game, set, match.

I walked down to the road and waved my Maglite at the patrol car. It crept forward, cautiously.

"I got it. It was still in the house."

"You sure?" the cop said.

"Well, I got *a* loup-garou. Is there another one around?"

"Not that's been reported round here. Kenner just reported there's one running around at the airport. Down on the runways and stuff."

"Joy," I said. "Call the coroners. And I need to figure out how to get into this house. Without using explosives, that is."

I rummaged in my trunk for a bit and pulled the Halligan tool and ax out.

"I really will need a hand with this," I said. "It's okay. It daid."

Between the cop and myself we managed to get the door hammered open. It was very seriously attached.

At one point I wondered if I was going to have to get out the C4. But we got it open.

The Metairie PD officer immediately bolted back to his car with the statement he wasn't going in until it was clear.

One dead in the living room. That was the loup-garou. Young male, probably the son. One dead in the hallway. Male. Torn to ribbons. Shotgun by his side, empty. Shells spilled out of a slung shell bag he never managed to access based on the number on the ground.

Bedroom door torn open. Closet door torn open. Two dead in the closet. Females. One shotgun. No shells on the ground, no powder smell, appeared unused.

Notes: 1512 Houma Boulevard. Loup-garou. Three victims. # U-148-239-J Receipt.

Mrs. Robinson would never make that packed lunch again. Because there was no one to make it. And no one to eat it.

Ever tried to find a werewolf somewhere out on the tarmac at an airport?

"Last we got a report, it was over by Gate C-6."

The speaker was Security Manager Randolph Everette, fiftyish, heavy-set, nice suit. Definitely a bureaucrat.

I was the first member of MHI to arrive. Mr. Everette did not appreciate the time it had taken me to respond. Louis B. Armstrong International Airport had a contract. We were very close to being in violation of said contract.

My excuse that I had already dealt with one werewolf this night was not well received. He seemed to feel I should have left that one to chow on common citizens rather than allow the Louis B. Armstrong airport to be shut down.

I suppose he sort of had a point.

According to witnesses, the problem had been one of their traffic directors. Which explained why there was a 707 half parked over at Gate C-2. It had, in fact, damned near run over another plane following the directions of a wand waver who all of a sudden fell to the ground and started writhing. The plane had turned to avoid running over him and nearly hit a DC-10. Fortunately, from the MCB's perspective, the pilots and passengers did not see the wand waver shred his clothes and turn into a werewolf. Some of the passengers on the DC-10 caught a glimpse of something but they weren't sure what. They'd been concentrating on, you know, the other plane trying to hit them.

The 707 was now stuck on the tarmac, and incoming flights were shut down until the tarmac was cleared. Everyone who could be unloaded, safely, from the planes had been. But they were all waiting on their baggage since the baggage crews weren't allowed outside until the problem was cleared. And planes were sitting, stacked up, on the taxiways since there were no Follow-Me trucks running and no wand wavers. Not to mention in the air. Planes short on fuel were having to divert to nearby airfields including the airbase across the river. Every entrance had been shut down.

There had been reports from other planes stuck at various points of "some sort of big dog" running around on the tarmac.

"We need to get this under control, fast," Agent Buchanan said. I still had him mentally pegged as Agent Three. "This isn't your normal New Orleans hoodoo. We're talking about a lot of uninitiated observers. Class Four event."

"I'm going to need to bring Honeybear onto the tarmac," I said.

"Honeybear?" Everette asked.

"His car," Buchanan said.

"No way," Everette said. "We cannot allow a civilian vehicle with an untrained driver onto the tarmac. It's unsafe."

"There won't be an untrained driver," I said. "If you want this fixed, you're driving. I have not a clue how to get to Gate C whatever."

"Uh . . ." Everette said, his mouth open.

"Sounds like a plan," Buchanan said.

In the end it wasn't Mr. Everette who drove Honeybear but one of the senior airport cops, Lieutenant Roy Gray. He had the look of a professional.

"Been doing this long?" I asked.

"Fifteen years," Gray said as he pulled Honeybear around the side of one of the terminals. "Ever since I got out of the Corps."

"Parris or Pendleton?" I asked.

"Please," he said. "Do I look like a Hollywood Marine?"

"One of the MCB is," I said. I was keeping an eye out for anything doglike. People were looking out their windows, clearly wondering why a 1976 Cutlass with a flashing purple light was able to drive around the tarmac and they couldn't.

"Which explains why he is MCB," Gray said. Apparently he had dealt with MCB before and was read in, which was why he got this job. "Parris, right?"

"Do I look like a Hollywood Marine?" I asked.

"With that haircut, you look like a boot."

I picked up my spot and rolled down my window. I was hit by a blast of muggy, JP4-scented air. I had a sudden flashback to being on the deck of the carrier the helo landed on taking me out of Beirut. It threw me.

"You okay?" Gray asked.

"Flashback," I said. I turned on the spot and shone it where I thought I'd seen a dog. No luck.

"Unit Four, report of possible canine, Gate D-12."

Another reason to bring one of the airport cops is they had local radios.

"That's on the other side of the other terminal," Gray grumped. "When were you in?"

"Eighty-one to eighty-four," I said.

"Three-year tour?" he said. "I thought they'd done away with those."

"I got medically discharged after Beirut," I said. "That was the flashback."

"Ah," Gray replied. He'd sped up but not as fast as I would have liked.

"There's a super-charger under this hood, you know," I said.

"There's grease and oil and jet fuel like you wouldn't believe on this tarmac," Gray said. "I'm not going to either spin out or make a spark and start a fire."

"The airport is shut down until I find and kill this thing and we've got three other calls," I said. "Please put the hammer down."

I could see the numbers up on the side of the buildings.

"Unit Four. Possible canine, D-8."

"Sound like it's moving down one side of D?" I asked.

"Yeah," Gray said.

We were passing D-12. Based on the numbers, we

were going to be approaching D-8 soon. I turned the spot back on but it was pointed the wrong way.

I rolled my window all the way down, climbed out on the door and shined the spot over the car towards the terminal. I caught a flash of brown fur.

It was headed our way.

"Turn right and head for the hills," I shouted to Gray. "Let's get it away from the terminal. *Hey, doggie! Over here! Nice fresh meat!*"

"This is not conducive to me making retirement!" Gray shouted, turning right and gunning it. Sure enough, we fishtailed. "Do you really have to egg it on?"

The werewolf was following us but we were outrunning it.

"Slow down!"

"Slow down, speed up! Make up your mind!"

"Stop here!"

I was nearly thrown clear as he hit the brakes, hard. I'd done some work on them before I left Seattle. Clearly it had paid off. We swerved—there really must have been some serious goop on the tarmac—then straightened out and stopped.

I slid out of the window and walked to the rear of Honeybear. Loup-garou, inbound.

We'd stopped, unfortunately, right under another DC-10. I was in the lights from the windows and I knew people were looking out, wondering why a person in full tactical rig had just dropped out of a Cutlass.

I'd taken a glance up. A few of them were kids. Parents always give kids the window seat.

I waited until the loup-garou was within fifteen yards and gave it a full burst from the Uzi.

It skidded to a halt at my feet. Right in front of

God and everybody. About six kids had just watched me shoot a poor little doggie.

I walked over and put two rounds in its head just to make sure.

Lights went away as parents quickly shut the shades and had to comfort their now-traumatized children.

Yes, I am the devil. Don't get me wrong. I love kids. Fried preferably but boiled works with a little hot sauce.

"Soon as we get the body cleared you're reopened," I said, tossing the Uzi through the window of Honeybear.

"Did you do that on purpose?" Gray asked.

Yeah, at the time I thought doing that werewolf right there was funny. Later, once I found out what I caused, I would regret it. But in the heat of the moment, I had made a bad call and someone else would end up paying for it.

"Hey," I said, opening up the cooler in the back seat, pulling out a Budweiser and popping the top, "you were the one that drove us right under a damned plane." I took a long pull. Gotta stay hydrated.

MCB was not happy. Mr. Everette was not happy. The airport got reopened. That's what the contract specified. Besides, I didn't give them much time to bitch. Before anyone else got out there, I already had another call. Coroner was on scene fast and the body was gone before you knew it.

They wanted me to stay to hear their bitching. Then Buchanan got a call. Loup-garou on Bourbon Street. Right in tourist town.

Yeah, I got to go, then.

LBA Airport. One LG. No vic. #114-8(Fed). Receipt Parish.

❖   ❖   ❖

Thursday night and Bourbon Street was filled end-to-end with tourists. Didn't matter if there was a werewolf running around. They were too drunk to notice.

Right up until it ripped their guts out.

Screaming? Hey, let's scream along! Woooo! Go Green Bay! Gunfire? Hey, is that fireworks? Let's go see the fireworks! Woooo! I love New Orleans!

Fucking tourists. If it's called tourist season, is there a bag limit?

It was all hands. The loup-garou was running wild through the center of tourist central. Some dead, number unknown so far, when I arrived. More injured and anyone bitten would have to be put down by MCB probably. And with tourists, MCB would have to do their full-on "if you talk about this, we'll kill you" routine.

We didn't know where it was, so my team was scattered all over the area. I ended up going the wrong way on Conti Street. I didn't care. I'd hit a hundred and twenty on I-10, purple light flashing and siren going *AHOOOGAH!* What, you thought I'd installed a pissy little cop siren?

I drove the wrong way on Conti Street dodging honking cars, stopped in the intersection of Bourbon and bailed out. Full rigged. Some douchebag in a Honda nearly ran me down. I seriously considered putting a magazine into his car as an incentive to learn manners.

"This is Iron Hand," I said on my radio. I might finally be in range of a teammate. "I'm at Conti and Bourbon. Any contact?"

"Hand, Ben," Ben replied. *"Last seen on Dauphine near Conti."*

Well, hell, Dauphine was a block over.

I got back in Honeybear, cars weaving around me, and just backed her up. Technically I was going the right way.

When I got to Conti and Dauphine, I bailed out again. Then, grumbling a little, I jumped up on Honeybear's hood, then onto the roof for a better look around.

Now, picture this for a moment. You're some tourist looking for a parking space to stop so you can go enjoy the fruits of New Orleans' night life. You're driving down a one-way street, your wife bitching at you that you should have just paid for parking, when you see a maroon 1976 Cutlass Supreme parked at a major intersection. There's a guy standing on the roof, holding a silenced Uzi submachine gun and dressed in tactical gear, up to and including a Kevlar helmet. Which, by the way, has a nasty set of gouge marks in it from troll claws.

Now, question for the audience. Do you go around? Do you back up to avoid the crazy person?

Do you stop and ask for directions?

"Hey, buddy!"

I looked around. There was a Cadillac stopped by Honeybear. It was blocking traffic even more, which, if there was a loup-garou inbound, was probably a good thing. There was a well-dressed middle-aged couple in the Cadillac. The wife was clearly pissed. The husband, driver, was just as clearly drunk.

"How do I find some parking around here?"

"Same way I did!" I shouted.

The man's window rolled up and I could vaguely hear the argument. Horns were honking.

There was screaming from up Dauphine.

I leapt off Honeybear and headed for the screams. Okay, so maybe I'm no better than the tourists.

Her name was Lindsey Carpenter. She and her friend Christina Hines had dropped out of college after one spring break and moved to New Orleans to enjoy the good life.

They were walking down Dauphine Street when from out of nowhere a huge dog creature rushed her and ripped her guts wide open.

Christina screamed and ran. The dog creature had to give chase.

She made it through the doors of a club. The dog creature followed. There, it attacked several patrons. It was indoors, surrounded by screaming people and confused by the plethora of prey.

It followed one of the prey back out onto the street.

I ran down Dauphine Street, in the road, dodging cars because it was easier than dodging people, when a man ran straight into a car. Just ran into the road full tilt and was hit by a late-model Impala. The impact tossed him fifteen feet through the air to land with a thud.

The loup-garou jumped onto the hood of the now-stopped Impala, pointed its snout at the sky and howled, long and deep.

I dropped the point-shoot sight onto its side and hit it with three rounds of silver .45. Couple more cracked the guy's windshield.

The werewolf turned, biting at the pain. The Impala suddenly accelerated, still with the werewolf on its hood. It was also headed right at me.

I dodged out of the way onto the hood of one of the cars parked on the street, rolled across and came back to my feet.

The Impala had to dodge Honeybear. The loup-garou rolled off as it did and, wouldn't you know it, thumped into the Caddy which was *still* blocking traffic. The drunk tourist was out on the passenger side trying to convince his wife that the cop or whatever had said it was okay to just park there.

The werewolf impacted on the Caddy's right-front quarter panel with a thud I could hear from halfway down the street. Then it got up. It was hurt but the rounds hadn't hit anything supercritical.

The man just stood there, looking at this massive wolf that had just hit his car.

I sort of wanted to let the loup-garou have the idiot but at the same time he was in that predicament in part because of my being a wiseass.

I jumped onto another parked car and lined up the shot. The wounded werewolf was getting ready to take down another victim.

There was the supersonic crack of a rifle. The loup-garou dropped with its brains splattered all over the quarter panel of the Caddy. The right front tire began to deflate.

"*Were you just going to sit there?*" Shelbye radioed.

"I was thinking about it," I said, touching my throat mike. "That guy's an asshole."

"*I'll cover up the wild animal, or whatever the feds will call it.*" Carter radioed. "*Hand, check on the wounded.*"

I walked back to the bar. There was a young woman lying in a pool of blood outside. She was still alive but she didn't have much time. Intestines were scattered on the sidewalk.

A friend was beside her, clearly with no clue how to handle a disembowelment. People were gathering around to gawk. Most of them were too wasted to realize this was real.

"Hoodoo Squad," I said. "Clear the area."

"The what?" some douchebag said, laughing.

The speaker was a fat man wearing a 'Bama T-shirt and ball cap.

"The guy with the Uzi and a *really* short temper," I said, putting the warm barrel of the silencer up under his chin. "Clear the fucking area! *Clear out!*"

That got through to him and he fled. I bent down on one knee by the victim.

"Hey," I said. "You're going to be okay." I looked at the nearly catatonic friend. "What's her name?"

"Lindsey," the brunette said.

Lindsey was pretty or had been. Five ten, one twenty...when all her guts were in place.

"Lindsey, this looks bad but you're going to be fine," I said, looking her in the eye. "Paramedics are on the way. You're going to be great."

I took out a morphine ampoule and slammed it into the inside of her thigh. I wasn't sure if it would spread through her body what with the ripped arteries in her stomach.

"That'll help with the pain. You just stay calm. Rest. It's okay if you pass out. Just stay calm and close your eyes. You're going to be just fine."

Lindsey trusted me. I knew what I was talking about. She was going to be fine. She closed her eyes and let the pain seep away.

A moment later they opened back up and her mouth fell open. Lindsey was gone to the Summer Lands where it was a party every night and no loup-garou came in to ruin it.

"You said she was going to be fine!" the friend screamed.

"She is," I said, letting go of the flaccid hand. "She's in heaven. We're stuck on this shithole. She's a lot better off than we are."

MCB arrived on the scene already talking about a "rabid dog." And because they were so helpful, the people who had been scratched or bitten would get this free easy "rabies test," only this was the kind of rabies where testing positive got you shot with a silver bullet.

I walked into the bar ignoring the rest of the mess. I walked into the bathroom. Plenty of people hadn't made it to the toilets to puke. I ignored the smell like I'd ignored the smell of spilled drinks, shit and iron in the bar.

I shoved my way up to one of the sinks. The guy I shoved didn't seem to like that but took one look at how I was rigged out and my face and didn't make an issue.

I wear Nomex flight gloves. They keep my hands from slipping on my weapons. They were covered in Lindsey's blood.

I took them off and rinsed them in the sink, wringing out the blood over and over again until the water ran clear. Then I rinsed my hands and dried them with a paper towel. I wrung out the gloves one more time and put them back on.

I reloaded my Uzi. I wasn't sure whether I had or not.

I walked back out.

The Caddy was gone.

CHAPTER 8
Let's Dance

For a change of pace, my next call was *not* a loup-garou.

"What the hell is a zoo-nu...?" I asked as I headed for Little Vietnam.

New Orleans wasn't just French. The French had settled on top of Native Americans. Then Americans, northern European/English derivative, moved in on the French. And there were two kinds of French. The Creole, who were descendants of the French aristocrats and such who were the early owners of trading companies and plantations, and the Cajun—Acadians—who were resettled from Newfoundland, before the British got Canada.

Then there were the slaves, West Africans from places like modern Ghana and Ivory Coast, by way of the Caribbean Islands and French Guyana.

New Orleans really was a land of immigrants.

And every immigrant population brings three things: its own native infections like malaria and yellow fever, its own food and its own hoodoo.

So, just as New Orleans had more different kinds

of food than you could find anywhere else in the US, at least at that time, it had more different kinds of hoodoo. We'd at least gotten rid of most of the infections. (Although AIDS was a bit rampant.)

Since the slavery days there had been more and more groups that came there for various reasons. Oil was and is big. Goes up and down but there's oil in them there bayous. Lots of fishing.

There were Hungarian enclaves and who knew Hungarians were fishermen? (The country is landlocked.) They'd brought their food, culture and hoodoo. There were pure African enclaves and they'd brought their kind of food, culture and hoodoo. Lots of Spanish influence. Food was good. Señoritas were foxes. South American hoodoo? Some of that is insane, brother. Guara hoodoo is fucked *up*.

Then there were the Vietnamese. They were recent transplants, refugees of a failed war. They'd settled, heavily, in the coastal regions of Texas and Louisiana to fish the fertile waters of the Gulf. And, yup, they'd brought their hoodoo.

Mostly they lived out US 90 in a little neighborhood near Michoud Boulevard.

I was already on I-10 doing my usual 130. Even though 90 was a main downtown street, it was actually faster to get on the 10 and go waaay out of your way then down to the 510 to get out there. At least if you could do 130 and the cops left you alone. US 90 was always chock-a-block traffic and streetlights. Yes, I'd blow red lights. Also a good way to get T-boned. I'd take the interstates.

"*Zoovnuj Txeeg Txivneej*," Trevor said over the phone. I could tell he was fluent whatever the hell the language was. "Man of the Forest in Hmong. Some villages treat them like minor fertility gods, and leave offerings to appease them. Sometimes they carry off the local girls."

I may be a little short but I always take no for an answer. "Vietnamese hob."

"Right," Trevor said. "*Orang minyak*, *kukobomo*, they're all over the world. There's all sorts of ritual offerings necessary to dispel it from an area. You're on your own for this one, but they aren't too dangerous if you know what you're doing. In Laos we discovered that filling it full of lead or silver just pisses it off. On the other hand, it also knocks it down long enough to throw a Willie Pete on it. And fire does for them."

"Roger," I said, sliding through the I-10, 510 interchange. I had to be somewhat aggressive with an idiot in a minivan at the merge point. He and his idiot family would live. The rest of the lane was clear, smooth, with a curve designed for about 75.

I did it at 112. Then I was on the 510. Traffic was light. My foot was not.

"It's outside *Tot Tot Thuc Pham*," Trevor said as if I knew what that meant. "Just go out US 90 past Michoud, look for the blue lights. Number 13612 Chef Menteur Highway."

"Got it," I said.

I finally made it to the 90, 510 interchange, blew through a red light at the intersection, nearly getting T-boned, and hammered it up Chef Menteur until I saw the blue lights. US 90 in that area was a semirural US four-lane highway. There were scattered buildings along the road, some strip malls, a set of crappy apartments. Lots of low scrub. Just to the south was the NASA Michoud Assembly Facility where they did the fuel tanks for the Space Shuttle.

It's generally considered to be about twenty minutes from downtown to that area in light traffic. I did it in seven. Did I ever mention how much I hate the double nickel and how much I enjoy violating the *hell* out of it?

I slowed down as I passed the state trooper car, then started looking for whatever was causing the issue. It was a sign that caught my attention. Most of the lettering was Vietnamese, which I hadn't learned, yet. Very small on the bottom it said TOT TOT THUC PHAM and even smaller was GOOD GOOD FOOD HERE.

Ah. Tot Tot Thuc Pham. Thanks, Trevor.

The building was long, low, cinderblock, painted salmon, with small windows, heavily barred, a heavy steel door and a window AC in the front. There was a flashing neon OPEN sign in one of the small windows. It looked less like a restaurant than a pawn shop. The parking lot was gravel and dirt.

The food was either going to be incredible, or kill you with botulism, and probably both.

There were a few parked cars. Off to one side, well to one side, was a cluster of people, Vietnamese, looking scared and ready to run.

Outside the steel front door was a small, bright purple, pot-bellied humanoid. It was screaming and ranting and pounding at the door. In front of the door were dozens of broken dishes and a bunch of scattered food. Not as much as should be from the dishes but the place was a wreck.

As I watched, the door cautiously opened and

another dish was shoved out. The humanoid dove into the food, gulping and chewing and in the process tossing bits of it all over the place.

When it was done, quickly, it shattered the plate on the steel door and started hammering again.

I got out, walked over and shot it in the back with my Uzi.

That got its attention.

It turned around. Its face was shaped like a bat with a very long nose and huge tusks jutting from its lower jaw. Call it a pig-bat face. Ugly. I'd seen *so* much worse in my time. I'd seen Fey queens and Huntsmen without their glamour. There ain't no ugly like Fey-ugly.

The Forest Man howled at me and charged.

I emptied the rest of the magazine into it. That put it down.

Purple haze was in the air from its blood but it was shaking off the effects quickly. It got back to its feet, shook its head back and forth rapidly, its jowls shaking and going *Blablablablabblable*, then hissed and charged again.

I'd reloaded. More .45. Down again.

This time it was far enough away from the building so I pulled a white phosphorus grenade off my belt, pulled the pin and lobbed it across the parking lot to land at its feet. I was just outside the bursting radius. I reloaded.

The Forest Man got up again, shaking his head, and looked at the hissing grenade at its feet. Then it picked it up and held it over its head, gobbling in Forest Man gobble, shrieking and hopping up and down as if it had captured my soul or something.

Then the grenade went off and it was covered in burning white phosphorus.

It ran around in circles, burning and howling, trailing white smoke.

I walked over and put a full magazine into its head. It stopped moving.

Just in case, I put a thermite grenade on it and walked about ten feet away.

Everything went white. Probably should have warned the witnesses to cover their eyes.

When the light died down I walked back. All there was left was a burned circle.

"Is it done?"

I looked at the building and just the cutest little Vietnamese girl was framed in the light from the doorway. She was wearing a skirt but no slip as was obvious. *What* a body! *Nice* legs!

"Yeah," I said, walking over. I handed her one of my *special* cards. The kind with my personal phone number written on the back. "Chad Gardenier. MHI," I said, shaking her hand. "All done. No need to worry about it anymore."

"Thank you," she exclaimed, throwing her arms around me. Nice boobs for an Asian chick. Very squeezable. "It had come for me! We were trying to appease it with the offerings of food, but..."

"Those things are a pest," I said smoothly, hugging her comfortingly and patting her on the back, "but we'll always be here to protect nice girls like you."

"Stay please, eat!"

I was starving. I hadn't eaten since three. I'd eaten a lot at Sasson's, but I'd also been expending a lot of calories. The Vietnamese food smelled great.

It was . . . and I didn't even get ptomaine poisoning. The owner—and the young lady's dad—wouldn't take a penny.

And she was very grateful. Very, very, very, wow, grateful.

I am such a schmuck.

The Goth club Orpheum was a shambles.

While we had been out chasing an absurd number of new werewolves recently, the vampires had come out to play. According to the survivors who had made it out, there had been at least two of them. One male was the leader and probably a higher form. One of the new vampires, female, was a regular at the unlicensed club. She was somewhat articulate and had talked their way in through the heavy security door.

To keep people from letting friends in without paying cover, the two other doors out of the basement were chained and barred. Classic example of the sort of club where a hundred people die in a fire. Some of the patrons had their throats ripped out. The rest made it out alive.

"This is going to be bad," Ben said.

"Why?" Greg asked. "Besides it being nighttime."

Jonathan was already in the hospital. Werewolf had shredded him up bad. Claws only, we hoped. So far the tests were negative for lycanthropy. Somebody had created *a lot* of new werewolves during the last month.

"Vampires almost never do anything this blatant," Ben said. "They're too good at surviving, so they pick off victims one at a time, people nobody will miss. Overt slaughter draws too much heat."

"So we've got a stupid or crazy vampire?"

It was barely 2 A.M. on the first night of the full moon. I understood now why Trevor was so insistent on everyone being in top form. I was beat up and I'd hardly had a single physical encounter.

"They won't have gone far," Ben said. "I'll put out the word to NOPD. But we need to find them, fast, or find their lair in the daylight."

MCB agents were already splashing gasoline on the club walls.

One of the survivors had a car phone and came running over as we were leaving the club.

She was about twenty at a guess—I'd want ID this time—heavy-set, dressed in a corset, PVC skirt, fishnets and stilettos. She had about two hundred pounds of make-up on and was just about popping out of her corset. Also nearly incomprehensible.

"The crypt!" she screamed. "The crypt!"

"There's about six million crypts in New Orleans, child," Ben said gently. "Which crypt?"

"The crypt, they're at the crypt!" she kept screaming, her black goop mascara running down her face.

"Now, take a deep breath, miss," I said calmly, looking her in the eye. "Where is the crypt?"

"On Decatur Street," she said, sniffling.

"There ain't no cemeteries on Decatur Street," Ben said.

"It's a club," she said as if we were morons. "I was calling around saying that Drusilla had turned to the dark side. She was my friend! And she turned!"

"That's what happens with vampires. More information, less sobbing."

"Lord Vordon called. They came to the Crypt but the Guardian would not let them pass."

"Bouncer wouldn't open the door," I translated. I spoke semifluent Goth. "Lord Vordon's probably the manager."

"Where on Decatur?" Ben asked.

"By Governor Nichols. About half a block towards Ursulines. Across from Fiorella's."

"Go home! Lock the doors!" I shouted to the girl as I ran for Honeybear. "Don't let a friend in unless they'll drink holy water!"

I got in and peeled out, hoping I remembered where Ursulines was.

As I was heading in the general direction, weaving in and out of traffic, siren and lights going, I got a call. It was Trevor.

"Chad," I answered, swerving around a Nissan that looked like the driver was drunk.

"This is even worse than last month. Another loup-garou in City Park. Vampires on Decatur. Choose."

"Fangs," I said.

"You'll be on your own. Can you?"

"They're as good as staked," I said. "Question is, can I find the club? And are they still there?"

The answer was, eventually, and no.

I banged on the door of the club with the butt of my Uzi. It was a good old-fashioned, metal security door with the good old-fashioned slide-bar vision slit. I decided I wanted one of those in my house if Madame Whatsername ever came up with one.

"Who dares disturb the Dark Portal?" the man inside boomed.

"Hoodoo Squad," I said. "Open up or I'll huff and I'll puff and I'll get two blocks of C4 and blow your house down."

He opened the door.

"Are they still around? If not, do you know where they went?"

Lord Vordon was tall, pale and wearing a top hat, tails, and carrying a silver-headed cane. He had implanted canines that nearly had me staking his ass but I'd run into that shit in Seattle. I was surprised to see it in New Orleans since everybody in this town knew damned well fangs were real.

"They did not pass the Dark Portal," Lord Vordon intoned over the caterwauling of the horrible Dark Wave band that was playing. I like everything about the Goth movement except the music. The Cure needed one. "We were warned that Princess Drusilla had entered the eternal night."

We didn't let them in. We got told Drusilla was a fang. Okay, and the weird pretensions. Just speak English for fuck's sake!

"I need you to call all the clubs she might go to and warn them," I said, passing him my card. "Give them this number. The moment she shows at one of them, have them call me."

One of the bouncers—a tall dude, with a shaved head, and a bunch of piercings, wearing fatigue pants, jump boots and an overstrained T-shirt—grabbed Lord Vordon by the arm and shouted in his ear.

"They have appeared at the Ossuary!" Vordon boomed, holding his hand to the sky. "The Dark Night has come to the Ossuary!"

"Where is the Ossuary?" I asked.

"731 Miro Street," the bouncer shouted.

I had no idea where Miro was and no time to read a map.

"You," I said, grabbing the bouncer by the shirt. "You're coming with me!"

"So..." the bouncer said as we were flying down Esplanade. His name was Dave King. He went by Decay. "You get paid for this?"

"Shit, yeah. Tons. And no time to spend it."

"Nice Uzi," Decay said. "I've never seen one like that before. Is that a full auto .45?"

"Custom design of mine," I said, passing it over. "On safe."

"Yeah. Sweet. How's the handling?"

"Great," I said, taking it back and clipping it on one-handed. I nearly sideswiped a Chevy, then nearly got T-boned in a red intersection again. Fucking minivans. They were the hot new thing. Bane of my existence. I'm probably going to die at the hands of some suburban housewife bringing her kids home from dance class. Damn you, Lee Iacocca.

"Get ready to take a left," Decay said. "I hear they shred .45 ammo."

"There's a fix for that," I said as he pointed to the turn.

"Up here on the right," Dave said.

"You in or out?" I asked. "You're in, you get part of the bounty. You're out, stay out."

"I'm in. I heard about the Orpheum. Guy on the door was my friend."

If he lived, I was going to point him in the direction of MHI. He'd fit right in.

I parked in the street and left the lights going. There was traffic. They could just go around.

I opened the trunk, rummaged, and came out with a shotgun for Dave.

"Think this explains itself?" I asked, handing him a bandolier of shells and stakes.

"Yep," he said, breaking the action. "You carry them loaded?"

"Always," I said. I handed him a Boy Scout canteen on a strap. "Holy water."

"That works?" he asked.

"That works. Just burns but it distracts them. Oh, wait."

I rummaged some more and came up with the dog collar.

"Best I can do for armor," I said, handing it to him.

It barely fit around his gorilla neck.

"That's your main and easiest-to-access artery. They like to climb. Keep an eye up. Stakes through the heart paralyze them. I'll take the heads," I added, tapping Mo No Ken.

"Works," Dave said. The guy had balls.

The entrance was around the corner.

So were the vampires.

Princess Drusilla, AKA Amanda Worthly, 17, lived in a nice house on Charles Street. She had attended private schools where the primary teaching was in French. Her father was a managing partner of Lornton, Crouse, and Barrande. Her mother and father were divorced. Her mother had taken off to India to "find herself." Amanda was trying the same thing through the Goth movement. Her father, a workaholic, gave her a generous allowance and essentially no management.

Princess Drusilla was well known in the New Orleans Goth movement. She always had money, always had access, and thus always had friends. At a club, she had met the absolutely fascinating Lord Mornington, AKA Tedd Roberts, originally of Durham, North Carolina—a vampire.

Princess Drusilla, starting to recover her wits after slaking her raging thirst on a half dozen of her closest friends, was not someone to be denied entrance to one of her favorite clubs.

"You will let me in or I will rip this door off, Thomas!" she shrieked. She was wearing a silk little black dress that barely covered her assets, fishnets, and stilettos. Her fangs were out and she was hungry again. "I shall not be denied! *Je vais boire votre âme!*"

There were two of them. "Cover up and six," I said, looking over my shoulder. Mo No Ken slid from its sheath with a nearly silent hiss.

"Got it," Dave said, a touch nervous. Good.

"Hunters!"

The other vampire had been a rotund man in his fifties with a heavy beard and dark brown hair. He was wearing an incongruous opera cape and top hat.

That's what she found attractive? Some girls just have daddy issues.

"Your silver shall not avail you!" he screamed and leapt, arms wide, fangs out.

Ben Carter had been right. Our senior vampire didn't have a very good survival instinct.

"How 'bout two-hundred-year-old Japanese folded steel?" I asked as "Lord Mornington's" head hit Dave in the arm.

"Incoming!" Dave said.

Now the newly turned Drusilla, on the other hand, was a beast.

It was on like Donkey Kong.

Three minutes later I was wiping down Mo No Ken with holy oil. Drusilla had been shot, staked, and was missing her head. Dave and I were both out of breath and covered in blood. She had bit him on the arm, but hadn't hit the artery.

I wrapped his arm up tight and patted him on the shoulder. The coroner was on the way.

"You just made about ten grand," I said. "Bad side is, when you die you'll rise as one of them unless your head gets cut off first."

"I can live with that," Dave said. "Ten grand?"

"Might be more," I said. "Part of it is based on kills and there are quite a few bodies in the wake of this group. Ten grand minimum."

"You guys hiring?"

I miss Decay. Good man.

I dropped Decay off at an all night doc-in-the-box, all he really needed, gave them a couple hundred for the stitches and headed back out. The zombies were rising in Greenwood and we'd just lost Greg Wise.

CHAPTER 9
Moondance

Anyone who has driven into New Orleans on I-10 and is not blind has noticed that at one point it is flanked by massive, aboveground cemeteries. If you're headed into town, Greenwood is the one on the left and Metairie is the one on the right.

Metairie is newer and fancier. The mausoleums there run to two stories and are real works of art. It is carefully maintained.

Greenwood is older. It is about one-third mausoleums and two-thirds sarcophagi, packed freaking cheek to jowl. It is not as well maintained but still a very nice place. Lots of history.

Both are absolutely enormous, complex, and one hell of a place to be in the middle of the night, more or less on your own, hunting undead. They are creepy as hell *without* zombies moaning in the moonlight.

There is a low, iron fence around Greenwood that was holding back some shamblers as I pulled up next to the NOPD car.

"Your guy went in," the cop shouted through his

window. "About thirty minutes ago. Haven't heard from him since."

I never want to be a team leader but if I ever run a team, its motto is going to be: *Habes intrare exire non habetis.* You have to go in, you don't have to come out.

"Greg," I said, touching my radio as I parked. "You there, Greg?"

No response.

Zombies can be a pain, but the kind someone raises out of a cemetery were slow and dumb. Greg had not been doing this for very long, but I had been told he knew his business. I didn't see Greg getting taken down by a bunch of shamblers. Not in a place like this. Which meant there was probably something else in there.

"Greg, if you can hear me, just hunker down."

"Your friend is one with us," a voice said on the radio. The accent wasn't local. Islands in general. Maybe Haitian. *"He has joined the darkness."*

"I don't know who you are, partner," I radioed. "But you are about to get a .45 caliber enema."

The man laughed, a booming psychotic laugh.

Jeeze, one of those, I thought. Another freaking necromancer thinks he's king of the world. Just my luck.

"You are weak and fragile compared to my chil-dren!" Cheeeeel-dren! *"You shall become one with the darkness."*

My first inclination was to go in there and kick his ass. There was one problem. Greg and Trevor had been right. I'd been going through .45 like water. Ten loaded mags were not enough. I had to top off before I could go in.

I opened up the trunk and collected all my mags, then started reloading. While I did that, more shamblers collected.

"Hey!" the cop boomed over his PA. "You going to do anything about this?"

The fence was only about waist height but had spikes on top. They were stuck on the spikes. It turned out that being familiar with the hoodoo, when they built cemeteries in this town, it was usually with the idea of keeping the residents inside.

I used semiauto to carefully tap every shambler in the head, starting with the ones who weren't stuck, then moving to the ones who were. From time to time I paused and did a 360. Still nothing major. I could hear more moaning in the graveyard. They were trying to come to the lights.

I went back to Honeybear, got out another can of Bud, took a sip and topped off the mag I'd just used. I decided I might need my night vision goggles and grabbed that heavy pouch too. As shamblers would find us, I'd walk over and tap them. It was getting silly. I finished off the shamblers at the fence, then went to find the gate. There are several gates to the massive cemetery. The one I was using was at the corner of Canal Boulevard and Rosedale Drive. Canal Boulevard was not to be confused with Canal Avenue, Canal Street, Canal Court, or Canal Way, by the way.

It was locked, so I walked back to the police car.

"You wouldn't happen to have the key to the dread... the gate, would you?"

"Your buddy took it with him," he yelled through the glass.

So much for the easy way. I called it in to Trevor,

then climbed over the fence, trying not to catch my balls on the iron spikes.

The drive there had trees on the right side and mausoleums and sarcophagi on the left. Beyond the trees was an open field, then the main buildings. Beyond the mausoleums and sarcophagi were more mausoleums and sarcophagi stretching beyond what I could see in the moonlight.

I had no idea where this necromancer shithole was hiding but he'd raised a fair passel of zombies. Every so often some moaning shambler would come stumbling out of the darkness. I was less worried about the ones on the tomb side than the tree side. There were bushes under the trees and they blocked my view.

I stayed to the middle of the road and used semi-auto. Cleanup was going to be a bitch on this one.

There were some shambler bodies already down. I followed Greg's path, keeping a careful eye out for what might have gotten him.

Then a shambler came out of the darkness and it *was* Greg. Shit. His throat had been torn out and one arm was missing. The wounds on his body were massive. That wasn't shambler damage. There was something far worse in here.

I gave him *requiescat in pace*, reloaded and kept moving.

I came to a set of tombs that were stairsteps. There was a sarcophagi, a one-story tomb and a two-story tomb. I bounded up and up and up.

I turned off my lights, pulled out my NVGs and looked around.

The goggles were huge, awkward, heavy, and had cost a fortune, but the cemetery was an eerie green under night vision, and it was amazing how much I could see.

There were shamblers moving between the tombs but nothing fast or that looked particularly powerful. A shambler horde *could* have done the damage. They can rip your arm off. He'd have to have gotten swarmed for that to happen. That's the first lesson of shamblers: don't let yourself get swarmed. And these were having a hard time even getting together in and among the complex layout of the cemetery.

I saw where the body trail turned left and headed deeper into the cemetery.

Moving on the ground was a danger. My vision was limited and if something could come out from between the tombs in a flash, I'd be toast.

But the majority of the cemetery was one-story marble tombs mixed with occasional nearly flat or waist-height sarcophagi. The two-story tomb I was on was a rarity. In fact, most of the tombs in the direction the body trail headed were one-story with very few sarcophagi. Most had flat roofs. A few were angled or curved but even those had narrow ledges on the side. That gave me an idea.

The first time I encountered zombies I was still recovering from being in the Marine barracks bombing in Beirut. It was at a tent revival (long story, look at the other memoir) and there were cars scattered outside. I used the cars, often hopping from car to car, to mess with the shamblers.

Pro-tip: Always try to fight shamblers on broken ground or where there are frequent obstacles. They can get up to a fair speed on a flat and in a direct line. Any change of direction or height messes with them.

Avoid fighting them on flats, where they can get a good run-up or where you can get easily swarmed. Always check six and never assume one is permanently down.

Being up on the tombs might also give me a chance to see what had taken Greg before it could close.

I stowed the goggles, because it is hard enough to walk when you can't see your feet, let alone do what I was about to. I jumped down to the next one-story, onto a sarcophagus, and back up on a one-story tomb. And I was off.

I was carrying a lot of weight in gear, ammo, and weapons. I'd been going hard pretty much all day and jumping from tomb to tomb was, to say the least, tiring. But it kept me up and away from any unseen shamblers. From time to time I had to get down to ground level since there were roads between the groups of tombs. A few saw me, and I would just pause, aim, and shoot them in the head. In the Marines you're taught to conserve ammo. One shot one kill. In this case I was pretty sure I was going to need it.

I stopped about halfway down the length of the drive when I could see the body trail terminate about fifty meters from my position. I was at the intersection of two broadways, roads not walkways, called Jasmine Avenue and Metairie Road. I took out some of my partially expended magazines and refilled them from my assault ruck. I was beat, I was out of wind and I was hot as hell. I also was about to meet whoever had killed my teammate.

"Greg, this is Alvin, come in, over."

"Alvin," I said quietly. "Iron Hand. Greg's down. Turned. Cleared. Necro on site. Has his radio, so listening."

"Roger," Alvin said.

"Ah, another Hunter come to join my children," the necro radioed. *"Come. My children shall feast on your flesh as the Dark loas feast upon your soul."*

I tried an idea and switched to Spanish.

"Hey, friend. Go to the road where I killed the vampire in the strip mall. Come in from that way. He is near Live Oak and that road. You understand?"

"Yeah, I understand," he radioed back in Spanish. *"Okay. Give me five minutes."*

I took a big drink of wine from my canteen, took a whiz since there weren't any shamblers around, ghosted back a couple of tombs, crossed Jasmine, then back up on tombs. I was back to being the Hunter.

I moved soft from tomb to tomb, searching for the necro SOB and whatever he was using for a heavy hitter. Finally, I spotted him. He was, in fact, at the corner of Live Oak and Metairie. Up on a tomb. And he was looking right at me.

"Come to me, my friend," the man boomed. He was big, fat, and as far as I could tell, black, but he'd painted his face to look like a skull. He was wearing a top hat and tails. What was with that idiotic look this night? "My spells are more powerful. Tonight, the Dark loas bring me the greatest of gifts! I have sacrificed to them and they are come!"

That was when I noticed the body on the top of the tomb. It wasn't rising because its heart had been ripped out.

"Oh, you did not," I said, lifting the Uzi. Human sacrifice never ended well.

The bullets bounced in every direction. *Warded. Shit.*

The necromancer started to chant in a deep, guttural

tongue, raised the wet blade of his knife to the moon and cried aloud. He was answered by a loud roar as something came over the tombs.

I think that it's the case with most experienced Hunters that we have things we prefer and things we don't prefer. And I think most of us like big shit that succumbs to sufficient firepower. I know that's what I like. Big shit like that shelob that you just keep hitting with more and more firepower until it dies. The one reason to join MCB for me isn't the importance of their jobs. It's that they can call in a fucking *arclite* strike when they need one. They can bring in a battleship or B-52s. Cluster bombs!

I'd like that kind of power. Not the killing-and-intimidating-witnesses power. There've been times I really wanted to bring in a full-on broadside from the USS *Iowa*, you know?

What most of us don't like is shit that is partially incorporeal, mostly magic, and doesn't want to die.

The moon was a silver glimmering outline behind fleeting clouds as the giant shadowy monster came to eat my soul. It was a black nightmare of webs and teeth. I wasn't sure what the hell it had once been, but it didn't seem to mind .45. And it was fast. Shit, it was fast.

The blow came out of nowhere and knocked me off the tomb I was occupying and into one on the far side of the walkway. I managed to slap-fall the sideways impact and my helmet saved my head, but I was going to feel it in the morning.

The thing came over the tombs and blotted out the moon as my Uzi went *click*. I decided it was pointless to shift to 1911 and drew Mo No Ken as I rolled away from its descending bulk.

I came back up to my feet and slashed as the nightmare thing approached. The blade went through the inky darkness as if it wasn't there. There was a slight sizzle from the consecrated oil it was coated in but nothing really useful. A massive claw appeared out of nowhere and ripped into my right arm. The straps for my Uzi parted and the weapon dropped. Mo No Ken went flying.

I thought the wound was minor, until there was a sudden spurt from my brachial vein.

Bullets did nothing. My sword did nothing. That left only fire as an option. It was right on me and I was bleeding like a stuck pig.

I backpedaled and it let me, making this strange whispering giggle noise that had to be a taunt. It crawled slowly forward, a black shadow amongst the shadows. I pulled out a thermite grenade, yanked the pin, and tossed. Then I clamped a hand on my bleeding arm and ran like the devil was chasing me.

When the light flared I turned around. The nightmare thing was gone. I held one hand up to shield my eyes from the fire, but there was nothing there.

Then it slammed into me from atop one of the tombs.

Those massive claws ripped into me again, shredding my assault ruck and armor. I reached around, pulled out a canteen and splashed it backwards.

There was a keening wail, a hissing sound and then the sound of fast wings. It was gone again.

I rolled over and propped myself on one of the tombs. I keyed my radio. First aid could wait.

"Some sort of black shadow demon," I said in

Spanish. "Fast, powerful, claws. Likes to come in from the side or above. Holy water seems to work. Guns, no effect. Fire possibly, but too fast to tell."

The radio clicked twice. I started fixing my arm.

In a situation like that, I don't fuck around. I mashed on a bandage. Then I pulled out a partial roll of rigger tape and taped that puppy down hard. The bleeding was at least reduced.

"It just flew back this way. I got a look. I think that's an Agaran."

I didn't know what an Agaran was, but Alvin knew what we were fighting. He might know the answer to my very important question: "How do we kill it?"

I got up and made my way back to my scattered weapons. I got Mo No Ken sheathed and picked up my Uzi. No major issues but it wasn't very much use in this situation. I reloaded anyway. Shamblers.

"Fire and light, I think. Or kill whoever called it up."

"The summoner's the fat guy in the face paint. He's warded against bullets. Can you take him?" I sure hoped that asshole with Greg's radio didn't speak Spanish.

"Shelbye's here. We're on it."

"You cannot defeat me, mortals," the necromancer radioed. Still in English. He sounded annoyed, so he probably couldn't understand us. *"I have the blessing of the Dark loas! Never before have they granted me such power!"*

I spotted the Agaran; it had collected along the ground, a rolling puddle of black. The holy water must have really hurt it.

Then I threw another thermite grenade right at it. The thing let out another unearthly wail. This time I managed to follow what happened—the flash revealing something that looked like a terrestrial squid; then it hopped away out of the light. It seemed to have shrunk.

Only I was going to run out of grenades, holy water, and blood pressure, long before it ran out of shadows. It was slinking around the tombs, trying to flank me.

"I see the necromancer. Is that ward impenetrable?"

"I don't know. From what I've read, that sort of magic will stop anything fast or living."

"What about thrown?"

Fire in the hole.

The necromancer never saw the frag grenade coming.

Pro-tip: For everything there is a season. A time for swords, a time for holy water, and a time for small bundles of explosives wrapped in notched wire.

Knowing what season it is, is the essence of Hunting.

There were twenty-six zombies in the cemetery, including poor Greg, and one Agaran which had melted into an oily puddle. We had a hard time finding that in the PUFF lists but the bounty was nice, higher than a shoggoth. Plus a bonus for the necromancer who'd raised all of them. The way you get paid on them is based on how much havoc they'd caused.

I left Shelbye and Alvin to cover the coroners on cleanup and took myself to my favorite all night doc-in-the-box to get my brachial vein sewn up.

CHAPTER 10
Doctor My Eyes

The cute doctor took one look under the bandages and said, "Uh-uh." I insisted I needed it working tonight and vascular surgery was not her gig. She also warned me I might not be *able* to get it fixed. Certainly not at 3 A.M. on a full moon.

Shortly before dawn I walked out of Memorial Hospital. A little woozy, maybe, but ready to roll. Or close enough for day two of the full moon. And I'd picked up a PUFF.

Wait. What?

Lots of people in New Orleans knew about Hoodoo Squad, because we were the thin green line between hoodoo and them or their families and friends. The drug dealers and innumerable burglars, muggers and other lowlifes of New Orleans treated us like we were royalty. How do you think doctors and nurses felt?

When I got to the emergency room, they were waiting for me. The security guard was real polite and deferential about all the guns.

"You really can't keep them, sir," he said. "It's not

just that it makes the doctors and nurses nervous. Sometimes there's drug reactions and stuff."

"Got that," I said. "I agree, even. But how far do you want me to be from my weapons in the event somebody turns into a loup-garou in reception?" The way my night had been going it wouldn't have surprised me.

We compromised. They got stacked in the room. Just in case.

The emergency room was overflowing. Standing room only.

I never even sat down. Not because I was one of the standing only, but because I never even went to intake. I went straight to one of the curtained alcoves. I heard some muttering.

"Why's he so special?"

"Hoodoo Squad."

"Oh."

That was the locals. The few tourists that said anything were told to shut their stupid tourist yap.

I got out of the top of my gear and got the wound looked at right away by a nurse.

"That's a bad cut," she said. "Normally we'd stitch the outside. Veins heal."

"I need to be going. I need the vein. Tonight."

"I'll get the doctor."

The doctor was the attending, not an intern. He looked at it and shook his head. "To get you up and going, I'll need to call in a vascular surgeon. And it won't be one hundred percent."

"I just need some mobility, Doctor." I put it in the formal *You're an MD* tone. "We're down to four people."

"I heard about Mr. Baldwin," the doctor said, holding the vein closed with a hemostat. "Who else?"

Jonathan's test had come back positive. He was officially a werewolf. I was told later that Agent Higgins had done the honors. I'd have done the same.

"Greg Wise, Doctor," I said.

"Oh, not Greg!" the nurse said. "I liked Greg."

"Sorry, miss. He's gone."

"I'll put up his cup," she said with a sniffle.

Hoodoo Squad really did have their own coffee mugs in the emergency room. I didn't have one—yet. I had one the next time I got carried in.

And when one of us would buy the farm, they'd put them up on a special shelf. It was like the memorial wall at the MHI compound. They showed it to me one time. It was sobering.

"I'll call Dr. Einstat," the doctor said. "It may be some time."

"Understood."

Some time turned out to be about twenty minutes. Dr. Einstat, wearing scrubs, was still blinking sleep from his eyes but looked sharp enough to repair an artery in his sleep.

"I came out on the full moon for you, young man," Dr. Einstat said, examining the wound. "You'd better be worth it."

"Doing the best I can, Doctor. Any chance you can get me up and going at thirty percent on the arm? Tonight?"

"Might be able to do better than thirty," Einstat said. "You'll need surgery, you understand."

"Any chance on a local? I really don't have time for recovery from general."

"Light general," he said. "Valium drip. And you look like you could use a unit of blood..."

It's amazing how much better you feel after a unit of whole blood. Vampires have a point.

I got an alcohol sponge bath from an old nurse's aide who had clearly been around the hoodoo block a time or two.

"I heard Mr. Wise has gone to the Green Lands," the nurse's aide said, continuing to sponge off all the various crap I'd gotten on myself. "A terrible business."

"Green Lands is a good description," I said. "Been there briefly once. So green."

"We all go to the Green Lands someday, son," she said. "If we do not fall to the Shadow."

"Working on it," I said.

A few minutes later they wheeled me out, still in my stinking, ichor-covered armored pants, and wheeled me upstairs into a small surgical suite. An anesthesiologist came in, hooked a valium drip into my IV and I sort of drifted off.

I really like valium drips. I hope heaven has valium drips.

I woke up a while later in recovery. My arm had a heavy set of sutures on it. Much heavier than normal. About every millimeter. Also a very strong clear bandage encircled my right bicep. Which was comfortably numb.

"You're going to have to favor it," a young doctor said. "I know you have to be mobile and have some use, but you're going to have to favor it."

"Tell Dr. Einstat thank you," I said. "Can I get up?"

"I wouldn't recommend it, but that's up to you," the doctor said.

"I've got to go."

A pretty nurse's aide helped me to my feet. My gear was right there in the recovery room. It was torn to shreds, literally. My tactical vest was ribbons. I realized I'd left some magazines back in the cemetery. God knew what else.

All I wanted was to lie back down. Whole blood or no, I was exhausted.

Death is lighter than a feather, duty is heavier than mountains.

I started getting my gear back on.

While I was getting dressed in my stinking combat suit, with the help of the nurse's aide, the same security guard came in and cleared his throat hesitantly.

"We've got a situation downstairs," he said.

Her name was Sylvia Parks.

Despite the awful necessity of what MCB does, awful is an accurate description. As the Doctors Nelson insist, victims need care and understanding to overcome their experiences. MCB sort of makes that impossible in the main. If you run into the supernatural and go to a counselor talking about werewolves or vampires or the boogie man, they get the nice young men in the clean white coats.

Sylvia had been a captive of vampires. Are there worse things, supernaturally? Yes. Is being a vampire captive bad on toast? Yes.

She'd been physically rescued but her mind was pretty well gone. She couldn't restrain herself. She had to talk about it. A county counselor had recommended her for admission. Because everyone knows vampires aren't real.

She spent months in a psych ward until she was convincing enough about no longer believing in vampires to get discharged. She got into drugs to help with the nightmares. She slid down the ladder into prostitution and wound up in New Orleans as a down-and-out streetwalker.

She'd been found in a cheap motel room, dead from a heroin OD. Just another statistic.

She was taken to the hospital, pronounced DOA in the ER and shipped downstairs to the morgue for processing. No ID and not from around here. As a Jane Doe she was left in the morgue until identified or they gave up, usually ninety days. Where she hung on a hanger until she woke up.

Uh, hanger?

Yeah. Forget what you see in TV shows like *Quincy*. There are roll-out trays in most morgues but they're for bodies which are undergoing advanced autopsy requirements where the MEs are going back to them multiple times.

Most big city morgues have a large cooler where bodies are on shelves, sometimes stretching up twenty feet. Those generally have some rotation system. But even that takes up a lot of space.

The morgue downstairs in the main hospital in New Orleans at the time had a hanger system. Bodies which were sufficiently together were held with a strap, like what they use to lift people up in a helo in rescues, wrapped in plastic and hung up on a pulley system. Very space-saving and efficient. Which was, clearly, necessary.

I don't think New Orleans in the mid-eighties had, officially, the highest death rate from murder in the nation. But remember the MCB. Most supernatural deaths were recorded as something else. In fact, when I was in the emergency room, an intern came for the *question and answer period.*

Every emergency entry had to have a reason for injury for statistical purposes. Federal law. I later ran into some people in the federal government who compile those statistics and *hated* the MCB for throwing them off. You might run across the statistic that the most dangerous place in the world is your own kitchen or bathroom? That's because MCB's most common form of death, when there's a supernatural event at a house, is "Died due to electrocution in bathtub/slipping in shower" or "died due to slipping while replacing kitchen fixture." Fire imp in the house? "Kitchen fire started by frying oil." Every agent gets the suggestion in training and uses it assiduously.

Yeah. Your *bathroom* is the most dangerous place in the *world*. Sure.

By the way, Mr. Robinson whose son turned into a loup-garou? He wasn't a hero who tried to hold the line and save his wife and daughter from a werewolf. He had gone nuts over dinner being burned and killed his whole family. That was the official story. Keep that in mind the next time you see "father kills whole family then commits suicide."

But back to the point. When I was still in emergency, a young intern had come in with a clipboard. Before he could even open his mouth, I said: "SOCMOB. Sierra Golf Kilo. Oscar oscar November."

"You've done this before," he said, grinning and writing it down.

What did I just say?

SOCMOB.

"Seriously, Doc, I was just Standing on the Corner, Minding My Own Business."

That was and is the most common opening for "I

got into a fight." It is never the fault of the person who is injured. They were just Standing on the Corner Minding their Own Business. SOCMOB.

Who had attacked me?

"Some Guy with a Knife." SGK.

Where did this guy come from? Were you confronting him?

"Out of Nowhere." Oscar Oscar November. OON. That's what the doctors write down.

Individual: SOCMOB.

Assailant: SG or SGK or SGG (some guy with a gun) or, often, SGs. (Some guys.)

Where did they come from? OON.

SOCMOB, SGK, OON.

Q&A done.

Emergency doctors say that the most dangerous places in the world are street corners, not bathrooms, and the worst possible things you can do to cause assault with bodily harm are:

- Stand on a corner, minding your own business.

- Be walking home from prayer service, especially if you are carrying a Bible.

- Be sitting on your own front porch. Again, holding a Bible is a sure sign you're about to get beat up or shot.

And Some Guy is an elite ninja assassin that travels the world harming perfectly innocent people for no good reason. Out of nowhere. Then disappears. Like it's magic. MCB needs to put Some Guy on the PUFF list and the "MCB Most Wanted."

I love emergency room personnel. They're the only group on earth more cynical than Hunters.

But back to the vampire in the morgue.

I hadn't been in the New Orleans General Morgue yet but I was impressed. Compared to Seattle, they had it down. The hanger room was behind a heavily sealed door with a fancy new electronic keypad. No zombies, vampires or other forms of undead were getting out of there. It was like a bank vault.

"What if you accidentally get stuck in there?" I asked the morgue attendant.

That, by the way, New Orleans or anywhere, is not a job I'd ever take. Or funeral home attendant. Just saying.

"There's a call button and a phone," he said dyspeptically. His name was Phillip Wohlrab. He was a dead ringer for Dave, the daytime coroner's shift lead. Short, chubby, very pale. Thinning hair and he had to be not more than twenty-two. He reminded me of a mole rat.

The vampire was clearly hissing at us from behind two inches of armored glass. You couldn't hear her but she was clearly hissing. When people woke up as vampires, they were usually confused and insane. Being tangled up and dangling from a bunch of straps probably didn't help.

"Any chance this could wait till daylight?" I asked, looking at my watch.

She hit the armored glass so hard it broke her hand. Then again. Because it just regenerated back to normal.

He pointed to the stack of bodies that were piling up in the room.

"Day shift will shit a brick," he said. "And we've got more coming in from Greenwood. I hate having to reprocess the already buried."

I probably should have called for help, but last I heard, everybody else was busy too. I worked my right arm for a second and drew Mo No Ken with my left. It was set up for a right draw and it was a harder reach, but once out, eh. I'm fairly ambidextrous.

"Yeah, sure," I said with a sigh.

He tapped the keypad and started to swing the heavy door open. He needn't have bothered. It nearly crushed him against the wall.

The newly awakened female vamp was all hunger, strength and fury. Not much in the way of brains. Then again, that also described genius vampire Tedd Roberts, and he had been a vampire for a month. Since she was trapped in the straps, and I didn't have a clean shot at her head, I just started slicing at limbs until I could get a good angle at her neck. It was more like hedge trimming than regular monster hunting.

"Now I'm supposed to clean this up?" Wohlrab said. There was vampire ichor all over the morgue and the body was starting to deliquesce.

"I just make the mess," I said, reaching for my cloth to clean Mo No Ken. That hurt. This was going to suck. "Besides," I said, pointing to the arm, "I'm injured."

"Always excuses," Wohlrab said with a sigh. "You're worse than day shift."

"Don't you have a janitor or something?"

As I was walking out of the emergency room, Agent Marine came marching in. He was in full tactical rig-out, including helmet with FBI in big white letters on the front, and followed by a very confused-looking junior agent in the same gear.

He was probably there to do the honors for some poor schlub who'd gotten bit or to intimidate some out-of-town witnesses.

"Hey, Bob," I said, half waving.

"Hey, Chad," he said, walking past. "Sorry about Jonathan."

"What?"

He stopped. "You didn't hear?" He looked around to make sure none of the patients were close enough to eavesdrop. "Doctors found a bite. Lycanthropy test immediately came back positive. I ran a couple strips to be sure."

"Shit."

"Baldwin was a good guy. I made it painless. That's all I could do."

"Thanks."

Bob nodded, then went back to work. The MCB agents were the only people having a busier night than we were.

In Seattle, MCB turned up for every damned incident and read us the riot act most of the time. In New Orleans, under Castro's leadership at least, they just waved and met us at Maurice's for drinks. I ended up having them over for grill-outs and vice versa. When the time came, MCB and MHI fought shoulder to shoulder to save Mardi Gras and died in a single pile.

I think the relationship in New Orleans is something that needs to be fostered. I get where the Nelsons and Shacklefords are coming from but . . .

Never mind. Enough preaching. Back to the monsters.

CHAPTER 11
Radar Rider

There's a smell. Any experienced Hunter learns it quick.

I talked one time to an old European Hunter who had been in World War II and had been one of the supernatural specialists called in to assess the Nazi concentration camps. He said it was the same smell. The smell of concentrated, starving humanity in desperation.

It was the smell of a vampire feeding pit. That same smell.

Ben and Shelbye had been chasing a werewolf in Elmwood when they'd smelled it. They broke off from the pursuit to identify the particular warehouse it was coming from. Then they tracked down the loup-garou and made their PUFF.

It was just past dawn. I'd already been up for twenty-four hours. I was beat to shit, my arm was in ribbons, my gear was in ribbons.

Trevor had rolled out when we were down to four. He still couldn't move much but he could shoot and communicate and he was a serious monster killer. He was working much like Shelbye, taking the sniper position. After the night we'd had, Trevor had called Ray for reinforcements. Hunters were on their way, but that would take time.

When we met up at the warehouse, we'd agreed to break down to three teams: Shelbye and myself; Trevor and Ben; and Alvin, as the least-injured close combat specialist, would be the monster position, pardon the pun.

But we'd all meet at the warehouse. Which, naturally, was locked.

"It's been on long-term lease," the real estate agent said, "and the locks have been changed. They're not supposed to change the locks. What do you think is in there?"

He wasn't from around here. He'd been in contact with the FBI and gotten clearance but was looking askance at the heavily armed "federal contract security officers" that wanted into the building.

"They're suspected of smuggling counterfeit Teddy Ruxpins," Trevor said. "Very serious charge. We'll take care of opening it up."

I had entry tools in my trunk. So did Ben, Alvin and Trevor. I just watched, ate, and drank sweet tea.

I'd stopped by a Waffle House and picked up a few bacon and egg sandwiches. I needed the calories.

The door was duly opened and Alvin took point. I had the number two position, then Ben, Shelbye and Trevor limping along behind.

The warehouse had once been used as a cold storage facility for meat. In the center was a separate concrete building that was the cold storage. It had a big, hermetically sealed door on it. Heavy steel.

To the side was a shipping container. One of those

big metal containers they stack on ships. The smell was coming from that.

There were six people in the container. Two of them were already dead. I managed those with Alvin's assistance.

We called in SIU and medical to evacuate the survivors, then checked out the cold storage building. That was certainly where our vampire was hiding. The heavy door was locked from the inside and, shall we say, resistant to entry tools. The walls and ceiling were heavy concrete. We'd spend all day chipping through.

"If we could get some C4 into the cracks, we could blow the door off," Trevor said, rubbing his chin as he regarded it. "But there's not a crack."

"Got a cousin with a 'cetylene torch," Shelbye suggested.

The hinges were recessed. Getting into what was essentially a vault was going to take time. Jonathan had been our explosives expert. Trevor was former SF and no slouch. But this was difficult. We couldn't just wait to see if anything came out at nightfall, because we were all exhausted, and who knew what was going to happen on the second night of the full moon.

"I've got this," I said. "I'm going to need a few things."

"*Ce qui* want?" Lieutenant Salvage said. He was one of three lieutenants with Orleans Parish Special Investigations Unit. Short, stocky Cajun. When he got tired, and he was already there, his accent got thicker and thicker, then he'd start breaking into Cajun patois French.

I thought for a moment, regarding the storage locker.

"A lift just to get up and down," I said, pointing at the arm. I had it in a sling at the moment. "A ladder. A box of lawn and leaf bags. A hose long enough to reach the middle of that roof from the nearest outlet. And...fifty boxes, at least, of corn starch. Better make it a hundred to be on the safe side."

"Okay," Salvage said, making notes with a quizzical expression on his face.

"That should do it. I've got the rest in my car."

We walked out and I went to my trunk and started rummaging. After a moment I came up with four green-cloth shoulder bags.

"Claymores?" Shelbye said.

"Nah," I said. "But the bags are handy."

Inside, I set the bags down on the floor, well separated, and dumped one out. It contained two blocks of C4 plastic explosive and a roll of detonation cord.

"You keep C4 and det cord in your trunk?" Shelbye asked.

"Sure," I said. "Don't you?"

Trevor understood what I was going to do. "You're going to need a lot more explosives than that. I'll send Alvin back to base to see what Jonathan had stashed."

"Help me roll this out, Shelbye."

Rolling out a cigar of C4 with one arm stitched up on the bicep was a challenge, but Shelbye made quick work of it. While we were working, a guy turned up with the cherry picker and an extending ladder. A cherry picker, for those who don't know, is sort of a rolling, pneumatic scaffold/elevator.

I'm not sure he knew what we were working with. If he did, he was the most unflappable guy I've ever met. He just delivered the cherry picker and left.

About twenty minutes later a Sheriff's deputy showed up with a bunch of bags from A&P. He *did* know what we were working with.

"Holy shit! Is that *C4*? I'm out of here," he said, walking away quickly.

Alvin got back with a bunch more C4. We took all the stuff to the roof of the cold storage with the cherry picker and got to work.

First I taped the cigars of C4 to my emergency stash of det cord with rigger tape. Then I laid it down in a circle on the roof. The circle was large enough to get the extending ladder down into the room below—barely. I made a mental note to carry around more det cord. I extended the last bit of det cord out from the circle, then we got to work on the tamping.

"Lay out the trash bags around the circle to overlap," I said, waving my arm. "Please."

Shelbye got out the bags and laid them down.

"Okay," I said, considering the situation. There were seven bags. "Ten boxes of corn starch in each bag."

She duly poured ten boxes of corn starch in all of the bags.

"Now we need the hose."

The bags were partially filled with water, the tops tied and a second bag was put around the outside.

"Okay, I'm going to ask," Shelbye said as she was filling the bags.

"If we just blow the C4, all the force will go up," I said. "We need something holding it down. It's called tamping. Usually, that's sand bags. You can use bodies if you have them. But getting sandbags filled and brought up here would take more time and effort. Water is incompressible, but with that much force, it will only remain incompressible for an instant, not long enough for the full force of the cutting charge to cut through the concrete. When mixed with corn starch, however, it forms a non-Newtonian liquid under pressure. The corn starch acts as a quantum binding agent just long enough to hold the material in place. Voila. Instant sandbag. You get some of the rigidity of sand and the combined mass of the corn starch, not much, and the water, a lot."

"That's sort of . . ." she said then stopped.

"I got a perfect F in high school physics," I said. "Have you ever taken a multiple choice test where you didn't study and weren't sure of the answers?"

"Yeah," Shelbye said. "I wasn't all that much on schooling."

"Ever get every single answer *wrong*?" I asked.

"No," she said. "Even if you pick C as the answer on all of them, you get something."

"I got every answer wrong in physics," I said. "Every single one. Not one correct answer for an entire semester."

"Why?" she asked.

"I was taking chemistry," I said. "I really liked the teacher. He told me I had to get an A or I couldn't come over to his house anymore. So I got every single answer right. But I'd set out to make a perfect C average. So I had to get every single answer wrong in physics."

"That is just plum crazy," she said.

"I really like physics," I said.

Finally, she had the bags filled and in place over the charges. I had her go down to the floor while I hooked up the detonation sequence.

I always prefer to use chemical detonation. It's just way safer than electrical. But in this case, I didn't have enough det cord. I resolved to find someplace in the trunk for a decent-sized roll in the future. In the meantime I had to go electrical.

"Turn off your radios," I yelled. "And go tell the cops to turn theirs off!"

Electric blasting caps work by way of exploding bridge wire. When sufficient current goes through—like a 9-volt battery—the EBW has enough resistance that it heats up and pops. That little pop is enough to initiate the blasting cap. In turn, the cap has enough pop to initiate the main charge. But the caps themselves have two little wires coming out of them, and theory was that stray EMR— like from a radio—could potentially cause an initiation.

I waited until she got back to hook up the detonator. I crimped it to the C4 then attached the leads to a long wire spool from a claymore with wire caps. I'd already run the wire over the roof and down to the floor of the warehouse.

"I sort of need the cherry picker," I said.

When I was down on the ground again, I hooked up a claymore clacker and put in some earplugs.

"Fire in the hole!"

Alvin had brought back a lot of explosives, and we'd used extra since we were cutting through the anticipated rebar. (Yes, I'd thought of the rebar.) The thump was still fairly muted. We were showered with watery corn starch and there was a *CRASH* as the blown-out circle of concrete hit the floor inside the storage facility.

"You can tell them they can turn their radios back on."

There had been two vampires in the cold storage room. The circle of concrete had landed on the head of one and that took care of that. The explosion pulverized the other. I just needed to take its head off before it could regenerate.

I told Shelbye to be ready with the ladder, tossed in a flash-bang, drew Mo No Ken left-handed and dropped through the hole. My arm might have been injured but there was nothing wrong with my legs.

It was noon on the second day of the full moon. The call had come in the previous night. A short check by an SIU sergeant had determined that it looked like it was all over and nothing had come out. So we waited until we had time to check it out.

The house at 4030 Eagle Street was single-story with the usual heavily barred windows and doors. Right next to it was a bright pink house with an American flag flying proudly. When we pulled up there was crime scene tape across the front of the house and the elderly neighbor was out on his porch with a shotgun.

I walked over. Okay, I limped over.

"You see what happened?" I asked.

"Heard it," the man said. "Just crashing and screaming. I came out to check on it. Lights had gone out in most of the house. I flashed a light in. Just tore up. Johnsons were gone. I called the police. Sheriff's deputy come by, said they'd get to it when they could."

"Been a tough night, sir," I said.

"Can tell, son," he said. "You need a Coke or something? Sweet tea?"

"Sweet tea would be much appreciated, sir," I said.

"And one for me," Shelbye said. She was cradling her M14.

"Sure will, miss," the man said. He looked at the house for a moment. "Nothing's come out. Nothing gone in. What the hell did it?"

"That's what we're here to find out, sir," I said.

We had to get out the Halligan tool and ax to get

the door open. Then I entered cautiously, Uzi held in my left and at the ready.

There was nothing to see. The front room had been torn to shreds. There was a large pile of dirt and broken concrete on the floor of the living room and some blood splatter on the walls. There was some sort of weird mucous or ichor all over the room. It smelled like shit, I'll tell you that.

"What the hell?" I said as Shelbye followed me in.

"One of these," she said, shaking her head.

"One of whats?"

"We don't know. We call it a basement boogie. Called it in to Cazador and they don't know. We get one from time to time. Houses. Cemeteries. One office. Daytime, nighttime. Never been surviving witnesses. Best we can guess is shoggoth or a grinder, but there's never a reason someone would sick a shoggoth on the victims, and grinders don't like a water table like we got in New Orleans. Generally, just regular folk. They just up and disappear into those holes far as we can tell."

"The hole's not big enough for a shoggoth."

"That's what Trevor said," Shelbye said. "Most of the stuff he's heard of that digs up from underground, don't like a bunch of wet and ain't nothin' but water down there."

"Ever try to dig out the hole?"

"You think?" she replied. "They go deep. We've tried drilling them and we lose the line. They just up and disappear."

I was really starting to hate New Orleans. And "we don't know" in this business is a very bad line. It's the things you don't know that tend to be the biggest problem.

Definitely turned out to be the case in New Orleans.

Those little holes turned out to be the manifestation of a *very* big problem. But it took us some time to figure that out.

We left the house to whoever wanted it. God knows I wasn't going to be buying it.

It was 2 P.M. the last day of the full moon. One more night and this insanity would be over. Hopefully.

Ben Carter was in the hospital having received a major head wound from some sort of big imp. Trevor was still in his soft cast but out plugging bad things right and left at range. My arm was starting to swell from the exertion and I was about delirious. More members of MHI had arrived from Texas and Georgia to backfill, and Trevor had put them to work.

We'd had more loup-garou, another vampire, more zombies and a ghoul outbreak.

I kept having to stop to sharpen Mo No Ken.

And now I had a call that Alvin and Shelbye were in the shit with "something really damned big." Trevor was on scene and it was all hands.

The incident was occurring near the corner of Oleander and Monroe in Holly Grove—what was still called, by locals, the American Quarter versus the French Quarter.

I never figured out what the other two quarters were.

When I got near, I started to pick up radio transmissions from the team.

"We need a Pig for this thing," Trevor radioed. *"Fall back. Fall back!"*

He wasn't referring to something that goes "Oink, oink." The Pig is a nickname for an M-60 machine gun. They needed belt-fed.

NOPD had a ten-block perimeter set up and were evacuating people from the edges. This was serious.

"Trev, Hand," I radioed. I was coming in from Leonidas Street, which I thought was pretty cool in my sleep-deprivation and pain-induced stupor. "Bring it down Oleander if you can. Lead it towards Leonidas."

"*Roger,*" Trevor radioed. "*Alvin! Load up! We are didi mao!*"

"Can I get a description of the entity?" I radioed, parking my car sideways on Oleander.

"*Probably a flesh golem but it's fucking huge. We're loading up. Hopefully it will follow.*"

"*I don't know if I'd say hopefully,*" Alvin replied on the radio.

I got out and sort of distantly noted it was raining. Just a light rain but the fact that it wasn't until I stepped out that I noticed was sort of weird. I was really tired.

I went to the trunk, opened it up and started rummaging. All the way at the back was a large green hardcase. Getting it out with the arm was a pain but I managed. I opened it up, pulled out the Barrett M82A1, flipped down the bipod legs, loaded a magazine and carried it over to the driver's side. Then I hefted it up, painfully, onto the roof. I'd used this shooting position before. Previously I had glued little rubber booties on the end of the bipod legs to keep them from scratching Honeybear's roof. I ran the charging handle—used my right arm for that, winced again—and went back to the trunk to do more rummaging.

I saw Trevor's big Coronado come around the turn backwards. Shelbye was leaning out the window, firing with her M14 at something.

Then *it* came around the corner. Futhermucker.

Flesh golems are normally stitched-together humans, like Frankenstein. This was a stitched-together . . . at the time I didn't know what. Later we figured out it had bull legs, a silverback gorilla's body and a bull's head, plus some extra stuff for filling. I thought maybe a really outsized minotaur at the time, only the necromancer who'd enchanted it either got ahold of Babe the Big Blue Ox and King Kong or somehow managed to get the whole thing to expand. It was huge.

I prefer the big things I understand. Strange shadows in a dark cemetery? Thousands of poisonous spiders? Gnomes? Those piss me off. I like the *big* stuff. There should be more really *big* monsters in the world. Out in the open on a street at midday in a light rain where everyone had locked their doors and hidden in closets till the bellowing big thing got taken care of by Hoodoo Squad.

Coroner was going to have to bring the *big* truck for this thing. And lots of plastic bags. At least when I got through with it.

Trevor's battered blue Coronado came backing up next to me and I waved with my left hand.

"I hope you've got an idea," he yelled.

I reached waaaay in the back again and pulled out a light antitank weapon.

"You keep LAWs in your *trunk*?" Trevor said.

"Don't you?" I asked, handing him one. I pulled out another for myself. "Extend that for me, will you?" I asked, waving my injured right arm.

The flesh golem was charging towards us, bellowing in rage. They had hit it a bunch, and chunks were hanging off, but it was still coming.

I fiddled with the LAW for a few seconds and figured out it was easier to fire right than left despite the injury.

"You gonna, you know, *shoot*?" Alvin asked.

"Getting there," I said, putting the LAW on my shoulder. "One Gigantor Stew coming up."

I waited till it was about seventy-five meters away, adjusted the angle and let go.

The light antitank weapon hit it in its massive belly and it mostly disappeared in a cloud of flame.

"Wooo-hooo!" Shelbye yelled from the passenger side window.

Trevor had extended the second one. Sure enough, it was getting up. He hit it again.

The thing was *still* trying to get up. It was mostly blown in half but it was a game one.

I walked over to the Barrett, got a good cheek weld, leftie, and fired at its head. It dropped. Struggling back up. Second round through an eye. Struggling back up. Lost the other eye. Hey, I'm a Marine. Shelbye might have been our designated marksman but Lee Harvey Oswald showed what Marine marksmanship is made of.

A few rounds later it lay down and was a good monster.

Just to be sure, I got on the hood of the Coronado and we drove up cautiously. I hoped it wasn't getting back up. I was out of LAW rockets and we had used up our C4 on the vampire bunker.

It wasn't moving. It wasn't struggling. It wasn't breathing but some monsters like this don't. There was a lot of blood on the ground and guts everywhere.

"That's *my* trophy, Shelbye!"

"I'll get my boy to do it up right," she yelled back.

That thing's head has looked *great* up on my living room wall ever since. I just call it Babe.

CHAPTER 12
Veteran of the Psychic Wars

The third night of the full moon was, for New Orleans, uneventful. We *only* had two calls and no more casualties.

Trevor had called and said to meet at Maurice's at 10 A.M. All I wanted to know was when I could have some actual rest. I'd caught a few minutes' sleep the day before, I think, and a catnap that night. Napping in a car in a park where you'd just cleared zombies wasn't exactly restful.

But he was insistent and told me not to bother to derig. I finished up with the coroner and got in my car, trying to remember where Maurice's was.

When I walked in...

Picture, if you will, an open-air bar off a street I shall not name at the edge of the French Quarter. Dark wood, dark interior, long bar on the left wall. The entrance is on the right.

Sitting at the bar is a group of individuals. At least half of them are sporting bandages. There are guns, knives and clubs on the bar and floor. All of them are in stinking tactical gear, most of them covered in blood and various juices and ichor.

All except two women have shaved heads. Helmets line the bar. Beside the helmets are shots of bourbon. The barmaid, same as from my first visit, cannot pour fast enough.

"Hey, Chad," Trevor said. "Food's about up. You met Salvage. Tremaine and Carter," he said, gesturing to two parish lieutenants in tac gear. Tremaine was the other female besides Shelbye. Hard-faced brunette in her forties with a scar that ran across her cheek and nose. "You know the MCB cats."

"Hey," I said, sitting down painfully. I pulled off my helmet and laid it on the bar with the rest.

"Since you're here," Trevor said, picking up his drink...

"Absent companions," I said, raising the shot. I downed it.

"Absent companions," the group chorused.

The bourbon chicken was outstanding. I'd have eaten the asshole out of a pig at that point. This was heaven.

"So you survived your first full moon in New Orleans," said Special Agent in Charge Castro. He sat down next to me. "Congratulations."

"What the fuck is going on here?"

"That, I truthfully do not know yet. Call it an outbreak? An epidemic? Beats me." He tipped his glass toward my teammates. "Regardless, thank you for your timely efforts. The truth remains contained for one more day."

"Cheers?"

Castro gave me a hard look. "You coherent enough

for the real, no shit, behind the scenes explanation of the MCB's First Reason?"

"I wouldn't call myself coherent, but go," I said, spooning up my second plate of bourbon chicken.

"Magic, of any kind, requires a few things," Castro said. "First, knowing you can. After that, basically, materials, time, money, and the ability to learn more about it."

"The benefits are obvious," Agent Higgins said. "With magic you get stuff that you otherwise couldn't."

"The downside is there's always side effects," Trevor threw in. "When you get enough houdoun, bad things just start happening."

"And the more that people get into it, the more crazy they tend to get," Castro said. "Often, serious necromancers start off with high-minded intentions and then go off the rails. Some of the strongest wizards MCB has dealt with started off as pure-minded as Albert Schweitzer. But that's not the real secret. To understand the importance of the First Reason, you have to understand history and economics. Do I need to go over the changes in lifestyle brought about by the industrial revolution?"

"Not really," I said.

"It was the combination of the printing press and the industrial revolution that changed the equation when it came to magic," Castro continued. "Prior to that, the Roman Empire had the highest per capita income of any civilization in history. Well, except the Carthaginians which they wiped out. But even then, only a fraction of the population were readers; most were hardscrabble farmers or slaves. Without the printing press, information was limited, everything had to be slowly hand-copied, and less than five percent of the population had what is currently a middle-class lifestyle. Roman emperors had about the same lifestyle as, and less available capital than, an upper-middle-class American."

"Hmm..." I said, thinking about it. "So Gutenberg comes along and suddenly information is everywhere. And then, with the industrial revolution, the capital changes start to create actual leisure classes which had not existed prior to it. Where before, everyone was living hand-to-mouth and dog-eat-dog, there were suddenly lots of smart people with time on their hands, no real security issues and access to knowledge."

"Most of the people who were messing with magic would have been serfs or slaves or living in mud huts. You'd have one witch doctor with almost no access to materials or knowledge except what was passed down by word of mouth for dozens of villages. Now, there's one on every corner with access to anything they can afford and there's these things called books. Need the bone of a saint? People can get that. Vampire blood? Do you have the money? How powerful a vampire? It's a fricking nightmare. All sane nations have agreed to suppress public knowledge of the supernatural. Soviets, Chinese, Indians, everybody is on board."

Castro paused to get another drink. Apparently this was a pet topic of his.

"One of the benefits to, say, communism is the combination of poverty and tyranny makes it tough for most people to play with magic. In the industrialized western world, we can't do that. For the believers, we contain or control. For the nonbelievers, we can suppress, disinform, and debase the very idea that magic and monsters exist."

"The idea that the supernatural is real is a joke. It's hokey. Who believes in monsters?" I nodded. This was finally making sense. "And thus not eliminate but at least reduce the number of people who try to raise zombies to go kill their vice principal."

"Exactly. You're a bright guy," Castro said. "Not to mention open up portals to the Old Ones. Some people say we don't think we should engage in suppression. I've heard arguments based on the Second Amendment. People can be trusted with houdoun, it's just another weapon. Despite the term 'gun nut,' guns don't actually have the direct effect of *causing* psychosis. Most magic does. Certainly all the necromancy associated with the Old Ones does. The more you study it, the crazier you become. And the proof? New Orleans."

"It doesn't explain all the fucking loup-garou," I said. "That was insane!"

"No, that's a werewolf on a mission," Higgins said. The former Marine took another shot. "There's a couple of asshole loup-garou in this town who *know* they're cursed, and spreading it around to be dicks. They must hole up during the full moon to avoid detection. But during the month they go out and get into fights and bite people. When I find them, and I *will* find them, they are not going to enjoy the experience. MCB has a special place for werewolves like that. A place where doctors...experiment. It's amazing how much you can *cut* on one of those things in the name of science."

"So that is the reason for the First Reason," Castro said. "That's the reason we have to threaten people, defame, *kill* them to keep this from becoming commonplace. And we'll keep on doing that until hell freezes over, the second coming, or God Himself tells us not to. Because as much as we *hate* our job, the alternative is *worse*."

"And we are very good at cover-ups," Higgins said.

"Best way to lie is to tell the truth badly," I quoted.

"Uh-huh... By the way, Chad, because you're so clever and *now* you get it..." Castro stood up to leave, and put some money on the bar. His manner went from friendly to grim rather quickly. "At the airport, did you think it was cute when you shot that werewolf right next to that plane in front of those passengers? Did it *amuse* you?"

"Hey, I—"

"Those weren't hicks in the swamp or superstitious poor folks in the ghetto. Those were upstanding taxpayers with jobs, relatives, and contacts who will run their mouths off... Don't worry. I convinced most of those passengers it was just a wild animal. But there was this one guy, turned out he was a bit of an animal lover, zoology degree or something. He knew better. Him, I had to lean on. The usual threats, you know, ruination, death. I'm a pretty good judge of character. Kind of meek, nerdy, I figured he would shut up. But minutes after I left his house, he was calling a reporter, trying to spill the beans."

"Hey, Castro, man," Trevor started. "It's been a rough few days. Go home, get some sleep."

"Naw, it's cool, Trev. Chad should know. I just came from our animal lover's house. I don't like to farm this kind of thing out to my agents if I don't have to. They've been through enough as it is. They don't need any more bad karma."

"Thanks, boss," said Higgins.

I felt sick.

"He was a nice guy, no enemies, no criminal activity,

looks suspicious if you just shoot 'em. No history of drug abuse so an OD was out of the question. No depression or suicidal tendencies... So he slipped in the shower and broke his neck. An avoidable tragedy, but you know the bathroom is the most dangerous part of the house." Special Agent in Charge Castro patted me on the shoulder, leaned in close, and whispered in my ear, "That one is on you, buddy."

And then he left.

The MCB agent's departure had kind of killed the mood.

"Mr. Gardenier!" a familiar female voice said from behind me. "Meeester Gar-den-ee-yay!"

"Madam Courtney?" I said, looking around, wandering what my real estate agent was doing here.

"Come, come!" she said. "The loas find you home! We close at one! Must hurry!"

"What?" I said. Confused really doesn't cover it. Whiplashed is closer. I'm all about flexible minds but at that point my brain was overcooked spaghetti.

"You should see your home before we close, yes?" she said, her eyes sparkling.

"Close?" I said. "On a house?"

"*No*, on a *canoe*," Madam Courtney said. "Come. Come. We go see! You will like! The loas have taken great interest in you!"

"Go on," Trevor said. "I've got the tab."

The house was perfect.

It was three-story, heavy stone, classic French architecture on the edge of the French Quarter. There was a pull-in for a vehicle with a wrought iron gate.

No more parking Honeybear on the street. The front windows were not only heavily barred, there were hurricane shutters that looked like wood but turned out to be steel. All the ground floor was as solid as a bank building. It was even constructed more heavily than the upper floors. You'd have a hard time ramming a bulldozer through it.

The ornate front door had a view slit to check who was outside.

The interior was stunning and more or less classically Japanese. Very minimalist. I loved the furnishings. All very nice.

"A senior member of the Japanese consulate has been transferred," Madam Courtney said. "He and his wife wish to sell the home as is, including furniture? You like, eh? Trust the loas."

There was a small, walled mediation garden in the back with a classic stone hot tub and a wading pool for sitting in the heat and socializing. The thought of soaking off my injuries in a hot tub was so overwhelming I thought I might faint. Of course, after the last few days I was thinking that most of the time.

There were things I'd need done. I needed a gear room—there was one that was perfect—and a guns and ammo room, again, that was perfectly situated.

The house was perfect in every detail.

Then I realized where it was. Dauphine Street.

Jesse's sister had been named Dauphine.

Yeah, I gotta have this house.

"Trust the loas," I said. Okay, maybe there was a point to magic after all. Call it a sign.

Oh, crap.

The address was 2057 Dauphine Street. When I'd

died, fifty-seven had been the sign I was supposed to watch for.

Okay, God. I'm listening.

"Come, come," Madam Courtney said, taking my uninjured arm. "We must not be late to the closing."

I was exhausted to the point of brain damage when I arrived at the lawyer's office.

"I apologize for my appearance," I said to the well-dressed Japanese couple on the other side of the table. I was, of course, speaking Japanese.

"We are aware of the heavy burdens of the Hunters of the dark," the consular official said, nodding.

"So you know who I am?"

"The way of the warrior is the way of duty," the official said. At least the lawyer didn't have a clue what we were talking about. "We could postpone. You are injured."

"I was injured two nights ago," I said, nodding. "I believe I can with humility wield a pen."

I had never closed on a house. It appeared to be a matter of signing lots and lots of papers. I should have read them. I just signed.

"Your house is very beautiful," I said as I signed. I had no clue what I was signing. I might be selling my soul to the loas. I didn't care. I *wanted* that house. "You must have had some excellent craftsmen. Are any of them local?"

"Many of them were local," the consul's wife said. "This is a town of excellent craftsmen."

"I will need people who are craftsmen," I said. "I am a craftsman but have little time with my duties for such actions. May I humbly request their information?"

"We met many of them through Madam Courtney," his wife said. They were signing papers as well.

"You are very comfortable with Japanese," the consular official said.

"I had many friends who were Japanese in Seattle," I said. I didn't mention one of them was yakuza. "I became a great fan of sushi. Unfortunately, it is virtually unknown in New Orleans."

"Oh, there is a very good sushi restaurant right around the corner," his wife exclaimed.

I had to have this house.

In about thirty minutes of passing paper around, I owned a home.

"I look forward to moving in. I will keep your fine home with honor."

"I understood you intended to move in today," the consular official said in English, looking at Madam Courtney.

"He is!" Madam Courtney said. "He must have a place to relax after his many battles!"

"Very well. I am humbly eager to lay my head to rest."

"You appear very weary," his wife said.

"Must I fight for an eternity at such a pace, such is the path of duty. But in truth, I could use some rest."

"Rest well in our former home," the official said. "It has been shielded by the finest Shinto priests. It is warded against all *akuma*. And the bars are very strong. Rest well."

When we got back to the house, there were a bunch of young men wearing long baseball jerseys and ball caps on sideways just sort of lounging around outside.

"Oh, crap," I said as we pulled up. I was following Madam Courtney in Honeybear.

I still had my .45 on. That was probably enough for some gangbangers. Of course, my right arm wasn't exactly a hundred percent.

I started to say something when Madam Courtney slapped her hands together twice and snapped her fingers.

"Where's Mr. Hoodoo's bags?" she snapped. "Get them in the house!"

"We was just waitin' for the keys, Madam Courtney!" one of the thugs said, tugging at his brow.

"Unload his car! What are you waiting for!"

The gangbangers even took off their shoes when they went in.

There was a bench by the front door and a place for shoes. A bunch of overpriced running shoes were already lined up. I took off my boots, my feet sighing in relief, and put on a provided pair of tatami slippers. Then I went and found Madam Courtney.

"The house is perfect," I said, pulling her to the side. "The loas are wise. The porters are...*what*?"

She just laughed merrily.

"Everyone has problems with the hoodoo, yes? To have a hoodoo man in the neighborhood is a great honor and privilege! These thugs they shoot all day and all night long and not kill the hoodoo! You Mr. Hoodoo! Dauphine Princes more than glad to help! Others come by. They help too. You rest, Mr. Hoodoo. Trust the loas! Trust Madam Courtney! Rest! Rest! Put your feet up! Get in hot tub! Let Madam Courtney handle this!"

I'm a Marine. I'm a Monster Hunter. I'm fucking MHI. I'm tough as nails.

My overnight case from the trunk was up in the main bedroom, open. Nothing was missing. I took a long shower. I didn't even really scrub or shave, just rinsed long and hard. I went downstairs and failed to resist the temptation of the hot tub. I fell asleep in the hot tub with the house full of Orleans Parish jail's finest graduates. I forgot to clean my weapons and no drill instructor showed up in dreams to chew me out.

I woke up in the middle of the night with no clue where I was at. I thought about it for a little bit. It wasn't the bunk room at Team Hoodoo. It wasn't a motel.

Had I bought a house? That *was* a dream, *right*?

No, I BOUGHT A FREAKING HOUSE!

I went downstairs. There was a night-light on in the very Japanese kitchen. All the paperwork was lined up on the bar. Yes, I'd bought a house. For a surprisingly reasonable sum I was fairly sure.

I felt much better than I should have, all things considered. My right arm still ached but that was just a matter of time.

I was still starving. Just in case, I checked the fridge.

You'll start to realize that I was unsurprised it was partially stocked. There was beer, condiments, sandwich makings, and two bento boxes.

I pulled them out and checked the contents. They were apparently from a sushi place I didn't know existed on St. Ann Street. Based on the address on the boxes and the address on the deed I'd signed, it was right around the corner. They were dated and timed from that afternoon.

The sushi was heaven. Not as good as Saury but not much was as good as Saury.

I ate it with Budweiser which is sort of sacrilege in some groups but Bud is actually a great beer with food.

I finished, burped, wondered if I should check in. If they wanted me, they could damned well find me. They knew police. I was somehow sure Agent Castro would know how to find me. Apparently that guy knew everything that went on in this town.

I did check the doors and windows. Everything was locked. I slid the interior deadbolt across the front door. It was apparent that was where the... Did a drug gang just move me in? Where the movers had left. I had more stuff in Seattle I'd need to move down.

I decided I didn't care. Mo No Ken was on the dining room table. My guns, all the stuff from my trunk, even the remaining explosives, were in a side room I'd tentatively set aside as a gear room. Honeybear was sitting in the carport. My spare gear from headquarters was stacked with it. Neatly. Including all my other guns and spare ammo. I had a hard time believing that a drug gang of all things just put that stuff in my house and left. There was a large cash bag for that matter. Hadn't been touched.

And they took their shoes off to enter.

I grabbed Mo No Ken and a 1911, went upstairs and went back to bed.

The phone by the bed rang. I groaned, looked around, wondered where I was. Reached to pick it up, winced, used the other arm.

"Hello?" I said blearily. I rise, automatically, at 0430. It's ingrained. But sun was peeking through the curtains of the window in whatever room I was occupying. Late morning sun I hoped.

"Hand, it's Earl, how you doing?" Earl Harbinger said.

"Fine, sir," I said, sitting up. Where was I? I was pretty sure I was still in New Orleans, but the room looked like it had been transferred from Hokkaido. "I'll be right as rain in about a month and a half. Just joking. I'm sorry I overslept. On my way in."

"Take the day," Earl said. "I'm in town. We've got this."

"I'm at least partially functional, sir," I said.

"What part of take a day was unclear? The whole team is hammered. Be in tomorrow about ten. Not earlier. Rest. We'll talk tomorrow."

"Roger, sir," I said. "Hate to say 'thanks' on skipping work but...thanks."

"You've all earned it," Earl said. "We'll handle the funerals tomorrow."

"Roger," I said. That was right. We'd lost Greg and Jonathan. We were down to five people. Trevor would be off his cane soon but...Jeez, I hadn't seen Ben but I'd heard his head injury was bad. Four people. And I was still injured. Yeah, bringing in reinforcements was the right call. I'm sure if Trevor had known just how bad it was going to be, we would have had them here sooner, but there was no way he could have predicted that.

"Get some rest," Earl said, then hung up.

I didn't. I went downstairs. Three stories. The room was on the second floor, in the back. I wasn't sure what was up top but there was no sound of movement. Big place. I was the only one there. It was eerie. Sort of dreamlike. You just didn't find Japanese interior design in New Orleans in the 1980s. Someone else *had* to live here. Someone Japanese or really into the culture. I'd love to live in a house like this one. Which meant, yeah, this had to be a dream. Okay. Maybe I'm supposed to tell Madam Courtney or something. But why would it start with a call from Earl? That was just weird. Nothing made sense.

There was a bunch of paperwork on a bar again. I started to look it over, hoping I wasn't digging into someone's private affairs.

"I did what?"

CHAPTER 13
Sledgehammer

I'd grabbed a beer and headed out to the hot tub, but the front door bell rang. Simple, it replicated the sound of the bell in a Japanese shrine.

Sighing, I went to the door and peeked through the vision slot. There was a middle-aged, light-skinned, black gentleman wearing formal morning wear down to white gloves standing there. Very distinguished. Straight back, short graying hair. He looked like an Army colonel I had met at Bethesda.

"May I help you?" I asked through the vision slot.

"Mr. Oliver Gardenier?" the gentleman said. "My name is Remi Prosper Girard, Mr. Gardenier. Madam Courtney has recommended me as your gentleman."

I took all the bolts off—I'd left the heavy duty bar off anyway—and opened the door.

"My what?" I asked.

I was wearing a bathrobe and holding a .45 in my hand but he didn't even blink.

"Your gentleman, sir," Mr. Girard said, proffering a card.

I took the card and read it carefully. All it said was his name and "Gentleman's Gentleman."

"I have references, sir," Mr. Girard said.

"I've had a really tough few days," I said, rubbing my chin and realizing that for the first time in years I was unshaven. "I woke up this morning and just realized I bought a house. Could I ask for a clue? Maybe buy a vowel?"

"A *butler*, sir," Remi said, making a face. "I detest the word, as it is incorrect. But it is the most common referent. A gentleman's gentleman."

"Okay, hate to do this, but hang on a sec," I said. I shut the door, locked it, and walked into where I vaguely remembered putting my stuff. Or people putting my stuff. I'd let unauthorized personnel into my personal space. I really needed rest. And my head examined.

I found the jug first, poured some of the water in a cup and went back to the door.

"I need you to take a sip of this before entering the house," I said, holding out the cup.

He took the cup and drank it.

"Would that be a common courtesy of the home, sir?" he asked.

"Holy water. Not a one hundred percent test but pretty good. Come on in."

"I shall ensure there is a font installed," Remi said, entering. "Your home is very beautiful, sir."

"I wish I could take credit for it but I'm still trying to realize I live here."

I was casting around for where you interview a butler. And trying to say "I don't need a butler."

"Perhaps in the downstairs parlor, sir," he suggested, waving one glove-covered hand.

We sat in the parlor. I was vaguely aware I should offer drinks. Or maybe not. I dunno. I'd have to dredge up local customs. I started to open my mouth.

"Sir is about to state that sir does not need a gentleman," Remi said. "I am not lacking for employ, sir. However, if I may state the case."

"Shoot."

"Sir has had, as sir noted, a 'tough few days.' Sir was clearly preparing for the bath. Would it not be better if someone else was to answer the door, sir, and inquire if sir was, in fact, in?"

"Point," I said, starting to open my mouth again.

"Has sir eaten?" Remi asked.

"I think there was some bento at some point." My stomach rumbled. I'm a serious eater and Hunting takes it out of you.

Remi withdrew a leather-covered notebook and made a note. "Sir is a proponent of sushi?" he asked.

"I . . . yes?"

"Very good, sir. Any other particular favorites?"

"All the food in New Orleans is good. Look . . ."

"Is sir familiar with the ancient Spartans, sir?" Remi asked.

"Yes." I owned a house. I was starting to vaguely remember talking Japanese to someone in a lawyer's office. Most of my memory of the last few days was sort of a continuous montage of flying through the nighttime streets of New Orleans, teeth, fangs, and horrible black darkness with claws.

Now it was being explained to me in meticulous English why I needed someone to put on my socks.

"Did the ancient Spartans take care of all their own equipment, living arrangements, and so on, sir?"

"No, but..."

"You are a Monster Hunter, sir," Remi said. "You may have other abilities, other skills, but your time is properly applied to controlling the houdoun and other forces which have always made life in New Orleans a trial. Has your gear been washed and repaired, sir? I am sure sir has cleaned his weapons but, given his recent experiences, even that may have been overlooked. Is sir intending to do his own laundry and cooking when he could be fighting the forces of darkness, sir?"

So that's how I got a butl—a gentleman.

I hated the idea at first. Hunters are a paranoid lot by training and experience. If you weren't paranoid, you didn't survive. Having someone I really didn't know in my personal space was worrisome.

But Remi's points were valid. Maybe not most places, but in New Orleans in the '80s, definitely. We were busting our ass, day in and day out. We did not have time for the little shit. I'd been dropping my laundry off at a wash-dry-fold place. My gear was in tatters. And, no, I hadn't cleaned my weapons. Turned out I hadn't even *cleared* some of them. For a Marine that's the ultimate sin. I had been too wiped out to even care.

Remi moved in like he'd always lived there. I went to the hot tub. While I was in there, nude, he came out with delivery from the bento place, Mamoto's. It was carefully arrayed on a china plate.

Pro-tip: If you're an elite Hunter, you make a lot of money killing monsters. Get support staff. You're a specialist at monster killing. Let other people handle the little shit.

And get a freaking butler. They follow you around

and take care of stuff like making sure your equipment stays in shape and you eat and drink and generally are supported. Don't think of them as an extravagance. Think of them like the squires and pages of the Paladins. They're there to take care of the little shit so, like Charlemagne's Paladins, you can go do the job and not worry about it. Call them a "personal assistant" if it makes you feel better.

Of course, good help like that is hard to find these days. And he wasn't cheap. But any really good Hunter ends up making a packet off of monster killing and if you're really busy, you don't have many ways to spend it. Get one who knows how to take care of guns, obviously.

There are worse ways to spend your earnings than on someone to answer the door. Just make sure they know the protocols.

Remi knew most of them. He had been Army, draftee, one tour, back in the days when it was still largely segregated. He had been an officer's "boy," in the parlance of the time. A troop designated to take care of a senior officer's stuff, a full colonel in Remi's case. His family had been "help" going back to the slavery days.

Five years ago his wife and youngest child had been killed by a loup-garou. He was quite pleased to have the opportunity to be gentleman to a Monster Hunter.

He knew how to strip, clean and reassemble the 1911 and M14. The guy could practically spit-shine a 1911. He picked up the Uzi quick. We talked while cleaning weapons. He had a spare pair of white gloves and made notes from time to time. He mentioned he knew a sewing lady who could fix my vest right up.

I mentioned I had a spare in my gear but it would have to be reconfigured. He mentioned that was his job. I admitted I needed a replacement for my assault ruck. He made a note. I had stuff in Seattle that still needed to be moved down. Note.

I finally just laid it out while he made notes. Gear room with a way to clean all the gunk off the gear. Maybe a good way to hang it. I probably needed spares based on the last full moon. Armory. Light one near the front, main one in a protected area, probably up. Primary magazine, fully prepared since it would include explosives, and secondaries. Probably ground floor. Weapons in every room. Weight room.

I'd like to have put in a shop. Not at the house, there wasn't really a place. But I knew my days puttering in a machine shop were pretty much over. Not in New Orleans. In New Orleans I had two jobs. Kill monsters. Try to survive.

I had gotten my gear more or less fixed up and Honeybear more or less reloaded. I had a list of stuff I had to pick up at the office.

Pro-tip: Keep an inventory list of your gear. Note things that are expended or damaged and get them replaced as quickly as feasible.

Remi had taken the inventory list to make a copy. I noted the things he could get, like more holy water, a backpack, and what I had to obtain, like more C4, detonators, det cord and silver ammo. Oh, yeah, and a couple of LAWs.

Who *doesn't* carry light antitank weapons in their trunk? Honestly.

Pro-tip: If you're in one of those areas where MCB

is all about discreet, get a golf bag. Great for carrying long guns and rocket launchers covertly.

I mean, seriously, who actually plays *golf*? And if you want to pick one up, pick the pawn shop closest to a high-end neighborhood. 'Cause when some long-suffering golf widow finally sues for divorce, the first thing she does is pawn his golf clubs.

If you do actually golf (seriously?) it's also a great place to pick up high-end clubs cheap.

End pro-tip.

Repacking my trunk was a pain. It was less of a pain with help. Remi had set a price which I considered reasonable. I'd have to check with my accountant to make sure I could afford it along with the cost of the new home. My accountant was still in Seattle. I asked Remi to ask Madam Courtney about an accountant as well as people to work on the house.

Repacked, fed, prepared, I won't say recovered because I wasn't, I headed to the office.

The meeting was in the team room. Trevor was still in a soft cast. Alvin was in a sling, left arm, from something the flesh golem had thrown at him that he'd managed to mostly dodge. I think it was a motorcycle. Shelbye had a bandage on her head. I was wearing the sling. I didn't absolutely need it but it sure felt better than not. Bottom line, everybody was injured.

But Happy Face had arrived. *I* was making a happy face.

Ray IV and Earl were here with Hoodoo Squad, catching up on our busy week.

"I'll be damned," Earl said, pacing up and down and

flipping through receipts. As he'd finish one, he'd pass it to Ray. He wasn't smoking for once. Trevor had quit and the building was nonsmoking which suited me fine. Shelbye, Ben and Greg had to go outside. Well, used to have to in Greg's case. Ben would be back. Hopefully.

"No kidding," Ray said, flipping through the receipts. "And we were in Montana chasing one damned skin-walker. Okay, I don't even know what an Agaran *is*."

"Yeah, I haven't seen one of those in a while and only heard that name once," Earl said. "I knew it as *títeres de sombra*. Shadow puppet. Agaran."

"I'd have been killed just like Greg if Alvin hadn't known," I said. Okay, probably not. I'd have dropped back and regrouped, gotten holy water, waited for backup. Nah. I'd be dead as a stump. Or, rather, a zombie.

"It's code 41638-B," Earl said, making a note on the receipt. "Add Agaran, minor, extradimensional. PUFF adjuster will recognize it. These fricking werewolves piss me off. Not the new ones. They're just . . . new. The ones that have been around for a while and are spreading the curse. I'm going to do something about those punks. How's your relationship with MCB?"

"I was getting to that," Trevor said delicately. "We've got a *great* relationship and, Earl, I'd *really* like to keep it that way."

"I won't piss in their Cheerios. Especially since we need their help. We need to track these sons of bitches down. We need to know if they frequent certain bars to get in these fights. That's police work. We don't have the time or people to do that legwork. They'll need to do it. But find a pattern and we'll find the werewolves. And then we'll deal with that situation."

"Question?" I said. "Do we get PUFF for a live capture?"

"Yes," Ray said. "Why?"

"One of the agents said something about turning them over to their scientific division," I said. "Apparently they dissect them to see how they tick. Without anesthesia."

"Yes, they do," Earl said, frowning. "And tempting as it is, no, we'll just put them down. Simpler. But we've got to find them first. You called in on these disappearances."

"Basement boogie," Shelbye supplied.

"The descriptions don't match anything I'm aware of. Ray did some digging in the archives. Ray?"

"There have been similar instances in other times and countries, but nothing that seems exactly the same. Our archives don't have anything that really matches."

"I'll call Oxford," I said. "There may be something there."

"Do that," Earl said. "We're here until y'all are fully recovered and we get more permanent Hunters on your team. We've put out the word before and we're putting it out again. There's a lot of reasons that people don't want to move. You get accustomed to your team and you don't want to leave your team."

"True that," I said. "Unless you gotta."

"True that," Ray said, grinning. Earl showed no reaction, so apparently Ray hadn't told him why I'd been eager for the transfer.

"People have homes, families," Earl said. "I ain't gonna force the issue. Unfortunately the most flexible about moving tend to be the least experienced. Not a good thing in New Orleans, obviously. I'm twisting some arms to get good folks down here. Huge PUFF payments should help. We're staying here for a spell, absent some major catastrophe elsewhere. At least through the next full moon. I've got business I have to do during that time, but the rest of my team's here for the duration."

"Happy to have them," Trevor said.

"Wish we could put a loup-garou on a leash," I said. I don't know why I said it.

"What do you mean?" Earl asked, his face hard.

"They're seriously bad news," I said. "I'd love to have been able to unleash a loup-garou on some of those zombie herds."

"We had that a couple of full moons ago," Alvin said, grinning. "Loup-garou got into a cemetery full of zombies. Jonathan and I pulled up, realized what was happening and just let the loup-garou handle it. Then when it was finished, we finished off the loup-garou."

"You can't *manage* a werewolf," Earl said. "On the full moon they're out of control. No way to handle them. You'd have to put it down like you did. Right call."

"What about darts?" I asked. "Have one in a cage, maybe with a remote? Set the cage down, back off…"

"Drop it," Ray said.

"But…" I wasn't picking up on hints.

"I said, *drop it*, Chad," Ray said. "We're not going to try to use a werewolf on a full moon. It's been tried. The results were not really good if you know what I mean. Drop. It. Chad."

"Dropped."

"Back to the point," Earl said. He was looking… weird. His head was down and he had a hard expression. Not anger. As if he was trying not to express something else. "The point is that we're not, really, that big of a company, and we're spread over the whole country. And while New Orleans clearly needs reinforcements, probably two teams, minimum, we don't have the people to do that. Regardless, no more solo bullshit. I don't care how tough you boys think you are, you can only look in one direction at a time. Minimum of two, or you don't go in."

"We've got contracts to keep, Earl," Trevor said. "And this city is—"

"Wise, alone, dead. Baldwin, alone, dead. MHI wins because we fight as a unit. You getting me, Trevor? Because if you ain't, I'll find a team lead who does."

"We were adapting to circumstances," I said, not liking Earl's attitude. Trevor was a good boss. "It's worked for me."

"That's a mighty compelling argument." He nodded toward my sling.

"You do what you have to do. There's lots of stories about you taking on monsters by yourself."

"But you ain't me, Hand." Earl scowled and leaned forward in his chair. "Hotdog bullshit works like a charm until the day your luck runs out." He turned to Trevor. "Until this damned freak-show city returns to normal, everybody rides with a partner. One of your team who knows their way around, with one of mine."

"Got it, Earl," Trevor said.

"Good. Now let's get back to figuring out how to staff this place, because apparently New Orleans opened the seventh seal or something."

It was quiet for a minute. I raised my hand.

"Go, Hand." Earl sighed. It was clear he needed a cigarette.

"Two things. One, I know someone who would make a great recruit. The bouncer who helped me out with a group of vamps. Two, we *can* advertise."

"MCB would shit a brick," Ray said.

"*Truth Teller,*" I said. "We'll even be paying MCB for a change."

"The what?" Earl asked.

"That is a truly bizarre suggestion," Trevor said, laughing. "I like it."

"Someone want to fill me in?" Ray asked.

"Better if you see it," Trevor said and looked around. "Shelbye, I think there's one from last week in my office?"

Some more of Earl's team had joined us—specifically Milo Anderson—and they had split up the pages of the *New Orleans Truth Teller* and were passing them around.

"Who's got page nine?" Milo asked, grinning from ear to ear. "Chad, that's you, right? Japanese sword."

"Made the front page," I said. "Just aced out Ben." I frowned at that. Ben always liked making the front page. I was sure he'd make it again. He'd be back.

"Monster Control Board allows this?" Ray asked, more perusing than reading. He handed his page to Milo and picked up another.

"MCB publishes it," Trevor said. "Their local motto is 'the best way to tell a lie is tell the truth, badly.'"

"Reading this is making my head hurt," Earl said.

"You jumped through the window?" Milo asked, crowing.

"And came back out holding a skull," I said. "Thing is, we *can* recruit in there. There are plenty of people in New Orleans who have shot zombies, or bashed their heads in with axes. A few who have managed to at least tag loup-garou. We'll get quite a few crazies. We'll also get people who aren't. That's what interviews are for."

"They'll still be green when they come from training," Ray said, frowning. "New Orleans is not a place for green troops."

"Send them somewhere else for a while. Then they'll come back."

"Natives will," Trevor said. "Natives always come back to New Orleans. They can't stay away. It will take some time for the pipeline to fill, but I'd say we'll be able to fill it. And they'll already be familiar with the town."

"Half my time is spent looking at maps and asking for directions," I said. "Damned canals in this town screw you up."

"That...makes a certain amount of sense," Ray said.

"I'm not just a pretty face," I said.

"You're not even a pretty face," Milo quipped.

"Yes, I am, and you know it," I said, grinning.

"Nope." Milo shook his head.

"I'd like to add something," Trevor said. "And someone, someones, who aren't really going to be active Hunters but can handle positional defense and, most importantly, paperwork. I'm swamped. Just filling out all the PUFF paperwork is a nightmare. I need an office manager."

"Got it. We'll work on that, too," Ray said, making a note.

"We need to meet with MCB anyway," Earl said. "Ray..."

"I'll take him," I said. "We'll talk to Bob Higgins. He might be a Hollywood Marine but once a Marine, always a Marine. Are we a go on advertising?"

"Yes," Earl said. "Reluctantly."

"We don't want recruits coming here," Trevor said. "We'll need someplace to do the interviews."

"We'll set up a temporary office," Ray said. "Need to get that in place first."

"I know just the real estate lady," I said, smiling.

"How's the house?" Trevor asked.

"Fan-fucking-tastic. And I now have a gentleman as well."

"Told you she was a wizard," Trevor said, grinning.

"A what?" Milo asked.

"You got a *butler*?" Ray said. "Who's got the big head?"

"I'm trying to picture Chad with a house. Like a grown up."

"I may not live long in this job," I said, "but I am now living in *style*. Trust the loas," I added in a Jamaican accent.

"Loas? Are you nuts?" Milo asked. He knew a loa was a houdoun spirit.

"All blessings extend from God, Milo," I said gently. "A blessing is a blessing. No positive power can extend from evil."

"Evil can be really convincing though, up until it eats your face," Milo said.

"I'll explain 'trust the loas' later. But, yeah, got a house. Great house. Fantastic house. I'd love to show it off while I'm still alive. Feel free to have the memorial service there."

"*Sic transit gloria mundi* is all well and good," Earl said. "But that's not a great attitude, Hand."

"Did you *see* what the last few days were like?" I said. "I'm going to gather every possible rosebud. Eat, drink and be merry 'cause it's only twenty-four days till the next full moon."

CHAPTER 14
Lawyers, Guns and Money

I took Ray Shackleford and Milo Anderson to meet with MCB. Milo didn't drink but he liked bourbon chicken. Earl just really hated Feds.

We were happily eating Maurice's chicken when Higgins sat down wearily at the bar.

"I hate the freaking lawyers," he said as the waitress poured him a shot. It turned out her name was Melisent, and I still hadn't got her number yet.

"Everybody hates lawyers, Bob."

"'This is an *a priori* restraint in violation of the First Amendment!' Yeah, it is. I nearly popped him just *pour encourage l'autre* but the paperwork is a nightmare. Instead, I pointed out that we could get his bar license revoked and if he made waves, we'd point out that he was clearly a nutcase which would destroy his career. Oh, and we already had pictures of him with an underage girl. Goodbye marriage and it would kick in the rider on his pre-nup and he'd end up penniless, disbarred and in prison for pedophilia. We knew the judges to do it. The fix is in, get over it. He shut the hell up."

"I wish it could be a different way," I said, remembering what Castro had told me the other night.

"So do I," Higgins said, taking another shot. "Three of the people from that vamp container you guys found, we just did the commitment paperwork. They're about to spend a very long period of time in confinement being repeatedly told that vampires aren't real...after having spent a very long period of time in confinement being snacked on by same. It's wrong. It's awful. It's horrible. It fucking sucks ass. It's necessary."

"Are you sure?" Milo said angrily. "Is it *really* necessary?"

"I've had the full brief," I said. "New Orleans is what happens when everyone starts accessing hoodoo. You start fucking around with this shit and you go bat-shit. There's more to it than that. But, yeah, sorry buddy, but I got to agree. Could it be handled better? I'm not sure. We really need a central place to send people like that where the doctors, experienced with the supernatural, say 'Yes, vampires do exist. And giant spiders and all the rest. But you can't talk about it outside of here.' Until then? We hold the line."

"Hold the line," Higgins said, picking up his glass and downing it. "You called this meeting."

"Few things," I said. "First, introductions. Bob Higgins, MCB, former Hollywood Marine, Raymond Shackleford the Fourth and Milo Anderson, MHI, couple of my best friends. Ray, Milo, Bob."

"Hey," Higgins said. "Heir apparent at MHI, right?"

"Yes," Ray said.

"Your people do good work," Higgins said, shaking Ray's hand.

That surprised him. Our relationship was usually a lot more adversarial.

"Milo is MHI's resident mad scientist," I said, grinning.

"Hey," Milo said, waving. He was on the other side of Ray.

Bob glanced at Milo's wispy red beard. It was trying so hard, and someday might be decent. "Is he old enough to drive yet?"

"I got into monster hunting at a young age."

"Mad science, huh? Hope that doesn't include hoodoo," Higgins said.

"He's the company's token Mormon," I said. "So, no. Any luck on the loup-garou? Specifically the ones that are biting off moon."

"No. I will find them and make sure they are repeatedly dissected," Higgins said. "I know people."

"We need to find out if there is any pattern," Ray said.

"Not that we've seen or we'd have tracked them down by now," Higgins said, shrugging.

"Any bars that the victims frequented?" I asked.

"There are a few," Higgins said. "But . . . how do you find a loup-garou in human guise in a crowded bar? We've tried. Also, people rarely go to the hospital for minor bites. We track those. Found a few. Never been able to capture the guys. From the descriptions we've had, there's two, both plain and normal. Then they get into a fight, often not one they've started, and someone gets bit. It's pissing me off."

"Just get us the list of bars," Ray said. "We're pretty good at spotting werewolves. We'll track them down eventually."

"I'll get you the list," Higgins said.

"Next item of business, we want to advertise for recruits," I said.

"What?" he asked, choking on his chicken. He took a sip of bourbon. "Okay, you *can't* be serious, Hand. No way DC is going to go for that."

"In the *Truth*."

"Oh," he said, then laughed. "Oh, God, I'm going to have to tell Bill this personally. MHI wants to advertise in the *Truth*." He gave a full belly laugh. "'Want to make money killing hoodoo?'" he said, in a worse Jamaican accent than mine. "'Join the Hoodoo Squad!'"

"Recruitment is our number one Achilles' heel," Ray said. "Because, well . . ."

"Us," Higgins said, nodding. "Fair cop."

"And we only recruit people who have had experience of . . . hoodoo," Ray said. "Not being practitioners, you understand."

"Got it. No, I get the point. Makes sense. I just hope you give them some training."

"We train the shit out of people," I said. "Marine Basic? No. But good training. And they'll have to be willing to start somewhere else, first."

"Unless we absolutely have to, no inexperienced Hunter is coming to New Orleans for the foreseeable future," Ray said. "But once they go to another team, they tend to want to stick there. Team bonding, and they often end up in their own region. Hunters with remaining family tend to want to be around family. We'll recruit here, train, send them somewhere less dangerous, not that this job doesn't have casualties *other* places, then they come back here. Probably be a year before we get them coming back. Assuming we have any recruits."

"In the meantime?" Higgins said.

"We hold the line," I said, downing a shot. "Or you guys figure out what is driving this town nuts lately and fix it."

"Our main team is in town now," Ray said. "We're MHI's heavy hitters and if someone needs us more, we have to go. But we're here for now."

"Good," Higgins said. "When your team was down to four injured people, I happen to know that Bill was ready to pull the grab bar and call our Special Response Team. Only no SAC wants to call up SRT."

"It's a career ender?" Ray asked.

"More like a life ender. SRT does not fuck around when it comes to coverups. They will burn *neighborhoods*. Bill—that's Special Agent in Charge William Castro to you guys—he loves New Orleans. He gets this city. An outsider isn't going to be lenient when it comes to our superstitious locals. If SRT realized how much the people in this town believe in hoodoo, they'd be tempted to break a levee and flood the place."

"Even then, I would have *kissed* Franks sometime on Thursday," I said. "I would have been *so* glad to see his happy and smiling face."

"You've met *Agent Franks?*" Higgins asked, sounding a little awed.

"Yeah." Apparently he had a reputation in MCB circles. "I like him."

"You've got to be joking," Milo said.

"About the happy and smiling face . . . maybe. I don't think Franks can smile. But I bet he wouldn't have blinked at the fact I was carrying a LAW in my trunk."

"You were carrying a LAW in your *trunk*?" Higgins said.

"Two," I said. "How the hell you think we took that flesh golem? Why do people keep being surprised about this? I bet Franks carries LAWs in *his* trunk."

"I do," Milo said.

"Next thing you'll be bitching about the claymores and C4."

"Wait," Higgins said. "*Claymores and C4? I thought you were joking about that!*"

"See? *See*?"

"Who *doesn't* carry a LAW in their trunk?" Milo asked.

Remi opened the door before I could knock.

"Welcome home, sir," Remi said. He had donned a pair of tatami slippers. I hadn't had the heart to ask him to take his shoes off before. He was wearing white silk stockings. I could tell my days of being a slob were numbered. Eh, I'm sort of a clothes horse to be honest.

"Do you mind?" I asked, sitting down on the bench and taking off my boots. "Fine to go with socks."

"The way my feet feel?" Ray said, sitting down.

"You're weird, man," Milo said, but he took off his Birkenstocks for, come to think of it, different sandals.

"Nice place," Ray said, looking around. He touched the holy water font and just touched his forehead.

Milo frowned at it. Remi had gotten, somewhere, in about three hours, a traditional font of the Virgin Mary holding out a basin. Apparently Milo didn't like gilded idols or something, but he stuck a finger in the holy water and touched his head to be polite.

"Parlor and study," I said, pointing to the two rooms. "I can't wait to get all my books from Seattle. I'll finally have almost enough book shelves."

I showed them around the house, pointing out where I was going to put in a gear room and armories. Finally we ended up back in the upstairs living room overlooking Dauphine.

Remi had laid out a selection of pastries along with both coffee and wine as choice.

"Mr. Anderson is Mormon, Mr. Girard," I said, clearing my throat.

"I apologize, sir," Remi said, unflustered. "I believe we have some apple juice. I shall obtain some root beer, if sir prefers."

"Apple juice is fine, Mr. Girard," Milo said. "Or water. Whatever. I'm easy. Heck, I'll get it." He started to get up.

"Please allow me, sir," Remi said, nodding as he left.

"Don't want to be a bother," Milo said, making a face.

"Remi lost his wife and youngest son to werewolves, Milo," I said. "He's thrilled as hell to be able to help. There's two strains in this town: those who support houdoun and those who oppose it. Remi's on the oppose side. And he more or less crowbarred his way into this job. Wouldn't take no for an answer."

"Guess you've got it all," Milo said, frowning. The servant thing was making him uncomfortable.

"Milo, are we friends?" I asked.

"Sure, Chad," Milo said. "Always."

"Then don't get a burr under your bonnet. I'm a Marine. I'm all about taking care of myself. But you weren't here for the full moon. When the shit hits the fan in this town, we just don't have time. I got maybe thirty minutes' sleep from the morning before the full moon to about 2 P.M. the day after. I'm going to get a spare set of everything, because by the time I was done, every bit of my gear was trashed from claws and teeth and just getting in the shit. And I did not have one moment to do anything about it. This way, if I'm passing by, I can stop and pick up new gear and just keep going. And if it can be repaired, washed, prepared in time, Remi handles it. 'Cause, no time."

"We've got to get away from that," Ray said, frowning. "I get the point. But the fact that you were mostly fighting solo is insane. Solo hunting is one of the main reasons for the casualty rate. And that tempo is going to burn people out. Burned out people make mistakes."

"Preaching to the choir, Ray," I said, taking a sip of coffee. Unsurprisingly, it was great. "All you need to do is get us about three times the personnel."

"Preaching to the choir," Ray said.

"Milo, we good?" I asked.

"We're always good, Chad," Milo said. "Just sort of threw me is all. I grew up on a farm. Milk in a box is fancy by my standards."

Remi entered on cat feet and set down a pitcher of apple juice and a glass.

"Shall I pour, sir?" Remi said.

"Sure," Milo said. "Sorry to hear about your family, sir. My sincere condolences for your loss."

"I had another child, sir," Remi said calmly. "And Cherie and Jason are with God, sir. But I am pleased to be able to contribute to the hunt for the unnatural and unclean. This is for me a calling, sir."

"Then I'll just get over letting you pour, Mr. Girard," Milo said, smiling.

"Please to call me Remi, sir."

"Only if you call me Milo."

"I shall endeavor. Will sir's guests be staying, sir?"

"Milo? Ray?"

"I really need to stay at the team headquarters," Ray said reluctantly.

"Earl's in charge of the team. Let him stay in the ghetto. Or not. Up to you. Duty is heavier than mountains. Milo, I'll be hurt if you don't."

"Well," Milo said, looking around at the minimalist splendor, "when you put it that way."

"Are the gentlemen's bags available, sir?"

"We'll get them later," Ray said. "And we can tote our own gear. And, hell, I'll stay. Better than a motel or the team barracks."

"It's central," I said. "And we can leave your cars on the street. We'll need a permit. I'll get that fixed. Don't worry about theft. The local gang watches our stuff."

"The local gang?" Milo said, boggling.

"Welcome to New Orleans, gentlemen," Remi said. "I shall endeavor to ensure your stay is as comfortable as possible."

Madam Courtney had been willing to make a house call. After listening to Ray's requirements, she snapped her fingers twice and waved her hand.

"*Too* simple," she said. "A simple office. Downtown. St. Charles Avenue is the only place to have such an office! That the recruits understand the *majesty* of their duties! This will keep away the riffraff!"

"Some of our best people might be considered riffraff, Madam Courtney," Ray pointed out.

"I resemble that remark," Milo said.

"Do you think? So, you have some people with record, eh? Do you think that did they want to fight the hoodoo, they would be turned away by going to a nice office, Mr. Shackleford? But the crazies? The scam artists? The ones who are weak of determination. They see the majesty of the building. They wonder, should they enter? Is this the right choice? Would you have those who have such questions, Mr. Shackleford? Would not most fail your intense training?"

"She has a point, Ray," I said.

"Trust Madam Courtney," she cried, laughing. "Trust the loas. They are not the Dark loas," she said, looking at Milo. "Mr. Gardenier would call them *saints*, yes? Trust the saints, Mr. Shackleford!"

"Okay," Ray said. "We'll trust your loas."

"Do you have a Standard and Poor's grade . . . ?"

When we got back to the team shack, the rest of Earl's team had arrived. And the only one I knew was a surprise.

"Franklin?" I said. "Long time."

Franklin Moore was one of the members of the MHI team dispatched to Elkins, West Virginia, to clean up a zombie outbreak only to find it had already been cleared by a badly injured, recently discharged Marine named Oliver Chadwick Gardenier, call me Chad.

"Look at you," Franklin said, getting up from the couch. He hadn't changed much. Couple more scars. Five eight, one-eighty, black as the ace of spades. "All growed up and a Monster Hunter!"

We shook hands left-handed and back-patted.

"I didn't know you two knew each other," Ray said.

"We met in Elkins," I said. "When I was still all busted up."

"And you're walking without a cane and everything," Moore said.

"Thanks to intense physical therapy and a kappa," I said.

"Kappa?" Moore asked.

"Storytime later," Earl said. "Introductions, then update."

I didn't know the others. "Where's Marty Hood and Dwayne Myers?"

"Marty died in a training accident," Ray said quickly.

"Shit. That happens. Too bad. He was a nice guy."

"It was a little while ago. Dwayne quit. Don't know what he's up to now..." Earl didn't look like he wanted to talk about them. "Hand, you know Moore. Meet Adam Greer, Thomas Steele, Katie Rogers, and Jamie Castillo."

"No relation to the lieutenant on the TV show," Castillo said. Castillo was about my height, bit short, Hispanic with dark brown hair and equally dark eyes. Really nasty facial scar. Probably a story there.

"You've met the rest of the local team," Earl said. "This is Chad. Goes by Iron Hand."

"Iron Hand?" Greer asked. Short. Real short. Serious muscles of a body builder/power lifter. Blonde hair in a crew cut. Bit of dip in his cheek.

"Insult from a kendo instructor," I said.

"That custom Uzi Milo built for you, Thomas?" Ray said. "There's a reason he called it the Iron Hand special."

"That's your design?" Steele said. He was tall and angular like a stick insect. I had to wonder if he didn't break in a strong wind. "Nice."

"So, introductions complete," Earl said. "Update?"

"We made friendly contact with MCB," Ray said.

"That'll be the day," Greer grumped.

"That's something to cover, Earl," Trevor said.

"On the agenda," Earl said. "Continue."

"We got an all clear from the local supervisor for open recruiting," Ray said.

"What?" To this point Katie Rogers hadn't said a word. Tall, brunette, she had a closed look. Or possibly shy. She didn't have the sort of confident attitude normal for a member of the main team. Cute, though. Not beautiful like Susan but cute.

"Oh yeah," Earl said. "New Orleans is different. Trevor?"

Trevor spent most of the next hour giving them the lowdown on the oddities of New Orleans, like having a significant chunk of our populace not only believing in the supernatural but knowing about Monster Hunters, a friendly and cooperative local MCB office, and our mysterious recent record-breaking activity level.

"Currently the entire Team Hoodoo is pretty much out of commission," Earl said at the end.

"Excuse me," I said. "I was fighting this way for most of two days! I can still shoot one-handed and swing leftie."

"So they're going to *take some time*," Earl said definitely. Time for a cigarette? "But based on the experience this morning, we will all need guides and help interacting with the locals."

"How was I supposed to know we were supposed to take extra PUFF from the coroner?" Moore said. "That's a violation of federal law!"

"Smoothed over," Trevor said.

"What?" Ray asked. "Padding PUFF?"

"The coroner tends to pad the PUFF," I said. "When we get a receipt from them and when they can. Six zombies instead of five, that sort of thing."

"Because we have to pay them for prompt response," Trevor said. "Under the table. And local politicians, including the Sheriff and SIU, to keep our contract. And the Parking department to keep them from towing our cars. It's a long list."

"Oh, great," Ray said, shaking his head.

"Welcome to the Big Easy," Trevor said.

"All taxes are bribes," Earl said. "Just roll with it."

"Got it," Moore said.

"So we're going to have one of the locals ride along," Earl said.

"Leave me out," I said. "I'm still getting the hang of this place."

"Thanks for volunteering. You're up next," Earl said. "Team will be Ray, Milo, Katie, Adam and you. You're along to advise, interact and show them how to get there."

"It took us nearly an hour to get from here to..." Thomas said, then paused.

"Metairie," Katie said.

"We took side streets," Castillo said. "It looked more direct."

"And got stuck behind a parade," Katie said.

"Fucking parades," I said, shaking my head.

"Hey, we got to have some culture," Trevor said, grinning.

"And then we ran into this canal..." Thomas said.

"Oh, yeah," I said. "The fucking canals throw me. I think they always will."

The phone rang. We all looked at it. Katie was the closest.

"They say there's a... pissed-off giant crocodile in the 17th Street Canal?" Katie said, nodding as she listened to the caller.

"Oh, not *another* one," Trevor said.

"And here we go," I said, standing up. "Since I'm not directly involved, I don't have to put on all my crap. I might even be able to stay in air conditioning!"

"Hot damn!" Shelbye said. "Let me roll on this one! Those things are *tasty*!"

CHAPTER 15
Shoot to Thrill

"That's a sight you don't see every day," Milo said.

"Around here?" I said. "Not *every* day, but..."

The sobek—so called after the Egyptian deity—was not particularly happy. It was taking serious issue with the Maryland Drive pumping station on the 17th Street Canal. It apparently had someplace to be and the pumping station was in its way.

The sobek was about fifty feet in total length but didn't seem very well designed. Crocodilian, but it kept trying to stand upright, trying to climb up the levee to the pumping station, and failing.

"We need that thing dealt with." The speaker was the representative from the Army Corps of Engineers. He pointed to where it was tearing at the structure of the levee. "That does much more damage, we're going to have a major incident."

"I think we already do," Ray said, pointing to the crowd of people up on the railroad bridge. They were pretty far away, but it looked like plenty of people were taking pictures.

"MCB's problem," I said. And the witnesses had been here before us, so we weren't going to get blamed for it. At least the monster was mostly concealed by the canal, so the people on the bridge were the only ones watching. "Trevor told me about this. These things get summoned out of Lake Pontchartrain every few months. You can see the damage from the last one. Some houdoun priest or priestess probably has a case of the ass with someone downstream. Thing is, if it gets to the boat pullout, it can walk ashore. That will be bad."

"All it takes is some heavy firepower," Adam Greer said. "We've got a McMillan Tac-50 in the truck."

"Fifty cal bounces off the head bone," I said. Shelbye had got me up to speed on shooting giant crocodile monsters. "Unless you get a shot in the sweet spot on the back of the head. And you've got to get it right in the brain, which is surprisingly small. We could get up on the railroad bridge, take the shot from there. Angle's about right."

"That works," Ray said, looking up at the crowd. "Katie?"

"I'm up," she said.

"I'll tote," Greer said.

"Why, such a gentleman," Katie said, batting her eyes. Damn. So much for making a run at her.

"I'll bring a spotting scope," I said.

I hadn't dealt with a sobek yet, but I'd had plenty of description from Shelbye. She really did consider them delicious. Of course, she thought you could eat a naga if you got it cooled off fast enough and kept it from deliquescing.

Cajuns.

We all walked up onto the bridge. There were about twenty people up there. Fortunately, school was still in session or there'd have been twice as many.

"It's Hoodoo Squad," one of them said.

"Hey! Hoodoo Squad! Can I get your picture?"

"Please don't," Ray said, with a pained expression. "The FBI is just going to confiscate the film."

"And we need to take care of this little issue," I said. "It's about to get very loud."

"Which one are you?" a girl in her twenties asked. Cute. Very cute. Five six, brunette, cheerleader body, white shorts and an AC/DC tank top. No bra and didn't need one. Like the song said: "Points on their own sittin' way up high." She looked like she'd done her hair up just to run out to see a giant crocodile. And maybe see the Hoodoo Squad in action.

"The sword guy," I said.

"The one who jumped through the window with all those vampires?" she asked, eyes wide.

"Yup," I said. There had only been one blinded vampire, but she didn't need to know that.

"These things are a pest," an older woman said. "This is the third time this *year*!"

"We find whoever's calling them up, we'll take care of it, ma'am," I said.

"Which one are you?" Points Girl asked Greer, flirting.

"Uh..." Greer said.

"They're from out of town," I said. "You'll probably read about them next few weeks. But if you have *any* problems, little lady, feel free to give me a call. I've got a house on Dauphine." I handed Points one of my *special* cards. With my personal number on back.

"I'll do that," she said, grinning. She tucked it into her shorts. In the front. Personal like.

In like Flynn, baby.

"Get your shit together and point out the sweet spot, Romeo," Ray said.

"Okay, Mr. Shackleford." I went prone and looked through the spotting scope. "See the two curved lumps behind the eyes?"

"Got that," Katie said, looking through the scope of the McMillan. It fired the same heavy round as my Barrett, but since it was a bolt action instead of a semiauto, it was more accurate.

"Right at the base where they flatten out. Directly in the center, but . . . Wait." The clumsy monster had fallen down again.

"So when *do* I make the shot?" Katie said. She was pushed into the McMillan. Calm and comfortable, ready.

"When it gets back up, we'll have the right angle," I said.

The beast finally regained its footing and . . .

"Fire," I said, sticking a finger in my right ear.

The round impacted perfectly. The sobek was down.

"And we're golden." I winced as I used my right arm to get to my feet.

"What happened to your arm, Mr. Gardenier?" Points asked, looking at my card.

"I was wounded while battling the forces of evil to protect the good people of New Orleans," I said. "And please call me Chad."

"I'd like to hear about it," she said, eyes sparkling, "Chad."

"Maybe over dinner? What are you doing this evening?"

"Nothin' much."

"Oh, hell," I said, frowning. "Probably should take a rain check. My boss is staying at my place." I nodded back over my shoulder where Ray was explaining to the Corps guy that cleanup was not our job. Agent Higgins had just arrived and was already taking people's film away.

"I've got a couple of friends," she said, grinning.

"He's married and the other guy staying with me is seriously religious. Good friends, don't get me wrong, but . . . yeah, come by this evening. Bring a bathing suit. I've got a hot tub."

"Why do I need a bathing suit?" she asked, batting her eyes.

"Lemme get your number as well," I said, pulling out my notebook.

In. Like. Flynn.

We'd gotten pictures. MCB had shown up and taken them, including Katie standing on the massive crocodilian with her rifle. Ray had asked about that.

"We'll put it up in a gun magazine like *Guns and Ammo*," Agent Three said. "Do some bad retouching. Maybe do it as an advertisement. When other pictures surface, people will say it's the same picture doctored. Don't worry, mon. Be happy. We got this."

Shelbye had already called and requested at least part of the tail. If MCB could get some freed up, her family was planning something called a "Fais do-do," whatever that was.

"Do you really think hitting on girls at an incident is a good idea, Chad?" Ray asked, as we were driving back to the team shack.

"In every other town in the world, it's probably a bad idea." Not that I wouldn't anyway. "In this town? Girls in this town freaking *love* Hoodoo Squad. *Milo* could get laid in this town. Not that he would. And stay that way, buddy. Not meaning to be a jerk."

"Got it," Milo said, shaking his head. He thought fornication was a sin.

"I'm Catholic. My father confessor gives me real bonus points for fighting the forces of darkness. So I'm covered. She's coming to dinner tonight. She offered to bring a couple of friends, but I told her one of you was married and the other was religious."

"Thanks," Ray said. "I think."

"Also, this job has kept me so freaking busy I've lost all my hobbies. I decided after my first day to pick a strip club and become a regular. Haven't even seen the inside of one yet. So at incidents is the only time I *could* meet girls. And you know I hit on any woman not wearing a wedding ring."

"And flirt with those," Ray said. "Susan says hey, by the way."

"Can we stop by the hospital?" I asked. "I'd like to see Ben."

"We'll drop you off."

Trevor was there too. The doctor said a lot of big words. They boiled down to "Too much damage."

"It's still possible he'll pull through," the doctor said.

"I understand," Trevor said. He was still using his cane. He was supposed to be out of the cast in a week, maybe two. Couple more weeks of physical therapy to be fully on his game. Trevor would be back for the next full moon. Ben would not.

Ben Carter, the man who first showed me around New Orleans, died about two weeks later, never having come out of the coma.

We had the funerals to deal with. Back then they were simple affairs. We had a crematorium we used and it always made time for us.

Greg and Jonathan were on side-by-side pneumatic slides in wooden caskets. Fine ones but unadorned.

The remainder of Team Hoodoo gathered around and Milo had asked to say a few words.

Great guy. Love him like a brother. Sincere. Honest. Godly in a way I'll never be.

Worst freaking public speaker in history.

Milo finally stumbled to a very sincere, heartfelt, badly-delivered close and stepped aside.

The funeral director hit the button and started the flames. Their caskets rolled in. Doors shut. There were glass windows so you could watch your loved ones burn to ash. It was one of the high-end crematoriums.

We had better things to do. The ashes would be delivered in preselected urns.

I made a note in my notebook.

22MAY85 1530: Memorial service, Greg, Jonathan. Ming vase ashes.

Translation: buy a Ming vase for my ashes.

What the hell, I didn't have much to spend my money on anyway. Speaking of which.

I called Remi on the car phone on the way back to the shack.

"What's the chance you could throw together a small informal event for about sixteen this evening?" I asked. "Something simple. The boss is not into fancy eats. Overestimate rather than under. Impromptu housewarming party."

"As sir prefers," Remi said. "Would sir be referring to sir's teammates and the new team in town?"

"That is what ... Yes. And some friends. Be advised: big eaters, heavy drinkers. Simple beer. Budweiser will do."

"I shall endeavor to provide, sir," Remi said.

"Sixteen?" Milo said. "Aren't but twelve if I'm counting right."

"Alvin's got a girlfriend," I said. "But I'm going to ask Points to bring more friends. Having a few cuties around livens up the party."

"Yeah, I think the team would appreciate that," Milo said.

"I just want to show off my new house."

"Hi, uh," I glanced at my notebook, "Cheryl? Chad from Hoodoo. This evening's still on, but ..."

Remi had gotten catering from a barbeque place. Tons of it. And help serving. There were iron washtubs full of a selection of love-in-a-canoe beers.

The girls turned up wearing cocktail dresses which sort of put Katie and Shelbye on the defensive at first. All they had were jeans and T-shirts. Points, along with most of her friends, turned out to be "professional cheerleaders" which is a subculture I won't even try to explain. Professional normally means you get paid. They don't.

Then most of Points' friends decided the place to be was the cold tub, given the heat, and, darn, *none* of them had remembered to bring bathing suits.

Milo withdrew at that point, blushing. Katie sort of faded with him. Shelbye just stripped down and jumped in. Ray was the most loyal husband I've ever known, and he just drank a bunch of beers and went to bed. The rest of the team was single. Alvin's girlfriend was from New Orleans and had no issues with it as long as Alvin stayed on *her* arm.

The team was in the rare position of being able to tell stories about hunts with people who weren't Hunters or family. The barbeque was excellent, the beer flowed and so did the stories. Trevor and the team told stories about Greg and Jonathan at what was both a housewarming party and a wake. Hell, after we broke out the bourbon even Earl got into the act, telling a story about fighting a houdoun priestess who'd called up a major Old One entity out in the bayou a few years back.

Say what you will about Hunters, we know how to party.

Then we got a call.

Zombies at a parade.

Fuckin' hoodoo.

CHAPTER 16
The Good, the Bad and the Stupid

Parades in New Orleans are like the heat and the bugs and the humidity: They are omnipresent. It seemed like every day, three or four times a day at times, there was a parade. Natives put them into two categories: parades, which are planned events that are advertised, have sponsors and are filed with the city; and "second lines" which are sometimes planned events, occasionally nearly spontaneous, frequently but not always advertised, often had sponsors, may or may not include floats and larger exhibits, and for which there is never any fucking warning.

Nobody but the natives could really tell the difference. They were both parades. The only thing with second lines was you were less likely to see the damned thing coming. Responding to a call, going like a bat out of hell and there's a fucking marching band in the middle of the street and a bunch of dancers in two bangles and a feather.

And the only thing that did *not* get out of the way for Hoodoo Squad was a parade. I ended up driving on the sidewalk one time to get past one.

But the thing about the parades—or second lines or what-the-fuck-ever—was they were and are the prime area of competition in New Orleans. Sure, they had a football team. In Green Bay it's all about the Packers. But this was the Big Easy. New Orleans is all about street theater and there was no better street theater than the parades.

Apparently at some parade a couple of months ago, one of the marching bands got a hoodoo man to curse another band's instruments so they would all be off-key. At least they were pretty sure it was a curse and not being toasted beforehand. Thus they lost the magic ribbon or whatever and were that pissed.

So when Band A was in a parade the next month, Band B went to a hoodoo man for a curse on them.

Said hoodoo man then raised the dead and attacked the whole damned parade.

No magic ribbon for you.

I told the girls to hang out. We'd be right back. Everyone had their gear handy. We did a one-hundred-percent call-out.

Half of us were drunk as loons.

When we pulled up to the parade at Harrison and Fochs, it was total chaos.

Bits and pieces of elaborate costumes were scattered on the street being trampled by a panicked mob. One of the band leaders was valiantly trying to brain a zombie with that big baton thing. Another shambler had a snare drum over his head and was wandering

around totally lost. Floats had driven into residences
and bars along the street.

Chaos.

"How the hell do you kill a zombie with a *drum*
on its head?" Ray said, laughing.

"Shoot it twice," Alvin yelled.

"Welcome to New Orleans!" I cackled, popping
my trunk.

People had spotted my purple light and the word
had got around. The crowd was shifting our way.

"HOODOO SQUAD! HOODOO SQUAD!"

And they were in the way of our shots.

"Get out of the way!" Trevor yelled. He'd somehow
managed to crawl up on his Coronado and was laid out
with an M14 on a bipod. "Goddammit, clear the way!"

"I'm going in," I said, dropping the sling and hefting
the Uzi one-handed. "Hell, I've *got* this," I slurred.
Ever heard of Dutch courage? Yeah, it was like that.

Trevor, Katie and Shelbye were up on cars for cover,
if they could get a clear shot. The rest of us spread
out and started walking forward. I started doing the
theme song from *The Good, the Bad and the Ugly*.

"Doolooloo, bwah whap, whaaaa..." I shot a shambler thirty yards away through the ear, left-handed.
"Oorah for Marine marksmanship!"

"Nahnah nanaanaaaah..." Milo said, dropping
another one with his M-16. "Mormon Brigade!"

"I don't know why you use that Mattel crap, buddy,"
I said. Shambler down. This one had been holding
down and chewing on a fat, screaming white lady
in a bright pink Chanel gown. Honestly, I probably
should have just popped her as well. Badly wounded
and going to turn. That was for MCB to take care of.

"That's coming from a guy shooting a twelve-pound pistol," Milo yelled. Shambler down.

"Mr. Hoodoo!" the woman said, grabbing my wounded right arm. Fiftyish, white, middle-class Cajun, in town for the party. "Help!"

"Ow, shit!" I snarled. She was panicked and just wanted someone to save her. We were working on it, okay?

"Get off!" I said, slamming her in the face with my elbow. She hit the ground like a sack.

Pro-tip: Hoodoo. People panic. When there's a crowd, you don't have time for finesse. You have to get the job done and if it takes *shooting* someone to get that job done, do it. Try to shoot them somewhere nonvital.

Most of the businesses had shut their doors when the shamblers showed up for the parade. One of the bars still had doors open and there was screaming coming from inside.

"Milo, Hand!" Earl bellowed. "Clear that bar!"

"On it!"

Two shamblers had gotten into the bar. One was down with its head blown off. The bartender had come up with a double-barrel and let go twice. He missed the second one. One of the critically wounded was being snacked on while the bartender was trying to reload with trembling hands and dropping shells all over the floor.

Drinks and tables were spilled everywhere. One guy was advancing on the shambler with a pool cue in his hand. In passing I wondered if he needed a job.

"Hoodoo Squad! Get out of the way! Move! Move!"

You know how sometimes you'll read a story about SWAT entering a house and the people in the house say they didn't hear SWAT identify themselves at all and SWAT said it was shouting as loud as it could? Both might be wrong. You see, when you're in a combat situation, your hearing gets all fucked up. You literally might not hear your rounds, but hear a fucking pin drop across the room. Not everyone has that reaction but it's common. And when you're in it, you think you're yelling but you're not. So you have to train and train to really *yell* at the top of your lungs. Forget how it sounds. You'll probably not even hear it. Just train yourself to yell as loud as you humanly can.

And you'll still probably be speaking in an *inside voice*.

I ran over and popped the shambler in the back of the head, right on the mastoid bone. Dropped. The guy with the pool cue looked at me as if to say: I had this, buddy.

I made a mental note to hand him a card.

"We need medics in here," I radioed, checking to make sure we were clear.

BOOM!

My helmet, shoulder pad and neck collar got most of it. But one round of number eight went between and hit me in the neck.

The bartender had gotten his shotgun reloaded.

"I'm hit," I radioed, holding my hand over the wound. That put it in good position to key the mike. "Hand is hit."

"*You dumb mother—*" Even that pissed off, Milo did not swear. He did, however, put his M-16 in the bartender's face. "*You . . . you . . . idiot!*"

"Sorry," the bartender said, dropping the shotgun and holding up his hands. "Sorry!"

"Milo," I said, dropping to one knee. "Not now."

I could talk. Trachea wasn't hit. There was no carotid spray. But I was bleeding like a stuck pig. Veinular at a guess. There's almost no place on the neck you can get shot and not die. I might have lucked out. Shit...more blood on my face, dripping on the ground. Where was that hit?

"I'm a nurse," one of the patrons said, running over.

"First aid kit," I said, choking a bit. I coughed up blood. Okay, trachea *was* hit. "Back. Belt."

"I think it clipped the right external jugular," she said, pulling out bandages.

"Back to see Dr. Einstat," I choked. I was kneeling and feeling a little faint. I coughed blood again. "Trachea."

"Try not to talk," she said. "Lie down."

"No," I said. "Car." I keyed the radio. "Need pickup. Car. Hospital."

"How bad?" Earl radioed.

I found it better to listen to the nurse and lay me down to sleep.

"Bad." Milo radioed. "He's hit in the neck."

"We're mostly clear," Earl radioed. *"Alvin, do pickup. You're local. Nearest hosp—"*

That's about all I remember.

Pro-tip on this one:

When they deal with the supernatural, people tend to panic. Which is why MHI only accepts recruits who have dealt with it proactively. The bartender? The lady outside? They panicked. Guy with the pool cue? Wasn't panicking but he was the only one in the bar who wasn't. Decay did well in the crunch. But people like them, people like us, are rare.

I've seen cops panic and shoot a half a dozen civilians

trying to hit one minor entity. Historically, soldiers, Marines, going back to some of the finest knights in history, have panicked when they deal with monsters.

So the pro-tip is, the only people you can really trust are your teammates. If you have to enlist a local, fair game. If you have to, you have to. But just because somebody can wave a gun around or even is a fair shot, that doesn't mean they can handle combat; that especially doesn't mean they can handle hoodoo.

I woke up in recovery at New Orleans General with an IV going in one arm, a unit of plasma going in the other and the comfortable feeling of being on morphine.

Heeeey, I thought, drowsily. *I made it out.* Morphine doesn't make the hurt go away, it just makes you not care. *Wheee . . .*

I turned my head a bit. That was painful. I stopped and moved my eyes around instead. There was one of those tables for eating in a hospital bed in front of me. On it was a mug with "Iron Hand" on it.

Hey, better than on the shelf. And way better than "Oliver."

Shelbye was napping in a chair in the room. I didn't want to wake her. I was thinking I probably needed to go to the bathroom and then realized I was catheterized. Sweet. Unfortunately, I was also awake. I really just wanted to sleep. Or take a drink. Bad thing about morphine—bad dry mouth. And I could tell I'd been intubated. That causes the worst sore throat in the world.

"Urgh . . ." Shit, that hurt, too. Yep, trachea had been hit.

There was a straw sticking out of the cup. I reached up, winced and used my left hand, winced again, looked to see the bandages there. Shit. Looked down. There were bandages on my nose. What the hell?

Bartender had been on the left. A stray pellet had clipped my nose. I was officially out of arms with which to masturbate and had a chunk taken out of my nose bone.

Peeing was going to be a trial as well. I was afraid Remi would insist on helping. I didn't know him well enough for him to touch me there.

And, shit, the girls had probably left the party already. Or, knowing my teammates, they'd dropped me at the hospital and gone back to continue. That's what I'd have done. There's a number you can call to see how someone is doing. I knew what they'd say in my case, "The patient is in critical but stable condition in ICU." I think I was about four beds down from Ben.

No reason to sit around with long faces. Just call the damned number. Stop by from time to time, preferably with a bottle of Kentucky sipping hid in your belt. Bring some books assuming I could pick them up to read them. Maybe smuggle in some Sasson's.

Pro-tip: The only three things you really need in recovery is decent food, something to read, and booze. You can't and shouldn't expect friends and family to stay by your bedside all day and all night. Maybe, maybe, if both arms are in a cast 'cause you can't hold the book or the bottle and can't feed yourself.

Okay, four things, but the fourth requires a very close personal friend or significant other.

Earl walked in about then and walked over to the bed. I gestured for something to write with.

He found a pen and pad and handed them to me, quizzically.

"Go party," I wrote. *"Beer warm."*

"We can hang out for a while, Hand," Earl said, shaking his head. "Besides, you'll be pleased to know there are half-dressed and undressed girls scattered all over your house last anyone checked."

"Score!" I wrote and grinned.

About then a nurse came in, took one look and went to get the doctor.

"Water?"

Earl lifted up the cup and I took a sip through the straw. Hey, my lips and mouth were still working. That was something. Legs, feet all seemed fine. Balls were still intact and that was the important part. Throat hurt like ever-living hell. More than just the intubation. A young intern arrived.

I'd been shot in the throat. Thanks, Doc, I was there. Sort of noticed. The round had clipped my external jugular vein and trachea and lodged against my esophagus. It was in a difficult place and the surgeons had elected to leave it in place. It shouldn't be a problem.

Which is why ever since I've had this weird feeling when I swallow food. No problem, just weird. Yes, to this day I have a round of buckshot in my neck. Not the only bit of metal, bone or whatever I've got in my body.

A vascular surgeon had repaired the vein—yes, it was Dr. Einstat—but it would need time to fully heal. I later had Dr. Einstat and other colleagues and family over to the house as well, bit more formal party, 'cause sucking up to your local surgeons is never a bad idea. A second round had slid under my shoulder pad and up along my back. That was a flesh wound. I may have aspirated some blood. That could cause secondary reactions.

You aspirate blood, you're probably going to come down with a killer case of pneumonia. It's probably killed as many people with throat or lung shots as direct effect. I was okay with that. I'm not suicidal or anything but I'm okay if I have to go to the Summer Lands. Just wasn't looking forward to the process. Tends to be really painful. Hopefully, though, I'd be fine. No signs so far. Breathing was clear. But I was sort of seriously dinged in both arms and the throat. I was pretty much out of action for a week or so.

I resolved that at this rate I needed to chat up a nice pretty nurse, as soon as I could chat, and not a "professional cheerleader." Paramedic, maybe, like Becca-Anne in Seattle. Somebody to help me pee, not Remi, and take care of other needs.

Shelbye had woken up, looking wasted and drawn. I pointed at my note to Earl. She shook her head and laughed.

"Gotta know when the party's over, Chad," Shelbye said.

"*Never,*" I wrote. "*Good. Need sleep. Pickup tomorrow. Go party.*"

"Will do, Romeo," Shelbye said. "See you in the morning."

I should have had a walking hangover but IVs are great for those. Mental memo. Pick up some more IVs. One way or another I was gonna need them.

I went back to sleep.

Earl put me out front as a dire warning to the recruits. The MHI ad had duly been dropped into the *New Orleans Truth Teller*. Along with it were lurid stories of the events of the full moon, both real and false. It was not true that a meteor had hit the 17th Street Canal levee causing massive flooding in Lakeview. Rescue operations were not still ongoing. Nor had a monstrous creature torn down the Pontchartrain Expressway during morning rush hour. But there was a very good, if blurry, Polaroid photo of the flesh golem, blown all over the street, with me standing there, face too blurry to recognize, holding a LAW tube. I've got a better 8x10 framed on my wall. That was taken by Bob with an FBI Nikon.

I'd made the front page again. Katie, of course, made the next one with the sobek.

Below the fold were memorials to both the lost members of Hoodoo Squad. They continued, with terrible misspellings and horrible grammar, on page three. There were lists of deeds, both real and false. Greg had never singlehandedly strangled a giant snake in Lake Pontchartrain. At least I was pretty sure he hadn't. Jonathan was not famous for stopping the infamous Black Witch of Allemands, I was pretty sure. Neither was named directly although they were referenced by previous famous exploits and the first letter of the first name.

More of the actual stories, in many cases damned near standard journalism, were in the interior. There was the story of how Jonathan bought it although he was "torn to pieces by a horde of loup-garou while saving a busload of children," not shot in the head by Agent Marine in the hospital.

And on the back page, terribly printed, was our full-page ad.

There was a cartoonish picture of a vampire, complete with opera cape, something bought from a costume store, and fangs out. The fangs were clearly Halloween false teeth. What I loved was that it was Agent Buchanan in the photo. I asked Higgins about it later and they'd first drawn straws, then argued if the short straw meant they lost or won. Never mind.

Hoodoo Squad was hiring. Training would be at a top secret location in a jungle in South America. Only the best need apply. Training was as intense as any commando school. Initial work would be with roving bands of elite Hunters, working in far climes. Those that passed those tests would be returned to New Orleans to join the Hoodoo Squad.

"Are you tough enough to face the hoodoo?"

I wasn't the interviewer. I was the guy who was supposed to drive off the scaredy cats. The interviews were being handled by Trevor while Earl's team answered calls. Shelbye and Alvin were out showing them around and "liaisoning" with locals.

Shelbye as a liaison. The mind boggles.

The kid was young and nervous. He was looking at a guy behind a desk who had both arms in slings, a bandage across his nose, two black eyes, and bandages on his neck like he'd been bitten by a vampire.

"Experience?" I croaked.

"I done kilt a zombie, Mr. Hoodoo," the kid said. "Up Bayou Road. Couple month ago. Come after my momma."

"What did you use?"

"Baseball bat."

That took either guts or stupidity. Could go either way.

I looked at his application form. He'd managed to almost spell his name right. Maybe. If that was his name. I looked at the list supplied by the MCB.

"Norbert LeClerc?" I croaked as best I could. Rs were hard. It was spelled "Noboot Laklurk," I think. Handwriting was not the kid's métier.

"Yes, sir, Mr. Hoodoo."

Recruit or not, the MCB had also helpfully supplied whether PUFF had been paid on the kill. It hadn't.

"President of the company is missing an eye and a hand," I said. "We just had two *kilt*. One more might not make it. I look like this. You really *want* this job?"

"Yes, sir," the kid said sincerely.

"Why?" I asked.

"Do it pay?"

The guy was medium-height, "big-boned"—okay, fat—brown hair and big bushy beard wearing camouflage BDU pants and a brown beret with an SAS flash. He had on a badly printed T-shirt that read "Elysian Field Hoo-doo Squad."

"Experience?" I asked.

"I've been fighting the supernatural for *years*," the guy said angrily. "Tired of catching shit about it from the *man*! If I have to join some special interest group to get some recognition, I guess I'll just have to cop to the man!"

I looked at his application. Neat handwriting. Could spell. Name Jon Glenn.

I looked at the MCB list.

Holy shit.

I started doing some calculations.

"You've been doing this for *free*?" I asked...croaked.

"Someone needs to! The supernatural is out of control in New Orleans! It's just getting worse every year! The damned government won't do anything about it! Corrupt politicians and special interests keep us from defending ourselves! We have a right to keep and bear—"

I tuned him out and pulled out the basic PUFF table to check a couple of things. The guy was telling the truth. The first kill was three years ago: five shamblers. That had continued. All single hunts as far as I could tell. Based on back PUFF, the guy was sitting on a quarter of a million dollars. Also noted "extremely hostile to authority." Yuh think?

He looked like a poser wannabe. Looks could be deceiving. We could use that kind of can-do attitude.

"When can you start?" I croaked.

"Is sir in?" Remi asked.

I was in the hot tub with both arms propped up. I could kind of use my left one to lift a can of beer with a straw in it up to my lips.

I'd had a long day of popping painkillers while croaking to recruits.

"Is it work?" I rasped.

"It is one of the ladies from the party, sir," Remi said. "A Miss Points I believe you called her."

"I am in." *Like Flynn*, I hoped.

"Oh, Chad," Points said, leaning over the hot tub and carefully putting her arms around me. "When I heard you were hurt, I was so worried!"

I thought about all my smooth lines. My throat hurt.

"I always use protection," I croaked. "You're on top. Take off your clothes and get in the tub."

Turns out she really liked the strong, silent type.

CHAPTER 17
Cool Change

I was spending most of my time at the house, recovering. That gave me time for other stuff. My stored shit came in from Seattle and I could finally start to fill in some missing items in the house. I hadn't realized how many katanas and 1911s I owned. I might need a twelve-step program there. There were enough guns in the shipment that I could put at least one in every room. They weren't perfect choices, though. Damn, I was going to have to buy more guns. Problems, problems, problems. Speaking of which.

I gently explained to Points that I wasn't a one girl kind of guy and my rationalizations for that. When that didn't work, I slept with one of her friends from the party and the message got across. I hate doing that sort of thing but since she knew where I lived, I had to do something. She still "forgave" me but the relationship cooled slightly. That was okay; there were plenty of girls who liked knowing a Mr. Hoodoo Squad.

Thing is . . . how to explain?

People, especially women, say that women are more

complicated than men. A bit, perhaps, but not as much as many people, mostly women, think.

Men in terms of reproductive needs tend to be driven by things which most people call shallow. Is a girl hot? I want to bang her. "Men only want one thing." Not true. More like a sliding scale. Depends on what's going on. In the middle of a firefight, what men mostly want is to survive and kill the enemy. At a pickup bar? Yeah, the scale has expanded the screw portion and reduced the fight portion. Generally. Depends on the guy. There is also eat, drink, read a book, study monsters, build a boat, go fishing, play computer games, whatever. Guys *do* want more than one thing. I've seen nerds pass up opportunities to get laid to play D&D. I think they're nuts, but it's proof that guys want more than one thing. Just depends on the circumstances. But back to why "hot" is not "shallow."

Though it tends to be culturally adjusted, "hot" also tends to describe certain physical criteria. And those physical criteria, in turn, tend to be "a woman who is likely to produce good babies and survive." That wasn't guaranteed evolutionarily. Lots of women died in childbirth prior to the invention of modern medicine. Having one that would probably survive the experience was a good thing.

High hip-to-waist ratio, common trend of "hot" in Western cultures, indicates a high likelihood of being capable of carrying babies. Think Marilyn Monroe. That's a girl who could have popped out a few. Raquel Welch, again, good potential breeder. Good hair, especially long, shows long-term quality diet and condition. (Think about someone with cancer and hair loss as a counterexample.)

Good skin? She lacks diseases and is young enough to provide many babies. Unk! Unk! Gronk like!

I could go on about this stuff. I've analyzed it, spindled it and folded it. Bottom line, men aren't as "shallow" as they're made out to be. They're analyzing things subconsciously for the best reproductive partner.

Women do the same thing in choosing potential reproductive—these days more pseudo-reproductive—partners. Women's tendency to be more "complicated" is more complicated but only slightly. They have different drivers rather than more. Sliding scale again. Men have as many "things" on the scale but tend to focus on one at a time, that one becoming "big" on the scale. Women tend to distribute. Thus it looks more complicated but isn't.

But one key factor in women tends to be "security." Evolutionarily and anthropologically, men tend to be the aggressors and defenders of a tribe. Tend. Isn't universal. Nothing in anthropology is. But feminists who trot out exceptions are cherry-picking. They are, note, *exceptions* and every one is susceptible to analysis if you know enough about the individual example.

It's one of the reasons some girls tend to go for jocks and thugs. They're violent and rough. "Pretty girls out walking with gorillas down my street." The girls tend to feel protected from *others*, even if the guy they're dating uses them like a punching bag. In many cases *especially* if they're being used as a punching bag. I don't know how many times Shelbye, one very bad-news chick, came in sporting a shiner that wasn't from fighting monsters.

Women tend to also be driven by perceived social status and this counts even with women who are not drawn to being punching bags. Because in evolution-ary times, the man's status tended to equal how many resources were available to the woman and her child. "Marrying up" meant that your children were more likely to survive. And women who were good at that tended to pass on their genes.

This is why rock stars get laid a lot.

This is at the deep, subconscious level which is immune to logic. And it's that deep level, immune to logic, where the lounge lizard must dwell. Fortunately, I *am* dangerous and rough. Probably my one problem with dating is I tend to be *too* much of a gentleman.

As to social status, Hoodoo Squad in New Orleans was right on the same level as a member of the Saints. I was a very-high-status guy, decent-looking, the growing facial scars only helped, obviously could provide security, and had a nice house.

Bottom line, just as the drug gang was thrilled to have a member of Hoodoo Squad on their turf, 'cause they scare away the hoodoo, the women of New Orleans tended to be more than happy to spend a night in my arms. Fishing for hotties in New Orleans during my time there was like fishing with Pete in heaven. I was Hoodoo Squad. They swam right up to the line, took the bait and jumped in my arms.

The real problem was getting them to leave.

Thank God for Remi.

I wasn't just banging hotties, finding places to stash guns and books, and rearranging the furniture. (Well, directing Remi in that.)

There are mourning traditions all over the world, ways to say goodbye to the dead. Ways to find closure.

Humans have always wondered if we are truly gone when we die and hoped that we were not. Hoped for themselves, hoped for their loved ones.

> *In the end, is my soul laid to rest with what's*
> *left of my body?*
> *Or am I just a shell?*

The balloon ceremony is none of those traditions. It is my tradition and one that I really like. It is based on two: one Japanese, involving a kite, and one Chinese, where you write a letter to the dead, then burn it so that the smoke would carry your words to heaven.

When my arms were sort of working I asked Remi to find me some really good stationery. Something solid and preferably handmade. Did not need to be personalized.

Then I sat down to write.

First, I wrote a letter to Jesse. I told him I missed him, hoped he was doing well. I'd stopped by and talked to his parents. I liked his family and I swore I hadn't hit on his sister. Despite having bought a house, which I talked about a little, it being on Dauphine Street, I was continuing to send some money to his family. He shouldn't worry about them or me; we were all doing fine and hoped to see him soon.

It wasn't "I hope you're in heaven" or anything. More like writing to a friend in India or something back in the days when you knew you probably weren't going to get a reply any time soon.

Handwritten, did a couple of drafts on regular paper, wrote it as clearly as I could, sort of calligraphed.

Then ones to Jonathan and Greg. Told them I hoped

they were doing well. Discussed that the company had made sure Jonathan's younger cousin was okay financially. He'd been looking out for her, long distance, since her parents were killed by hoodoo. Apologized I never had the time to get to know them better but promised we'd sit down and talk when I got there. Told them not to worry, we were doing fine. I even told them we were recruiting in the *Truth* and it was funny as hell.

Then I took all three letters and wrapped them up tight in scroll form with a fine red ribbon.

I walked down to the river by Jackson Square. The whole way from the house. Not a huge distance but this wasn't something to just jump in Honeybear. Arms were still tender and I was trying manfully not to talk much but the legs were working fine.

When I got there, I found a balloon vendor and bought three plain rubber balloons. Then I tied each of the letters to an individual balloon and let it fly up to the heavens. I watched until the last balloon was out of sight, then went home.

After things had gotten settled down enough I could quit croaking my way through recruiting duty, I made an overseas call.

Back when I'd been in Seattle and had, you know, time, I'd spent quite a bit of it in England. The Van Helsing Institute had been around about as long as MHI but had a slightly different approach. They, too, had archives but they shared them with Oxford which was a premier center for the study of the occult, at least as it referred to fighting it. Cambridge was the "give vicious, violent monsters who want to rip our throats out a chance" university.

I'd picked up a master's, long distance, from Oxford already based on my existing bachelor's and University of Maryland correspondence courses. The thesis was an analysis of the Sasquatch language and its relationship to Tibetan yeti. I'd started working on another degree when I'd chosen the wrong elf chick to bang.

Bottom line, again, I had good relationships with both Van Helsing Institute and Oxford. And Oxford had been studying monsters back in the Dark Ages. The British Ethnological Society and the Royal Society for the Study of the Supernatural had done reams and reams of papers on every kind of hoodoo found in every corner of the world. Often the information was wrong, but it was something. They were bound to have something on our tunnel borer.

So I gave VHI a call.

"Van Helsing Institute, Clara speaking, how may I help you?"

"This is Mr. Gardenier," I croaked. "I'd like to arrange a consult call with Dr. Rigby."

"Dr. Rigby is out at the moment. When would be convenient?"

"I'm recovering at the moment and home most days. If he cannot reach me for some reason, you can speak to my gentleman and arrange a better time."

He called the next day. I'd told Remi I was in.

"Chad," Dr. Rigby said. I could picture his massive, bushy eyebrows going up and down. "Are you seriously wounded, lad?"

Dr. Rigby had nearly the same reputation in British circles as, say, the Old Man, Raymond Shackleford III. For good reason. WWII British Marine commando running ops into occupied France, then Special Operations executive working with French and German Resistance where he got involved in the supernatural. Got out after the war, completed his degree and joined Van Helsing. Top Hunter in his day.

"Gah," I croaked. "Flesh wounds. I already had one injured arm, when some asshole shotgunned me, panicking over mincers." Mincers was the preferred English term for zombies. Mincers referred to the term "mincing" as a form of walking. Also "to mince" as in to cut up food. They also called them sergeant majors and ministers. The latter referred to the Monty Python sketch, "the Ministry of Silly Walks."

Brits, what can you say? They've got an odd slang for, like, totally anything. What-ever. Gag me with a spoon.

"Asshole got me in the *other* arm. Also in the throat, which is why I sound like this. Worst part is, I'm out of arms to pleasure myself."

"I'm sure you'll find someone to help with your dilemma," he said, chuckling. "From experience, also rather painful to sleep on either side. You needed a consult?"

"Want to fax some reports and descriptions of a recurring event," I said. "MHI, MCB, nobody can figure out what is causing it. Want you to look."

"Be happy to," Rigby said. "What is it?"

"Something burrowing from underground and taking people out of their homes, but the details don't match any creature we know of."

He didn't insult me by suggesting something obvious like a grinder. "Interesting."

"Might take Oxford," I said. "Must be rare and odd."

"Fax the report to me," Rigby said. "I've seen my

fair share of rare and odd. And I'll send a copy to Dr. Witherspoon at Oxford."

"Thanks. Cheers."

"Cheers."

Worst part of the ordeal? It wasn't being unable to sleep on either side comfortably. It wasn't being unable to "pleasure myself." I had Points and Company visiting frequently. Wasn't being unable to scratch my ass. Nope. Trevor called me in to help with the PUFF *paperwork*.

You got any clue how much paperwork is involved in PUFF? It's the Federal Freaking Government. Guess.

Take a standard shambler mob. Say, fifteen shamblers. (Okay, there were twelve but this is New Orleans.)

We'd get a receipt from the coroner. Fifteen shamblers, Federal Unearthly Creature Code Number (FUCCN and you know how that's pronounced) 51487-A. Dave's squiggle. Parish stamp. We'd get the parish incident number or other police entity. All good.

Each and every walker required a *separate* piece of paper. Form 248-36-C. Generally called a 248. The 248 had to have the FBI incident number, which was different from the state or local. This was a "Federal Incident Number, General." (FING to which we'd add the "r" in general. Thus FINGr.) There was a box for state or local incident number but it was "non-binding."

Generally, MCB in New Orleans would fax over a sheet with their incident numbers (generically called "Giving us the FINGr") and the corresponding state or local along with Confirmation of Kill number. (COK, again, you know how it's pronounced. "We finally got COK'd on that cockatrice." Not like the cola, put it that way.) Sometimes there were incidents missing. You'd have to call one of the agents and get the FINGr and COK. Quite frequently, especially after the full moon, we'd have to wait a couple of weeks on COK. You couldn't file until you had been COK'd. I frequently just used codes with Agent Marine when we were waiting on COK. "Come on, Bob! I've got the FUCCN, I've got the FINGr! I need my COK, man! This is FUBAR!"

But anyway, back to the paperwork issue...

Back in the ooold days, you'd laboriously fill in each piece of paper with the information. A few years back, MHI went "up-scale" and got software and computers to do this. Uh-huh.

This "custom designed" POS, Supernatural Unified Computing Spreadsheet (SUCS) was possibly the *worst* piece of software in the history of bad software. First of all, it was designed to work with the Commodore 64, even then a system so out of date it was a plesiosaur. Second, it had no databases and no relational structure. If you could type, it was better than filling it in by hand and possibly, not sure, better than a typewriter. If you could get it to work at all. And the way it worked, you had to fill in the information, then carefully insert a 248 in the printer and hope like hell that all the print lined up in the right boxes. The one good feature, it's only "selling point" (hah!) was that if you had fifteen shamblers you, supposedly, only had to fill in the information once and it would generate all the forms for you.

Supposedly. Because, get this, *it didn't save*! I mean, it had *no* save feature *whatsoever*. So if you had fifteen shamblers and were on your sixth 248 and it was misaligned, you had to do a complete refill of *all* information! Assuming it didn't crash on you in the middle! In which case you had to start all over again! And for the 248, if there were fifteen shamblers, each of the forms had to be numbered 1-n. So imagine if you fucked up sheet six of fifteen. The actual box wanted "X of Y." In this case "1 of 15." You had the choice of either doing fifteen more sheets or saying you wanted fifteen, only printing one, whiting out the 1 in 1 of 15 and writing in 6.

Side note: The spot on the 248 had the "of" in it and two very small spaces to either side. When I was working on it, I realized that at some point the Nelsons had had to do this for a couple hundred freaking giant spiders! I called them and asked them how they'd done it. Especially since with the computer font we were using, you could not fit a three-digit number in the "of blank" blank. It would only take at most two.

The answer was, they'd done one sheet, whited out the "1 of 1," written "158" very small in the provided spot, photocopied it then laboriously hand-entered "1 of," "2 of" et cetera.

After I talked to the Nelsons I suggested to Trevor that we just run one sheet of whatever number it was supposed to be, photocopy it then hand number the increments. He was so relieved at the suggestion I thought he was going to kiss me. Hated freaking paperwork.

But the bottom line was that the damned program was crap.

Oh, and after doing all that, we then had to fax it all to Cazador where someone, usually Susan, did the actual filing. And send signed copies later. 'Cause, of course, everything had to have a legal signature. Gah!

Look, I'm a swordsman in every meaning of the word. I'm a cunning linguist. I'm not a computer geek. But I'd spent two years in Seattle, not quite Silicon Valley but closer than Cazador, and had spent half that time, I swear, in the basement of Microtel cleaning up their messes.

Compared to Trevor, I was Bill Freaking Gates. Or Ray, for that matter, who had been the guy who arranged the software buy. And programming is a language. I'm a linguist. I'd taken programming classes. I looked at the code and nearly puked. It was the code equivalent of the *Truth*. Misspellings, bad grammar, no syntax but in code-speak. And absolutely zero documentation or notations. It sucked.

So once my throat was getting better, I sat him down in the office, put my hand on his knee, looked him square in the eye and said:

"Ray," I said. "Buddy. Boss. You're a great guy, really. But you are a freaking *moron* when it comes to computers."

I told him we needed new software. He agreed. Everybody hated it. I told him we needed an updatable relational database of all the Codes with an automated query look-up and daily polling. He started to look a bit confused.

Look, Ray is an incredibly smart guy. I don't know anyone better at reading musty old tomes of hoary dark lore. Not even the guys at Oxford. He gets hoodoo at a level I don't. Possibly too good a level. Thankfully he's so clearheaded or I'd be worried about how much dark shit he knows.

But computers? Not his thing. I had to try to put it in terms of a card file system in a library. He nodded like he understood what I was saying but I could tell from the slightly vacant expression I was using one of those languages that just doesn't translate.

"I'm out for a couple of weeks," I said finally. "You guys have got this. Let me go look for an alternate solution. May cost more but it's going to be right. If we don't have the budget, we don't have the budget."

"Okay," he said. "Works for me. We really do need something better. I know that. But..."

"Yeah," I said. "Computers. I'll find the right solution."

CHAPTER 18
Working in a Coal Mine

This presented the problem: Where do you find a software developer who is "read-in" on the existence of the supernatural? A good one, that is. Not the idiot who'd written this. I had worried it was Milo but he wasn't into computers. Hate to have insulted my best living friend.

Well, I thought, the government has to have some computers to handle this stuff, right? I later learned the answer was "Sort of and you don't want to know how bad." The actual computers that handled PUFF management, then, were the main-frame equivalent of a Commodore and I don't think they've ever been updated. I'm pretty sure they're still using punch cards.

But where would the government *go* for computers?

The answer, see previous memoir, is whoever had bought the right congressmen and senators. But the basic answer was probably a large vendor.

After thinking about it, I called IBM. Fuck trying to find some little dink developer company where the owner and only programmer happened to know about PUFF. IBM was bound to have some department for it. And it wasn't like we weren't a potentially awesome client.

Look, we were what's called a "mid-cap" business. Medium capital. We weren't Fortune Five Hundred but MHI was and is, non-publicly, about Fortune One Thousand. Yes, family-owned and operated for, at this point, approaching one hundred years. We're established and wealthy. Just the sort of client IBM likes. We weren't a "small business." We were pushing millions of dollars in PUFF every year. I didn't know how many millions at that time; I found out as part of this side job. Proprietary is the answer but, whoa! If I'd had Ray's money, I'm not sure I'd keep hunting!

It took me about two days of talking to different departments looking for someone who was read-in on PUFF. I finally found it in one of their departments that wouldn't disclose who their customers were except "Entities of the Federal Government."

"I need a salesman on the commercial side read-in on PUFF and we'll probably need custom development," I said. "We need individual turn-key systems at multiple offices, probably polling, probably Microtel-compatible systems with other office software compatibility, training, support and ongoing PUFF update. We're a mid-cap, private firm."

I'd asked, along the way, for the right terminology for what we were and what we wanted without getting into exactly what we do. When people asked, I'd use either "classified contractual work for the Federal government" or "proprietary" or just "classified."

"Can you tell me the general area of your business?" the guy asked.

"Can you tell me the meaning of the third word in PUFF?" I asked.

"Forces," the guy said. *"First word?"*

"Perpetual. We're a Hunter company."

"Which one?" he asked. *"Honestly, you're going to need to be pretty big for IBM to want to look at custom dev."*

"MHI."

"Oh. I've heard of you guys. I'm going to get such a nice bonus from this referral..."

I don't know if he did or not, but about a week later, a salesman and a development specialist were dispatched from IBM home office to New Orleans and met with Ray and me. I fobbed the salesman off on Ray and I sat down with the developer. Both had experience with entities. The salesman had lost a family member. The other had been in development long enough to have had his own little issues.

"I used to work in Seattle," I told him. "We had the Microtel account."

"Their QC department?" he asked, eyes wide. "Good heavens!"

"More like hell."

"Nobody ever comes out of there alive," he said grimly. "Nobody."

IBM didn't have the same issues as Microtel, nobody had the same issues as Microtel, but they did have issues. They had a Hunter company under contract at the time. We ended up snaking the account based on the fact that we had nationwide coverage and they had nationwide issues. We picked up some of the employees from the NY-based company that had handled their main research farm so it wasn't all downside for them. Company president ended up as one of our team leads. Never mind. Hunter business is like any other. Mergers, acquisitions. It's just that *hostile takeover* has a whole new meaning. The pen, trust me, is *not* mightier than the sword.

One aspect was the question of what the maximum possible Y was in X of Y? One of how many maximum?

I asked Earl the question one evening.

"Earl," I said. "We're working on this new software package."

"That damned thing," Earl growled. I don't think the guy knew how to just speak in a normal tone. It was like he barked and growled *everything*.

"Thing is, what's the most number of things MHI has ever had to file of one type in one incident? How many of whatever? One of three hundred? Five hundred?"

We were eating dinner at my place. Earl had declined the invitation to stay. Most of the team were in a pretty decent motel. New Orleans had plenty of them and even if there were prior scheduled guests, even the Hilton in New Orleans was glad to have Hoodoo Squad on premises.

He thought about the question while masticating some shrimp étouffée. I'd asked Remi if I really had to get a cook. He'd tried to keep the offense off his face, then cooked dinner.

Anyway, Earl thought about it for what seemed a very long time then cleared his throat.

"One thousand, eight hundred and twenty-six," he said, then went back to eating.

"Wait. One thousand, what? Seriously?"

There were things that swarmed. Certain types

of small, supernatural, deadly insects mostly. I hated those but most of them were susceptible to Raid. I'd heard there was one, a swarm of cannibalistic locusts, that had taken a crop-duster. I'd heard of some major killer-frog swarms, but, again, swarms? You listed those as "swarm." As individual *items*?

"Those zombie squirrels?" Ray asked.

"Nope," Earl said.

"Come on," I said. "Story time."

"Ah, hell," he said, taking a sip of beer. He refused to drink it from a glass. It had to be from a can or bottle. Remi just put the can or bottle out in a little holder. I think they cordially liked each other but Ray refused to be "highfalutin'" and Remi refused to allow him to be entirely redneck. It was a game I loved to watch. But to the story.

"We were down in Ecuador. Been a bunch of weird things going on. Middle of another civil war so we had to be on our toes. Bunch of gringos running around and about six sides in the war killing each other, some of them using gringo mercs, which was what we looked like. That was before your..."

He'd gestured at Ray but paused and cleared his throat.

"It was a while back. Anyway, me and a team were down there checking out a bunch of undead that kept popping up. Thing was, we couldn't track down the necromancer that was causing it. Creative fella, turned out he'd been a professor. Anyway, we tracked him down to this little village down in the jungle side of Ecuador. And he spotted us and ran. We followed him up into the hills and he finally went to ground in a cave. Sun was falling and we were closing in."

He paused and frowned.

"We knew we had him dead to rights. We knew he had some kid with him but we didn't really know what we were facing. Sun set as we got up to the cave. We weren't worried. He wasn't a vamp, we knew that. He'd been walking around in the sunlight. Thought he might plan on turning the kid but we'd only be facing one undead and an old man. No problem. Then, right as the sun set, there was this just godawful unholy flapping of wings. They landed on Joey first..."

"What?" I asked.

"He'd used that poor kid as a sacrifice to power some necromantic spell that killed and reanimated all the *fruitbats* in that cave. And I ain't talking mere zombies, but vampiric."

"Holy shit," Ray said. "I never heard that story."

"*Actual* vampire bats?" I said. There was a species called a vampire bat that would cut wounds into victims, including humans, and lick the blood. But they weren't *actual* vampires. I'd heard of zombie animals but never vampire animals. "Were they infective?"

"Yep," Earl said. "Just like any vampire. One bite and you were infected. Sucked blood, big fangs. Powerful, nasty, everywhere. Killed and you rose from the dead. Blotted out the sky. One thousand eight hundred and twenty-six as it turned out. Wingspan like this," he added, spreading his arms wide. "We had some armor, but they were all over us. Hitting every major artery. On our faces, arms, legs. I swear they picked Saul up in the air and nearly flew off with him."

"How'd you survive that?" I asked. I'd once faced one hundred and fifty sassus giant spiders with a similar team but we were prepared and it was on a single vector. At the time I couldn't imagine what that must have been like.

"Shotguns," he said, shrugging. "Knives. Machetes. You ain't the only guy who knows how to swing a blade, Hand. Everyone went to killing until our arms gave out. We were waist-deep in bats by the end, but I was the only one who survived. Then I went into that cave and chopped that guy to pieces.

"But, yeah, one thousand eight hundred and twenty-six. We'd never seen it and I filed as 'previously unknown entity.' Then an adjuster turned up. He actually *had* heard of something similar, even had a name for it. That was before all this code bullshit. I tried to convince him it was a swarm but we had to file one piece of paper for every single damn bat. Financially it was worth it. Made a killing. Most of it went to families. Vampiric, infective *and* flying? Even back then they were worth a thousand dollars apiece. And back then for a thousand bucks you could buy two ca—Made a packet."

I thought about the story later as I was getting ready for bed. I wasn't a huge student of South American history. There were plenty of others who could beat me in that category in Jeopardy. But I didn't recall Ecuador having a civil war in . . . It had been a while. Coup d'etat maybe? Sometimes those dragged on in the country.

It was puzzling at the time. I'm sure at least some of my gentle readers know the answer.

The salesman and developer stayed for three days. The salesman, realizing that Earl was one of the decision-makers, tried to schmooze Earl. Hit and bounced. It was funny as hell to see.

The developer was good. In the opinion of a power user, a good developer is one who looks at the existing process, might suggest some improvements, but develops a custom solution that fits the process rather than creating a solution that's his idea of how it *should* work or taking a completely different process and trying to ram it down the customer's throat.

Despite some qualms, see below, he hung in there, studying what we had to file and how we had to file it and eventually a team at IBM developed a really good system. They do good work and MHI has stayed with them ever since. Because, well, IBM.

Not that there weren't some...issues.

One issue that was funny as hell was their reactions to the team. See, we were meeting at the team shack. First of all, they were less than thrilled about being in the ghetto. We told the boys on the block to keep an eye on their rental. "Yes, Mr. Hoodoo!" Mostly anything parked out front was okay, but some idiot might come by and break into it since it didn't have a Hoodoo sticker.

But then they were in the office the first day when one of the teams came in from an "incident," covered in blood and ichor and smelling like a mortuary.

"Five shamblers, and one dumbass junior necro," Shelbye said, tossing the receipts on the desk. "Bagged and tagged."

She was still carrying her M14, her face was splattered with blood and she generally, from the point of view of a nice salesman and a computer geek, must have looked like the reincarnation of Morrigan.

"Right," I said, looking at the receipt. "No incident number."

"Shit," she said, pulling out her notebook. "Shee-yit."

She scrawled the incident number on it and handed it back. "There."

"Thanks," I said, putting it in the box until we got the FINGr from the MCB.

"So..." the developer said, looking at the receipt. It had a bloody fingerprint on it. "That's how it works?"

"Pretty much," I said. "At this end. Later we get a Federal Incident Number, General, from the FBI as well as a Confirmation of Kill. We talked about those."

"Okay," he said, his face green. "And shamblers are...?"

"Zombies, human, slow," I said. "FUCCN 51487-A. Pretty much our bread and butter."

"So they were just..." the salesman said.

"Out shooting walking dead in the head," I said, tapping my index finger into the side of my own. "Ever seen a Romero flick? You've got to blow their brains out, you know. And one human who raised them. Technically, you don't have to shoot them in the head, but we usually do 'cause better safe than sorry."

The developer retched a couple of times.

"Bathroom's that way. Or use the trash can."

He ran out of the room. There was a sound of vomiting from in the bathroom.

"Hey!" Shelbye said, banging on the door. "How long you gonna be? I gotta wash this guy's brains off'n my face!"

The salesman made it to the trashcan.

We are bad, bad people.

The developer and salesman were gone. I'm sure they heaved a sigh of relief. Trevor was out of his cast. I was starting to be able to do workouts again.

We got the call from the hospital that there'd been a "Code Blue" and they'd been unable to revive Ben Carter.

We'd been taking turns going to the hospital but it wasn't a twenty-four-hour watch. Nobody was there when he passed.

Our usual funeral home picked up the body. Trevor did the honors of taking off his head. The funeral was going to be tomorrow. Milo, God help me, wanted to say some words.

I asked Shelbye who you called for one of those big New Orleans funerals. The one with a marching band and all. She knew people.

The next day there was a second line. The whole team plus most of Earl's team turned out. We all went to the crematorium and this time waited for our friend to burn to ash. It takes a surprisingly long time. We waited.

When we walked out, there was one of those big New Orleans marching bands and a carriage followed by a caparisoned steed, boots reversed. There was a flag bearer carrying the banner of Team Hoodoo—a shrunken human head—and another carrying an American flag. We placed Ben's urn on the carriage, took our places behind it, Trevor took charge of the Team Hoodoo flag, I took the American, Shelbye and Alvin acted as flag guards and we started walking.

It is a long damned way to the riverfront at Jackson Square. Right through, if not the busiest part of town, then an extremely busy one.

The band played slow dirges as we walked. The main one was "When the Saints Go Marching In." Most people don't understand that hymn. What it refers to is the Final Battle when the Warrior Saints fight by the side of the Angels. When all the warriors who have gone to Heaven or Valhalla or the Summer Lands, rise up to return to earth to fight the hordes of Satan.

Ben would be there that day. I would. Jesse would be there. Those guys that Earl talked about in Ecuador. We'd *all* motherfucking be back *that* day. That last fine day of Perfect Battle.

Ben was going to march back in at the side of the angels "When the Saints Go Marching In."

People stood by the side of the road and bowed their heads. They did that anyway for a funeral, but this was a member of Hoodoo Squad.

Cars honked as we blocked traffic. There'd been no planning, no official filing. Second line. Suck it, bitches. Fuck you and your minivan. I don't care if your precious baby is late for soccer practice. Slowly state troopers and Sheriff's Office and NOPD cars turned up to block intersections and wave cars onto alternate routes. Officers got out of their cars and stood at attention as the urn passed. At one intersection Bob and Jody, along with a couple of junior MCB agents, joined the procession.

Finally we reached Riverfront. I'd asked everybody to write a letter to Ben. Mine, as with most I think, included apologies for not being there when he died. But he understood, I'm sure. Death is lighter than a feather . . . I told him it was fun hunting with him and he'd been a great guide. I told him I'd see him soon.

Everyone wrapped their letters in ribbons and we got balloons. Finally, together, we released them into the air. We watched until they were out of sight, then struck up the band.

The wake at Maurice's is still the stuff of legend.

CHAPTER 19
Back in Black

I was off physical tyranny, out of the office and back on the job. Thank God. I swore then and there I'd never be a team lead.

There are reasons to want to be a team lead. Some people really like being the boss. Nothing against them. Earl's like that as are both adult Rays. Trevor was a natural-born leader. There are jerks who are that way, but MHI's "corporate culture" generally avoids them.

Team leads get paid more. They get a cut of the entire team's action even if they're sitting in an office or at a conference in Maui. That's nice. Money for nothing, right?

They also have to inform the family of the departed, make arrangements thereof, and, notably, handle most of the paperwork. I never even got into the paperwork for being end users for the sort of ammo, weapons and explosives we use. That's another nightmare.

I have stated definitely I will never be a team lead. Have zero desire. Some people think I have leadership skills. Okay, I'm fine with leading a field team.

I'll train newbies on an area or back at Cazador if I must. I'll do that stuff. I don't really have a problem with taking responsibility for the deaths of people I'm leading.

I don't know anyone who likes informing the families, and I hate the freaking paperwork. I make enough money and I really don't like the responsibilities.

Doctors, not knowing the *horror* they had unleashed, had cleared me for real work. I was once again free to kill shit and make money. Telling me I could go back to work was practically a violation of the Hippocratic Oath. "First do no harm." I was about to do some *serious* harm. Just as soon as I got a fricking call!

"Please, God, I'm begging You, gimme a call!" I said, watching *Sally Jesse Raphael*. "Can you imagine if some of us went on this stupid show? 'Well, Sally, my problem is I haven't shot a zombie in the head in *weeks*! It's driving me nuts!'"

"You need to cut down on the coffee, Chad," Milo said.

"Don't you even start," I said, taking a sip of coffee. "Next thing you'll tell me is to quit fortifying it!"

"Alcohol cuts down on fine motor skills," Milo said, "which is why I shoot better than you."

"Oh, you did *not*," Shelbye said, making an "oooh" face.

"Since *when*?" I shouted. "Are you disrespecting Marine marksmanship?"

"No," Milo said. "Just yours."

"*Oh!*" I shouted, pointing in his face. "Oh! It is on!"

"We got a call," Trevor said.

"Thank you, God," Shelbye said. "I was afraid they were going to get into a shooting match right here."

"What we got?" I asked, popping to my feet.

"Some sort of giant frog problem over on St. Charles," Trevor said, handing Shelbye the slip.

"Hoooweee," Shelbye said. "We goin' *uptown!*"

St. Charles Avenue is the ritzy part of New Orleans. There are some questionable areas but by and large all the "right" people tend to live in and around St. Charles. Where it goes downtown as Madam Courtney pointed out, it is also the "right" area for offices.

The street is double one-way with a trolley line running down the middle. It is tree-lined and shaded along almost its entire length and it's a very long street. The buildings are an eclectic mix of residential and commercial. The residences trend towards mansions on large lots, some Victorian era and neo-classical with a few newer that had replaced ones that had succumbed to time. It was a very upscale street, but this was New Orleans and even upscale areas had their issues. Especially if you were a politician, businessman or lawyer.

In New Orleans in the 1980s, if you really wanted to mess with somebody, one popular method was hexing. Hexing could range anywhere from, yes, temporary impotence to death if you hired a crazy-, evil-enough practitioner. Premature baldness was often considered to be a hex by people who had a family history thereof. Instead of, you know, being a baldy.

But if a person had strong wards against hexes, or an example needed to be made, stronger measures were called for. Like attacking their house with a bunch of giant, acid-spitting superfrogs.

In this case, it was a lawyer who had the "issue."

His name was Reginald Katz, Esquire, and he was an immigrant. He'd been sent to New Orleans as part of a merger of an established New Orleans law firm with a much larger NYC-based law firm. Basically, he was there to show these yokels how it was done in the City. He bought a big mansion on St. Charles Avenue, installed his bottle-blonde, fake-boobed, nineteen-year-old trophy wife, rolled up his sleeves in City fashion and went to work.

Part of the shake-up had involved a long-standing property dispute. There was a relatively small piece of property in Marigny. The title was disputed. The current resident, one Odette Lefebvre, 87, insisted that the property had been deeded to her family in perpetuity in the time of her great-grandmother by the last listed property owner. A large NYC-based property company had bought a bunch of dormant titles, including 911 Marigny Street, as part of another merger. They were, on paper, the legal owner. Miss Odette claimed it as right of long standing and on the basis of some rather worn documents of questionable legality.

See, back when the damned Union won the War of Northern Aggression, Odette's great-grandmother had been the mistress and hoodoo woman of one Côme Fred Lestrange. When the slaves were ordered set free, she simply continued her residence at 911 Marigny and her previous positions.

Mr. Lestrange had unquestionably owned the property. However, Lestrange died without official issue. And at the time the property had simply languished legally. Other properties were seized by the Damn Yankees and sold off, but for some reason 911 Marigny was overlooked.

There were other issues. Like Miss Odette had never paid taxes on said property. She was, from a legal POV, not much more than a long-term squatter.

Nobody had brought that up in her long life though, because Miss Odette was a hoodoo woman of some note.

I've talked a lot about the bad side of hoodoo and some people, Milo, would tend to see hoodoo, technically houdoun, as nothing but bad. But the truth is, it's a very nuanced sect.

Houdoun is not a black and white religion. They have the Black and the White but they also have the Dark and the Light. Most practitioners wander in the realm between these four. Some are strongly White or Light but may occasionally wander into the Dark or even the Black. They don't find this "wrong." It's more or less a matter of personal choice.

I'll try to explain that in real terms and try to give some idea of the nuances.

Necromancy derives, almost assuredly, from the Old Ones. They are very very bad. Nobody wants the Old Ones to reappear and I've had to kill enough freshly risen zombies to really want that power to disappear.

But think about this. Say that you've got one last thing you need to do. You've been killed and your family is in danger. You're the only one who can save them. But you're dead. Nothing you can do. Even heaven's got to kind of suck. Or they're not even going to be killed. Enslaved. Held by vampires. Choose something really bad on toast that only *you* can prevent. But you're dead.

Would you choose to come back as a revenant? They have their memories. Soul gets tricky and it might damn you to hell. But would you choose to come back to save your family? Lots of people would choose yes.

So in some circumstances even the power of the Black, necromancy, has some semilegitimate uses.

I wouldn't, by the way. It's not that I wouldn't care, I would. But from the POV of eternity, no matter how bad it was and how long it lasted, it's better for them to not have me come back and potentially damn my immortal soul. Or maybe I'm just a hardhearted bastard. Unless God sends me back, I'll just wait in the Green Lands, thanks.

The Dark is casting hexes and summoning things. Also talking with and using the Dark loas. Those are generally believed to be human souls damned to hell, or demons. The fire imps that I'd faced in the cemetery my first day in New Orleans were from a Dark casting.

On the other hand, the minor hexes that a few of the team used—on the down low, because the Shacklefords would flip their lids—were also Dark casting.

Wards, blessings, healings were from the Light and the White. The White was generally considered to be God or Saints. The Light I suspected was close to Fey magic. Not that all Fey, or any Fey, were goody two-shoes.

Miss Odette was a well-known Light priestess. She did fortunes, minor healings, provided herbal medicines and warding charms and spells. She was right around the corner from where I lived and even I had picked up a couple of her charms. They were good charms. I've seen them work. And it was well known that the more good you do for someone the more power you get. And in houdoun, power is power. White, Black,

Dark, Light, it's all power. She was a very powerful hoodoo woman and just because that power had generally been Light didn't mean she didn't have contacts on the Dark and Black sides.

So it being New Orleans, everybody knew not to rock the boat. Because even the Light can get pissy when it's being disrespected. Nobody pointed out, officially, that taxes were not being paid. Nobody asked who really owned the property. Judges were easy with continuances on Miss Odette's side and her lawyers were pro bono. You don't mess with hoodoo and you hope to gain favors in general.

Enter Reginald Katz, Esquire. Reginald was fifty-five, on his third trophy wife and had come down here to shake things up. He was a big guy, heavy set, dominating, great suit and tie collection, very good in a courtroom and did not give a flip about hoodoo. The case had been languishing for years. The real estate company, with which he'd worked in NYC, wanted it resolved in their favor. When he came to town they switched representation, their local representation having been, yes, dragging their feet, and Reginald Katz, Esquire, went to work.

He demolished every argument on Miss Odette's side. He had the law on his side and knew how to work the court system. He quickly had it moved to Federal Court, which was a bit less wary of hoodoo since the Feds had really good warding charms and counteragents, and within a month of arrival had won the case. Congrats, Reggie, an 87-year-old woman was going to have to move out of the house she had literally been born in that was almost certainly legally hers based on genetic inheritance. You're the man.

When the Sheriff's deputies arrived they were really apologetic. She was nice to them. She understood they were just doing their job. They and neighbors and the local "neighborhood association" (drug gang) all helped her move to a new home nearby.

Two days later, giant acid-spitting frogs descended in force on the home of Mr. Reginald Katz, Esquire, who along with his trophy wife died screaming.

Agent Higgins really wanted to list it as "Act of God" for reporting reasons.

The house was two stories and large, probably ten thousand feet. De rigueur for the area, it had a low wrought iron fence out front that prevented entry to the grounds and, notably, driveway.

When Shelbye's cousin was working on the grill of Honeybear, he'd sort of automatically installed a heavy steel brush bumper. Another way to describe that is a ramming bumper. Two thick pieces of horizontal tubular steel with intervening vertical smaller pieces attached firmly to the frame. Sort of thing you see in *Mad Max*.

I really didn't like the look and it made the front end heavy. Then I realized I was working for Hoodoo Squad and he'd known that and done me a favor. I had to wonder if maybe I should get heavy screens over all the windows and maybe the same thing for the windshield. Whatever.

That flimsy, weak, pathetic fence was no match for Honeybear.

"Hah, hah!" I bellowed, pulling into the driveway. "I am the Honeybear!"

"We could have checked to see if it was open," Milo said.

"Screw that, my fine moral friend," I said, getting out. "We are the Hoodoo Squ—What the *fuck*?"

That exclamation was caused by looking at the roof and what was on it.

You ever see one of those photos of Amazonian tree frogs? They call them "arrowhead" frogs. The ones with all sorts of psychedelic colors? Electric blues and purples and the brightest orange on the face of the earth? The ones that sort of seem to reflect the sunlight, big bulbous eyes, like something on an acid trip?

Okay, imagine you're looking at the front of this big Victorian mansion that looks like Disney's idea of Tara in *Gone with the Wind*. Manicured yard, nice trees...

And on top of it has hopped one of those frogs. Mostly an electric blue with green markings and big, bright pink circles in the markings.

As big as a rhinoceros.

And it's *looking* at you.

Miss Odette was one powerful-as-*shit* hoodoo woman. This is why in New Orleans, you don't fuck with the hoodoo.

"Son of a..." Milo said, his mouth hanging open.

"Oh, these is gonna be *good* eatin'!" Shelbye shouted. "We be havin' a fais do-do for the whole *family* after this'n!"

There was a crack of an M14 and the thing jumped straight up.

Okay, again, picture if you will. This frog the size of a rhinoceros has jumped straight up. Ever seen one of those things hop? Regular ones it's sort of unreal. This one? It wasn't really straight up. It just looked that way. It went up and up and up and...

"It's a bird..." Milo said.

"It's a plane..." I intoned.

"It's SUPERFROG!" we both said.

The fucking thing just kept going. And going. And... it was gone. I mean, we were near the corner of St. Charles and Joseph and the next report was from *Daneel*! The damned thing jumped a block and a half! I swear at apogee it was spread out and catching a breeze off the river. It was like half frog, half bat, all insane.

"Oh," Ray said, in *that* tone. "Even MCB *New Orleans* is going to have problems with *this*."

"Yeah," I said. "But it's guaranteed to make the front page of the *Truth*."

"More like *Time Magazine* if we don't stop them quick."

I went back to Honeybear, opened up the trunk and rummaged until I had Bertha the Barrett out.

"We're gonna need the big guns for this," I said.

"I got one in the van!" Milo said. "Whoever bags the most wins!"

It was ON.

CHAPTER 20
Time of the Season

Reginald Katz, Esquire, and his new trophy wife, Claudine, were in the back by the pool. They were quite dead. They were both nude. It was midweek but perhaps he'd come home to celebrate after chucking an old woman out of the only home she'd ever known.

They were also mostly bones and those were dissolving.

There were huge, wet traces around the pool. From indications the superfrogs must have generated in the pool, come out and proceeded to pronounce the doom of the hoodoo on the twosome.

There were three frogs left in the backyard, throat sacks inflated, mournfully calling for mates. The sound was as insane as the rest of the mission.

BOOORAAAGAACK! BOOORAAAGAACK! BOOORAAAGAACK!

I had hearing protection in but still shook my stomach and bones. It was like being at an AC/Dfrog concert.

I didn't wait long to open fire.

Milo, the pussy, was lowering his Barrett into the prone. It wasn't but fifty yards. I leaned in and fired offhand.

You can, yes, do that with a Barrett. You actually can get back into battery, back on target, faster offhand than in prone. But the damned thing is heavy as hell and you'd better have a really good stance.

The first round hit the frog on the left, right square in the kisser. One down. No princess for *you*, Superfrog!

That caused the other two to go full-on superfrog and head for points unknown. By the way, turned out there was another one which had already superfrogged away.

We all opened fire as the frogs took to the air. I don't know if that was the right move or not. Yes, rounds come down and do occasionally injure or kill people. That wasn't really the problem. The problem was, so do frogs the size of rhinoceri. I was pretty sure they could adjust their landings to land on something other than people. I mean, they might land on some minivan carpooling a soccer team, but I could just see one of those things coming down in a crowd in downtown, which wasn't far. That would be bad.

Whether it was good or not to hit them on the way up, I was sure I had.

"I tagged the one on the left!" I shouted. I'd taken off the scope and was firing iron sights. It was like shooting skeet. Enormous, psychedelic skeet.

"So did I," Shelbye said. "That one's mine! What we bettin' for?"

"Bragging rights," I said.

"Whatever we're betting for, they're gone," Ray said. "Okay. I'm calling up everybody. We need to get these things under control. Fast. Right now we'll split into two-man teams. Uh..."

"I get Shelbye," I said. "Sorry, bud, but we're in competition."

"I got Ray," Milo said instantly.

"Team comp," I said. "I'll call Trevor and get him started on the pool."

"This is not a..." Ray said. "Okay, fine. Whatever." He paused and looked at Milo for a second. "Tell Trevor I got fifty bucks on Team Shackleford," he said quickly.

"Done," I said, trotting for Honeybear. "You comin', Shelbye?"

"Jist about," Shelbye said. "This is gonna be fun! And I got a hunnert says we get more!"

"Call dispatch," I said. "Tell Juliette over there we're in a betting race and she needs to call us before she calls Trevor. Fifty-yard-line tickets for the first Saints home game."

Bertha was sitting across both our laps with the muzzle brake out the passenger side window. I wasn't going to lose a shot 'cause I had to get her out of the trunk.

"That's cheatin'!" Shelbye said, picking up the car phone. "I lahk it!"

Now I just had to get fifty-yard-line seats for the first Saints home game.

"I think that first one went towards Isidore," I said, turning on lights and sirens and making the turn onto Octavia. I think the posted speed limit's like twenty-five. I was doing seventy by the time I got to the stop sign. I slowed for that, honking my horn as well as hitting the *AHOOOGAH* siren, and pushed through. The next block I saw a heavy-set woman running. Fat women don't run. Not even while jogging.

"Hey!" I yelled out the window. "Which way'd that giant frog go?"

"That way," she screamed, pointing back over to the right.

"Thanks," I yelled as we sped away.

"Best way that way?" I yelled to Shelbye.

"Hang a raht!" she yelled.

There were a couple cars going way too fast *away* from the direction of the Isidore Newman School. School would get out soon. That meant more traffic, and more potential victims. Also, for the MCB, more witnesses. I thought of the animal lover from the airport. Would Castro murder a school kid? Probably. I made the turn at Saratoga.

Some kids were running.

"I think we're close!" Shelbye yelled.

"You think?" I asked. "What gave you your first clue?"

I drove up on the sidewalk, laying on the horn and trying not to kill kids, maneuvered around a bus, nearly hit two kids, and stuck my head out the window.

"*Where is it?*" I yelled.

"Ball field," the girl yelled as she ran...away...fast.

Smart kid.

"You know where the ball field is?" I asked.

"Yeah," Shelbye said. "We played Newman one time. Kicked their ass, the snooty pansies. Get back on Daneel. Raht!"

There was a lady hurriedly walking in the opposite direction. She was holding a young teenage boy in a school uniform by the hand. He didn't look as if he minded. You could tell he'd normally be like "Ah, Mommm" but at the moment he was happy with the reassurance.

"Where's it at?"

The lady just looked at me in shock for a second.

"The damned frog, lady," I said, pulling Bertha out of the front seat.

"It went that way," she said, pointing back over her shoulder.

"Ball field's that way," Shelbye said.

"One frog stew, coming up."

"Beeg damn frog stew," Shelbye said, grinning. "Gonna have us some good eats tonight!"

Imagine if you will.

On a standard football field there are two groups practicing. At one end is the male lacrosse team. At the other end is the female field hockey team. They are kept well dispersed to keep the players focused on their game. But, you know, there are looks. Hey, he looks good in shorts. Wow, Amanda is really hot today…

Suddenly, a fucking frog the size of a rhinoceros drops out of the clear blue sky.

Her name was Miss Janet Windersly. I mean, that wasn't her fault or anything. I've had to suffer with Oliver Chadwick my entire life.

She was the assistant field hockey coach. Miss Windersly had never married. She lived in a house in Metairie with a very long term roommate, Claudette. To the extent that there were men in her life, they tended to be the type to steal her ball gowns.

Miss Windersly was athletic, muscular, horse-faced and just a touch manly. She was a force of dominance on the field hockey field, always bellowing at the girls in what might, kindly, be called a contralto.

She also made sure to stay near the *center* of the field so as to ensure that the girls kept their eyes on their play and not things on the other end of the field.

When what we will hereafter call Sierra Two, on its second hop, did, yes, use a bit of gliding ability to adjust its landing, it was looking for something big, clear and preferably green.

Why, look down there, Superfrog! A big, green spot to land!

So what if there were a few minor insects on it? It was using up a lot of calories in this weird place. Might as well pick up a snack.

Sierra Two landed within ten yards of Miss Windersly with a massive *THUD*.

Sierra Two maneuvered around a bit, assessing is surroundings. Then a twenty-yard-long tongue lashed out and Miss Windersly was sucked into its enormous maw.

Its mouth slapped shut with Miss Windersly's field hockey stick still jutting from one side and a couple of thrashing legs out the other. The tongue rotated around a bit and both disappeared from view. A moment later the hockey stick came spitting out like a cherry pit and landed thirty yards away.

There was at this point a certain amount of screaming and running. Fortunately, both groups were athletic.

We happened to be coming in from the direction which was disgorging the field hockey players. A surprising number of them had retained their hockey sticks.

I suppose if it was the only weapon I had in the face of Superfrog I'd probably have held onto it as well.

"Where?" I asked, grabbing one of the cuter hockey players by the arm. "Hoodoo Squad. Where?"

"Who?" she said, jerking her arm. "Let go of me, you *pervert!*"

I grabbed the next one coming along.

"Where?" I asked.

"Hoodoo Squad?" she asked.

"Well, duh," I said, jiggling Bertha.

"Thank God," she said. "Middle of the field last time I looked. It was heading the other way."

Sierra Two had landed between the late, unfortunate Miss Windersly and the charges over which she kept such a personal and proprietary eye. It had, however, been pointed in the general direction of the other end of the field, the reason that Miss Windersly, standing guardingly on the fifty-yard line, had come to its attention.

But in that general direction it pointed was the male lacrosse team. And when they screamed and ran, it gave chase. 'Cause all this exercise was making it hungry. And, well, FOOD.

Frogs generally think like this: Moving, food. Not moving, not food. Smells right, sings right, fuck it.

That's pretty much frog motivations. Pro-tip if you will.

We ran onto the field and looked around. No frog. We could see a gym at the other end of the field and some figures inside.

"Scope that front," I said, pointing.

"Just a bunch of kids and some coaches," Shelbye said.

"Tell me it didn't hop again," I said, running that way.

Know how much a Barrett weighs? Thirty-five pounds. Know how much one round of .50 caliber weighs? Four ounces. Doesn't sound like much. I was carrying *forty* rounds of .50 caliber in magazines. The magazines alone weighed a pound. Six grenades. More .45 mags. And I'm not a big guy. And I was just getting back in shape. The heat, the humidity. I was sweating my ass off running down that damned football field.

"Wait," Shelbye said, holding up her hand. *Shelbye* was outrunning me. But the hell if I was facing Superfrog without the reassurance of Bertha the Big Blue Barrett. She looked through her scope again. "They're trying to signal something..."

"What?"

"They keep pointing... Up?"

I looked at the top of the gym.

Superfrog looked back. Then it jumped.

At us.

I missed the head. I mean, give me a break, hitting the head would have required another miracle, but the .50 caliber round hit Superfrog in the body and really messed it up.

Unfortunately, we now had an enraged and wounded Superfrog headed right for us in mid-air.

When you have a good shoulder weld with a Barrett it just pushes you back. When there's a gap, it has time to accelerate into your shoulder. Felt like being kicked by a mule. I still got the fuck out of Superfrog's way.

It hit in a slide on the 45 line, leaving behind a trail of blood and some guts. Then it got up and now it was pissed. And looking at *me*. It looked like it was either choking or gathering up a loogie. *Guphf, guphf, guphf.*

I was on my back with Bertha five feet away and that might as well have been in the end zone. I scrambled back.

The acid loogie landed where I'd been lying.

The two of us shot the hell out of it. I emptied Bertha, then pulled my .45 and put a few magazines into Superfrog.

It finally croaked.

Sorry. You had to know that was coming.

"Fuck, yeah," I said, grinning. The Superfrog was splayed flat out with its tongue hanging out.

"Oh, I bet they taste great," Shelbye said, walking over. *"Laissez les bons temps rouler!"*

"Careful," I said, reloading Bertha. "The skin on those is poisonous. At least the regular ones. I'd bet this one is, too."

"We'll figure out how to skin it," Shelbye said. "Pump it full'n air prob'ly."

"I get the trophy from the other one," I said. "I wonder if somebody has a camera?"

Then it started to get up again.

Fucker's regenerated.

"What do we do now?" Shelbye said. "Cain't take its head. It's poisonous. We'd need gear."

"I should have brought Mo No Ken," I said, still covering it. It started to get up again and I put another .50 round in it. "I got an idea. Cover me."

I walked away, set Bertha down on her bipod and pulled out a white phosphorus grenade. There was another shot from Shelbye.

"You best hurry," Shelbye said. "Three-oh-eight seems to jess piss it off."

"Get ready to pry open its mouth," I said.

I walked back over, pulled my pistol and shot it seven times in the head, right where you pith a frog.

"Now, pry open its mouth," I said, holstering and pulling the pin on the incendiary grenade. While I was doing so, my .45 rounds started to pop out of its head, one by one.

Tough amphibian.

Hey, I'd just found a new way to do ballistics tests!

Shelbye inserted the barrel of her M14 into the thing's mouth and pried it open. I knelt down, put the grenade into its mouth, let go of the spoon, shoved my hand and the grenade into its throat and then tried to pull my hand back out.

These days there's a movement afoot to stop teaching kids dissection in high school biology because it's a bad thing. But even if you've taken dissection, you generally gloss over the details of frog anatomy related to the esophagus. Thus even I, world expert on fucking everything, perfect C in frog anatomy, was unaware that there was a bit in there that was designed to make sure that food only went *one way*.

Which, in part due to a human leg, was trapping my right hand.

"Oh, hell. I'm stuck."

"That ain't good," Shelbye said.

But I had an ace in the hole. I was wearing Nomex flight gloves. And they might be stuck but my hand wasn't. I managed to wriggle out of them and backed off, fast.

There was a *Poof* and the most hellish smoke came pouring out of the damned thing.

Then the Superfrog started to deliquesce.

"AH, HEY-LL," Shelbye yelled. "Not one of *those*! Shee-yit!"

"Well, we still got the PUFF," I said. "That's gonna have to be good on one of these."

"I know, but still," she said. "All this shit that done turn to goo. Seems like a waste of good meat, yuh know?"

"Is it dead?"

The man yelling looked like a coach.

"It's dead," I yelled back. "But we don't know where the other ones went!"

"Other ones!"

We took a sample—there was a body in the stomach, which was the sort of thing we needed to prevent—and headed back to the car. By the time we got there, there was an NOPD car on scene. MCB was on the way. We left them to it and got on the phone.

"Trevor, Hand," I said when I got through to the office. "Be advised. These things regenerate."

"We know," he said drily. *"Fortunately it was MCB who was on site when the one you supposedly killed sat up and got…"*

"Froggy?" I asked. "Well, we just got one at Newman school."

"That's not good."

"It's croaked. On a serious note, did they lose anybody?"

"No, but Higgins ain't real happy with you."

"Well, tell him he's in on the pool," I said. "By the way, I got two hundred bucks on Team Bertha."

"Bertha?" Shelbye snarled. "Bertha?"

Shelbye was serious about watching her weight.

"The Barrett," I said, putting my hand over the phone.

"Oh," she said, mollified.

"We got any more reports?"

"All over the city. Dispatch has been going crazy. These things move."

"MCB must be loving this," I said, trying not to laugh. It wasn't a laughing matter. People were dying. But...Superfrogs.

My radiophone began to ring and Shelbye picked it up. She waved at my call.

"Hey, Trev," I said. "Gotta go. Call later. What?"

Shelbye was laughing like a loon as she hung up the phone.

"You ain't gonna believe this!" she said, laughing so hard she was crying.

"What?" I asked. "Where am I going?"

"There's one on the Superdome!"

"Well, shit," I said. "There's no way we're getting..."

I picked up the phone and called home.

"Remi," I said. "Didn't you say that one of your previous employers owned a helicopter...?"

CHAPTER 21
Fly Like an Eagle

Mr. Albert Aristide Lambert was a named partner of Lambert, Klein, Masson and Kempf, one of New Orleans' most prestigious law firms. The Lamberts went back to the second wave of Louisiana colonization, which was when the "better types," second sons of aristocratic French families, came to the New World seeking large land grants.

The Lamberts had never blown their money, or had a son addicted to gambling, or lost it all in any number of speculative ventures that had cost their peers their fortunes over the years. They had by and large been on the smart side in such things. They had thus over the centuries amassed a considerable fortune.

By the way, in contrast to Mr. Katz, Mr. Lambert had been married for forty-two years to the same woman. Mr. Lambert was not a believer in "trophy wives" and distrusted partners who engaged in such foolishness. They should just get a mistress like any intelligent fellow. Mistresses were much less costly to turn over than wives. And if the fires were damping on their wives, clearly they just needed a new pool boy or possibly lady's maid as the wife preferred.

The bourgeois annoyed Mr. Lambert.

Remi had been a junior house manager to the Lamberts for five years before gently asking to be released from employ to take up a new position. The Lamberts were aware of his loss, they had sent a very kind wreath to the funeral of his wife and son. They gave him an excellent recommendation and a quite generous severance despite it being his choice to leave.

So when Remi called and delicately asked his former employer for the loan of his helicopter, after explaining the issue, Mr. Lambert politely agreed.

All this hoodoo was bad for business. And it turned out that he could see the damned thing from the window of his top-floor corner office on St. Charles Avenue.

However, as his grandfather once told him, hoodoo was simply one of the costs of doing business in New Orleans. Giant killer frogs could never break out in the pool of the Lambert residence. It had the strongest wards possible. Only idiots from New York City didn't have wards on their homes and businesses. Not to mention were idiotic enough to bring suit against a powerful houdoun priestess.

The chopper set down at the Daneel Playground shortly after. Agent Buchanan had arrived at the school and was busy trying to collect the names of witnesses. I had no idea how Castro was going to spin this. Every time people had come around us, Shelbye had waved them back. Most of them wanted to know if the killer frogs were coming back.

Not if I could help it.

I'd brought Mo No Ken this time, loaded a couple of magazines of tracer and had lots of thermite grenades on my vest. I intended to shoot a Superfrog off the Superdome.

The dome of the Superdome was made of cloth held up by internal pressure. I wasn't sure how much fire it could take. And actually killing the Superfrog might be tough. That might require landing on the dome itself. We couldn't land the chopper, obviously. But I might have to get out and burn the thing. There was a technique for that I'd practiced a couple of times in the Marines. It wasn't getting *out* that was the problem, it was getting back in.

Also that I'd be dropping onto some sort of balloon roof.

As the helo landed, I realized we had another problem right away. The doors didn't slide open. They opened like a car door. So opening them to take a shot was questionable.

I ran over to the pilot's door and waved to open it. The engine was still going, the rotors turning and I had to shout to be heard.

"You understand what we're doing? I have to take a shot from this. With this," I added, hefting the Barrett.

"We'll have to remove the doors," the pilot yelled. "And, yeah, I know how to do this. You?"

"Never," I said. "Marine but not this kind!"

"I used to be a Nighthawk! We need somewhere to put the doors."

"Will they fit in a car?" I asked.

We drove Honeybear up on the field as a crowd gathered. NOPD had been dispatched, realized it was

Hoodoo Squad and set up a perimeter. They weren't sure what was going on and generally didn't want to know.

I was in a hurry. I wasn't sure how many Milo had gotten by now but my two had turned into a one. I needed to put another point on the board. And I needed to be sure that people in the City of New Orleans were safe, of course. That was the main point. Definitely.

And beating Milo like a stump.

The doors fit in Honeybear. We loaded all our gear and put on headsets. We were in the air seconds later.

"I'm fine with you talking me through this," I said. "We've got one target on the Superdome that I know of."

"Not the first time I've done something like this."

"Do I ask?" I asked.

"No," the pilot said. "You know what Nighthawks are?"

"No," I admitted.

"Special Operations Aviation Regiment. Plank holder. Let's say I've carried a lot more Rangers than lawyers. And I've seen a lot more weird shit than you'd think."

"Want to switch jobs?" I asked.

"I got married and had a kid. Reason I got out. So, no. The main thing I want to do is not bend the bird. We're not insured for this. I pointed that out to my boss and he said he understood. But if we bend the bird I guarantee you, your firm will be facing one hell of a lawsuit."

"Then let's not bend the bird. I really want to make money on this job. And beat my best friend like a piñata."

"Oh?" the pilot said.

"We're in a race to see how many we can get," I said. "Teams. He insulted my shooting. I'm a Marine. There's no worse insult. Major problem. These things regenerate. That's . . . oh, you probably know, don't you?"

"Yes," the pilot said. "And it's an issue. Especially given where your target is. Look to port."

The size of the massive dome was evident by the fact that a rhino-sized frog on it looked like it was a normal-sized, even tiny frog.

"Tiny little baby frogs," I said in an English accent.

"I saw it on the way over. It hasn't moved since it landed there."

Special Agent in Charge Castro would be glad of that. Maybe he could say it was a neon weather balloon that had gotten stuck there or something. It was just kind of hanging out. The only movement was when Superfrog's throat sack inflated. I couldn't hear it from up here but I suspected you could on St. Charles, which was about a mile away.

"This is fun," Shelbye said.

"Other issue. No safety harness."

"I got some 550 cord," I said. "What about the side blast?"

"Compared to, say, the rotor blast?" the pilot asked. The interior of the chopper was already filled with it and I got his point. "You're going to be shooting downward at a very steep angle. Can you calculate for that?"

"Yes," I said simply.

For angle shooting, the bullet only sees the flat ground distance between you and a target (effect of gravity). So when you place yourself at an angle to the target in elevation, you are seeing the target along the hypotenuse of a right triangle. So to get the elevation difference between the distance you perceive to the target along the hypotenuse of the right triangle and the distance the bullet is actually affected by the gravity (which is the flat ground distance), you must multiply the range along the GTL by the cosine of the angle to the target. This will give you your actual true range that you need to adjust for to hit the target.

For example, an angle of 45 degrees has a cosine of .7, which means that you actually have the range of 70 degrees of whatever your observable distance is from that angle. For a .50 machine-gun round, that means an impact difference of about 20 inches at 500 meters with a 45 degree angle.

Ballistic calculations were what drove most sniper school candidates nuts. Fortunately, I got a perfect C in trigonometry.

"I'll try to stop about five hundred meters out and in as steady a hover as I can get with these wind conditions," the pilot continued. "Try to get the sucker with the first shot."

I used some parachute cord, colloquially 550 cord, to secure my vest to the helo. Then I used more to secure Bertha to my body. I put in a quick release knot on both so I could undo them.

"How's the wind?"

"The way we're coming in?" the pilot said. "From right to left more or less, about ten knots."

"I'm not sure about how to finish it off. I can do a dust-off onto the roof but... Can you keep your footing on that?"

"Hold on," the pilot said. "Hey, girlie, there's a phone back there. Hook the intercom into it."

"How?" Shelbye asked.

The frog hadn't gone anywhere. It was still mournfully calling for a mate. Must be the time of the season in whatever dimension they came from. Or maybe they were just like me and mating season was any season.

I had to think it was getting dried out up there. It wasn't humid enough for a frog like that to appreciate direct sunlight. They preferred nighttime and shade. Then I realized I was trying to equate normal frog behavior to a giant, acid spitting, regenerating Superfrog. Maybe it preferred the sunlight for the heat?

We got the phone hooked up and the pilot had Shelbye dial a number.

"Gary, Tom," the pilot said.

"Hey, Tom. What's up?"

I had no idea who Gary was.

"Boss loaned me to take care of a little problem *your* boss has at the moment," the pilot, presumably named Tom said. "We're up here over the Dome."

"Thought that might be you. I'm inbound at your eight. Hoodoo on board?"

"Roger. They want to know if they can do a dust-off on the roof."

"It will support them, but—stand by, putting on my onboard. This is Bart Tocca, he's one of the facility engineers. Bart, what about standing on the roof?"

"Can't you just shoot it?" someone, presumably Bart, asked.

"I have to get to it physically and either put a fire grenade in its gut or cut its head off. Come to think of it, forget the problems of standing on that gas bag. They melt into acidic slime when they die. I just realized either of those could be bad."

"Yeah, you make a major cut and you're going to

go for a several-hundred-foot drop," Bart said. *"And what kind of fire?"*

"The kind that will be guaranteed to burn right through. I may be able to do the cut without cutting into the roof. But . . ." I thought about it and then realized there was something else to consider. "Oh, by the way, I need fifty-yard-line tickets to the first Saints game. You can get those, right? But I suppose that's not important right now."

Everyone on the connection laughed until a voice broke in.

"Goddamned right it's not," the voice said. *"You bust my roof, I'll sue the crap out of you!"*

"You want this thing off your roof or no? 'Cause there are three more wandering around the city and I can chase *them.*"

There was a long pause.

"Get that thing off my roof without a major hole and I'll get you season Goddamned tickets to the fifty-yard line," the voice said.

"You want to after this is over, go and look at the big blob on the forty-yard line of Isidore Newman School. I'm pretty sure it's still burning a hole in the ball field."

"Isidore? Why there?"

"Frog landed on their ball field."

"Any casualties?" It wasn't "boss tone," it was "worried tone."

"A coach. No kids luckily."

"Get this damned thing," the man said. *"And we need to finish this call. Fast."*

The Superfrog still looked content. "I've got an idea. I need NOPD or Dome security or someone to clear the area on the shady side. When that's done we'll try to herd it off the roof either to the ground or onto the side. Then we'll take the shot, land and dispatch. Sound like a plan, Tom?"

"As long as this bird comes no closer than five hundred meters," Tom said.

"We need to go back to intercom. Can whoever I'm talking to get the area clear? I don't want civilians getting hurt when it comes down. Oh, and I'm going to have to put bullet holes in the fabric. That's a must. So you need to clear the interior."

"Got that," the boss said. *"That we can repair. Acid burns not so much."*

"Call us when the area is clear. Out," Tom said. "Okay, we're back on intercom."

"These things regenerate fast. When we get it down, we need to be on it fast to take it all the way out. At short range, .45 will keep it down. Enough in the right place, anyway. So once it is out, yeah, I need you to drop us as close as you possibly can."

"There's a reason I got out of this shit," the pilot said with a sigh.

It was about fifteen minutes later when the air-phone rang. The MCB was going nuts. *They* were even out hunting the things. So far only Team Bertha and Team MCB had a definite score up on the board. Ray and Milo had been chasing one and nearly run the van into a canal. Milo had nailed it from across the canal, anyway, only to see it sit back up and jump away.

"We've got the interior and most of the exterior cleared," boss voice said. *"And, by the way, thank you."*

"Why?" I said, thinking about the shot.

"I just got ahold of my daughter. You the guy carrying 'the biggest gun I've ever seen in my life, Dad'?"

"She a really level-headed brunette, five two, plays field hockey?"

"No. Blonde. Bit of an airhead."

"Oh, yeah, she did great," I said, rolling my eyes.

"Thanks to you two. Now get that thing off my roof."

"Okay, let's go in for a shot approach. Every time these things have been dinged, they jump. So far, enough up and back it can't get us and I'll shoot it. Try to drive it off the roof."

"Hope it doesn't spit," the pilot said.

"Me too," I said. "I owe somebody tickets."

We approached from up and back and Tom came to a hover at five hundred meters distance.

We were practically right over it. The distance over ground was about ten meters. There *were* no ballistics as such. The bullet was both firing and falling straight down.

"Winds?" I asked.

"Picking up a bit," the pilot said. "Hang on."

The craft drifted a bit.

"Thirteen knots here," he said.

"You're good."

"Yes, yes, I am."

I spotted the big frog in the scope. It was massive at this range. I didn't want to actually harm it. Just get it to hop. I aimed at its tail and fired.

The round missed and hit the roof a few inches behind it. But the wind of its passage and the supersonic crack must have spooked the thing. It hopped.

I tried the same thing. I was further away this time and it didn't move. Then it turned and hopped back in the general direction it had come from. Shit.

I adjusted based on those two shots and tried again. That time I hit it in the leg. That caused it to hop, sort of sideways. And it started limping towards the side of the massive building.

A few more shots, one reload, and it crawled over the side into shade.

"Get us in position, Tom! Quick. Right over it."

Tom slid the helo sideways like it was on rails. The guy really was amazing. Then he pivoted so I could get a shot in.

The frog was climbing quickly down the exterior of the building. The wound on its leg was already closed. Damn, these things regenerated like nobody's business.

I lined up the shot and considered the ballistics. We were out from the Dome, at an angle and further away.

The bullet went right through the sweet spot. Superfrog dropped off the side of the Superdome and did a Superimpact into the super parking lot.

"Whooo!" Shelbye shouted.

"Get us down. Fast."

"I gotta drop you on a car." The people might have been evacuated but this must be an employee parking lot. It was packed.

As we dropped down and I hit the thing again, I swear it was already starting to move.

Tom hovered directly over a car. Shelbye wasn't tied in with paracord and got out before I could. I undid the fast knots on my harness and on Bertha. I dropped Bertha on the floor of the chopper and jumped out.

I hit the roof of a new model Mercedes and rolled down onto the hood, then onto the ground landing on my feet. I ran for the frog as fast as I could, charging up to it as it was starting to get to its feet. Shelbye was pumping .308 rounds into its head.

I pounded a whole magazine into its pith point, again. It dropped. Again. Reload.

Then I took Mo No Ken and, wincing at what would happen if I hit the acid sack, sliced into its head.

I got most of the way through and then sawed the rest off. Mo No Ken dug into the concrete of the walkway it was on and I nearly cried.

The frog began to deliquesce.

"That's two, Milo!" I shouted.

I looked at the goop on my sword and swore. I wasn't sure if I could wipe it down with my usual silk cloth or not. And I had to get it off before it fucked up my sword or dried.

"Fuck it," I said, and wiped it with my remaining glove, hoping the stuff wasn't poisonous.

Pro-tip if you ever have to deal with a Superfrog.

Yeah. Yeah it is. And it penetrates Nomex flight gloves and skin. But it takes a while.

Milo had one up on the board and they were hot on the trail of another. With the one that Higgins got, that only left one more. All the teams were hot on its trail but the fucker kept moving. But my team had a helicopter.

Then Juliette called. She was just thrilled to get fifty-yard-line tickets but they'd gotten a call and there was one in a backyard in Central City on Josephine Street near the intersection with Clara. She was getting around to putting it out where MCB and Trevor could hear but, darn, she'd just broken a nail. It might be a minute or two.

"Head to Josephine. Near the corner of Josephine and Clara."

"I'm not actually from around here," Tom said. "Where?"

"I think I can figure it out," Shelbye said. "It ain't but right over that way," she added, pointing.

"Turn to seven o'clock," I said.

"Ain't far," she said.

Tom turned the helo and put the nose down. Shelbye leaned in and looked out forward.

"See that there canal?" she asked, pointing forward and down. "Slow down as you cross thet."

"Got it," the pilot said.

"Thinkin' it's over there," she said. "Go slow round here . . ."

"There," the pilot said, gesturing with his chin.

"Yeah," I said, spotting the giant neon thing. At least this one wasn't parked on a giant landmark in front of the whole city.

"What the hell is it doing?" Tom asked.

The frog had its rump in the air and its head down in some sort of hole. It seemed to have its tongue down in the hole like an anteater. A moment later something came out of the hole, stuck to the tongue and struggling. I could just get a flash of a red hat and it was gone.

"Heh," Shelbye said, chortling. "It done found a gnome burrow."

"Oh, now I'm conflicted," I said. "I mean, killer frog terrorizes city, sure, go kill it. But it's getting rid of a *gnome* infestation. Damn, to kill or not to kill, that is the question? Whether 'tis the nobler path to allow gnomes to be consumed or follow the path of duty? Gah."

"If Milo gets it, we're gonna have to split the pot," Shelbye said.

"Oh, yeah, that," I said.

I picked up Bertha off the floor.

"Let's try the same thing," I said as the frog started rooting around in the ground again. Seriously, gnomes. Apparently you can't eat just one. "I'll hit and drop it at height. Then we drop, hit it again. Then drop all the way down."

I leaned out and sort of swayed.

"Oooh," I said, my vision blurring.

"Don't fall out!" Shelbye said, grabbing my harness.

"You okay?" Tom asked.

"I think the frog juice is kicking in," I said, slurring. "I sort of got some on my hands on the last one."

"You okay to make the shot?" Tom asked.

"I dunno," I said. My vision was getting *weird*. "Pretty colors! Whoa! It's got *pretty* colors! Okay, I'm good...I'm a Marine. I can do this..."

I lined up the shot and fired just as another gnome was pulled up from the burrow. It was getting sucked into the Superfrog's mouth on the end of its psychedelic pink tongue.

I hit the gnome.

Ever seen what happens when you hit a gnome with a .50 caliber round?

You can't, really. Not unless you've got one of those stroboscopic cameras on it when you do, in which case you're a very very bad person.

But it was pretty much like that film of an apple getting shot. But...splashier.

"Oops," I said. "Missed."

"At least it was quick," Tom said.

Well, the little dude was about to get eaten anyway. The frog was clearly confused by where its snack had gone. One second it was struggling on the sticky end of its tongue, about to enter its maw and the next second it was just a fine mist of blood.

It stuck its head back down the hole. Gnomes must be tasty as hell.

The next shot went through the back of its head and it dropped.

We dropped down. I put another one in. All the way down.

I tumbled out, much less graceful than my usual entry, and stumbled over to the Superfrog. I pulled out my .45 and pulled the trigger. Oops. Didn't reload? Chuckle. That's funny. I pulled out a mag and looked at it, wondering what it was.

"Let me handle this," Shelbye said. She put a round of .308 through its skull.

"When'd you get out of the . . ." I looked at my fingers and worked them like I was counting. "Word. Thingy on top. Goes round . . ." I said, swinging my 1911 around in a circle. "What's that thingy called?"

"Man, you're *seriously* stoned."

"Pretty colors," I said, reaching for the frog. "Feel the pretty colors . . ."

That's about all I can remember. Well, okay, I remember a *lot* of stuff after that but I'm pretty sure the giant purple porcupines were just part of the trip. You never can tell in this business.

I swear this next part is true.

"I have to report what happened," Dr. Ransom said, holding his pen over a form on a clipboard. "It's a federal requirement."

The doctor had dealt with a lot of odd cases in his time in the emergency room but the . . . little person currently occupying the bed in the emergency room seemed to be a special case.

Paramedics responding to one of several incidents of temporary release of a mold toxin that caused brief hallucinatory periods, which only occurred under certain very rare weather conditions which New Orleans *had* briefly experienced and there's no real danger and it's passed, go back to your normal lives, or *possibly* the giant frog attack that hundreds had witnessed, found the much-gang-tattooed little person, heavily bearded and bald, wearing only a pointed red cap and blue jeans, unconscious, lying in the middle of Josephine Street in a very distressed condition. Multiple contusions, lacerations and some sort of weird burn that appeared chemical.

His ID listed his name as "Lyfta Barmhärtigast" but he insisted his name was "Bun-Bun."

"Doc," Bun-Bun said in a squeaky voice, lifting his left arm to swear since his right was in a sling. "I swear on a stack of Bibles, as God is my witness, I'mma just standin' on the corner, mindin' my own damn bidnitt when this giant fuckin' killer frog just *drops out of the clear blue sky*!"

"SOCMOB," Dr. Ransom wrote. "GKF, CBS."

CHAPTER 22
The Mob Rules

Seagulls churned in a squawking mass as some tourist threw them crackers, their wings a deep salmon from the setting sun. Couples walked hand in hand along the beach, shoulders and hips occasionally bumping in a pavane as old as humanity. Older men, the burning passion of youth long damped, sat on chairs with rods in holders, drinking beer and hoping to catch the big one. There's always more fish in the sea.

The first sliver of the full moon was rising over Lake Pontchartrain.

The frog toxin turned out to be a leeetle more dangerous than I'd realized. I spent a few days tripping like Timothy Leary and hooked up to an IV drip before it finally cleared my system.

The good news was it gave me plenty of time to heal up my various hurts. My bicep was as healed up as it was going to get. And, well, the trip while occasionally bad was actually pretty cool. It's not something I'd do voluntarily even if I was into drugs. But it wasn't all bad. And the "bad trip" aspects were mostly sort of banal compared to my actual job. Giant carrots with teeth? Piffle.

Apparently, a big neon parade balloon had been sucked up in the wind and gotten stuck on top of the Superdome. Pretty crazy stuff. The other frogs had been moving fast through residential neighborhoods, so those were either hallucinations, explainable phenomena, or intimidated away. Special Agent in Charge Castro had been so pissed off at having to bully an entire field hockey team that he had personally gone to see Miss Odette about her hex gone wrong.

The old priestess had explained that her spell was not supposed to have been so strong, the frogs so big, and they should have melted back into the pool when their job was done, not rampaged and taken lives of folks not cursed! But the hoodoo, Agent Bill! There's just so much more power building lately! Bad spirits everywhere! Even the weakest of hexes was raising the dead and making monsters bold!

Did Miss Odette know why?

No, Agent Bill, but something was hiding in the dark, making the hoodoo extra strong and out of control. Summon a little thing, it turns *big*. A weak practitioner who would normally struggle to summon an imp would get a mighty Agaran shadow demon instead. It was a mystery, but she knew in her bones it would be worse on the full moon.

And Special Agent in Charge Castro had nodded, agreed that was extremely unfortunate, then drawn his sidearm and shot Miss Odette right between the eyes. On her porch. In broad daylight. He didn't even bother trying to make it look like a suicide. It was Castro's way of leaving a message to the practitioners, that MCB New Orleans had been lenient under his watch, but he was getting really sick of this shit.

Besides that, Juliette got her Saints tickets, but most importantly, Team Bertha won bragging rights.

Another full moon was upon us.

Earl had some business back in Cazador, so Ray and Trevor were in charge. We hoped it wouldn't be like last time, but we hadn't managed to find the werewolf assholes who were biting people—Earl had said they knew how to cover their tracks with wolfsbane—so odds were we'd be facing a whole bunch of new loup-garou again. Plus, more out of control hoodoo raising shamblers and growing giant monsters like Miss Odette had warned of. So safe bet was that it would suck.

The plan was this. We'd break into two-man teams. Ray was adamant that we would not be going in solo and whenever possible we'd use a full team. At least six by preference.

When that was trotted out, I'd raised my hand.

"I get Milo! As long as he's not driving."

While I was in the hospital, we'd gotten some new recruits. They weren't new to MHI, just New Orleans.

Everett Christiansen was tall and slender with thick, curly, beautifully-styled short beige hair. He had that look. I could tell he was going to be competition for ladies at incidents. He was a real shotgun-aholic. Had a Beretta he seriously thought could take down anything in the world. Thought subguns were for pussies. His sidearm was a Bren Ten which he also thought shit gold.

I wasn't sure we were going to get along. He had that tall guy attitude. He was from Chicago and thought anywhere else was pussy work. Chicago had the baddest monsters in the world. He was kind of snotty about Mo No Ken.

I was looking forward to seeing his expression at Maurice's in three days. Assuming he survived.

Fred Ramsey was shorter than I am, had really beady blue eyes and a curly black beard and long black hair he wore in a ponytail. He had the definite feel of a cutup which I was fine with. He was built like a carrot. Narrow waist, really weirdly broad shoulders. I almost asked him if he was actually a dwarf and did he count for PUFF. He'd taken a transfer from California 'cause he was "sick and tired of granola eaters getting in the way of killing monsters." Must be even worse than Seattle.

Brent Waters was a big, heavy-set, good ole boy from North Carolina which he pronounced "Noath Cahrlahner." Brown beard, bald, he had a perpetual wad of chew in his left cheek. Beechnut Wintergreen was his preferred chew and he always had stashes when he went out on call. He had been working the Carolina teams and took the transfer 'cause things were slow and he was looking for the PUFF.

A freaking Winchester lever action .30-30 of all damned things was his primary. He did his own silver reloads. I was looking forward to him trying to keep the damned thing loaded in the crunch. Not to mention I told him he'd better have a couple thousand rounds already reloaded. He laughed. I told him I was serious.

And that gave us seven again. The Magnificent Seven, since I was the only wannabe samurai. With the seven from Cazador, we had fourteen. Should be enough, right?

I'd invited Milo to join my personal ritual for preparing for the full moon. He'd been working pretty steadily the last week but was willing to play along.

He was sort of uncomfortable going to a Catholic church, but he was glad that at least I was giving religion the old school try. He lectured me on sins of the flesh all the way to dinner and I pointed out I was far more of an expert on the subject, thank you. I had to explain the concept of shriven. He didn't think much of it. Mormons. Can't live with 'em and they're heavily armed so killing 'em's actually sort of tough.

We had our last supper at Marchal's. Milo wasn't really into fancy food but he agreed it was good eating. The restaurant wasn't crowded at 3 P.M. but during our seven-course meal various people stopped by and wished us luck.

Milo was starting to get the picture that it might be a bit different.

After the fine meal which I washed down with wine and Milo washed down with a Coke—because, yes, apparently they can drink caffeine—we drove out to Lake Pontchartrain to watch the moon rise.

"This isn't a bad ritual, Chad," he finally admitted.

"I know you're supposed to live for the next world, not this," I said seriously. "We see enough hell on earth, I try to find as much heaven as I can in the middle."

"I suppose there's some sense in that."

"I think you're a great guy, Milo. I'm glad you've got your faith. Just can't quite wear a hair shirt myself. Or green socks with sandals for that matter."

"Hey, my sandals are super comfy. Besides, I wear hiking boots when I'm working."

"Actually, if there's one thing I'd change it would be your wardro—"

The phone rang. The moon was up. And it starts.

❖   ❖   ❖

Tilford Road was typical suburbia. Lower-middle-class working neighborhood. Single-story ranch homes, mostly brick. The one New Orleans touch was most of them had barred windows.

The loup-garou dad had gotten the whole family, again. One of the sons had managed to make it out of the house and onto the roof using a ladder, then cleverly pulled it up. Problem being, loup-garou could make that jump.

Milo was shining a spot out the open window trying to spot the werewolf. Three of our cars were patrolling the area.

"Hoodoo, if you're listening," the scanner squawked with Juliette's voice. *"Code seven-two, Tilford Road. Code seven-two, Spain Street. Code seven-two, St. Charles Avenue, uptown. Code seven-two, Eleventh Street, Gretna. Code seven-two, Wichers Drive, Merera. Code nine-six, General Fochs. Call me. Unit nine-four, respond Ten-niner..."*

There was a flurry of shots. Three-oh-eight, by the sound of it. From behind us. Then some pistol.

"Werewolf's down," Katie radioed.

"You're waiting on coroner, then," I radioed back. Katie had taken Brent Waters, the big North Carolinian, as her partner. "We're out of here." I hit the lights and sirens and peeled out.

"I'm trying to find those streets," Milo said, unfolding a map and putting on the overhead light.

"Trevor will give assignments." We had barely started. So much for Ray's hope of six men at each event.

The phone rang and Milo picked it up. He listened for a second.

"Okay, we're on it," Milo said and hung up. "We're

supposed to go single team on the werewolf on Spain Street."

"Seventh Ward it is," I said skidding through the turn onto Lake Forest Boulevard.

"Where is Spain Street?" Milo said, looking back and forth at the map. He let go of it for a second and the wind whipped it out the still-open window. "Son of a . . . gun!"

"Spare in the glove compartment," I said, laughing. "I'm good to the 10. Not sure which is the best exit off the 10. So you've got till then."

I put in a cassette as I blew through the red light at Crowler. This called for some Golden Earring. Right turn and the damned Honda that thought it had the right of way should have paid attention to the sirens. He stood on his brakes and honked his horn. I gave him the finger and kept going.

"Take . . . Elysian Fields," Milo said a couple of minutes later.

"Dammit," I said, sliding right through three lanes from the left. I cut off a Caddy that stood on its horn. I swear to God it was the same asshole who'd asked me for directions last full moon. I nearly lost Honeybear getting onto the exit but the tightened-up shocks held it together. Then I was on the off-ramp and going like a bat out of hell. I stood on the brakes as we came into the intersection and stopped at the light in a cloud of blue. I made a mental note to get new tires. There was heavy traffic this time of night on Elysian.

"Go . . . left," Milo said, moving the map back and forth again. It's like he'd never heard of folding them.

"I know go left. What then?"

It was one of those funky intersections with a median in the middle of the road and you had to go about fifty yards and there were all these freaking lanes...

I just drove out into the oncoming traffic slowly and dared them to hit me.

When it was clear the front cars were getting the picture, I floored it to the other side and repeated the performance.

"I think..." Milo said, still trying to figure out the New Orleans map.

"I'd let *you* drive but you drive like an old lady."

"I do not drive like an old lady. Just because I am a decent, cautious driver does not mean I drive like an old lady."

"You just described an old lady," I said, cruising down Elysian Fields Avenue. I thought that was apropos. The Green Lands. I was mostly looking for blue lights. I knew Spain Street was around here, somewhere.

"It's left," Milo said suddenly. "Turn left."

I'd just passed a cross street. The next one was one-way, the wrong way. And it had traffic.

"Buckle up," I said, turning left, across oncoming traffic into Johnson going the wrong way on a one-way street. Again. This was becoming a pattern even I didn't like.

"Oh, *heck* no!" Milo shouted, putting both hands on the roof, like that was going to help.

"Hey, we're right by the office," I said, reaching down and picking up a canteen. I opened it one-handed as I weaved through oncoming traffic at about 45. "Thought this area looked familiar." I took a drink. "Keep an eye out for Spain," I added.

"There!" We nearly crashed into a station wagon.

It hit the brakes and its horn. Didn't the idiot see the violet lights? "There! Turn right!"

"Now, *where* on Spain?" I asked as we got onto Spain in one last blare of horns. It was a long street and I wasn't seeing any blue lights.

"How the heck should *I* know?" he asked, shuddering. "You are f... insane, Chad. *Billions of blistering blue barnacles in a thundering typhoon!*" he shouted.

"What?" I said, looking around. "What kind of a cuss is *that*?"

You could tell there was hoodoo in the neighborhood. Spain Street was a street street. It was one of those places cars should be cruising up to corners to do deals. There were always people peacefully sitting on their porches, walking down the street carrying a Bible, or just standing on the corner minding their own damned business. The kind of place where some guy just jumped out of nowhere and did a smack-down.

The ghetto, in other words.

And there were always people out on the street, especially this time of night. This was getting on to prime street time. But not tonight. They were locked up tight behind barred windows and heavy doors. 'Cause there was hoodoo in the night.

I nearly got T-boned crossing Robertson. But in a few blocks we saw the NOPD car, buttoned up tight.

"What's the last report?" I yelled through his closed window.

The cop cracked his window a bit.

"Headed over towards Urquhart," he yelled then closed his window.

"Shit," I swore, doing a three-point turn and nearly getting hit by an old Chevy. I hit my *AHOOOGAH!*

siren and the guy held up his hands as if to say "Sorry!" He'd finally noticed the purple lights. I needed some on top and back.

I headed back to Urquhart, then started cruising slow, looking for any sign. Nothing.

"Screw this," I said, stopping at the corner of St. Roche and Urquhart. I got out and pulled out a bull-horn from behind my seat.

"Best get up and out," I said. St. Roche is another one of those double one-way, large median in the middle, tree-lined roads. Nice place. Big live oaks, shady. Pity it was in the ghetto.

"Why?" Milo asked, getting out.

"'Cause we got at least three more loup-garou run-ning around and a vampire," I said, holding up the bullhorn. "We don't got time for this shit. Let's try some challenge howling."

"You have got to be kidding," Milo said. "Okay. If you're going to try to piss off a werewolf, how about we do it somewhere we don't have a bunch of people driving by on a busy street catching our stray bullets and being witnesses?"

"That's..." I sighed. He was right. "The bathroom is the most dangerous room in the house."

"Huh?"

I picked a smaller street, drove down it a bit until it looked quiet, and parked. We got out. I turned the bullhorn on, put it up to my lips and howled.

Oh, wow, it was loud. Not as loud as those damned frogs, but really loud.

"That oughtta bring him out." Then I howled again, turning in place to get the sound spread around.

"That is the *worst* werewolf call I've ever heard in

my life," Milo said, disgusted. "It sounds like someone's got your testicles in a vise."

There was an answering howl from somewhere northeast. It sounded pissed. This was its territory. Other loup-garou were not welcome.

"What were you saying about my awesome wolf call?" I asked.

"That it's idiotic?" Milo said.

I howled in that direction and added a growl for good measure. The loup-garou howled back. It was closer.

"You are officially insane," Milo said, shouldering his rifle.

Then a howl came from the southeast. It was closing in. I turned that way and howled.

Suddenly it was there. The werewolf appeared on the roof of the nearest house. It jumped off the top of the house in an enormous leap. Milo even got off a couple of shots while it was in midair. Then he had to dive out of the way because the werewolf crashed right into the middle of Honeybear's roof.

It hit and skidded on Honeybear, its daggerlike claws ripping the hell out of my roof. But Milo must have managed to wing it, because it rolled off, leaving a bloody smear.

"Oh, you did not," I said, dropping the bullhorn and lifting my Uzi.

Then it was back up, wounded and pissed. I riddled it with an entire magazine of .45 silver hollowpoints.

"Oh, Honeybear," I said, rubbing my hands on the roof. "Did the big bad wolf hurt you?"

"You are too weird to even..." Milo said, getting up and shaking his head.

"At least I don't wear green socks with Birkenstocks," I said.

"Those are my casual wear."

"Cover my six, please." I reloaded, took a drink and shook my head. "Never a cop when you need one. You okay?"

"All good," Milo said.

As the werewolf died, it changed into a middle-aged black woman. She was skinny but flaps of skin indicated she'd recently lost a good bit of weight.

I picked the bullhorn back up and did a couple more calls. No response.

"Okay," I said. "I'll call dispatch. Seems like that was the only one in the area."

I'd had to put the cooler in the back with Milo riding with me. I pulled out a can of Budweiser, popped it open and picked up the phone.

"The hoodoo gone, Mr. Hoodoo?" someone called from one of the houses.

"Looks like it," Milo yelled back.

And in seconds we were in the middle of a mob.

I was talking to Tremaine from the Sheriff's office SIU while Milo was trying to persuade a guy in his twenties that, no, he didn't need anything.

"No, thank you," Milo said as the guy showed him that he had first-class crack. "I don't do drugs."

"Did a howl," I said. "Don't think there's any more around."

"People round here know if there's hoodoo," Tremaine said, taking off her helmet and rubbing her hair. "We've got a bunch already tonight. Seems worse than last month."

"I gots weed, too, man," the guy insisted, pulling out a nickel bag. "You want it, I gots it. Primo stuff, man. Colombian."

"We're working on tracking down the source," I said, taking another pull on the Budweiser.

About sixty people were gathered trying to get a glimpse of the dead lady. There was blood spilled down my door and into the seat. That was going to suck. We'd covered the body with a sheet while we waited on the coroner. Speaking of which.

"Any word on coroner?" I asked.

"They're busy as hell," Tremaine said. Like Shelbye, when she got tired, her accent got nearly unintelligible and she'd occasionally break into French. "Three other loup-garou and a big kill over in Metairie and we just got a report from Fourth in the Garden District."

"Seriously, I can hook you up, man," the guy insisted. "You want girls?"

"Look!" Milo said, losing his temper. "I don't want your crack or your hookers or your crack hookers or your hooker crack! I'm annoyed and I'm armed!"

"Who's the red-headed kid?" Tremaine asked. "He new?"

"New here. Milo's actually been a Hunter longer than I have."

"He don't look like much."

"His hobbies are climbing mountains without ropes and interpretive bomb-making," I said.

"Just say *no!*" Milo shouted at the dealer. "You should listen to Nancy Reagan!"

Tremaine's radio squawked. She listened for a bit, then shook her head.

"Coroner's over on Kerlerec. They want to know if you can transport to the morgue."

"Okay, that's even got me boggling," I said.

"Hey, it's cool, man," the drug dealer said, holding up his hands. "Just bidnitt. I know there's something you wants, man!"

"I don't have room in the trunk," I said. There were too many weapons and explosives in there. "Could throw her in a body bag and carry it over on the hood I guess."

"Even for New Orleans that's a bit much," Tremaine said. "If you've got the body bag, I've got the trunk space."

"You got any bottled water?" Milo asked, giving up and realizing until he bought something from the guy, he wasn't going away. "Like *spring* water? In a *sealed* bottle?"

"I can hook you up, man," the guy said, nodding. "Be right back."

"Hey, Milo, help me get this lady in a body bag," I said. "But I'll have to follow over to coroner's to get the receipt."

"Hey, man, I can get the best water," another guy had now sidled up to Milo. "Like, trippin' water, you know?"

"I'll get the receipt," Tremaine offered. "Either run into you at some point or you can get it at Maurice's."

"Oh, please just go away," Milo said wearily.

"That works," I said, making a note. I already had the local incident number. "Try to survive so I can pick it up. MCB's a bitch if we don't get receipts..."

CHAPTER 23
Living in America

"I've dealt with weird things from shadow dimensions," Milo said, draining a bottle of apple juice. "I've killed more vampires than you can shake a stake at. I'm pretty darned good at monster hunting. But I'm not sure I'm cut out for New Orleans."

The bottle of "trippin' water" had cost ten dollars. And the cap wasn't sealed. I was pretty sure the guy had grabbed an empty bottle and filled it with tap water. Milo was an even worse negotiator than he was a public speaker.

"The drug dealers here have a real serious work ethic. Hardest working sons of bitches in this town. Very competitive business. They're always looking for new clients."

I crumpled up the Bud can and tossed it out the window. I hate littering, but Milo was taking up the spot where my trashbag usually sat and I wasn't going to just drop it in Honeybear. Although the way the interior was starting to look, I might as well. I usually rolled with a thick quilt on the front seat to sop up the blood and shit from my armor. It was sopped through with blood at the moment. Honeybear was going to need a serious detailing after this moon.

"Right in front of a cop," Milo said in a wondering tone. "He was trying to sell me drugs right in front of a cop."

"Special Investigations Unit don't give a shit about drug dealing and he knew it. They've got more important things to do. And besides, even if he did get busted, he spends a couple of days in county and he's back on the street. They think of it the way we think of being too injured to work. Three hots and a cot, see some old friends. It's like paid vacation. Now get your game face on. We're almost there."

Fourth crossed St. Charles and continued on. Homes tended to be a bit smaller with smaller yards. But it changed quickly. In a few blocks we were in the ghetto again. It really looked exactly like Spain, same ratty cars, same ratty houses, same bars and heavy doors, scraggly yards, devoid of people.

The address Tremaine had given us was 1828 Fourth Street. Single-story, what would be called in Pennsylvania a mill house, that had been split into a duplex. Usual heavy front door and barred windows.

One of the windows was shattered and the bars had been ripped out.

"And it's a roamer," I said. "It's nice when we can get them in the house."

"Going to do your really bad werewolf call again?" Milo said.

"Hey, it works," I said, cruising down the street. "Get out the light, maybe we can spot it."

We rolled along slowly, looking for signs of loup-garou. Running people and blood splatter were the usual ones.

There was some blood splatter on the road and a red hat.

"Oh, Christ," I said, stopping the car. "Not more of these little bastards!"

The sign was right by a brick building that was definitely a duplex. There were chain-link security fences on both sides between it and the neighboring houses.

Just inside the narrow passage to the right of the house was more blood splatter and another hat. I could hear what sounded like one hell of a dogfight going on behind the house. I pushed through the weed-choked passage between the two houses, and reminded myself to do a tick check after this one. I'd picked up a bunch at the cemetery my first day.

The backyard was a shambles. Bits and pieces of gnomes were scattered in every direction, at least ten more were seriously injured and a three-headed dog was just getting its last head finished off by the loup-garou. Red pointy hats were everywhere.

"Living in America" was playing on a boom box in the corner of the yard.

The loup-garou turned, snarling. Milo hadn't even made it into the yard and I was blocking him.

I took a good stance and opened fire full auto, starting more or less pointed at the ground and riding the rounds up.

A couple dug dirt. The rest dug doggie.

The loup-garou skidded to a halt as the silver bullets shredded its body and spine. I slid sideways to let Milo get through, then dropped my mag to reload.

Milo stepped over and put two in the head of the panting and whining werewolf.

One of the gnomes stood up, shaking his head. He already had a sling on one arm and stitches over half his body. Now his leg had been badly ripped by claws. Whatever had happened to him before this, that gnome was having one bad week.

"Fuck you, Tall," the gnome squeaked. "What the hell you doin' on our turf? We *had* this!"

"*Sure*, you had this," I said. "Lawn ornament."

"Who you calling a lawn ornament?" the gnome squeaked, trying to pull a cheap-ass pistol out of his waistband with his left hand.

I walked over and stuck my Uzi's suppressor in his puffy beard.

"You're PUFF-applicable. You're just a little bundle of green to me, short ass. Draw it! I double-dog dare you!"

"Hey, no problem, man," the gnome said, holding up his good hand.

"Sorry about your dog," I said, lowering the weapon. I wondered if we could file PUFF on the thing. It was probably worth a few shekels. "Where's your burrow? We'll help you get your homies out before the SIU gets here."

"Hardly no burrows in New Orleans, man," the gnome squeaked. "Too wet. Gots to get them up in the house 'fore the man gets here!"

Milo and I picked up the wounded gnomes, even I could carry two at a time by the ankles, and tossed them in the house. They were tough, say that for them. Their Momma would handle things from there. Gnome Mommas were grade-A healers. If the gnomes were up and in sight, SIU might just get the urge to "handle" the gnome infestation. SIU hated gnomes more than I did.

When we had the scene cleared up, we called SIU.

"So all the surviving gnomes were gone when you got here," Salvage said, turning a red hat over in his hand thoughtfully. Tremaine had passed my receipt to him at some point, so we were good on that front.

"Yep," I said. "The cerb was still kicking and there were bits and hats everywhere but the gnomes were all gone. We finished off the cerb so I'm going to file on that."

"Looks like the scene's clear," Salvage said. "Coroner's on the way. You going to file on the gnomes?"

"Depends on if we can figure out how many there were," I said. PUFF on a gnome was ten grand, which was just insane. The three-headed dog was half that. Generally, it was 'cause they were hard to catch. Unless you were a werewolf crashing the party. "Lotsa bits. Not sure if the Feds will pay on a hat count."

Turned out that Shelbye had already filed on the gnome I accidentally shot with the killer frog. I hated to get paid for killing innocent bystanders but you couldn't call gnomes innocent so all good.

"Coroner's on the way," Salvage said. "With your reinforcements in town, they're having a hell of a time keeping up."

"The good news is we're getting it shut down faster," I said.

"Yeah," Salvage said, dropping the hat in gnome splatter. "I've got another call. You gotta wait on coroner this time."

"Works for me," I said. "I'm gonna go grab a beer. Milo, want an apple juice?"

"Yes," Milo said.

I was getting an apple juice out of the back for Milo when I heard a "Psssst."

Sure enough the much battered gnome was up by Honeybear's tire, hunkered down to keep out of sight of "the man."

"Hey, humie," the gnome said. "Sorry 'bout earlier."

"No problem," I said, pulling out the apple juice and grabbing another Bud. I popped the top and handed it to the gnome. "I'm Iron Hand. You?"

"Bun-Bun," the gnome said, taking a deep drink of Anheuser-Busch's finest. "Shit tastes like camel piss. You need to get some Dixie!"

"Speaking of camel piss," I said. "What you got, shortie?"

"Big Momma says we owe you one," the gnome said, making a face.

"If I need a cheesy decoration for my garden, I'll let you know," I said.

"Well, fuck you, then," Bun-Bun snarled. I could tell he wanted to toss a table. Assuming he could reach one.

"Just kidding." Gnomes could be good snitches. "Gots nothin' I need right now," I said, then paused. "Actually, the one big question I gots, only one might be able to answer is Big Momma. Gots somethin' weird going on."

I was a Monster Hunter. I was talking to a gnome. You have to understand I have a different definition of "weird."

"Big Momma don't like t' talk to humies," Bun-Bun said. "Hell, I think humies all need a cap in the ear, you know? But Big Momma don't talk to humies none at all."

"Fine," I said. "When I need a lawn ornament, I'll call."

"Up yours, Tall." The gnome vanished.

"I can't give you a receipt based on number of hats!" Dave said.

"Hey," I said placatingly. "Gnomes never leave a hat behind! If there's a hat, it's a dead gnome!"

"I'll try to figure out how many pieces there are," Dave said. "MCB's been looking over our shoulder lately, you know? Castro's been in a bad mood since the frog incident."

"I'm good with not padding. I've never liked it anyway but I'm not from around here. Just try to get a count of the bits and give me that."

We had to borrow a ladder from a nearby house. There was a gnome head, still in the hat, on the roof.

"Seems like it mainly was leaving behind the heads," Dave said. We had seven battered gnome heads lined up on the back porch of the house.

"Not much eating in a gnome head," Milo said, nodding sagely. "Mostly bone."

"I'll give you a receipt for one loup-garou, one medium cerberus, and seven gnomes," Dave said, scratching at a receipt.

"Works for me," I said.

He pulled off the yellow slip and handed it over.

"I think we can fit all the gnome bits in one bag..."

❖   ❖   ❖

"Totally bogus," I said, tucking the receipt away as we drove off. We'd had to wait until coroner cleared the scene. "Like that hat on the street? That one got completely gobbled up. Maybe if they find some heads in the stomach contents we can get the rest of the PUFF."

"Chad," Milo said. "Gnomes aren't all bad. And we didn't even kill them."

"Know who Horatio Nelson was, Milo?" I said. We had a call over on St. Charles Avenue. Another loup-garou that two teams were already trying to track down.

"I went to high school," Milo said. "And I didn't get straight Cs."

"Getting a perfect C is hard," I said. "He was one badass fighter. Ship, personal, you name it. Took a Spanish ship-of-the-line with the crew of a brig by boarding from the stern and fighting his way to the front—at the front, leading his men. Just swinging a sword most of the way. One of his quotes I always keep in mind: 'I could not have tread these perilous paths in safety were it not for a saving sense of humor.' If I don't laugh about this shit, I'm going to suck start a twelve gauge."

"That's fair," Milo said.

"And it was bogus. You got any idea what the PUFF is on a gnome? I've got a house to pay for..."

We cruised St. Charles for a bit, then got the call that Ray's team had finished that one off. Then the phone rang again.

"Think you can find Loyola University?" Milo asked, juggling the car phone and a map.

"I think so," I said drily, speeding up. There was traffic. I hit the purple light and the sirens and made a U-turn. A Toyota had to turn desperately to avoid being run over. It would not have survived the Honeybear. "It's on St. Charles Avenue."

"Vampire attack," Milo said.

"This should be fun."

"Why?"

"Loyola's a big center for monster lovers. We're probably going to catch some shit."

CHAPTER 24
Crazy on You

"Vampires are sentient beings!"

The speaker was a portly man in his fifties with a big bushy beard and thick brown hair, wearing a tweed jacket that must have been hot as hell. He looked like the late and unlamented Tedd Roberts. Who wears a tweed jacket in a town like New Orleans in *June*?

"So are you," I said. "Doesn't mean I won't blow your brains out if you don't get out of my way."

The attack had taken place over on the Academic Quad. From what we'd gleaned, the vamps might still be on the premises.

"University property is a sanctuary zone!" the man shouted. He was some sort of dean. "Entry of common law enforcement is forbidden!"

"Good thing we're not law enforcement," Milo said.

"That's right, we're bounty hunters," I said. "Different breed of cat. I can quote the Supreme Court rulings. Seriously, if you think we should not enter and deal with the threat, go reason with them. From my experience, vampires can be reasoned with. We'll follow and stay back. You go talk them down."

"Well, uh . . ." the man said, grabbing his collar and pulling it.

"So, you're fine with your students getting their throats ripped out but not willing to take the chance yourself? I mean, 'cause they're only students, right? Plenty more where those came from. They just clutter up the place."

"That's not at all—"

"Both my parents are professors. I've heard the discussions since I was a kid. Now, for the last time, you got three choices: Get out of my way, go try to talk the vamps down yourself, or personally experience the violence inherent in the system. Choose."

Back in his twenties he'd probably have been more than willing to take a beat-down to prove a point. Give peace a chance. Stick it to the man by showing how the entire system was based on fascism.

That was then, this was now. He got out of the way.

As we were walking away, Milo told him, "Sentient just means they feel stuff. You meant they're sapient beings. Read a book, professor."

Luckily, this time of night the campus was pretty deserted. We found the campus cops next to a mangled body. From the number and savagery of the bite wounds, we were either dealing with several vampires or one really aggressive one. Milo identified us and started talking to the cops. I started looking for a sign of which way they had gone.

"*Hand, Trevor,*" my radio hissed. "*Location?*"

"Peace quad. Credit union. One KIA so far. No count on vamps yet."

"Alvin and Moore are coming in from the north. Me and Shelbye are at your six. Hold your position until we get there."

I spotted bloody footprints. I could hear music coming from that direction.

Milo came over. "Witnesses saw at least two, definitely sounds like vamps. And the cops just got a radio call, something about a party over there." Then he saw the bloody footprints. "Three...four...Oh boy. They're hunting in a pack."

"Negative, Trevor," I radioed. "We need to get this shut down fast."

There was a long pause. *"Continue sweep."*

"Hand out," I said. "Let's keep going."

"Two of us going up against this many vamps in the dark is insane," Milo said. "Not saying I'm not coming, but..."

"We have to go in," I said, stepping into the darkness. "Nothing says we have to come out."

We'd been sweeping east of the bookstore when we heard a series of shots and screams to our right. Small caliber handgun. Mixed screams. A more powerful gun, fairly rapid fire. Panic fire in both cases.

The campus cops had been armed with .38s.

We sprinted between the bookstore and the Jesus School. Behind it was a well-lit set of basketball courts and a "scene."

There had been a bunch of kids out on the court playing basketball under the lights. Most of them looked to be university students. Guys playing, girls mostly watching. Bit of a party. Coolers filled with beer. Stereo going.

Then vampires decided to crash the party.

Two fraternities had gotten into some sort of friendly argument and decided to hash it out with an equally friendly game of basketball. Their associated sororities had turned out to act as cheerleaders.

Many of the Loyola students were from other states. Mommy and Daddy would pay to get them out of the house and send them off to New Orleans to get some education, hopefully, and have a good time when they were still young. Gather ye rosebuds. Sweet yet swiftly pass the halcyon days of youth.

Locals in both groups recommended against it. They knew that bad things were happening on the full moon lately. One of them even came armed. He had a .44 Automag—a present from his parents—which he was carrying illegally. Because he was a superstitious local, he'd rubbed silver nitrate in the hollowpoint cavities. Not that a small amount of silver nitrate would actually do anything to a loup-garou. Has to be pure silver, not any sort of alloy. I'd say "pro-tip" but you should have gotten that in training.

But you couldn't blame the local boy for trying.

Problem being, bullets aren't much good on vamps. Even young vampires swallow bullets and spit out the bits. Hitting them in the head would disorient them. Breaking bones would slow them down, at least until they regenerated. But the only way to really shut down a vamp was to stick something big through their heart, and killing them required taking off their heads.

As it was, the kid's pistol didn't do much good at all. Not noticeably.

He still did better than the campus cop, though.

The campus cop, who survived, later explained that

he'd come to the group to get them to leave. They were having too much fun to listen to some fat old security guard talking about a "security threat on campus." They were mostly drunk, the music was going, and they hadn't heard the previous victim's screams.

When the vamps appeared and ripped the arms off of the first basketball player, the cop had drawn his revolver, turned tail and ran, firing over his shoulder. Full-on spray and pray with all six rounds. He hit two students, one lightly, the other died in the hospital, and not a single vamp.

Most of the students, live ones anyway, were running when we arrived. One was limping away, bullet in the leg, one coed was down and bleeding. Five were down, covered in vamp. The one with the gun was trying to get another magazine in the well. Props for courage at least.

I took a look and called to Milo.

"Fade left and cover," I said, drawing Mo No Ken.

Like I said, guns only sort of disorient and piss off vampires. You have to take off their heads.

One of the vamps glanced up from her meal, and turned towards me. Female, looked not much different from the coed she'd been feeding on. Shorts, crop-top shirt, barefoot.

The tape in the radio changed to "Crazy on You" as I charged.

She came at me, slower than normal, bloated with blood, arms spread to catch my shoulders, pull me in and bite. But even a slow vamp was crazy fast. I swung up from a down and left position, taking off her right hand at the wrist. She still tried to claw my face off.

Milo's bullet went through her cheek, shattered her teeth, and blew the side of her skull off.

She stumbled past. I leaned left and came down with Mo No Ken from behind and took her right leg out from under her, cutting it in two through the thigh. That caused her to buckle sideways, right in line for a one-handed return upstroke.

Sweep back and the blonde head was rolling in the sodium arc lights.

It was like that kill flipped a switch, and every other vampire's head snapped up, staring at me with red eyes. They all looked like kids, new creations, feral, not smart, but still mean as hell.

The nearest male leapt up from his victim and charged me. I spun away in a *pirouette à la seconde*, came around and took his head from behind. It flipped through the air, splattering ichor in every direction.

There are times like this when I'm in the zone I wish there were cameras rolling. It must have been beautiful.

Milo was firing: rapid, aimed semiauto. Every round hitting a skull. A female vampire flew through the air from my right, hissing like a tea kettle. A bullet went up her nose and out her forehead. I slashed upward and rolled out of the way. She landed behind me. I took a quick look over my shoulder. The female vamp was on her knees and hands, trying to figure out why her legs weren't working right. That was because both lower legs were lying in a pool of blood.

Before I could take her head, a vampire tackled me.

It was like getting hit by a rhino. Mo No Ken went flying as the vamp started ripping at my throat guard, trying to get it free while I tried to push his face to the side. Not much chance of that with a vamp, but I wasn't going to fight fair. I got a thumb into his eye and gouged until blood squirted out.

The vamp grabbed my left arm and twisted it, nearly breaking it. Even a weak new vamp is as strong as a power lifter.

But the eye gouge was just a distraction. The whole time I was scrabbling for a canteen. I opened the lid and tossed the holy water in his face. He shrieked and rolled off of me. He probably hadn't experienced pain since being turned.

I crawled for my sword, wondering why Milo had stopped shooting. I got my answer when he was hurled past, to bounce off the chain link fence and land facedown in the basketball court.

The vampire with the melted face *flew* back to his feet. He was on me in a flash. I reached for Mo No Ken, but I was dragged away, my left arm ripped by his talons. That would have to wait. Amazing how you can ignore things like that when you're running on pure adrenaline.

There were several shots. Then dozens of them. I was splattered with blood as the vampire was *riddled*. It jerked and twitched, pieces of meat flying in every direction, until it fell flat on its back in a cloud of smoke and blood vapor.

That thing I said about bullets only disorienting and pissing them off? That's why we use a *lot* of bullets.

Franklin Moore ran past me. He stopped at the vampire and drove a stake through its ribs, pinning it there and leaving it paralyzed. Then he drew a military surplus machete from his belt and started hacking crudely at its neck, like he was clearing brush. As a swordsman, it was painful to watch.

"Damn, Franklin, sharpen that thing or something."

Half a dozen chops later, the head rolled off.

I got up and retrieved my sword. Shelbye was helping Milo up. Alvin and Trevor were finishing off the last wounded vamp.

The student with the Automag had finally gotten the magazine loaded and lifted the weapon, searching for targets.

"You point that at me, my friend will put a round through your head," I said.

He'd been so concentrated on reloading his gun he hadn't even realized we were there.

"Oh, shit," he said, slumping down, the gun dropping from nerveless fingers. "Shit, shit, shit..."

"Yeah," I said, wiping Mo No Ken. "Welcome to our world. What's your name, kid?"

CHAPTER 25
Bad to the Bone

I let Trevor handle the scene while Milo gave my injured left arm a little TLC courtesy of Betadine and lots of bandages. I swear, bandages and ammo had to be our two biggest costs.

Oh, and funerals.

When vampires roam in a pack, it can be bad news, but our timely intervention had saved a lot of lives. Some of the kids would die, but we'd interrupted the feeding frenzy early enough that most of those bitten would probably be saved. Alvin and Franklin had followed the ambulances, so if any of them died in surgery they'd get decapitated immediately, and not give Wohlrab, the night shift morgue attendant, any more surprise wake-ups in a few days.

As Milo was expertly wrapping bandages around my arm, there was a voice behind me.

"You're Hoodoo Squad?" a girl asked.

I wasn't worried about my six. I'd noticed Milo look up, then back down. No threat. I was watching his, he was watching mine. Nice to have a brother at your back.

"The same," I said, grimacing as Milo tied the bandage tight. "Watch the arm!"

"Quit being a sissy," Milo said.

"This stuff is real," she said in a shell-shocked voice.

"Yep. You were there?"

"Yes," she said, sitting down on the bench I was occupying.

My immediate reaction to a girl that pretty is normally "woof, woof!" I guess I was tired. I didn't even pull out a card!

"You'll get past it," I said, shrugging. "There's so many worse things in this shit, you wouldn't believe."

"It's hard to even think."

"Know that guy over there?" I said, gesturing with my chin at the kid who'd had the Automag.

"I think he's a Sigma Nu. I don't really know him but I recognize him."

"Go make friends. He might not have stopped them, but he was the only one really trying. Guy like that should get some moral support and he'll be a good shoulder to lean on."

"Okay, I guess," the girl said.

"You're going to need somebody's shoulder to sleep on for a while," I said. "Helps keep away the nightmares."

"I'm not that sort of girl," she said, frowning.

"I said sleep, not fuck. Make friends. Some guys from the FBI will be here soon to tell you that you can't talk about this. You can with him. Make friends. What you do after that is up to you."

I'd been putting on my gear as I was talking and when I was done, I stood up.

"I'm impressed. You didn't hit on that poor

traumatized girl," Milo said. "That was nearly gentlemanly. I must be a good influence on you."

"More like you kill the mood. Come on, we have more monsters to put to bed."

"You good to keep going?" Trevor asked.

"You kidding?" I asked. "'Tis only a flesh wound. Besides, there's PUFF to be collected. You got any idea how much good help costs these days?"

Full moon in New Orleans is like Christmas season in retail.

"It sounds like zombies in St. Louis Cemetery," Trevor said.

"Please tell me we're going one team on shamblers," I said. "I got a mortgage to make."

"Nope. As soon as another team is open, I'm sending them after you and Milo."

"The day I need backup for shamblers is the day I quit," I muttered.

"That's exactly what Greg Wise told me."

St. Louis Cemetery was another old one off of I-10. It was in three sections, bisected by roads. The shambler outbreak was in the center section between Conti and Bienville.

All three cemeteries were surrounded by high walls, which acted as tombs themselves. The interior walls were lined with grave markers marking the bodies behind them. The rest of the cemetery was entirely tombs, with none of the low sarcophagi common in other cemeteries.

There were heavy iron gates at three points on the cemetery.

Honestly, it was clear whoever set the place up knew what they were doing when it came to undead outbreaks. It was half cemetery, half undead prison. No damned shamblers were getting out of that place. Wights, maybe, those things could climb like spiders, but even a ghoul would have a hard time with that fence.

"Whoa," Milo said, looking at the gate. "This place is a fortress."

"Back then people knew how to build a cemetery to contain the occasional undead outbreak."

"Accent on occasional. Man, we really need to figure out what's making the hoodoo go haywire, because I really don't want to die in Louisiana."

"It's not so bad," I said.

"The town is below sea level. I need mountains, Chad."

The NOPD car had been parked about half a block away over on Conti. He'd already gotten a key to one of the gates. It was over on Claiborne, which was a hell of a walk, so we drove. Oops, had to go the wrong way on a one-way but there wasn't much traffic this late.

So we had a key to this gate but I was thinking I didn't want to use it. I could see that the place was another maze. And there were shamblers already waving their arms through the gate.

"You miss climbing," I said, gesturing at the wall. "Let's draw them in with lights and noise, then just shoot them from up there."

Here's a very important pro-tip that's an extension of earlier ones.

Pro-tip: Bring shamblers to *you* and use any height or complexity advantage to keep them from getting to you and bringing them to where you can kill them easily. Don't let them close unless you absolutely have to. And if you do, be aware you're probably going to have to ask a friend to shoot you in the head.

"We can just shoot them through the gate," Milo pointed out.

"We're going to have to use it to get the bodies out," I said. "Why block it? And from up there we can draw more in."

"That makes an amazing amount of sense," Milo said. "Especially coming from you."

"Well, I suppose we could take ten hours to machine a special flamethrower for them if you'd prefer. In the meantime, why don't you come up with some inventive way to get us up there?"

The wall was about sixteen feet high and there were no available handholds. Well designed, as I said. So we decided to drive around it and see if there was a way in.

The back side was a chain link fence surmounted by barbed wire. No way in there.

However, by the corner of Claiborne and Conti, there was a short section of brick wall. It was short enough to hop up onto and from there, we were up on the main wall. It was still high enough to hold in the walking dead. *Really* well designed.

A couple of zombies came around as we were climbing up. We ignored them and walked along the wide top of the wall to the gate.

The horde by the gate noticed our lights and came shambling over. So did the ones that had reacted to our getting up on the wall.

We both opened fire . . . slow, aimed fire. I had

brought plenty of extra ammo. I'd learned my lesson on that at the battle in Greenwood.

"This is shooting ducks in a barrel," Milo said. There were twelve shamblers down and we hadn't come near being scratched.

Which is the way you should fight monsters. Fair is for children on a playground. Monster hunting is about efficient and fast. Kill monsters. Get paid. Live to collect the fat check.

The maze conditions of the cemetery meant that not all the shamblers had gotten over to us. We could hear more moaning down in and amongst the tombs. Somebody's hex had gone horribly wrong. *Again.*

"Hey!" I yelled. "Over here! Come here, you idiots! This way... That's right... Come to Papa Smurf... Your shot, Milo."

"Thanks," Milo said.

Shambler down.

"And I am not a smurf."

"If the Birkenstocks fit," I said. "Smurfette, then. This is going to take all night," I said. "Those things are too stupid to all get over here in any decent time. And there's other calls."

"First you want to play it safe," Milo said. "Now we got to get down off of here?"

"There are times to play it safe and others to take it to the ground," I said. That's another pro-tip. "Sounds like about six more. I say we go to them."

Milo thought about it for a second.

"Sure," he said. "Why not?"

"You want point or six?" I asked as we walked back to the low wall. We probably could have made the jump but why take the chance?

"Point, of course," Milo said. "Who wants six?"

"Rock, paper, scissors?"

He won. He always wins. I have no idea how he does it.

There were seven more. Took about ten minutes.

"And now to get coroner."

"Hey, Tim," I said as the coroner's assistant came over to the gate. It had only taken about half an hour which wasn't bad. "Nineteen."

"All old desiccated corpses. You sure you don't want to break open some tombs and drag out some extras to shoot?"

"Thought about it, but it's too hot." I laughed like Tim had made a joke, because Milo would flip his lid at the idea of padding.

"You *sure* it's clear?" Tim said as his assistants lowered the flat. "One of your new teams said Metairie was clear and it wasn't."

He sounded offended, but the coroner's job was nearly as dangerous as ours and they weren't as well-armed. Technically, they weren't supposed to be armed at all. But all of them carried a gun when they worked. They weren't stupid.

"Totally clearing Metairie is a daytime job," I said. "You know that. And it's why we stay for security. This one is clear."

We'd walked the whole thing calling for more undead, but none showed.

"Okay," Tim said. "Just keep an eye out. This job doesn't pay enough to lose people."

"Milo," I said, "head back and call Trevor or Ray. See what's up next."

"Next?" Milo said. "Seriously?"

Our promised backup had never arrived which meant it was still busy out there.

Tim looked at Milo like he was a moron. "On the way in I heard there were some ghouls in Lafayette."

"You have got to be kidding me," Milo said, shaking his head as he walked to the car. "This town sucks!"

"I'll cover," I said. "You ready?"

"Nineteen," Tim said, handing me the yellow slip. "Thanks for stacking most of them in one spot."

"And we made sure the gate was clear," I pointed out. "But you're welcome. Now away to the next call. See you in a bit."

"What's next?" I asked, pulling out a can of Budweiser.

I'd refilled my canteens and stuck them in the trunk. My arm was hurting like hell but it was time to roll.

"Everybody else is chasing down leads or waiting for coroners. It's starting to quiet down. He's got a weird call for us to check though," Milo said. "In Carollton, according to Trevor. Last spotted near Fern and Jeanette. But he said the witness who called it in sounded stoned, so it might be nothing."

"What did he see?"

"Some kind of giant rat."

"Okay," I said. "This is even affecting my sangfroid slightly."

"Giant rat" was an understatement. It was the size of a small elephant. Naked and gray with pink eyes and really big teeth. As we watched, it was using those huge teeth to chew through the wall of a two-story brick house. The house next door had already been reduced to rubble.

A little hex had given us really big frogs. Out of control hoodoo was probably the cause of our weird bull-gorilla flesh golum, and probably the sobek too. But what dumbass had been using magic on this hideous thing?

"I think it's time to break out the LAW," Milo said.

He was spotting the thing with the spotlight but it wasn't noticing. I was pretty sure it was a giant mole rat and they're basically blind.

"Bertha maybe," I said, getting her out. "But if it's an actual animal and we mess it up, Shelbye will kill us."

"What?" Milo said, getting out of the car. He kept the light focused on the massive rat.

"She's going to want to eat it or stuff it."

"I know you're not big on asking for help, Chad, but..."

It was a mole rat the size of an elephant.

"Oh, I'm okay with it this time."

Milo got on the radio, and started to call it in. Then he paused. "Uh oh. Listen." Somebody was screaming. It was coming from the house the mole rat was demolishing. Imagine waking up to that. "Shoot. We're on."

The mole rat stopped for a moment, pointed its snout at the sky and let out a weird, high, squeaky cry. It was bizarre coming from such a massive beast.

It's hard to transliterate "monster sounds" but it was something like:

"*DOC! DOC, DOC, DOC, DOOOOC!*"

I got out Bertha the Barrett and loaded up a magazine. I got out both LAWs as well and put them in the front seat. Just in case.

"You drive. Drive up parallel to it." I sat on the hood. "If the first shot doesn't do it, we take off and stay at range. If that don't work, speed up, we get away, unpack the LAWs and finish it off."

I had the little rubber bipod booties for when I had to shoot across the roof, but then I actually looked at Honeybear's roof. The loup-garou had done a number on it. I loved that car. I'd rebuilt her so many times all by myself. It was just a shame. The impact of the werewolf had driven the top in two inches and it was scratched to shit. We were way past booties.

"Why am I driving and you're shooting?"

"Well," I said, "first of all, *I* won the marksmanship competition with the frogs."

"Just because you cheated and got a helicopter. That's not a real shooting competition. That's a 'who has the best contacts' competition."

"Second, 'cause this is *my* Bertha and *your* Barrett is in the van. Now shut up and drive, Smurfette."

"I'm armed you know," Milo said. But he got in the car.

"Also," I said, yelling, "'cause would you trust *my* driving with you on the hood?"

"*No!*"

I held up a hand as we came parallel to the gargantuan beast. The real question was where to shoot it. I was sort of familiar with rat anatomy courtesy of a perfect C in biology. The heart should be right behind the shoulder.

The mole rat had gotten its head into the house and

was pushing through the wall with the aforementioned shoulder. The inhabitants were not enjoying the experience. I heard a blast from a shotgun but that was pissing in the wind. It was past time to take the shot.

Then I made a mistake.

Pro-tip: You can fire most big powerful rifles from any of several positions. Prone is most people's preference. Offhand—standing—works if you've got the upper body strength. You can even do it kneeling. I've tried it.

Seated, the recoil is going to rock you back. Especially when you are seated on a waxed metal car hood.

It made the most sense for what we were planning. I'd just never actually tried it with a Barrett before. The problem is traverse. When you fire an M82, you *are* going back. I'm not a big guy. Someone with arms like Trevor can shoot a .50 offhand and barely move. When I fire it offhand, I have to lean into it. Then I ride it back about four or six inches. Very fun and very effective.

It turns out you don't have that distance, and keep your balance, when you're in seated position on the edge of a slippery car hood.

I fired and found myself rolling backwards trying to control 35 pounds of steel that had just aggressively shoved me over the side.

I ended up on the ground on the street. I'd managed to hold onto Bertha and even protect the scope, but at the cost of a bloody nose and my dignity.

Offhand, yes. Kneeling, maybe. Prone, definitely. Sitting, never.

I'd say end pro-tip but there's a second one.

Pro-tip: If you've ever hunted, say, deer, you may

have noticed that heart shots, even perfect ones, rarely kill immediately. If you're smart, when you know you've nailed a critter and it takes off, you just let it run and wait a minute. That way it goes a little ways, stops to see what hurt it, and drops dead. If you chase, it will keep going on adrenaline for a long way.

Humans can even survive getting shot in the heart for a bit if they are accustomed to violence and pumped up. Emergency personnel call gang-bangers "human cockroaches" for a reason and long-term professional Monster Hunters get the same way. After a while it gets harder and harder to kill us because we've been nearly killed so many times, our bodies get used to trauma and adjust. Just like animals. Ditto professional soldiers in a long-term war. And I'm of the personal opinion that having some alcohol in your system helps. Just from watching who does and does not survive severe trauma.

Whether the mole rat was drunk as a loon, or just very robust, or regenerated, was, at that point, unknown. What *was* known was that it could hear, could figure out that loud noise and sudden pain were probably connected and did *not* drop right away from a heart shot.

"Get on the car!" Milo yelled. *"Get on! Get on!"*

I was sort of dizzy from getting kicked off the hood by Bertha. I got up and looked to see what all the excitement was about.

The mole rat was running at us faster than anything that big should be able to run. I mean it was getting bigger and bigger and bigger as I watched.

Adrenaline is an amazing drug. One moment I was standing up, shaking my head, wishing I could maybe, you know, go home and take a long shower, maybe a nap... The next instant I was up on the hood, lying on my back on the windshield and pulling out Bertha's bipod.

Adrenaline is amazing stuff. Don't even know how I got there.

For once, Milo did not drive like a little old lady. Honeybear peeled out in a cloud of blue smoke and burning rubber smell and the chase was on!

Oh, that mole rat was pissed! Damned near hit us as we peeled out, then turned faster than it should have been able to and followed the smell of burned rubber and the roaring sound of a Delta 88 at full rev.

"*DOC! DOOOOOC!*" it was squealing. I didn't speak mole rat but I think that meant "I'm going to kill you and eat your bones! Bwahahahah!"

"Slow down. We're losing it!"

"Good!" Milo shouted. But he slowed down. Because he was coming to a *stop sign*. And if you're a little old lady, you STOP at stop signs.

As I lined up the shot, I noticed something. We were at the corner of Fern and Birch.

"You're driving the wrong way on a one-way street!"

BOOM! Another .50 cal round right through the chest. It kept running. I was starting to think this thing regenerated.

Milo was carefully checking both ways for traffic as I lined up the next shot. Either this one had better work or Milo had better, you know, *go* or we were about to be mole rat chow.

Problem being there was another car in the intersection.

A minivan.

We just *sat* there. I looked over my shoulder and could see the lady in the minivan signaling for Milo to go through.

I suspect Milo was signaling frantically for her to go through. If we went first she'd be in the intersection when the mole rat arrived and it would probably eat her and her soccer spawn.

She was probably thinking she wanted crazy people with guns as far away as possible and not realizing there was a reason I was firing over the back of the car. This was Louisiana. People do that sort of thing for fun.

I fired off the rest of my magazine, rapid aimed fire, then leaned back to pull out another mag from my vest. I knew no matter how fast I went, I wasn't going to stop the mole rat before it got to us and did one hell of a lot of damage to Honeybear. Not to mention, well, *eat us.*

Milo bailed out of the driver's side with a LAW. But it takes a few seconds to pull the pins, get it up on your shoulder . . . I really should have had it extended.

The mole rat reached Honeybear and *bit my fucking trunk!* Its massive upper teeth went *right through my trunk lid!* The bastard!

Fortunately, it was concentrating on killing the big metal thing that had hurt it. Honeybear shook back and forth and I heard my bumper give way.

I got a mag seated and aimed right between its beady pink eyes. *Boom*!

Brains splattered out of its tiny bullet head. Who knew a mole rat even had brains?

But that got it. It dropped, its head still attached to Honeybear's trunk lid. My car settled on its leaf springs with an unpleasant metallic noise. *Grinnngg.*

Fucking mole rats!

I heard a squeal of tires as the minivan peeled out of the intersection and drove away as fast as mommy could manage.

I didn't even know you *could* peel one of those out. Learn something new every day.

The tow truck was the sort usually used to tow semitrailers. It had a flatbed trailer attached on back.

A chain had been gotten around the mole rat's neck and it was being dragged onto the trailer by one big-ass crane. It had not deliquesced. Shelbye was going to be ecstatic.

The teeth were still embedded in my trunk lid. We'd cut them off with a borrowed axe to get the head off Honeybear's rear end. Which was absolutely trashed. Fucking mole rats.

"You know Shelbye's going to want it," I said, taking the yellow slip from Tim.

"As long as Dr. Henry gets invited to the fais do-do," Tim said.

"I think you can bring the whole department," I said. "And SIU. MCB. Them Cajuns gonna be eating right for a month."

Recipe for giant mole rat jambalaya.
1. Catch one giant mole rat.
2. Dice fine.
3. Make jambalaya.

CHAPTER 26
I'm Alright

"I think I'm starting to like it here," Milo said, taking another bite of donut.

Mormons won't consume anything containing alcohol or tobacco. But don't ask them about refined sugar. Boy could eat more donuts than an entire SWAT.

The sun was rising over Lake Pontchartrain. There was another loup-garou running around somewhere. There'd been a vampire attack that we'd missed and we were going to have to track down the vamps. There was something else going on in some place.

I really didn't care. I was munching on a breakfast burrito and there were four more in the greasy sack from Germaine's.

Monster hunting builds up an appetite.

"It grows on you," I said, taking another bite of burrito. I'd asked for extra jalapeno. That was probably a mistake. I was going to pay for it, for sure. "Like mold."

The phone rang.

"I'm *eating*," I said, without asking who it was.

"Got that," Ray said. "When you are done eating, head to New Orleans Country Club. We missed a couple last night. The zombies from Metairie Cemetery got out and are wandering around the golf course. We're getting complaints. It's interfering with tee time."

"Try to hit them in the *head*, Milo," I shouted out the window, rocking my weight from side to side.

You can drive a car on golf cart paths. You can even get up a fair turn of speed. I hadn't been too sure about the occasional bridge and whether it could take the weight of Honeybear—especially with everything that was in the trunk—but they handled us fine.

I'd let Milo do the shooting this time. I mean, it wasn't like he was a *good* shot or anything, but I was tired and he was still fuming over the mole rat. And that way I could stay in the air conditioning. We had the windows rolled down but any little bit of cool helped.

So he was up on the much mangled roof of Honeybear with his M16, trying to pot shamblers that were wandering around the New Orleans Country Club. Currently the object of his attention was a probably African-American male—it was hard to tell with the advanced decay—in a very nice if faded suit wandering near the water hazard. The shambler was missing an arm and didn't seem to have any clear goal in mind.

"I would shoot if you'd stop rocking the car!" Milo yelled.

"No idea what you're talking about," I yelled back, rocking from side to side and trying not to laugh.

Obviously, MCB had closed the place, but there was still a foursome of golfers watching from the nearest tee. Since they hadn't been run off, that meant they were read in on the supernatural somehow, and probably connected enough that MCB had to be polite to them. More than likely judges or politicians. They didn't seem perturbed by a few zombies, but they were clearly impatient to continue their game. One of them was already doing practice swings.

They change it every so often, but in 1985 the Monster Control Bureau had two different ranking systems for monster-related events. One was on the basis of the threat to citizens and national security. That was a color-based ranking system ranging from green, one monster, couple of victims, no big deal, to Extinction Level event, which was, obviously, bad.

The sobek, even though it hadn't managed to kill anyone, was classed as a Yellow event. If it had managed to climb out of the canal, lots of people might have died.

The second was based on how hard it would be to cover up. When a few homeless people saw a vampire, no big deal. Class One event. Everybody knew homeless people were crazy and it was just a few of them. Godzilla attacking the Democratic National Convention on camera live would be a Class Five.

In any other town, zombies in broad daylight on a major golf course used by high rollers and Very Important People—who could not easily be dismissed or defamed—was considered a big damned deal, probably a Yellow Three. In New Orleans, Agent Higgins just ran off the know-nothings, shut the gate, and put up a CLOSED FOR MAINTENANCE sign, while his boss, Castro, drove a golf cart over and schmoozed with the foursome from the donor class. Castro waved when he left. I doubted they'd even bother writing up anything in the *Truth* for this one. It was like Class Beige Negative One here.

There was another shot.

"Dang it!" Milo yelled. "Quit rocking the car!"

"Don't know what you're talking about," I yelled, but I quit rocking the car. "Have you considered getting your eyes checked? Take a comfortable breath. Slow trigger squeeze. The shot should come as a surprise..."

There was another shot. The shambler dropped.

"There you go!" I yelled. "Before you know it, you'll be almost to the level of Marine marksmanship!"

"Just find me the next one," Milo said. I could tell he was grumbling.

As we pulled away, the guy with the driver let fly. I will never get the allure of golf.

I'd gotten a map of the course at the pro shack and marked where all the zombies had fallen, but when we went back with coroner, the one at the water hazard was missing.

"I swear there was one right *here*," I said, looking around. You could see the trace of brains on the ground. "Right damned here!"

"No zombie, no receipt," Dave said.

"The brains are all over the ground," I said, casting around. Milo had hit it square in the head. Finally.

"Excuse me, you there in the armor!"

I'd heard the golf cart coming up behind me but ignored it.

"Yes, sir?" I asked politely, turning around.

The speaker was a gentlemen in his sixties, distinguished, well-dressed, with iron gray hair and blue eyes.

"If you're looking for human remains, young man, you may have your work cut out for you," he said. "A gator took it."

"Oh, son of a bitch," Dave said, shaking his head. "Not that again."

"Any idea where this gator went, sir?" I asked.

"Somewhere in the water hazard," he said as he drove off. "Good luck."

"Well, shit," I said. "What do we do now?"

"Gotta get the gator out of the water hazard," Dave said, shrugging. "Cut it open, see if there's a body in there."

"So . . . how do you catch a gator, again?" I asked.

I had already come to the conclusion that there were three answers to any question along the lines of *how do I/we get something done* in New Orleans?

1. Ask Remi to make arrangements.
2. Call Madam Courtney.
3. Shelbye had a cousin.

These even fell into three broad categories of the gumbo that was New Orleans but that's a big digression. Simply put, of those three, which would *you* choose to get a gator out of a water hazard?

You guessed it: Shelbye had a cousin.

More like some sort of third cousin, tenth removed or an uncle or something. The guy was about a hundred, short, his head far too large for his body, bow-legged, walked with a stoop and his arms out and seemed to have been inexpertly carved from teak by some alien race that had *heard* of primates, had them described certainly, but never actually *seen* one. I was relatively certain they'd used some sort of nonprimate monkey as a basis. His face was probably based on a proboscis monkey and his body on . . . lemurs? Possibly? He was another one of those characters in New Orleans I wanted to check if they were PUFF-applicable.

"Ooh, gator eatin' zombie nouveau!" he exclaimed in the same accent Tremaine used when he was really tired. Cajun so thick you couldn't cut it with Mo No Ken. "*Être pas bonne!*"

He then said something in what Cajuns thought was French. It sounded disappointed. Even when they used close-to-French words, Cajun accent was just as thick in French.

"Lost that," I said. "Something about a donkey?"

"Buyers won't take them if they've eaten humans or human remains," Shelbye translated. "What he actually said was 'You get more dick from a donkey.'"

"Ah," I said. "Well, how much to get it out?"

"Oool, two hunnert?" he asked.

"Done," I said. "How long?"

"Long'n it take," the possibly human said with a shrug.

"Rock, paper, scissors?" I asked Shelbye, holding out a fist hopefully.

"Oh, no," she said. "Your kill. *You* gotta stick around. I ain't sittin' here for one damn shambler."

I didn't want to stick around for one damned shambler, either. Full moon was prime hunting season even by day. There were things to kill and money to be made. Girls to save. The last place I wanted to be was stuck on a golf course waiting for Methuselah to fish a gator out of a pond.

"What if I need a translator?" I asked.

"When Cousin Badouin gets it out, pay him two hundred dollars," Shelbye said, walking away.

Cousin Badouin walked to his green pickup truck, slowly and arthritically, and rummaged for a bit before pulling out a weighted treble hook attached to a long line. A bit more rummaging and he came up with a long-barreled pistol that looked like a .22. Then he slowly and arthritically walked back. I swear it took him five minutes just to make the round trip.

When he got back to the water, he squatted down and appeared to go to sleep. He seemed to just be napping in the sun with the hook dangling in his hand.

"Need any help?" I asked.

He answered in what I took to be the negative.

I'm a really good linguist. You need a lot of exposure to Cajun to understand it. One of the reasons is it is a closed metaphorical dialect. What's that mean?

There are closed metaphorical dialects in English. Take the Deep South. One of those places where you want to paddle faster if you hear banjoes. If you go into a corner station and ask the owner for directions, the answer might be: "Don't take a hound dog to know the weather."

What this actually means is "You should probably buy a map, Yankee."

Unless you understand the metaphors, the colloquialisms in other words, you may be able to cut through the accent, you may be able to understand the words, but the metaphors are only understood by a closed set.

What does the term "being bus-left" mean? What is a "spare tire" besides the obvious?

You more or less have to guess based on the context. And you are entirely unable to communicate on your own terms, fully, because you do not have the necessary metaphors to relate.

This was my issue with Cajun the entire time I was in the area. Even if I could cut through the thick accent to understand the mixture of French and English, the metaphors were only fully understood if you were raised in the culture.

At one point when I was recuperating, I dug into the anthropology and linguistic texts on Cajun and came to the conclusion that the anthropologists and linguists who were Cajun—there are Cajuns who go to college—were incapable of explaining it and those who were from outside were incapable of understanding it. So that was no use.

Or as a Cajun would say: *"Raccoon dans un arbre n'est pas le souper."*

More or less.

I went back to Honeybear in a less than good mood.

"This wouldn't have happened if you weren't rocking the car," Milo said in a superior tone.

"I wasn't rocking the car," I said. "You just can't shoot."

"You were rocking the car," Milo said, getting angry.

"Was not," I said.

"Were too!"

"Not!"

"Were!"

I shoved him. Lightly. With my elbow. He shoved back. Harder. We shoved back and forth for a while then both started laughing.

"See!" I said. *"That's* rocking the car."

"How long's it going to take?" Milo asked.

"No idea. And rocking the car was funny."

"See!" he said. "You *were* rocking the car!"

"Duh," I said. "I was waiting for you to get down

on the ground in exasperation. Then when you were going to get in, I was going to drive away and make you chase the car for a while."

"You . . . jerk," Milo said, laughing. "I don't know why I like you."

"Same reason I like you," I said. "I have an *actual* asshole of a brother and you *lost* all of yours. We both gotta find family where we can."

"Point," Milo said.

I rolled up the window and cranked the AC.

"I am going to get some shut-eye," I said, sliding the seat back. By then I'd taken off my armor and gear and was just in the Kevlar and cotton combat suit. "Wake me up if Methuselah catches anything."

I was having a nightmare about spiders when Milo shoved me and started shouting.

"Werewolf!" he shouted. "Loup-garou! Get out of the car!"

I'd kept my .45 on just in case and hit the door in an instant, totally awake. Then hit the ground on my face as my boots caught on something.

"What the fuck?" I yelled, rolling over and trying to get to my feet again. And down. And up . . . and down. And I finally looked at what my feet were caught on.

My freaking bootlaces were tied together.

"You son of a bitch!" I shouted. *"Milo!"*

Milo was on the other side of the car laughing so hard he was choking. He'd had the good sense to cower behind one of the tires so I couldn't get a shot at his ankles, the coward!

"That's for rocking the car, jerk!"

I tried to come up with an acceptable insult and

gave up. I started untying my boots. He'd knotted them thoroughly. "Okay, okay. Even?"

"Even," Milo yelled.

"Hoooweeee!" Cousin Badouin shouted. "Ooooh! Eeets a beeg one!"

Methuselah, the teak proto-human, had caught something.

He was hooting and caroling as he dragged the gator up towards the bank. I had enough knowledge of gator hunting by then to know that on the bank was the *worst possible* place to have a gator. They had a very powerful tail in addition to their bite. Nobody in their right mind wanted to try to kill a gator on the bank.

I'd forgotten this was one of Shelbye's cousins. That put the question of "right mind" in perspective.

Sure enough, he had the gator caught on the tail with that treble hook. And, sure enough, he was dragging the damned thing up on the bank.

He yelled something at me in pseudo French. He had both hands on the line so he couldn't gesture. But I got the impression from head movements he wanted help.

I ran over, glad I had managed to get my bootlaces undone, and he pulled the line towards me.

"*Vigoureux!*" he shouted. At least I was pretty sure that was what he was saying. "*Vigoureux!*"

I decided he wanted me to hold onto the line. And pull *vigorously*?

I grabbed the line and pulled vigorously. The alligator pulled back even more vigorously and I was nearly on my face again.

"*Vigoureux!*" Cousin Badouin shouted again, dancing

around like, well, a proto-human design based on various forms of nonprimate monkeys. He'd drawn his single-action .22 and was waving it in the air. I noted in passing that, surprisingly enough, he had his finger off the trigger.

I kept pulling vigorously, dragging the recalcitrant gator onto the bank. Based upon the gabbling from Methuselah, I was now proceeding as desired.

As soon as the gator's head was in the shallows, Methuselah made a leap like a vampire and landed on the gator's back. The gator then became *extremely* vigorous. Then I stepped on one of my bootlaces.

I had gotten them untied. I hadn't gotten around to tying them again.

I was on my back with an angry gator on the other end of the line and an angry Methuselah on *its* back.

How do I keep getting myself into these situations?

Milo was no help whatsoever. He was laughing too hard.

I managed to keep pulling *vigoureux*, pushing along on the ground.

Methuselah finally managed to get into position and capped the gator in the back of the head with a .22. The gator thrashed a couple more times and was still.

"Laissez les bons temps rouler," I said, letting go of the line and rolling over on my back. *"C'était plus amusant que de manger des araignées."*

"Les araignées sont bonnes frites!" Cousin Badouin argued. *"Bon! Tres bon!"*

"What the heck are you saying?" Milo the cunning linguist asked.

"I was just explaining that you were my retarded cousin," I said, standing up. "Now we gotta try to get—"

Something hit me hard in the head. As I passed out, I distantly heard a male voice shout:

"Fore!"

I sat in the car, windows rolled up, AC on full blast, "Twilight Zone" playing, surrounded by the smell of decaying blood from the damned loup-garou that had bled all down my roof and all over my interior, drinking a Budweiser and holding an icepack on my head while I let Milo deal with Dave. From what I could see without turning my head much—the fall had wrenched my neck—there were bits and pieces being extracted from the belly of the gator.

Milo had duly paid Cousin Badouin who had presumably left satisfied. I don't know. I was comatic by Titleist. SOGCMOB, TGB, CBT.

"I got a receipt for one shambler," Milo said as he got in the car. "How's the head?"

I just looked at him balefully then removed the icepack for a second.

"Ooh," Milo said. "Nice goose egg! You can see the little dimples! That's gotta hurt."

"Thanks for your concern," I said, putting Honeybear in gear.

"It was hard to tell, but I think Cousin Badouin said seeing you get whacked in the noggin made his day."

CHAPTER 27
In the Air Tonight

I walked into Maurice's and slapped Everett Christiansen on the back. I hadn't seen him since the beginning of the full moon. For some reason, he looked a little tired.

"Still think the South Side of Chicago is the baddest town ever?" I asked, sitting down next to him.

"This place is insane," he said, picking up his shot and downing it with shaking hands.

"Just concentrate on those PUFF bonuses," I said. "And they call it the Big Easy for a reason."

It had become tradition, after surviving a full moon, Hunters, MCB agents, and SIU cops gathered at Maurice's, and Melisent had shots waiting for all of us. It looked like most of them had already arrived.

"We were at a call," Milo said, sat down, looked at the shot, then at the waitress. "Orange juice? Please?"

"Up to you, honey," Melisent said, pouring Milo orange juice in a shot glass.

I took his bourbon and downed it.

"I'm gonna need a basis for drinking, honey," I said. "And I still don't have your number."

"Food's almost up," Melisent said. "And that's 'cause I've got yours."

Milo looked over at Officer Tremaine. "Hey!"

"Tremaine," Tremaine said, raising her glass. "That loup-garou on Roche?" Her accent had gotten very pronounced.

"Tremaine," Milo said. "And this guy kept trying to sell me drugs! Right in front of a cop! With a dead werewolf up on the roof! There were thirty or forty people gathered around trying to get a look!"

"Drugs ain't my bailiwick," Tremaine said.

"We got more important things to worry about," Salvage said. "We take our time busting street dealers, we get *nothing* else done. Not in this damn town. Unless it's gnomes."

"Death to all gnomes," Tremaine said, raising her glass.

"Death to the gnomes!" the other two chorused and drank.

Melisent poured more drinks.

"How the hell do you handle this?" Christiansen asked. He had bandages on his face.

"Last couple times, with half as many people," Trevor said.

"We lose anybody?" I asked.

"No deaths. Some injuries, nothing severe."

"You expected more?" Christiansen asked.

"I wasn't expecting to see *you*," I said, grinning. "This was an *easy* full moon. Hell, I got some sleep."

We'd gotten a lot of calls over the last few nights, but with all the people we had in town, most of them had been easy to clear up. I'd even been able to stop by the house, take a shower and change into a new uniform.

"Alvin and a couple of Ray's guys are in the hospital," Trevor said. "Torn up by some ghouls."

"Steele and Castillo," Ray said. He was the only one from his team who wasn't looking worn to a frazzle. "Superficial injuries, they'll be fine."

"LT and Stick Insect," I said, nodding. "Ghouls are nasty. SOCMOB. F-G, O-O-N."

"What?" Greer said.

"Standing on the corner minding my own business," Tremaine translated. "Fucking ghouls. Out of nowhere. I've actually listed that in the ER before. 'Cause I *was* standing on a corner..."

"Hooooweee!" Shelbye said, sitting down at the bar. She had Fred Ramsey with her. He was in a soft cast and from the looks of the way he was moving, probably had broken ribs. Shelbye had a bandage on her arm but that looked like it. "We gonna be havin' a real fais do-do on Saturday! Y'all come on down my camp! *Laissez les bons temps rouler!*"

"Make a deal with Doc Henry?" Salvage asked.

"T'at one beeeg rat!" Shelbye said. "Gonna make a fine rat jambalaya! We bring some up to t'ee boys in hospital. Do t'em good. Put bone on t'eir bone!"

"Rat what?" Katie said. "You're going to eat a *rat*?"

"How come you always manage to get the big ones?" Trevor said. "When they said giant rat, I was thinking dog-sized, not elephant."

"Elephant *rat*?" Christiansen said, downing another shot. The shakes were fading at least.

"Mole rat," I said, shrugging. "We got an idea on PUFF on that yet? Should be decent."

"Real big," Milo said. "Real *real* big in your rearview."

"Use a LAW again?" Salvage asked.

"Figured Shelbye would want it for jambalaya," I said. "So, Bertha."

"So it nearly *ate* us!" Milo said. "I *said* we should go straight to LAW."

"Worst part was it half ate Honeybear. Trunk is that fucked up. 'Cause *somebody* drives like an old lady."

"Cousin Louis fix it right up," Shelbye said.

"If that stupid woman had just gone through the intersection..."

"You'd have looked both ways and slowly and cautiously proceeded," I said, "while *I* was busy trying to kill a monster rat..."

"Monster rats," Christiansen shouted. "What, a *hundred* zombies? Ghouls? Vampires hunting in *a group*? Fricking werewolf on every *corner*! *What the hell is wrong with this town?*"

"It's New Orleans," Trevor said, lifting his drink. "To absent companions."

"Absent companions," we all chorused and downed our drinks. Melisent was already pouring before they all hit the bar.

I tried again when she poured mine. "And, honey, I need some sweet tea and a phone number."

"I'll get you the sweet tea," Melisent said. "I'll even give you a phone number. It's to a mental hospital. You need it."

"We have a fais do-do Saturday." Shelbye declared. "Bring both teams, they free. Plenty of rat to go around! You guys sticking around?"

"We'll hang out for a while," Ray said. "See if things calm down, but eventually we've got to go. There are other areas we cover."

"Fair enough," Trevor said. "I still need more help. At least one more full-timer at minimum."

"Two," Christiansen said, standing up and putting money on the counter. "If I'm out of MHI because I won't do New Orleans, I'm out of MHI. Fine. But I'm not doing another full moon in this town. I want to live to spend the PUFF money."

"I'm sure Tony will take you back," Ray said, shrugging. "Up to him."

"New Orleans isn't for everyone," I said.

"No kidding," Trevor said. "See ya round, Chicago." Christiansen left without another word.

Good riddance. Fucking *shotgun?* Maybe that works in *Chicago.*

This next bit's gonna be kind of choppy. Much of it was "same shit/different day" and I'll skip most of that. I got injured, was out for about a month at one point. Dropped the Shackleford kids some special Uncle Chad presents. Spent some more time in England trying to track down what our mysterious digger creature is—no luck there—and did some research on swamp-ape language. Banged some hotties. The usual.

Things did calm down. New Orleans was still the busiest place in the country, and the company hot spot, but it wasn't the madhouse that it had been when I first arrived.

The hexes went back to causing impotence and baldness, rather than growing giant mutant animals or summoning powerful shadow demons. At least for a while. At the time we didn't know the cause of the out-of-control hoodoo, or that it would be back soon. But those assholes creating werewolves were still a pain in our ass, and every full moon there would be a few new ones.

We'd been turning over people like a treadmill. And it had been a revolving door, let me tell you. Our advertisement and recruiting started to pay off, and Ray kept finding us more help. Some, like Chicago, came in with background and knowing— just like I had—that the Big Easy was going to be easy. Then after one or two full moons would quit. Some quit Monster Hunting, some got taken back by their teams.

We'd lost Alvin. Not dead, lost his leg to a loup-garou, but fortunately didn't get infected. He retired back to Texas. Still there last I heard, got a job with a Sheriff's department doing the desk work and handling their supernatural stuff. With Alvin gone, Shelbye and Trevor were the only remaining members of the Hoodoo Squad from when I'd joined.

It was late summer and hot as hell day and night, when we got a call from SIU.

Earl Harbinger had been making regular visits, off moon, to the area. Most of the time he'd respond to calls but he was never around the team shack. Always gone. Off on his own. I asked him what he was doing one time and he answered "Enjoying the night life."

What he'd been doing was, literally, going to bars and clubs, drinking, and just hanging out.

If you're read-in on Earl, you'll know what he was doing. He was loup-garou hunting.

So we get a call from SIU. Our boss has up and shot some dude in a bar multiple times. Guy's dead. Earl's claiming the dead man's a werewolf.

Slow night. We *all* had to roll out on this one.

Dive's over in Metairie. One of the ones that had been identified in the very long list from MCB of having had at least one person bitten in it by a loup-garou. Earl's out front of the bar, smoking a cigarette, talking to Officer Tremaine, jacket undone. He's turned his weapon over to the first officer on scene but identified himself as MHI so the officer called SIU instead of locking him up. Earl's looking cool as a cucumber.

Inside the bar I expected a shambles. Nope. There were clear signs of hasty exit. There's a body under a sheet, blood leaking all over the already nasty floor.

Guy appears to be in his thirties. Sort of biker looking. Long hair, beard, hairy, heavy-set, bunch of heavy rings on his fingers which creates a sort of brass knuckle effect in a fight. No real indications, though, that's he's a loup-garou. Wearing all his clothes and stuff. I'd add description of his face but...wasn't much left of his head. And was leaking from a lot of holes. A lot.

According to witnesses, Earl simply gunned him down in cold blood.

So...what the hell happened? Took forever to drag it out of Earl.

He's in the bar, looking for one of, any of, the loup-garou that had been intentionally biting people off-moon and this one walks in. Earl knows he's a werewolf right off. Guy spots Earl. Walks over and bows up on Earl.

Earl explains there are rules about being a werewolf, at least in the alpha's territory. Which he was in. No messing with humans. Don't piss off the alpha. He'd violated both.

This guy suggests that Earl shove it and wants to fight. Makes a challenge.

Earl suggests they take it outside.

The guy says let's throw down right here.

"So I said, 'Okay, if that's how you want it,'" Earl tells us. "And I pulled and shot him with all six cylinders. Reloaded. Put those in his head. Amazing how fast that clears a bar."

Cold, man. Really cold.

For reasons that may be obvious to you or may not, this apparently surprised the hell out of the guy. He was expecting Earl to, you know, take him on physically.

I'd gotten some skinny on stuff by then so I asked Earl why he'd done it that way.

"I've seen more punks like him than all the bad werewolf movies ever made. He violated rule one *and* two. Wasn't going to waste my time."

The body, of course, tested positive for lycanthropy.

You do *not* bow up on Earl Harbinger. Certainly not if you're a loup-garou.

Later, it happens again. Slightly different. Earl walks into a club over in Lower Ninth, walks up to one of the club's regulars and just guns the guy down. In that case, other guns were pulled. Earl holds up his hands, identifies himself as being with Hoodoo Squad and calmly suggests they call the police.

We had a lot fewer problems with new loup-garou after that. It was just amazing.

But something happened *between* those two events. It was before Earl found the second loup-garou. I might as well finish the story I started this memoir with.

October and the weather was finally starting to cool off. At least it *had*. Then it got blazing hot again, what up north would be called an Indian Summer and down in the Big Easy was just called "hot enough for you?"

That night, you could feel the tension in the air. The feel that there was a front on the way and it was going to be *big* one. The feel that the temperature was going to break and break hard in a wall of thunder.

If you'll remember, I had rolled up on a single werewolf call, which had turned into a two werewolf call. And after I'd gotten injured killing those two, a pack of ghouls had crawled out of the ground to eat the corpses. Which it turned out really pissed off the *third* werewolf.

So there I was, limping back from calling the coroner, around the corner to see a pile of ghouls devouring the loup-garou I'd just killed. A blast of wind hit as the storm reached the cemetery. The heavens opened up and water poured from the sky.

The ghouls turned, hissing at my lights, and got up from their meal.

More were closing in among the tombs. Their outline was revealed as lightning pounded the Big Easy like Thor's hammer.

I was wounded, alone, stuck in a thunderstorm and surrounded by hungry ghouls. Then *another* freaking loup-garou, barely audible over the howling wind, thunder and pouring rain, bayed its challenge to the moon...

I've been dead. Dying doesn't really trouble me. Various *ways* of dying are my fear. Dying slowly in agony dissolved by spider venom while doctors try very hard and fail to save me. Having my soul ripped from my body. Being sacrificed. Ending up crippled, especially if I lose the use of my dick.

Screaming my way to death as the ghouls pile on and feast.

But there are times, for me, when I honestly long for a glorious death. When all the fear slips away. When I truly enter that zen state that is the point of all the martial arts crap. When the world focuses to a mind, a hand and a blade.

Okay, and a white phosphorus grenade.

I took one from my vest, pulled the pin and tossed it at the cluster that had been feeding. Ghouls don't like fire. They jumped away from it and it took their minds, momentarily, off of fresh meat. Then I took Mo No Ken in a two-handed grip and went to work.

The injury to my leg was a distant issue. A variable to consider like the pouring rain making my sword's grip slippery in my gloved hands. I would be slightly less agile than normal. The wet ground. The bloody mud that eventually started to suck at my boots.

The tombs were tight, here. There was no wall or brother at my back and damned little maneuvering room to crash through and attack at an angle. There were ghouls before me and ghouls behind. I had them right where I wanted them.

I knew this was not the battle where the Lord planned for me to die. This was no grand finale. This was just another skirmish in a war that would only end with the Final Battle. *This* might not be my destiny, but if I fell here, He'd find somebody else to be destiny, boy. I did not care. It was time for battle.

There was barely room to swing Mo No Ken as I turned back and forth, slashing and hacking at the undead, the rain pouring down my face and the battle illuminated by continuous sheets of lightning blasting the firmament. Lightning struck a nearby tomb, the bolt so close you could hear the *pop* beforehand then the massive CRACK as it hit. The lightning flashed from tomb to tomb, so bright for a moment I thought I was in a strobe-filled club.

I did a side kick left, slamming a ghoul in the stomach while thrusting right, one-handed, into the eye of one on the other side. Spin back and Mo No Ken swept up, then down, slicing the kicked ghoul from shoulder to stomach, out the right side, cutting the ghoul in half. Spin, sweep back up and another was sliced from groin to shoulder and literally fell in two, adding to the writhing pile of undead on that side. They were still slithering forward, grasping at my boots, snaggle-fanged maws chewing at my shin plates...

Then the loup-garou arrived.

Most of the ghouls were to my right where the body of the last loup-garou had been mostly consumed. That was, coincidentally, the direction it arrived from.

Ghouls will generally run from a serious fight. They smelled the blood and sensed the injury. They didn't have enough sense to realize that even wounded I was the more dangerous predator.

But they recognized loup-garou. Suddenly, the "heavy" side was just trying to get away and, to my left, they were running. Not from me. From the werewolf.

Couldn't have that.

I slashed off the ghouls that were holding my boots and gave chase. I wasn't finishing them off, you pretty much have to burn them, but a ghoul on the ground with no legs I could deal with later.

They're fast and agile but they weren't fast and agile enough. Some jumped up on the tombs and made it off into the darkness to safety. But not many. A couple that tried that ended up cut in half. Most I left crawling on their arms in my wake. They weren't getting anywhere fast that way.

But I could tell from the sound that the battle with the loup-garou was almost over.

Now the pain hit. My leg was on fire. I was weak and trembling in the rain as the loup-garou slunk forward. I was the last remaining prey in sight that wasn't running away and it wasn't going to stop until all the prey was down and easy to feed on.

Loup-garou are like that. They say that wolves aren't that way but they do the same thing. All predators do. Get a wolf around vulnerable prey and they'll kill everything in sight, then go back and eat. Lions and tigers and bears, oh, my.

"Thanks for the assist," I said as the werewolf slunk through the rain towards me. It was low, growling, ready to leap. It had been wounded by the ghouls, bitten and scratched, but unlike me, its wounds were already healing. "I don't suppose you'd like to reconsider? I could use your sort of backup on a regular basis."

I can be fairly persuasive. Apparently, I wasn't persuasive enough. The loup-garou leapt.

Mo No Ken slashed one last time as I stepped aside.

My savior was dying.

Turned out to be a middle-aged white lady. Looked like she would have been more comfortable in church. Actually, looked a bit like a "Bertha Better Than You" type.

"Go to God, madam," I said, turning Mo No Ken

against the downpour to clean it. "I'm sure you're forgiven all your sins."

So that completes the story I began with. If I was basing this book on the format of my previous memoir, that would be the way I'd end it.

But I've overlooked one very important New Orleans tradition, and the day when Hoodoo Squad met its match: Mardi Gras. The day the dinner table turned.

CHAPTER 28
Street Life

So there we were in Mardi Gras. People had warned me that if I thought a full moon was insane in New Orleans "just wait." They weren't kidding.

Of course, since our crazy monster activity had died down considerably, we were hoping it would be the normal kind of crazy, not the blood-soaked-massacre kind.

The parades and celebrations had been going on since before the Sugar Bowl. They just got more and more frantic and raucous as the month went by. Hoodoo? Didn't nothing stop the Mardi Gras krewes from turning out. So we were all on station waiting for something bad to happen.

All the parades and second lines and celebrations were just a warm-up for the Fat Tuesday parade. That one shut down the whole damned city. Every hotel from Bourbon to Baton Rouge was booked solid. Every street was packed with tourists and locals. And on every corner you could buy everything from a ten-dollar bag of heroin to a ten-year-old.

Ever try to respond to a supernatural outbreak when there are ten thousand drunken assholes in your way?

I'd say the worst part was I was missing the party, but honestly, I was just as glad to not be attending. It was fucking insane. No, the worst part, seriously, was taking thirty minutes to go two blocks only to find that the sighted vampire had already drunk a tourist and was long gone.

A week before, the SRT had arrived. Oh, what fun, what fun. Because Mardi Gras was such a big national event, and there had been such a suspicious spike in monster activity over the last year, MCB headquarters had dispatched their elite Special Response Team to keep an eye on things. SRT were the ones who could call in the battleships and B-52s, which meant they outranked everybody.

So while SRT was in town, Special Agent in Charge Castro was temporarily in charge of dick. MCB wasn't going to be lenient or understanding about anything.

With most of this giant crowd being made up of law-abiding citizens happily ignorant of the supernatural—who would go home and tell all their friends about anything weird they saw—Hoodoo Squad had been told to be discreet. No driving around with sirens wailing and purple lights flashing. It meant I couldn't carry my Uzi or wear my body armor in public, and the indignity of slinging Mo No Ken over my shoulder in a plastic map case.

Higgins had introduced me to a few of the MCB agents who would be stationed here for Mardi Gras. Unlike our locals, most of them had been stuck-up jerks who wouldn't give me the time of day. I was told Franks was in town too. I had first met him after my initial encounter with shamblers. I got the impression that most of the MCB were a little frightened of him.

The day before, Agent Marine stopped by Maurice's. He had been given a rookie junior MCB agent fresh out of their academy to be his temporary gopher. I was surprised to discover that it was someone I knew.

It was Dwayne Myers. He had been with MHI for a few years and had even been on Earl's team. Good reputation, had been tight with Ray. Like me, he had even rated having the little Shackleford kids call him uncle. I had heard he had quit after his best friend, Marty Hood, had gotten killed in a training accident, but I hadn't known that he'd joined the MCB. There wasn't traditionally a lot of crossover between our organizations.

I tried to talk to him, but Dwayne wasn't feeling talkative, looked like he didn't want to be there, and was basically being an asshole to everyone, but I bought him a drink anyway. Melisent poured us shots.

"Absent companions." I drank. He didn't.

"I'm on duty."

"Higgins doesn't seem to care." I pointed my chin at Agent Marine, who was being his usual self. "I heard about Hood's accident. Sorry, man."

Dwayne gave me an angry look. "So that's what Earl is calling it? An accident?"

"Why? Was it something else?"

"I don't know." He stubbed out his cigarette in an ashtray. "I don't want to talk about it."

"So why the job change, Dwayne? I know it can't be because the government pays better."

From down the bar, Higgins laughed.

"You really want to know, Chad? MHI is a bunch of

damned cowboys, pushing too hard, and getting good men killed in the process. They're not by the book. They don't even have a book. You're a smart guy. Get out of MHI while you still can." And then Dwayne got up and walked out of Maurice's, his shot untouched.

"That rookie needs to learn to relax," Agent Higgins said as he came over and finished Dwayne's drink. "Wound tight like that, he'll never last long in the MCB."

It was just after sundown and I was pushing my way through the drunken mob with a new guy named Caleb Warren. New to New Orleans, but not new to MHI. He was a big, blond Minnesota farm boy from hardy Viking stock. Ray had talked him into transferring here from our team in California.

We were responding to a vamp call right by the freaking Place D'Armes hotel. For those of you who don't know it, it's right on one of the busiest streets in New Orleans and right at the height of tourist season on freaking Fat Tuesday. And this vamp throat-bites a tourist right in front of God and everybody. Most of the other tourists thought it was street theater or something. The hotel shut its security doors up tight and screamed for help.

Caleb and I were over on Orleans Street when we got the call. Couple of blocks. Vamps right on the street was a "Go Now" from SIU. We were pretty much matched in terms of getting through the crowds. Caleb had more mass and longer legs and could bull through the tourists. I had agility and could slither through, but it was easier to follow the big guy. Nice to have a plow.

We forced our way across St. Ann Street to the

sidewalk on the Place D'Armes side and slowed down. We could see the victim down. Someone, a tourist I'm pretty sure, was doing CPR.

Uh, lady, if you *do* manage to get him back you are in for the last shock of your life.

Not really—it usually takes a few days for them to wake up, plenty of time to get them embalmed. That's one of the reasons people started embalming. Keeps the number of surprise vampires down.

As we approached, a young kid in a hoodie walking towards us turned around and started running. Then he jumped up onto a second-story balcony at 635, then up to a second on the corner building of Royal, and up to the third, then up to the roof. Fast. Not humanly fast. Supernaturally fast.

We'd found our vamp.

Now, when he went to the second story, the chase was on. Normally, a vamp easily can outrun a human, but I was going to run this fucker down. One vamp? I was Iron Hand, baby. I wasn't even going to bother with "stake." I was going right to "chop."

A lot of the buildings in the Quarter are flat-roofed. And I have always been agile.

"Boost," I yelled to Caleb, running up to under the balcony.

"Trevor said stick together!"

"Boost!"

"You've got to be . . ." Caleb said, then shrugged and stuck his hands down, interlocked.

A second later I was up on that second-floor balcony. By then the vamp was disappearing over the rooftop.

Screw that. I burst through the glass French doors into a party for the upper crust.

"Hoodoo Squad," I said politely. "Sorry about the door. Vamp on the roof. Where's your roof access?"

"This way, young man."

Their gentleman was another older fellow like Remi. As the party resumed, he politely but rapidly led me to the ladder to the roof. I could partially hear, partially construct the conversation as I left. The owners of the condominium had out-of-town guests visiting for Mardi Gras.

"What was that about? You just let him barge into your home? Shouldn't we call someone?"

"It's a New Orleans thing, cher. Don't trouble yourself. Henri will clean up the glass when he comes back. More cabernet?"

"It's a New Orleans thing" explains everything to out-of-towners.

"Please apologize to your patrons and their guests," I said as I climbed up the ladder.

"We do understand, sir," the gentleman said.

The vamp had run from the roof he'd climbed and onto the one I was on. But by the time I was up on it, he'd backtracked onto the roof of Place d'Armes and headed in the general direction of the corner of Chartres and Dumaine.

I, of course, gave chase. The weather, for once, wasn't blazing hot, and up on the roofs I could make good time, unlike in the street.

"Hand, where are you?" Caleb radioed.

"Headed towards Chartres and Dumaine," I said, sort of panting but not gasping. It had been a pretty decent run so far.

The fang headed over a few more roofs, jumped into the air in a tremendous leap and disappeared.

He was getting away. I ran faster, leaping across the few openings and up onto the edge of the roof he'd flown off of. I looked down. Alley. Dumpster. Top closed. No time to think. I hit it in a roll and then off and onto the ground, landing on my feet.

The vampire was waiting for me.

Correction, *all* the vampires were waiting for me.

Red eyes appeared in the shadows. They hissed and growled as they circled. I was surrounded.

"I've been watching the Hoodoo Squad for a while. I knew you would be the only one impulsive enough to follow a vampire by himself," said the one I had been chasing. He lowered his hoodie. The fang appeared to be a black male in his early twenties, and he was leaning against a brick wall under the one dim light in the entire alley, looking smug. "I took my time so you could catch up."

"You think you can kill me?" I drew Mo No Ken. Some of the vampires ventured into the light. They all looked young and made me wonder if we'd missed some of the kids who'd been killed at the university. "Come on then!"

"This is the one who murdered Drusilla!" That vampire, a white kid who was actually wearing a Loyola T-shirt, rushed me. "Let's turn him!"

Ichor droplets were still in the air when his head went flying into the festive night. There was a brief cheer in the distance that was entirely unrelated. Great timing though.

The expression on his face in the moment before Mo No Ken struck was perfect surprise. I expected him to say, "Wait. What just happened?"

"I am *Iron Hand*, bitch!" I shouted, spitting on

his deliquescing head. "My blood would *burn your undead soul!*"

"Enough, children," the leader said. All of the other vampires immediately froze. The severed head had landed between us. He began walking toward me, pausing long enough to dismissively kick the skull into a pile of trash with his Air Jordans. "If I wanted you dead, Hunter, you would be. This is my city."

"New Orleans doesn't belong to vampires."

"Spare me. I've been here so long that while I was still alive, we considered Andrew Jackson a tourist. You can call me Jack."

I struck. It was a blindingly fast downward slash that should have cut right through Jack's neck.

The vampire *caught* Mo No Ken. Mourning stopped abruptly, with an impact that I felt in my wrists like I had just tried to chop through a boulder. He had simply clapped his hands together, only he'd moved so fast I hadn't seen it. A bit of steam rose from between his palms from the consecrated oil.

Oh shit.

If Jack wasn't a Master vampire, he was probably close enough that it wouldn't matter. From what I had read on the topic, the best way to fight Master vampires was with artillery.

"I brought you here so we could talk," Jack said, not sounding upset or surprised that I had just tried to kill him. He didn't even show me his fangs, but I realized the temperature had suddenly dropped. There was another flash of movement and Mo No Ken went clattering down the alley. He'd effortlessly ripped it from my grasp.

"Okay…" Listening beat dying so I played it cool. "What can I do for you, Jack?"

"Here's the deal, Chad..."

"I prefer Iron Hand."

Jack raised an eyebrow. "Whatever, *Chad*. I'm here to do you a favor. I've seen Hunters come and go, and contrary to what you might believe about my kind, I don't mind you meddlesome little pricks all that much."

"That's kind of surprising." I nodded my chin toward the melting college student.

"Amusements and pets. The vampires you weed out are those too stupid to follow orders or too feral to listen to reason. Basically, Hunters keep out the riffraff. Too much human blood shed draws attention, and attention causes me inconvenience."

"Then you should tell your little minions to calm down."

"That's the problem, Chad. They aren't listening so well anymore. New Orleans has become a vortex, drawing the darkness in. The uncivilized of my kind feel compelled to come here, their hunger magnified. Every half-wit who has ever played at magic is suddenly a powerful necromancer. It is all the fault of a new player in town. Or perhaps I should say *old* player, but it has recently turned its malevolent gaze upon us once again."

"The activity spikes during the full moon..." Too bad, we had hoped things were actually calming down. Ray's team had even gone back to Cazador. "I thought we were through that."

"No. Recently you have merely been enjoying the temporary lull of a cyclical hunger. It was full, but now it's back. What you've seen before? It is nothing compared to what's coming to this town next."

It was so cold next to the vampire that I was

beginning to shiver. "How come you haven't taken it out then?"

"It is beyond my reach. It is incredibly powerful. It troubles me. This thing is an outsider. A trespasser. It's a...a..."

"Tourist."

"Damned right," Jack said. "Fucking tourists."

In Seattle I had learned that monsters had turf wars too. After we had taken out that lich, it had been chaos until I'd found our Fey princess to take its place. It sounded like Jack didn't like being deposed. What the hell? I had gotten monster intel from the yakuza. How much worse could this be?

Well, obviously a lot worse, but Jack the super vampire hadn't ripped me in half yet.

"Tell me where this thing is then, and I'll handle it."

"In time. Don't worry. I'll be in touch." With a nod from Jack, the other vampires retreated. I caught glimpses of them spider-climbing up the walls. In seconds they were all gone. "Right now, you've got more important things to deal with. A normally inept priestess has asked for a curse upon tonight's celebration, and our ambivalent yet powerful *tourist* god has granted her wishes beyond her wildest dreams. You'll want to gather *all* your forces and head toward Royal."

"What are we dealing with?"

"Something bad enough that if it breaks free, thousands of mortals will perish, and then my city will be crawling with so many government men that I'll never be free of the annoyance... Assuming the carpetbaggers don't just pull the plug and flood the whole place. Believe me. If they knew what was here, they would not hesitate. I've seen the entire world in ways your pathetic mortal mind can't even begin to comprehend, but this is, and always will be, my home. There is nothing else like this place, distinct and wonderful. I wish to keep it that way."

It's like Trevor said. New Orleans natives always come back.

"We'll take care of it," I said.

"Good luck, *Iron Hand*."

I blinked, and Jack had already vanished.

By the time I got on the radio, the temperature was returning to normal. Freakin' creepy super vampires.

Just as I finished warning the others, Caleb came running up.

"What took you so long?"

"Have you *seen* the crowds?" Caleb said, bending over and putting his hands on his knees to pant. Big guys. No stamina.

Jack had said we'd need all of our forces, so I was checking if anybody had eyes on the MCB.

"*I see some SRT from here dressed up like cops,*" Shelbye replied. "*I can shoot the big scary one to get his attention.*"

The big scary one was probably Agent Franks. Shelbye was up in the bell tower of St. Louis Cathedral with a Barrett, a .30-06 BDL and her M14. So she pretty much had the whole area covered. The bishop hadn't even blinked when I had asked if she could stay up there.

"*I called Castro directly and gave the SIU a heads-up,*" Trevor responded sharply. "*Hang on, Shelbye, river side. What the hell is that coming over the levee?*"

"*That's . . . crawfish? Big-ass crawfish! Whoo-hoo, we gonna be havin' another fais do-do!*"

"*I'm getting close to the water. There's . . . hundreds. The river is swarming with them. All teams to the riverfront!*" Trevor said.

I could hear fire starting from the bell tower as well as rapid fire from near the river. It was barely audible over the Mardi Gras madness.

"*Retransmit! All teams to the riverfront! We've got—*"

The call cut off.

CHAPTER 29
Rock'n'Roll Party in the Street

"Shit, shit," Shelbye radioed. *"Trevor is down. Who's in charge?"*

"This is Hand. I'm in charge."

I jumped up on the dumpster, did another jump to a window ledge, then up to the roof.

"Where are you going?" Caleb shouted.

This way would be faster, but Caleb probably wasn't athletic enough to make it. "Get to the car and grab more guns," I yelled down, then got back on the radio. "All teams converge on Royal. Shelbye, what are we looking at?"

"Crawfish? Giant lobsters? Hundreds? Thousands? They're coming out the river and... Shit. They're cracking people's heads open and sucking out their brains. I think they got Trevor."

"Who else do I have?"

They began to check in. Fred Ramsey and Brent Waters were heading for Trevor. Caleb was getting more weapons and Shelbye was above. That was all of Hoodoo Squad.

I was up on the roof of the Place d'Armes by then and could see what Shelbye was looking at.

They were arthropods, for sure. Similar to crawfish or lobster but they were multicolored, mostly white and red with some electric blues, and about a yard long. In addition, rather than having two smallish claws, like a crawfish, they had one massive one that looked more like a blunt instrument. Which was exactly what it was.

Decatur Street was crawling with the things right by Jackson Square. As I watched a middle-aged, short, balding guy was desperately trying to run away up St. Ann. One of the arthropods used its tail to jump through the air and land on the guy's back. The club-claw flashed blurringly fast and his head was cracked wide open. As he fell to the ground the...crawfish? lobster? no, *mantis shrimp* stuck a proboscis in the brains and sucked them right down.

Then it started crawling after more prey.

Most of the mass seemed to be heading into Jackson Square and up St. Ann. People had seen what was happening and were running for their lives. Unfortunately, the Mardi Gras crowds, drunk as skunks, were surging that way to see what fais do-do was going on over *there*! Woo-hoo! Love Mardi Gras! That was keeping the runners from getting away. Luckily when the gunfire started, that got most of the mob moving in the right direction.

Most of the businesses on the lower floors were closing their doors when they could. Panicked people were pushing in and preventing that. Mantises were flooding in behind them.

"All teams assemble near Royal and Ann. Get up

on the balconies. We can't fight these things in the crowds." I took my own advice and climbed onto a balcony. Elevation worked for shamblers, so hopefully it helped with killer crustaceans too. "Forget collateral damage on this one. We can't let these things get to Bourbon. They're some sort of killer mantis shrimp."

"*Copy,*" Shelbye said. "*Mantises moving through Jackson Square, up St. Ann and the alleys.*"

"Anyone passing SIU or SRT, drag them over here," I said. "We hold the line at Royal! We do not let these things get to Bourbon."

"*This is Fred. We're moving up Dumaine as fast as we can, but the crowds are insane and there's a parade in the way.*"

"Throw flash-bangs if you think it will help!"

I drew my pistol. The range was long for .45 but I'd been practicing constantly. The ones jumping were a no-go. The ones crawling—and most of them were—or feeding were targets I could hit. I nailed one that was feeding, blowing the crustacean away but hitting the already dead female victim beneath it too. The mantises weren't very big.

"Shelbye, concentrate on the ones in the park," I said. "Fred, status?"

"*Can't . . . get . . . through . . . Get the hell out of my way, you fat fuck!*"

"*This is Caleb; I've got some long guns from Honeybear.*"

"Caleb, Hand; get the hotel to get you up on the roof, then head to Chartres and St. Ann." I went back to shooting. Everybody for blocks would hear those gunshots. If it kept them moving away from the monsters, good.

"*MHI, cease fire! Cease fire!*"

"Who the hell is this?" I radioed, but I already knew. Trevor had given Castro our channels a long time ago.

"*This is MCB SRT. Cease fire! You will cease causing a major incident during Mardi Gras! Are you insane?*"

"You already *have* an incident!" I shouted. "And I don't have time to hold your fucking hand. You've got people dead already and a wave of angry, brain-sucking crustaceans headed *right for the parade*, which is being broadcast *live on national television!* So are you going to get your head out of your ass and *help*?"

"*Those are not our orders,*" the unknown agent said. "*Stand by.*"

"*Overridden.*" That was Special Agent in Charge Castro. "*I can see this from the chopper. This is a Class Four, Yellow, say again, Class Four, Yellow. SRT and all other MCB and SIU teams will deploy, immediately, to protect the parade. If it hits the main body of tourists, right on broadcast network, it goes to Class Five, Red.*"

"*Our orders are to—*"

A police helicopter passed overhead. That had to be Castro.

"*This will be essentially uncontainable if they make it to the parade, Special Agent, and I will absolutely kill your career if you sit this out. You know what? Fuck this desk jockey chicken shit. Somebody tell Franks the forces of evil are going nuts over here. We need SRT at Royal and St. Ann, stat. Everyone switch to MHI's channel to coordinate.*"

"*Moving forward to observe. SRT out.*"

I didn't understand MCB internal politics, but

invoking Agent Franks must have worked. I'd been potting crustaceans and reloading furiously as the conversation continued. The problem being, because we had been working low profile, I was getting low on rounds. We were going to have to finish this in minutes or the wave of mantises were going to hit Bourbon like an all-you-can-eat human buffet.

Frankly, all my pistol fire was pissing in the wind. We needed claymores and belt-feds for this. This was worse than Portland's spider problem. More mantises were making it up the street than the number I'd killed.

Suddenly, Caleb appeared at my side on the balcony. He passed over my Uzi and an assault vest full of magazines. While he began firing his M16, I threw on my vest. That was much better. There were so many mantises moving down the street that they were hard to miss. Together, the two of us started stacking bodies.

The mantises were scurrying about, each one about the size of a dog, but faster. They didn't appear to have any strategy other than to head directly toward the nearest living thing, club its head in, and slurp out the contents. There was a wave of them, and it was about to crash right over us.

Several MCB in SWAT gear ran up the street below. I heard them coming, because they were shouting at the fleeing civilians something about drug gangs getting into a shootout, and to get out of here. They were more worried about the people being witnesses than surviving.

"Oh, hell," the agent in the lead said.

"Sorry, did you think I was *exaggerating*?" I said, not taking my eye from the sights.

The SRT opened fire.

More down. I was getting about one kill for every two shots. And at that rate I was going to run out of ammo long before we ran out of mantises. Just filing the PUFF was going to be a pain in the ass. I think we might set a record with this one. Or someone else would if we all got killed.

I took out one of my white phosphorus grenades and tossed it at a cluster of the things in the road. It wasn't going to hurt any people. Everyone in the intersection was already dead. The Willie Pete had very little effect. A couple mantises were badly burned but the rest just kept on trucking or went around. So much for fire.

As I was thinking that, a mantis peered over the roof above me.

I lifted my muzzle and fired. It dropped past me and fell into the street. Then I looked around.

The fuckers were *climbing up the walls of the buildings,* and going in through second-story windows and doors.

The SRT agents were mostly using MP5s, and their subguns were chattering like crazy. But there were so damned many targets that we were still getting overrun by brain-sucking crawfish. Good news was, getting your skull crushed looked like a quick way to go. Better than fucking spiders.

Caleb's M16 was doing a fair job on the crustaceans climbing up the wall. I'd worried that the light rounds wouldn't penetrate their thick carapaces. But they were going right through and apparently doing a real number on them.

I wished right then I had an M16. First time I'd

wished that in . . . ever. Lots and lots of rounds would be good about now. We were piling up mantis bodies on the street below. But more were just going right by up St. Ann. We were completely surrounded and about to be engulfed.

"Caleb, climb for the roof. I'll be right behind you."

The mantises began leaping up at us, and man could they *jump*. MCB agents below screamed as they were dragged down, and bludgeoned or clawed to pieces. I pulled myself up onto the roof and discovered that there were already more mantises swarming up the other side.

"Fuck this," I said, drawing Mo No Ken.

I wasn't sure how well the sword would work. A mantis was skittering right at me. I swung, slicing right through its giant claw and deep into the top of its body. The carapace was hard but no match for Japanese steel. I jerked Mourning out and the mantis slid over the edge, twitching. I started slashing and kicking crustaceans off the roof while Caleb kept shooting.

And then more of the MCB arrived on the street below. Franks was just chewing gum placidly, as if all these tourists dying didn't seem to matter to him. He looked over the carnage and the swarm of monsters trying to rip us to pieces, and nodded, like *no big deal*.

Then he laid in with that pussy MP5 like nobody I'd ever seen in my life. In a second it seemed, the wall of the building, the balcony, the far building, were clear. Then he reloaded faster than any normal human should, went down the street, and went on a fucking rampage. One of the mantises leapt through the air at him. He grabbed it out of midair and hit it in what on a mantis would be the face. The thing shattered in a spray of blood, coating him in red.

I could see the mantises going into the apartment across the street. People were dying in there as well. There were screams from under our feet. The street was littered with bodies of the dead, wearing bead necklaces, their heads cracked open and so much blood and brains spilled out the blood was running into the sewers.

Down the street, a shotgun went off. The men from the dinner party I'd literally crashed were out on the balcony with double-barrel shotguns. Henri was standing behind the gentlemen, calmly holding a large satchel full of shells. I guess the visitors had decided to get in on this *New Orleans thing.*

"Hand, Shelbye," Shelbye radioed. "*Uh . . . these things climb.*"

I looked over at the cathedral. The walls and roof were crawling with mantises. And more were headed up the bell tower. She leaned out on one side, firing down. But there were more coming up behind her.

"*Tell my folks to have a right nice fais do-do with these. Gonna be a hell of a party. Sorry to miss it.*"

About seven mantises made it over the back side of the bell tower. We could hear her shots. The gunfire stopped. Then the surviving mantises started climbing back out.

"Shelbye. Come in." Nothing. There was no time to think about it. All I could do was go back to swinging.

I realized many of the SRT guys were already dead. The agent who had been calling the shots had been buried under a pile of falling claws. Franks was off in the intersection by himself, murdering piles of mantises. The big agent had drawn many of the monsters away, but it looked like the rest of the SRT was getting routed. Someone down there needed to step up and lead them.

"*Alpha, reinforce MHI and SIU,*" Myers said over the radio. "*Charlie, hook left and block Royal that way. Bravo, right. Stop these things before they get to Bourbon. We hold the line here.*"

The SRT listened and got their shit together.

"We got more crawfish coming up," Caleb said, pointing at the next wave. "I should have stayed in California."

"Stay up here. Stick and move. Don't let them cross Royal."

"What are you going to do?" he asked.

Most of the mantises were concentrating on Franks in that intersection. "I always like it when big guys plow the road for me," I said, stepping lightly onto the coaming then jumping off.

I landed with one foot on the railing of the balcony, just slowing myself, then jumped off again. Both jumps were about a story and a half. No way Caleb was going to follow me down. And I didn't want him to. Safer on the roof. Maybe he'd survive up there.

There was a clear spot where Franks had gone through. Well, clear of living mantises at least. And humans. Bodies of both were scattered everywhere.

Franks was bouncing around the intersection of Chartres and St. Ann like a rabid squirrel, dodging mantises, firing in every direction. From time to time slinging his subgun, and wielding two Bren Tens at a time. Nobody could do that. Not and hit anything worth shit.

Franks could.

I sliced an incoming mantis out of the air and closed in from behind.

"Angel six!" I shouted. Not sure why I shouted that. Just made sense. I definitely wanted him to know that a friendly was coming up from behind. Franks didn't seem like the kind of guy you wanted to surprise.

As I approached, a mantis managed to come in from behind as Franks was killing one to the front. It slammed its claw into his helmet. Lacking a cover, the helmet split in half, and fell to the ground.

That was bad news. I'd planned on *my* helmet protecting *me*.

Franks pulled the mantis off and tore it in half, but another landed on his shoulders as he was doing so. It lifted a claw.

I didn't even think about it. I drew my 1911 and fired.

The round hit the mantis, but it continued through, and struck Franks right in the back of the skull. It was a killing wound.

But Franks just turned his head, his face covered in mantis blood and nodded. I took that to mean *Thanks*.

"Got six," I said as I arrived. I holstered, hefted Mo No Ken and spun to cover the agent's back.

I don't know how long we fought in that intersection. I'd just try to keep up with Franks as he moved back and forth. It was tough. The guy was clearly inhuman and inhumanly fast. But he was facing the mass of the remaining approaching mantises. I'm pretty quick, but I only had his back.

That was bad enough, but having finished off the inhabitants, the mantises were pouring out of the nearby buildings. I could hear the continuous crackle of fire from up the street. Mantises kept leaping at us, but fortunately all the hits were cuts, nicks, and grazes. And we really didn't have time to deal with grazes.

There wasn't a moment to think. At one point in my early training, back in high school, Mr. Brentwood would toss apples at me and I'd try to slice them out of the air with an old cheap katana.

It was like that. But more like a bunch of baseball guns firing thirty-pound lobsters from random directions. When they landed, and several landed, they'd hit hard.

I stumbled as one hit me square in the right side of my head, and before I could even react, slammed me in the helmet so hard I saw stars. It was like being shot in the helmet with a pistol round. I was stunned by the impact. I could sort of hear the helmet crack and knew I was going to die. I fell to a knee and one hand, trying to prop myself up.

As the helmet fell away, carrying with it my commo, I sensed the weight come off my shoulders and heard another cracking noise.

I looked up as Franks was just done wringing the thing.

"You gonna lie there?" Franks asked, tossing the mantis over his shoulder.

I lunged up at him with Mo No Ken, drove the point within inches of his ear and speared the inbound mantis square in the brain.

"No," I said, flicking the thing off my sword.

The nice thing about a blade is you never run out of ammo.

But damn were my arms getting tired.

That was partway through our knock-down, drag-out party in the street. I couldn't even tell you how long we fought.

❖   ❖   ❖

Most of the monsters were dead. The street was littered with brightly dressed revelers, dead, their skulls split open, and fluorescent bodies of the mantis shrimp. I knew if someone could paint it properly, it would sell for a pretty penny at the Salvador Dalí Museum.

"We got more in the buildings," I told Franks, shaking my head and looking around. "And I'm about flat out of rounds."

A helicopter approached. I assumed it was Castro surveying the carnage.

Mais non. The helo dropped in close. I looked up to see my gentleman, Remi, hanging from the door. He lowered my spare assault ruck full of ammo from a rope.

Tom waved from the pilot seat. Borrowing that helicopter was getting to be a habit.

Once the gear hit the street and was grounded out, I unhooked the carabineer and thumbed for them to lift up again.

I made a mental note to invite the Lamberts to dinner.

"I need to link up with my people. What are you going to do?"

Franks didn't answer. He just started walking up St. Ann Street.

I let him go. There were more mantises to track down. Our male bonding moment was over and somehow I knew it was anything but.

I don't get Franks. I don't know what he is. He's not a human and not a werewolf, I know that. But the truth is, I like him. I don't like what he does most of the time but that covers MCB as a whole. All I know is when the shit hits the fan I'd rather have Franks at my back than Earl. And that's saying something. We honestly combat click better.

Even with Mardi Gras, NOPD had managed to set up a perimeter and close the zone to personnel or traffic. From St. Peters to Dumaine, from the river to Royal, there was hardly a soul left alive. Bodies were everywhere. Coroner was going to shit a brick.

And there were more mantises scattered around. I let those come to me, shooting them as they crawled into jumping range. I stayed away from enclosed areas, just wandering the deserted streets.

Choppers were circling. FBI, NOPD, Sheriff's office. Nobody came to my assistance. Bare is back without brother. I was out of commo but I was sure that if there had been a rest of the team, they'd have found me. I wasn't exactly hiding and was occasionally using my 1911 so they'd hear the shots. The only shots I was hearing were from up by Royal.

Occasionally I heard the distinct chatter of an MP5. It was coming from over by the front of St. Louis Cathedral. I knew who it was but there was no point in trying to link up with Franks again. He did his thing. I did mine.

The MCB being the MCB was already spinning some story, and New Orleans, being New Orleans, had returned to celebrating. I could tell when it was midnight, the official end of Fat Tuesday. The sounds in the distance slowly died and the party was over.

The party was never over. Not in my book. This party, this job, this mission, wouldn't be over until God let me go home.

I'm a Monster Hunter.

EPILOGUE
In the End

It was dawn of Ash Wednesday. The streets were covered with litter from the celebrations as tens of thousands of tourists and twice that many locals slept off their hangovers.

I watched the light grow as I sat on the steps of St. Louis Cathedral. National Guard was picking up bodies, human and mantis. Doc Henry, New Orleans Parish Coroner, was out there managing things. The survivors of the SRT were out spreading joy amongst anyone who had had contact with the incident. A rookie MCB agent had stepped up and taken charge. New Orleans would be the first of Myers' many commendations, but right then he was too busy telling the news that all that gunfire they had heard was from a battle between DEA and Colombian drug dealers. I was sure Washington would find some way to cover up all the dead and missing.

It was only SRT talking to the witnesses because MCB New Orleans was *gone*. Even Bill Castro had landed and fought the mantises. He had died herding a bunch of tourists to safety. While Franks and I had battled in the intersection, other mantises had spread out, up Pirate Alley, down Chartres. MCB New Orleans had fought and died, defending the people they normally intimidated. I'm sure that Higgins and Buchanan preferred it that way. They had been wiped out.

So had SIU.

And so had MHI.

I found Trevor's body. There wasn't enough left to cut off his head.

Fred Ramsey and Brent Waters had managed to make it to the intersection of Royal and St. Ann just in time to take the brunt of the mantis assault. SIU on scene, Tremaine, Carter, and four SIU officers, were already down. Fred and Brent held out until SRT got there and died with their boots on. Salvage had bought it stopping a probe up Pere Antoine Alley.

Caleb's position on the roof had finally been compromised.

Shelbye was gone. I'd gotten Tim to get her out of the bell tower. I had a little discussion with a National Guard lieutenant and all her stuff had been gathered up as well for delivery to her family.

They had stood their ground.

Six little Indians. Five little Indians ... then there was one.

I'd had a chat with Doc Henry when he showed up. He promised to both get our people to our funeral home, today, and save some of the fresher mantises for the fais do-do. I promised him Shelbye's family would like him to attend.

I wasn't sure what to do.

Duty is heavier than mountains.

I got up and went back to Honeybear. There was still work to do. I needed to report in to headquarters on the incident and tell them we needed some new monster chow ASAP. Just because MHI was toast didn't mean monsters were going to sit the next few days out. I'd have to contact the families. At some point, Doc Henry would have a count on the mantises. The PUFF paperwork on this was going to be complicated. We'd had support from MCB and SIU. I'd have to check with Susan how you shared that out. I wasn't sure if we'd set up the computer system for that.

Funeral arrangements.

There were going to be five members of MHI cremated today.

It was dawn of Ash Wednesday.